Also by Max Byrd

JEFFERSON

JACKSON

GRANT

a novel

MAX BYRD

BANTAM BOOKS

New York Toronto London Sydney Auckland

This edition contains the complete text
of the original hardcover edition.
NOT ONE WORD HAS BEEN OMITTED.

GRANT: A NOVEL

PUBLISHING HISTORY
Bantam hardcover edition published August 2000
Bantam trade paperback edition / June 2001

Bantam Books are published by Bantam Books, a division of Random House, Inc.
Its trademark, consisting of the words "Bantam Books" and the portrayal of a rooster,
is Registered in U.S. Patent and Trademark Office and in other countries. Marca
Registrada. Bantam Books, 1540 Broadway, New York, New York 10036.

PRINTED IN THE UNITED STATES OF AMERICA

BVG   10 9 8 7 6 5 4 3 2

*For my daughter Kate
and my son David*

With Love

EXTRACTS FROM A REPORTER'S NOTEBOOK
—NICHOLAS P. TRIST, *June 1880*

New York is for Ulysses S. Grant. Never defeated—in peace or
war—his name is the most illustrious borne by living man. Vilified
and reviled, ruthlessly aspersed by unnumbered presses—not in
other lands, but in his own—assaults upon him have seasoned and
strengthened his hold upon the public heart. Calumny's ammunition has all been exploded; the powder has all been burned once—
its force is spent—and the name of Grant will glitter a bright and
imperishable star in the diadem of the Republic when those who
have tried to tarnish it have moldered in forgotten graves; and when
their memories and their epitaphs have vanished utterly.

—SENATOR ROSCOE CONKLING
nominating speech, Chicago Republican National Convention, 1880

He was unquestionably the most aggressive fighter in the entire list
of the world's famous soldiers. He never once yielded up a strong-
hold he had wrested from his foe. He kept his pledge religiously to
"take no backward steps." For four years of bloody and relentless
war he went steadily forward, replacing the banner of his country
upon the territory where it had been hauled down. He possessed in
a striking degree every characteristic of the successful soldier. His
methods were all stamped with tenacity of purpose, originality, and

ingenuity. He depended for his success more upon the powers of invention than of adaptation, and the fact that he has been compared at different times to nearly every great commander in history is perhaps the best proof that he was like none of them.

—COLONEL HORACE PORTER
aide to General Grant, 1864–65

THE SECRET LIFE
OF U. S. GRANT

by Sylvanus Cadwallader

CHAPTER ONE
(not for publication)

START WITH HIS HORRIBLE MOTHER.

Hannah Simpson Grant, lately deceased. Not much missed.

In his eight full years in the President's Palace in Washington City, Hannah Grant never once visited her famous son. During the war, when a group of neighbors came rushing in one day to tell her about Grant's brilliant victory at Vicksburg—the single most intelligent act of generalship in American military history—she just stood up and left the room without a word: life was Fate, Hannah claimed to believe, whatever happened was God's will; to praise somebody for doing God's will was a sin. When Grant came home after winning the war, she met him at the door and said, "Well, Ulysses, you're a great man now, I guess," and went back into her kitchen.

Horrible mother, worse father.

Jesse Root Grant had arrived in Hannah's home town of Point

Pleasant, Ohio, in June of 1820, all alone, without encumbrance of family, to go to work in the tannery.

He was twenty-five years old. Two decades earlier his drunken, newly widowed father, Captain (from the Revolutionary War) Noah Grant, had moved out to Cincinnati from Pittsburgh, part of that first big emigration season of 1799, when land-hungry settlers started pouring west into Ohio like water through a broken dam. But Noah Grant was a restless and footloose man, and in the year 1805 he decided to pull up stakes and decamp again, this time in the direction of Kentucky. Before he took off, however, he simply deposited his five younger children on the doorsteps of various flabbergasted neighbors and relatives and left the two oldest ones to cope for themselves, Susan (age thirteen, who would soon marry) and Jesse (age eleven).

And if ever there was somebody born to cope, it was horrible Jesse Root Grant. If Hannah Simpson was silent and torpid, waiting passively with her hands in her lap for whatever God's will might turn out to be, Jesse more than made up for it with activity and obnoxious bluster.

Point Pleasant was a quiet township of almost two thousand people then, the majority of them farmers and Southern transplants, and as soon as he got out of the stagecoach and put down his valise on the hotel steps, Jesse set about enlightening them one and all on the great subjects of the day. He was going to be rich, he announced, and that would be a good thing for the town. He was a Democrat and a Mason. He was against slavery and in favor of abolition, and he had his doubts about the politics of that arch-Southerner Andy Jackson. One week after he climbed down from the coach his first Letter to the Editor appeared.

For all his bluster, though, Jesse was a shrewd man. He had chosen the tannery business because he correctly saw that a new territory, in the process of settlement, was going to have a growing demand for leather goods, and also because the vast green shimmering forests of the Ohio Valley (all gone now, stripped as if by locusts armed with axes) would give a perpetual supply of oak bark, whose tannic acid was what you needed to tan your hides. If he hadn't been such a self-satisfied, opinionated cuss, Jesse might have become the Leather King of the Middle West. As it was, despite his personal unpopularity he quickly prospered; he made some money and bought his own tannery, and at the age of twenty-eight, consulting a "life schedule" he had drawn up for himself, noted that it was time to go out and find a wife.

Three engraved illustrations from *A Boy's Life of General Grant,* published in that year of glory 1865.

Picture Number One   A two-room clapboard house, 16 by 19, the closest thing to a log cabin you could get in Point Pleasant. This is 1822, long before the invention of photography, so the artist is free to use his imagination. The front room has a fireplace where Hannah cooks and a few straight-backed chairs on a bare pine floor. The six-week-old infant General is sleeping in a crib made from a drawer. The rest of the family is pulled up in a circle by the fire. On Jesse Grant's lap sits an old black slouch hat crammed with slips of paper torn from a tablet—Hannah has written "Albert" on one of them because they're choosing the baby's name and for some peculiar reason she's always liked Albert Gallatin, who was Thomas Jefferson's Secretary of Treasury; Hannah's sister Anne has written "Theodore" on her slip because she thinks it's romantic; Grandfather Simpson considers "Hiram" a handsome name, but his wife and Jesse, who have both been reading in an odd lot of books that Jesse bought, want "Ulysses" after the great Grecian warrior in Fenelon's *Telemachus* (names are Fate). Anne, the youngest, is about to pull out a slip of paper, Jesse is bending forward to read. . . .

Picture Number Two   Hiram Ulysses Grant, age nine, on a horse—the army in its inimitable and intractable way will mistakenly change his name to Ulysses S.—bareback in his father's tannery yard in Georgetown, Ohio, where the family has moved from Point Pleasant. The prosperous new brick house is in the background, also the tannery sheds and the quiet tree-shaded brook that runs beside them, trickling down toward the Ohio River five miles distant. A pleasant scene, right out of Mark Twain's little book *Tom Sawyer*. What the artist can't show is the *blood* everywhere, specks and globules of red and drying blood all over the hides, the sheds, the workers' arms, clothes, hair, and faces, not to mention the stench of scraped and decaying animal flesh and lumps of fat quivering on the ground and the sharp counter-smell of tannic acid from the oak bark in the iron grinder. What he can't show either is the boy Ulysses in actual motion (we'd need one of

Mr. Edison's zoopraxiscopes), galloping his horse down the main street of Georgetown like a Tartar.

It is a celebrated fact about him, of course, as soon as he could stand up and walk Grant found his way into the company of horses. At West Point he was known as the finest rider of his era— set a record for the high jump that still stands—and in Georgetown he was known as little Grant who could ride, break, or train any horse he saw. When he was three a frantic Grant neighbor banged on the window to shout that the baby was swing-ing from horses' tails in the stable (Hannah merely nodded and went on with her business). At age eight he was driving his father's wagon by himself all over the backroads of the county, hauling in bark. At nine he bought his first horse, a dappled white mare, with his own money. (Grant could read a horse, somebody said, with the same natural fluency Dr. Johnson could read Latin.) If you are small and lonely and looking for power, and we all are, a tall, strong horse between your legs will do it.

Shadows of the future bankrupt: when he was twelve or so, his father sent him to buy a neighbor's horse, and he struck the bar-gain by saying, "Papa says I should offer you twenty dollars, but if you won't take that I can go to twenty-two and a half, and if you won't take that I should give you twenty-five."

Picture Number Three   Fourteen-year-old "Useless" Grant, as his fellow students call him, stands on the doorstep of his one-room schoolhouse. He's alone and the illustration makes him look dis-consolate: he does no better in school than his horse-bargaining story would suggest. Satisfactory in mathematics, a remarkable visual memory (for landscapes, terrain), which school doesn't test; poor in all other subjects. His ambitious braggart father nonethe-less declares him a "genius" and sends him to one country school after another, covering the same lessons over and over—I heard so many times, Grant says now, that a noun is the name of a thing that I even began to believe it—but "Useless" still doesn't shine.

If he walks outside the wrinkled gray border of the engraving and we follow him, we see him telling his father he will work in the hated tannery as required until the day he comes of age, never one minute after that. Now he goes down into the cellar of the new brick house. In a locked cupboard is some all-purpose home fever medicine, fifty percent alcohol—the world before the Civil

War was boiling with all varieties of fevers—and young Hiram Grant is kneeling down, undoing the lock.

Lincoln used to say that he was a product of the Kentucky backwoods of the 1820s (just the other side of the Ohio from Grant) and he didn't think there had ever been such heavy drinking anywhere in the world as there was back then—men, women, even children. I myself remember the cask of whiskey and the tin cup on every store counter. There were jugs at the end of furrows, for the plowman's comfort, at the end of corn rows for huskers. There were jugs in the fence corners for the farmhand's dinner. This part of Ohio grows grapes and makes bad but abundant wine. The town hotel is an endless gurgling tap room. Every kind of celebration centers around the whiskey barrel. If a man isn't dead drunk three or four times a year—on the Fourth of July, certainly, and Andy Jackson's birthday—why, he loses all standing in the community.

What leads young Grant furtively down the cellar steps? Well, inheritance maybe; his paternal grandfather was without a doubt a drunkard. Loneliness, too, perhaps, the feeling that he is unloved by his silent mother, misunderstood by his awful father. The village boys mock him because he won't go hunting and shoot a living animal with a firearm. They mock his prudery—no boy, no man in the army would ever hear Grant swear or tell an off-color story. A few years later, at age seventeen, he will stand only five feet one inch tall, weigh 117 pounds. He will not swim or bathe naked in front of anybody, he has a fragile, rather feminine delicacy of feature (pull aside the coarse beard and cigar—in the Mexican War the other officers called him "Little Beauty"). Put your face close to the picture. Under the shell of a mute, determined reserve do you hear a sad and sensitive little boy crying?

A child's feelings are like the stars, they never burn out. They have to be buried or drowned.

Thus great generals are born.

PART ONE

WASHINGTON,
CHICAGO

November 1879–April 1880

CHAPTER ONE

"AN AUTHOR," SAID MAUDIE CAMERON, AGED TEN, WEARING A crisp white pinafore and an expression of pug-nosed disdain, "is a dreadful person who writes books."

Nicholas Trist III scratched his chin stubble with the palm of his hand and studied a crystal decanter of amber-brown whiskey just to the child's left, on a tabletop otherwise uselessly cluttered with little colored porcelain figures of cats and dogs in bonnets.

"My father never reads books," Maudie said. "He says books are a damn-blasted waste of time."

"That's quite enough, Maudie." The child's governess was knitting or sewing or vivisecting something furry and blue in her lap, and without actually looking up she narrowed her eyes in a professional frown. Trist caught a glimpse of his own red-rimmed eyes in one of the room's six mirrors. He placed his hand on his knee and stood up and dropped his hat.

"*You* wrote a book," Maudie said.

"But nobody read it," Trist assured her. Despite himself he licked his lips. Three steps to the decanter. Five steps to the door. Five thousand steps back to the steamship docks at Baltimore. His hat somehow found its way to his fingers again. There were four separate kinds of malarial fever according to the drunken Arab doctor he had seen in Marseilles, and Trist had managed to come down with the least severe but the most persistent strain, though for the life of him just now he couldn't remember the technical Latin name of it.

"Are you, in fact . . . an author, Mr. Trist?" The governess had put down her knitting and was making apologetic little flutters with her hands. "I understood you were Senator Cameron's escort to Chicago."

"Journalist," Trist said. In the mirror, by a species of optical illusion, he swayed on his feet.

"Yes. Well." Doubtful flutters now. "I can ring for the Senator's wife—she knows the Senator's schedule, but he should be home himself any moment."

"You're per-spiring," Maudie announced, coming closer. "And your eyes are red." She cocked her head like a sparrow on a curb. "And you haven't got one arm *at all.*"

"Maudie—"

"I wonder," Trist said unsteadily to the governess, and stopped to rub his brow with his hat. "A little touch of illness from the ship," he said, "overheated, ocean voyage." He gestured vaguely toward the window, which opened onto the redbrick elegance of Lafayette Square, Washington, D.C., at present not overheated but overcast with low, fat afternoon clouds the color of avocados, at present showing no ship at all anchored under its leafless gray trees. In the center of the Square a colossal bronze statue of his stepfather's old boss Andrew Jackson reared his horse and tipped his tricorn hat to a squadron of pigeons.

The governess had tended a hundred feverish children. She pulled a silken bell cord behind the whiskey decanter and scooped young Maudie out of harm's way, germ's way. Instructions flew. Doors rapidly opened and closed; a black maid in a black uniform hurried down a hallway in front of him, pointed wordlessly to a door, and disappeared. Trist nodded his thanks to the empty corridor, then slumped his back against the wall.

In one pocket of his coat he had seventy-three dollars in new American greenbacks, a handful of useless French sous, and six paper packets of Dr. Susens' Patented Tropical Miracle Quinine Powder. In the other pocket he had a dented brass flasket of miracle brandy. The sweat was now running down his cheeks and neck and under his shirt; he was starting to melt from the top down, like a candle. This was the classical pattern—fever first, then Dizziness, Chills, Trembling Extremities, *La Nausée*. Dr. Susens listed the symptoms briskly and unsympathetically on the packet and recommended one dose every four hours, taken with two tumblers of water. Trist used his teeth to tear open a packet, licked the bitter quinine crystals from his hand like a dog, and then uncapped the flasket and swallowed steadily for as long as he could stand it, till brandy spilled over his chin and leaked out his pores. The Arab doctor had suggested a mixture of arsenic powder and chalk instead of quinine, but in the war Trist had seen arsenic used as a poison as well as a medicine; if he was going to poison himself, it might as well be with brandy.

He wiped his mouth with his sleeve and braced himself against the wall. Brandy worked fast. He could already feel his veins start to crackle and light up like burning twigs. Quinine made him excitable. He glanced at the dark little privy behind him—what else did you expect of a United States Senator in the year 1879 if not modern indoor plumbing?—and then pushed away from the wall and began to walk. Because he ought to be there, waiting, when Senator Cameron arrived, a journalist ought to be on time and waiting.

He passed one closed door, a second, turned a corner, and stopped. In a house ten minutes and lost. Trist took another swallow of brandy. The corridor was at least fifty feet long and ended at a heavily curtained window. There were three dim gas lamps spaced on brackets along the wall, but they did little to dispel the inky gloom. Trist had the sensation of walking downhill, as if into a mine. He passed another mirror where somebody's flushed and overheated face floated in the black glass like a burning moon. In his first command in the war, in the summer of 1863, three-fourths of his troops had caught either dysentery or malaria. He blinked at a pencil-thin streak of light creeping under the bottom of a door six feet away. In the war, Senator Cameron's father had been something important in Lincoln's cabinet. Trist moved toward the light and tried to remember the story. The older Cameron was a Pennsylvania politician with a reputation for wholesale thievery. When Lincoln asked a colleague if Simon Cameron was likely to keep it up in Washington, the colleague had scratched his head and said, well, Simon probably wouldn't steal a red-hot stove. When Cameron demanded an apology, the colleague declared, I did *not* say you wouldn't steal a red-hot stove.

Trist pushed the door open and walked into a lady's dressing room illuminated by two gas lamps that framed yet another mirror. The window on the right was blocked by dark velvet drapes. Beneath it was a blue-and-yellow Empire sofa, then a walnut *armoire,* a folded green dress on a chair, a row of women's high-button leather shoes on the carpet. Seated on a bench in front of the mirror was a young woman of perhaps twenty-two, with soft black hair curled into a bun on the top of her head, from the waist up entirely naked.

Against the murky shadows of the rest of the room her skin was radiantly white, lit up from within. Her shoulders were slender. Her back was straight, the indentation of her spine looked like a smooth recessed column of muscle. When she lifted her hands to her hair, her breasts rose in the mirror, their tips stiff, red-hot.

A clock in the shadows ticked. Somewhere in the house a dog barked.

"You've made a mistake," she said quietly, without turning, and Trist thought, yes he had, he had made a grave mistake; in the myth, poor stupid Actaeon had blundered into a sacred grove and seen a goddess bathing, for which he was transformed into a stag and killed.

Light blew off her body like foam from a wave.

In the corridor he turned left, turned right, met the black maid who had been sent to find him, and reentered the cozy parlor precisely at the moment Senator J. Donald Cameron of Pennsylvania spun furiously around on his heel and snarled, "Where the *hell's* my wife?"

THE BLACK MAID CROSSED THE ROOM SERENELY AND DID something delicate and domestic to a vase of cut flowers by the window. "Oh, she's still down in her sanctum gettin' dressed, Mr. Senator Don. The young ladies needs their beauty time."

"Who the hell are you?"

"Trist. Nick the hell Trist."

Cameron stared at him as if he had just gotten sick all over the rug.

"Then you're goddam late," Cameron said. "You were supposed to be here yesterday morning, nine o'clock sharp."

Over the maid's shoulder, two or three streetlamps flickered to life in Lafayette Square. Sarcasm was not a good start; a bad start. Trist heard his voice explaining apologetically, with passable sincerity, that he was very sorry indeed, the ship's crossing had been delayed in France, they'd only docked in Baltimore that day. The quinine fizzed in his blood like an electrical charge. When—or in senatorial language—when the hell had it turned so dark? And how exactly had feverish young Actaeon been killed? He couldn't remember. Torn apart by senators, no doubt, beaten to death by streetlamps.

The maid gave her flowers one last encouraging pat on the

head and left the room. Cameron, who had already snorted once, snorted again and strode to the decanter, where he found a single glass among the porcelain cats and dogs and poured himself a whiskey large enough to cure all four kinds of malaria at once.

"If you're sick," he said to Trist, "then I don't want you around my family. I don't want you anywhere."

"I'm fine. I'm ready to start right now."

Cameron didn't look mollified. He drained off his whiskey in three quick swallows and instantly poured himself another. Trist tried not to lick his lips. What had they called whiskey in the army? Oil of gladness? The Senator was a big, beefy, black-moustached man in his middle forties who might have been pickled half his life in oil of gladness.

"General Beale said he gave you a letter of recommendation."

In an inside pocket, behind the malaria packets, was his set of credentials. Trist fumbled for a moment, then handed the letter to Cameron, also his certificate of Good Character from the editor in chief of *L'Illustration* in Paris, written by himself and signed, as best Trist could recall, on the haunch of a giggling blond *gymnaste* in a hotel *de l'après-midi* on the rue de Varenne. Also his official and out-of-date correspondent's card from the *Revue des deux mondes* that simply gave his name and the two severe titles: *Écrivain. Éditeur.* Good Character threw a brief sop to honesty. "I actually only met General Beale last summer, when he was travelling in Paris."

"He knew your father," Cameron said, reading.

"Stepfather."

The Cameronian snort again. The Senator wiped his drooping moustaches with a sleeve. "Beale says you've lived in Europe ten years." His tone suggested that this was either an impossibility or an oversight.

"Off and on."

"Journalist in Paris. Three languages. Wrote a book. Wounded at Cold Harbor." Cameron looked pointedly at the empty left sleeve.

Trist opened his mouth to say something, decided simply to nod. Cold Harbor.

"You going to slander Grant?"

It was a crude but not unintelligent question. Cold Harbor, Virginia, June 3, 1864. The single bloodiest half hour in the history of human warfare. An open-field charge by Union troops against impregnable Confederate trenches, ordered by General U. S. Grant, miles away, sitting in his tent like Achilles, an attack so suicidal and pointless that the night before the battle the soldiers had pinned their names on slips of paper, to identify their corpses in the morning. Cold Harbor was the place where Grant had finally and truly earned his nickname "Butcher." Trist had been hit by three minié balls in his left arm, another in his ribs, and then lain almost a day and a half out in the open, in no-man's-land under the broiling Virginia sun, while Grant and Lee exchanged slow, gentlemanly notes about a possible cease-fire for removing the wounded. Sometimes Trist still woke up tangled in his sheets and soaked with sweat and trembling in a way that malaria couldn't begin to touch.

"Grant is," Cameron said, "the most famous man in the world."

There was no denying that. Victory obliterated criticism. Ulysses S. Grant was far and away the best-known, best-loved character on the planet, an amazing fact to contemplate. When Grant had left the presidency two and a half years ago and started on a round-the-world tour, he had been greeted at the Liverpool docks by the largest, most enthusiastic crowds in English history. Queen Victoria herself had invited him for dinner. Bismarck had come to his hotel in Berlin and asked advice of the Man Who Freed the Slaves and Saved His Nation.

"Well," Trist found his voice, "that's why I'm supposed to report about him, that's why the French press wants a correspondent here. I wasn't planning to write a word about the war. Everybody already knows about Grant in the war. The real story is that nobody in history has ever been President three times."

"Nomination first," Cameron said with brusque practicality. "Then election, then history." The newly filled whiskey glass made a short amber orbit around the window and Lafayette Square. "Beale lives right over there, on the corner. He bought the Stephen Decatur House. As you probably know. Tedious old fool, but we like his daughter."

"Beale's in California," Trist said. "I haven't seen him."

"I cabled you my terms," Cameron said, "nonnegotiable. You wanted an inside look for your magazine, you can come with me anywhere I go as campaign manager. I'll see if I can get you an interview with the General, but he doesn't usually give them.

If I don't like what you write I'll tell you. You pay all your own expenses."

"All right."

"I guess you can write with one hand."

"Yes."

Cameron had a big man's small feet and gingerliness of tread. He moved across the room, holding his glass to his lips so as not to spill a drop, and stopped at a bell cord hanging on the wall. He yanked it hard once. "Women," he said to the wall in general. "My goddam wife."

It seemed like an unanswerable remark. Next to the bell cord was a framed photograph of a train wreck, the third or fourth such photograph Trist had seen since stepping off the ship that morning.

"And does your wife travel along with the campaign?" he asked, as casually as he could, speaking of train wrecks, speaking of women. Because it had to be Mrs. Cameron, it had to be her "sanctum."

Another yank of the cord, a neighborly glower in the direction of General Beale's house. "You've been gone so long, I guess you don't know, Trist, Chicago may be about the biggest, most public goddam banquet of the century. Beale said you went to Yale."

Trist was becoming accustomed to Cameron's disjointed style of conversation. He risked another nod of his head and was pleasantly surprised to find no pain at all, which meant that the fever was on the run. Bless the brandy, bless the quinine. In the mirror he saw two of himself, but they were both upright and steady.

"Just for a year," he said. "I left to join the army. After Cold Harbor I seemed to lose interest." Cameron showed no reaction. "I had some other questions," Trist said and patted his coat in vague search of a notebook, pencil.

But Cameron only shook his big moustaches in impatience. He had already downed his second whiskey. Now he jerked the bell cord again and unsnapped the hunter's case of a thick gold watch.

"What I expect," he said, and as he pulled open the parlor door Trist realized that he was being simultaneously accepted and dismissed. "What I expect, Trist, is somebody *presentable*. Most journalists are riffraff, no manners, you know that, you went to Yale. Most journalists aren't people I can have around my family." He studied Trist's face for a moment. "Be at the B and O station tomorrow morning, six o'clock." In the hallway he stared at Trist again. "Bring a clean suit." He unbolted the door to the street. And as an afterthought: "Shave."

MALARIA, THE ALGERIAN DOCTOR HAD TOLD HIM, COMES AND goes like a cat.

Outside, the cool air somehow mysteriously revived his fever. Trist leaned against an ivy-covered column on Cameron's porch, wiped his brow with the back of his hand, and tried to regain his balance. Across the street, in the damp November twilight, the gas lamps of the Square cast pale slanting reflections off bare branches. The carriages clattering along Pennsylvania Avenue kicked up a brown American smell of horses and mud. Trist shivered. Home again, home again, jiggity-jog.

He crossed the street and opened the little iron picket gate into the park. At the first bench he came to he sat down. To the left, through the trees, he could just make out the dim white bulk of the President's Palace, as it used to be called in the far-off days when he was in the army and Lincoln was in the Palace.

He pulled out his brandy flask, only to discover he had no more brandy. A gust of wind made the glass panes in the nearest streetlamp rattle. He touched his cheek with his hand and wondered if he gave off a kind of orange malarial glow in the dark, like a human jack-o'-lantern.

He shifted on the bench for a better view of Andy Jackson's statue. Lafayette Square, of course, had nothing to do with Lafayette. Before the war they had simply called it President's Square, the social center of Washington. It was down on the southwest corner, if he remembered correctly, in sight of the Palace, that Congressman Dan Sickles had waited one Sunday morning in 1859 for Phil Key, son of Francis Scott Key, who had been, Sickles thought, unduly attentive to his wife. Sickles had shot Key dead on the spot, and the jury had acquitted him, and Congress had promptly commissioned him a brigadier general in the army.

Washington, Trist's stepfather used to say, was too small for a city, too large for a lunatic asylum.

Why in the world had he come back?

Because he was curious.

Because you get tired of being bitter and angry and far from home. Trist didn't exactly hate U. S. Grant, not anymore, and he didn't blame him anymore for the loss of his arm or the train wreck of his youth. But Grant still baffled him, Grant as an American problem. Grant might have "Saved the Nation," but he'd been a lazy and incompetent President, not corrupt himself but endlessly tolerant of corruption in his cronies and cabinet. His whole second term had been one long scandal—how could he still be so wildly popular? What kind of strange new country would choose Grant the Butcher to be President more times than Washington, more times than Thomas Jefferson?

Muffled voices could be heard now, from somewhere behind him, and Trist shifted around slowly on the bench. At the top of Cameron's steps somebody was rapping the brass knocker. When the maid opened the door, Trist could see that it was a couple, elegantly, formally attired, more European than American. The man wore a dark overcoat and Londoner's silky top hat, the woman was in sable furs. Both were so short that, framed in the doorway, they looked like children in adult clothes, come to a dress-up party.

He waited to see if anybody else would appear, but the door closed at once, the curtains were quickly drawn. After a moment Trist stood up, exhaled a long gray comma of a breath (like an author), and started down a bare path in the general direction of Willard's Hotel, where he had left his trunk and a two-dollar deposit for a room.

In the morning, he thought, he would quit. In the morning he would take an express train back to Baltimore, he would shovel coal back to Paris. At the corner of Pennsylvania Avenue and Fourteenth Street, shuddering with fever again, he stopped to grip a lamppost and admire the gleaming rank of politicians' carriages lined up before Willard's entrance, just as in the war. At the bright, noisy hotel bar he drank two more glasses of brandy and counted his change in French.

BUT IN THE MORNING, AWAKENING BOLT UPRIGHT AND FEVER-less, he climbed out of bed and started to dress for work.

At the Baltimore and Ohio Railway Station on C Street, three blocks north of the Capitol, he swung quickly down from the back

of his omnibus. He walked as fast as he could over a muddy ramp
and up through a canopied entrance porch into the terminal. It
was six-fifteen and the first trains from Baltimore were already
clanking and hissing to a halt. He squeezed past a crew of sleepy
porters stacking baggage. A conductor in earmuffs waved him on.
Three or four uniformed announcers stood by a gilded booth and
shouted train numbers through cardboard megaphones. Trist
dodged to one side to let a pair of Negro women in old blue army
greatcoats hurry by, pulling a steel tub of sausage meat between
them, and then he slowed, stumbled on the boardwalk, and came
to a complete, mystified halt. In front of him, spread in a line
before the main platform gate, several dozen men in coats and
melon hats blocked his way. And every one of them was holding
out a pocket watch and staring up at a row of clocks.

Trist turned and looked up with them. Seven clocks—he
counted—seven big black-and-white railroad clocks hung just over
their heads, suspended by pipes from a steel girder that ran cross-
ways under the roof. The nearest clock said "Washington–
Richmond Line." He put down his grip and stood on his toes to
read the others. "Baltimore and Ohio Co.," which was twenty minutes faster. Then "Philadelphia–Penn. Central," "New York Central," five minutes earlier than Philadelphia.

Trist lowered his head and saw that, like an automaton, he had
his own watch open.

"My husband says that going between Washington and San
Francisco you could reset your watch two hundred times if you
wanted. Because since the war every railroad company operates its
own particular clock. Seven different lines use this station, I
think."

Mrs. J. Donald Cameron stood beside him, dressed in a deep
emerald-green coat that clung to her bust and a black travelling
bonnet tied under her chin that did not, quite, obscure the matching green of her eyes. "Some Senators want to pass a bill for one
single national time, but the Western states don't want it. He
pointed you out to me," she said. Farther down the platform
Cameron was arguing loudly with a porter. "Since, of course, we've
never met before."

Trist felt his neck and cheeks flush as if he were a schoolboy.
He put away his watch.

"Have we, Mr. Trist?" she said with a cool, expressionless face.

Actaeon had been torn apart by dogs, he remembered now, that was the true story of how he died in the myth: transformed into a stag, hunted by dogs, the last thing he had seen in life was the goddess herself, now fully clothed, smiling down at him. There was no other word for Mrs. Cameron but dazzling. He cleared his throat, listened for the baying of hounds. "Well, if we had," he said solemnly, holding out his hand, "I would certainly remember."

CHAPTER THREE

THE MOST PUBLIC GODDAM BANQUET OF THE CENTURY WAS scheduled in fact to be a Grand Old Army reunion in honor of ex-President Ulysses S. Grant, just returned a month ago from his round-the-world tour and using the banquet, the cynical said, merely to drum up support for a third presidential term.

Sylvanus Cadwallader, decidedly among the cynical, watched the ex-President pass down the hallway of the Palmer House Hotel surrounded by a skulk of yapping politicians—Cadwallader paused to savor his noun; a skulk was a group of foxes—and made a note of the room they entered. Parlor Suite 21. He consulted the confidential list that had cost him five dollars and two pint bottles of E. C. Booz & Company bourbon whiskey in bribes, all of which he planned to charge, as usual, to the Chicago *Times*. Cadwallader had been a newspaperman since 1850, starting in the small somnolent towns of northern Wisconsin and Michigan. He had long ago found that a reporter's best friend, next to a good dictionary, was a generous budget of bribes. Parlor Suite 21 belonged to J. D. Cameron and party.

He leaned against the corridor wall and scribbled a little shorthand memo to himself. It was no news that Grant was sitting down in consultation with Don Cameron. The Camerons, old

Simon and young Don, owned Pennsylvania as far as Republican politics went. Young Don had even served for a time like his daddy, a most undistinguished time, as Grant's Secretary of War. But Cadwallader was much more interested in writing down his personal impressions of Grant, while they were fresh.

He enjoyed numbers. He thought numbers anchored unsteady minds in reality, so he closed his eyes and did a little calculation. He had known the ex-President . . . almost twenty years. For a period of thirty-one months during the war he had been, if not daily, at least weekly in his presence, and there had been a stretch of time, before Ingratitude Did Its Fateful Work, when he and Grant could have been said to be intimate friends. He licked the tip of his pencil and flipped a page. Grant was fifty-seven years old, four years older than Cadwallader. The General had put on weight during his world tour: he moved now with a fleshy ponderousness that came of too many days behind a banquet table instead of on top of a horse. The skin was softer, the hair and beard grayer. But the face was still Sphinx-like, blank and unsmiling. There was still the same small wart just above the right moustache line—Lincoln had had it, too, and so had Cromwell, if Cadwallader remembered correctly—the same nearly horizontal slash of the mouth. Grant's eyes used to be his most expressive feature: dark gray, surprisingly animated. But he had passed by too quickly for Cadwallader, pressed against the wall by all the foxes, to see his eyes clearly. Unmistakable was the square jaw and the wide forehead. Unmistakable, too, was the fact that Grant had been saying nothing and everybody else had been yammering like geese.

Cadwallader read over what he had written, struck out the geese as one animal figure too many, and slipped the notebook into his pocket. He would expand and revise it later on into something florid, the way the *Times* liked it. Easy enough, because U. S. Grant was a subject that always set his pen to smoking.

Which reminded him to mention the inevitable cigar clamped between Grant's teeth. He pulled out the notebook to add it. General Grant had very likely started smoking his trademark black cigars when he was a chubby babe in his cradle—Cadwallader had said that very thing to Mark Twain last night in the Palmer House bar, and that Grant-intoxicated man had nodded thoughtfully two or three times and allowed it was a striking image.

Cameron's door opened again. Cadwallader leaned forward

expectantly. But neither Grant nor Don Cameron came out, only a tall, skinny-boned young man, sweating as if he'd just left a steam bath. The young man stopped in the middle of the hall, opposite the door, and wiped his forehead with a handkerchief.

Bodyguard, Cadwallader thought first. Then, looking more closely at the coat sleeve: veteran.

"When I was with General Grant at City Point, Virginia, in 1864," Cadwallader said, strolling over and uncorking a reserve bottle of E. C. Booz whiskey, "he had a guard posted outside his tent to keep away all the curiosity seekers who kept trying to get in and see him." Cadwallader paused and took a swig of the whiskey. Up close the boy had a simple malarial pallor, common as a cold these days. "One day a strange comical old fellow, looked like an undertaker, came up from the James River docks and tried to reach the General's tent by ducking under a hedge. By granny, those guards were on him in a flash, guns out and cocked, and they damned near frog-marched him off under arrest, except just then the General poked out his head and said, 'My god, boys, that's President Lincoln!' "

Cadwallader chuckled and rubbed the top of the bottle with his sleeve. "Maybe he didn't say 'My god'—Grant don't swear, ever. But the rest is true. I didn't see you go in before." He nodded his head toward Parlor Suite 21. "So my first idea was that you must be guarding Don Cameron and not General Grant. I know that's Cameron's suite."

"Cameron's suite, but I'm not a bodyguard."

From yet another pocket Cadwallader came up with a cigar and a yellow-tip phosphorus match. "Well, I can see that now." He lit the match with a single practiced snap of his thumbnail. "Ever since Lincoln, half the Congress thinks they need a personal guard from Pinkerton's. The vanity of U.S. Senators needs to be measured in some special grandiose unit. A 'Jumbo' maybe, like Barnum's elephant. Or a boxcar, or a Goliath. Now your Senator Cameron I would estimate at twenty 'Jumbos' worth of vanity, minimum, which puts him about average for the Senate." Cadwallader leaned forward through a wreath of smoke. "Journalist?" he guessed.

"Yes."

"Got the noble fraternal look," Cadwallader explained. "Who do you work for?"

"A couple of foreign magazines, French." Nicholas Trist wiped his face again, then put away the handkerchief and took out a packet of medicinal powder and opened it with his teeth. His voice, Cadwallader thought, had a fine malarial rasp. Pity about the missing arm, but then that was about as common as a cold these days too. "The main one's called *L'Illustration*, from Paris. I came over to write about the campaign."

Cadwallader handed him the bottle to wash the powder down. Then out of habit he held out his business card with the two quill pens crossed like swords and the plain Times Roman type that said "Sylvanus Cadwallader. Special Correspondent, Chicago *Times*, New York *Herald*." "Skedaddled to France after the war, I suppose," Cadwallader said. "Lots of you boys did."

"Land of opportunity."

Cadwallader chuckled and recorked the bottle. "Well," he said, starting to saunter away, "you let me know if I can be of any help to our good French friends. The old-timer always knows where the bodies are buried, and that's a true thought."

AND ANOTHER TRUE THOUGHT—NEXT TO THE BUSY TEN-CHAIR hotel barber shop Cadwallader stopped to relight his cigar and stare at the lobby turned to bedlam in front of him. Another true thought was that a bigger, *noisier* crowd had never invaded the poor old Palmer House Hotel in its poor old life.

He skirted around a small hecatomb of undelivered luggage and trunks and took up a position beside a potted palm, under an enormous floating banner—the whole ceiling was one unbroken series of flags and banners—that said "VICKSBURG——GRANT—— 1863." Everywhere he looked, every nook and corner of the lobby was jammed with middle-aged, gray-haired men. He watched three Republican Congressmen sweep by arm-in-arm. He recognized regimental flags from the Army of the Potomac, the Cumberland, the Tennessee. Clearly, nobody in the country could stay away. Over by the famous State Street revolving doors they were pouring into the building like Hittites.

Worse yet, Cadwallader thought, more and more of them were showing up in their old blue army uniforms, newly enlarged and refitted paunchwards. (He complacently smoothed the flat-bellied black-and-white houndstooth coat he wore morning and night.)

They had their cigars in one hand, their drinks in the other. The spittoons at their feet were an overflowing god-awful brown mess.

He moved strategically around the potted palm to dodge a shouting bellboy. A brass band was playing patriotic songs. Wives and daughters were making endless circling promenades around the grand staircase and its three tiers of balconies. He pulled back a curtain. Outside, in a black stinging rain, the streets were likewise jammed with people. There hadn't been so many people on the streets of Chicago since Mrs. O'Leary's cow had tried to burn the city down, only these people were all waiting—they had been waiting since dawn—just to catch a glimpse of Ulysses S. Grant when he came out to review the parade, even though that wouldn't start until the rain was over.

Well, it was Grant's party. Cadwallader smiled at his pun. Upstairs he found a relatively quiet alcove furnished with a leather chair and table and sat down to rest his feet.

What had crazy old Sherman said? He would follow Grant into battle as if he were the Savior himself?

Across the hall a man hurried past with a poster: GRANT *WILL*!

Cadwallader smiled again, because that was the headline from one of the best-known dispatches he himself had ever written—at the disastrous Battle of the Wilderness in May 1864, when Grant lost fifteen thousand men in two days and everybody else in the country thought he was bound for defeat and disgrace. They talked about George Washington's *will* as the thing that had held the new Republic together in the first days of the Constitution. They talked about Andy Jackson's *will* that had crushed the Choctaws and the Cherokees, and knocked the British backwards at New Orleans. But they were nothing, Cadwallader thought, *nothing* compared to the will of U. S. Grant, because he had been there and seen it, and Sherman was almost right.

Down below, the band was winding in and out of the lobby, playing "Pop Goes the Weasel." Cadwallader drummed his fingers against the chair arm. Loyalty was a virtue too. They should have invited him into Cameron's suite for a visit, Grant himself should have spotted him in the hall and sent for him. There were other headlines he could write if he cared to. If he weren't such a corn-fed, true-blue patriot. Pop goes the—

"By God, Caddy, I think you'll be scratching in that notebook when you pass the Pearly Gates!"

Secretary of the Treasury John Sherman, younger brother of
William T., had the demented family grin. He stood in front of
Cadwallader's chair, hands on his hips, black silk top hat shoved
back on his head like Pericles's helmet, nodding cordially. Cadwallader put away the notebook he had just pulled out and sprang
to his feet.

"Mister Secretary," he said with a genial bow. "Here to greet
the General, no doubt?"

Sherman's grin stayed diplomatically in place. Even around
the Sherman family, "the General" referred only to U. S. Grant,
and if U. S. Grant had any important rivals for his third presidential nomination in the spring, one of them was John Sherman of
Ohio, thirty "Jumbos" minimum.

"You know my wife, Caddy," the Secretary said, and Cadwallader bowed again to the voluptuously gowned lady on
Sherman's left arm. "And Mr. Washburne."

"Congressman," said Cadwallader, and shook hands with Elihu
B. Washburne of Illinois.

"Just saw Bob Ingersoll," Washburne announced gloomily. Bob
Ingersoll, a former Union colonel, was to be the main speaker at
the banquet later that night. He was also a notorious atheist and
lover of whiskey, and Washburne was both a Methodist and a tee-
totaler.

"With that awful Mark Twain," said Mrs. Sherman. "Mr.
Cadwallader," she began, then broke off with a frown. "I can't hear
myself speak," she shouted into her husband's ear. Some spirit—
Cadwallader guessed it was not unconnected with E. C. Booz &
Co.—had seized the band, which was now marching up the grand
staircase and playing a brigade call from General Butterfield's old
command, while all around them grown men were raising their
glasses and chanting,

> Dan, Dan, Dan, Butterfield, Butterfield!
> Dan, Dan, Dan, Butterfield, Butterfield!

Sherman gestured toward a side corridor. At the next alcove Mrs.
Sherman tried again. "I have a favor to ask, Mr. Cadwallader," she
said. "The ladies are not permitted at the banquet tonight. I wonder if copies of the speeches—"

From the top of the staircase now came a new chant, to the deafening tune of the army mess call:

Soupy, soupy, soupy, without any bean,
Porky, porky, porky, without any lean,
Coffee, coffee, coffee, without any cream!

Mrs. Sherman gave up. "This stupid, *stupid* war!"

"Rain's stopped," Washburne called from a window. "Grant's outside!"

Fifty feet away the band wheeled toward them with a cheer.

Ulysses leads the van!
Ulysses is the man!
VICT-O-RY!

CHAPTER FOUR

GRANT WAS INDEED OUTSIDE, STANDING IN THE CANOPIED reviewing box that had been erected especially for him on the hotel's second-floor balcony. Cadwallader pushed out through the revolving doors and into the crowd, and shoved and jostled a hundred yards up State Street. The wind was whipping hard off the lake, ice-cold, and the skies looked as if the rain might start again any minute. But the parade was definitely under way. The first of the Illinois infantry regiments was already marching past to a deafening cheer, flags up, swords up, eyes right. Cadwallader watched from the curb for a moment, but found himself slowly losing ground, crushed back against a lamppost, it seemed, by half the shoulders and elbows in Chicago. The Springfield Marching Band came around the corner playing "John Brown's Body" out of tune, and he shivered and rubbed his face and thought of his nice warm hotel room on the fifth floor, paid for by the *Times*. He had stood in the cold outdoors just about long enough, he figured, to get the flavor of the thing.

Upstairs five minutes later, still shivering, he draped a blanket across his shoulders like an Indian and went over to the window. The Palmer House was nothing if not modern. Under the sill, next to the baseboard, was an iron-pipe central heating contraption for which a new word had recently been coined: "radiator." He squatted on his heels and turned a knob. Then he held his hands out, palms down, the way you might warm them over a campfire, until he felt the heat begin to spread from the pipes—radiate—and he braced himself on the wall and creaked to his feet. Fifty-three years old.

He pulled the blanket tighter around his shoulders and sat down in a straight-backed chair two feet from the radiator. Sylvanus B. Cadwallader had only been thirty-six the year he first met Grant, 1862. Working in Milwaukee as City Editor for the Milwaukee *Daily News;* in poor health and bored to tears. And he might be there yet, he thought, covered in cobwebs and bent over his desk like Ebenezer Scrooge, except one day early in October, out of the blue, a telegram arrived from the owners of the Chicago *Times,* and Cadwallader's world just flipped itself up and over, changed forever. Would he care to go down to Tennessee and write about General Grant's army for the *Times?* (And by the way, their previous reporter had been tossed in military prison by General Grant for publishing false information—could Cadwallader possibly get the man out?)

Cadwallader could and did. If he closed his eyes and shut out the noise from the street below, he could still picture the grimy little yellow stucco depot in Jackson, Tennessee, and hear the old wooden cars of the army train jerking and squealing to a halt. He could still see the pale consumptive face of Grant's personal aide, Major John A. Rawlins, as the Major sat in his tent on the outskirts of town and scowled his way through Cadwallader's stack of press credentials and said the General would talk to him some other time. And he could still see *Grant's* face when he finally did get to meet him two weeks later.

Cadwallader chuckled to himself. Thirty-six years old and full of conceit and vinegar—what Cadwallader had done was send off his first story to the *Times* even more critical of Grant than his incarcerated predecessor. The Union troops were in the process of maneuvering from Jackson over toward La Grange, getting in position for the cavalry clash that would ultimately be the Battle of Holly Springs. The stragglers and bummers in some of the regiments were plundering and burning every civilian building they passed, and they needed to be disciplined and punished, and Cadwallader, in the height of his newspaperman's military wisdom, said so.

Next day he was passing Grant's tent on his way to breakfast when the flap shot up with a crack and there was Grant, beckoning him to come in. The General had a mass of newspapers on his table, and without uttering a word he turned through them slowly till he reached the *Times*. Bylines were rare back then. He pointed at the lead article and said he supposed Cadwallader was the author.

Cadwallader was.

The General lit a cigar with a flint-and-steel lighter and blew a puff of gray smoke. "Well," he said quietly, "it's factually correct, and steps are being taken to remedy the situation. And if you never write more untruthfully than this, Mr. Cadwallader, you and I won't have any problems."

A great cheer came up from the Chicago street, and then what sounded like two different bands playing two different songs at the same time. Cadwallader stretched out his legs and wiggled his toes.

The thing about Grant was that he didn't *look* the part of a hero. He looked and acted exactly like what he was, a hard luck Western farmer, carrying with him the air of empty fields and dusty roads and the small-town harness shop. For the first two years of the war, in the midst of all those Eastern generals with their tailored uniforms and their polished manners, he was just somebody to ignore.

Only, by 1863 the little Westerner with the unkempt beard and the quiet voice had somehow or other managed to have two separate Confederate armies surrender to him—at Fort Donelson, at Vicksburg—and forced another into headlong retreat at Chattanooga, and when he took command of all the Union forces in 1864, a collective sigh had seemed to go up from the nation. "The *boss* has finally arrived," one private soldier in the Army of the Potomac told Cadwallader, and Cadwallader printed it in the Chicago *Times* for the whole world to read.

The other thing about Grant, of course, was that he was a thousand times more complicated than he looked, and that was the mystery of him. Lincoln knew it instinctively. Lincoln knew all about the mystery of character. In the worst days after Shiloh, when that jackass Whitelaw Reid had written his famous article about Grant the bungler and the butcher, the Radical Republicans had sent a Senator over to the President's Palace to demand that Grant be fired. And Lincoln heard him out, thought it over in silence, then shook his head: "I can't spare this man: he fights."

The one and only time Cadwallader ever saw Grant lose his temper was during the Battle of the Wilderness, May 1864. "Uncle" John Sedgwick's VI Corps had just been routed in a surprise attack and over five thousand Union casualties were already reported. Grant was sitting on a camp stool, smoking his cigar and receiving dispatches, when one of Sedgwick's surviving officers came thundering up on his horse. As soon as he spotted Grant the officer started stuttering that the army was in a terrible crisis, Lee was about to cut them off at the Rapidan River, and if he *did* cut them off all communications with Washington City would be lost for good, and then they *would* be doomed. And Grant stood up and took the cigar out of his mouth and flung it to the ground.

"I'm heartily tired of hearing what *Lee* is going to do," he said with genuine fury. "Some of you always seem to think he's suddenly going to turn a double somersault and land in our rear and on both our flanks at the same time. Go on back to your command and try to think what *we're* going to do ourselves, instead of what Bobby *Lee* is going to do!" Later that week he wrote General Halleck the famous letter where he said he proposed to fight it out on this line if it took all summer.

Rain pattered against the window and ran down the glass in silver bullets. Out on the street the parade sounded as though it was winding up in a hurry. Cadwallader pulled out his watch. Three more hours till the monumental goddam banquet. Plenty of time for a nap.

There were two reasons the people had elected Grant President twice before.

One was because in his simplicity and competence U. S. Grant embodied the perfect American allegory, rags-to-riches, log-cabin-to-the-President's Palace. Every man and boy in the country could see it and identify with it and feel some pride in a free society like that, where you might fail once or twice, but Virtue would be Truly Rewarded in the end.

And the other reason, of course, was Appomattox. If any image was going to live forever in American memory, right alongside

Washington at Valley Forge and Andy Jackson at New Orleans, it was surely the perfect glorious contrast of U. S. Grant and Robert E. Lee, sitting down in Wilmer McLean's brick house at Appomattox to end the war. Everybody in the world knew the scene. Silver-haired patrician Lee in his handsome clean uniform with his yellow sash and his jeweled sword. Laconic little U. S. Grant in his dirty boots and his mud-spattered old private's uniform with the three stars sewn like an afterthought on the shoulder. Grant writing out the terms of surrender the way he always wrote, without hesitation or pause, then handing them modestly over to Lee, generous, noble terms, Grant's own initiative and the first great step toward national reconciliation and forgiveness. It took a hard heart indeed to vote against Appomattox.

Cadwallader lay down on the bed and pulled the blanket to his chin. He set his mental clock to wake him up one hour later; yawned. There was one more reason, he thought as he drifted off to sleep, why the people had twice elected Grant as President, and might yet do it again. Grant was the country's last true connection to the martyred Abraham Lincoln. Grant was Lincoln's friend and Lincoln's heir. The two of them had walked side by side down the smoking streets of Richmond in 1865, the tall and the short of it, as Lincoln had joked. What Grant really represented, Cadwallader thought, was Atonement and Tribute at once.

If Grant wanted the Republican nomination, he could probably have it, as the cub reporter said, by spontaneous combustion.

CHAPTER FIVE

Y OUR FRIEND MARK TWAIN," SAID WILLIAM TECUMSEH "CUMP" Sherman, and he turned his head to the left and covered his mouth, "is a piece of *work!*"

Somebody whooped his name, and Sherman stood up and wagged his cigar and sat down again to a foot-stamping chorus of "Uncle Cump! Uncle Cump!" He leaned over to pour a little more coffee in Grant's cup. "Twain told me he came up the staircase tonight, into the hall"—Sherman swept his cigar across the spectacularly resplendent banquet room that the Palmer House Hotel claimed was the largest in the world—"found all those women lined up on the stairs to watch us go in. Says, 'Don't you think the General ought to come out for *female rights* tonight? Win some *votes?*' There he is now."

Grant saw him, three tables away, lanky on his feet, all red hair and red moustaches, glass of water raised in their direction like a gladiator giving a toast. Twain said something to the group at his table and they fell apart in raucous laughter, though you could only tell that from their pantomime, because by now there were five hundred men in the room, and what seemed like five hundred more waiters, and over the noise of the voices and laughter and glasses and silver there was still the orchestra playing every Civil

War march ever written. Twain blew a kiss to Sherman, and the table went to pieces.

"He's coming over," Sherman said.

And indeed he was. Grant studied his menu. They had passed the oyster, turtle soup, and salmon courses, and the waiters were starting to fan out with the roast beef servings, and as far as he could tell, Mark Twain had yet to take a bite.

"He's wild as can be," Sherman said.

Grant smiled at the thought. He had carried *The Innocents Abroad* with him on his round-the-world tour, and he enjoyed the idea of Mark Twain running wild anywhere. He looked at Sherman, who was now standing up again and leading the orchestra with both arms. He looked past Sherman, down the head table, where little Phil Sheridan, brand-new father of twins and the fiercest cavalryman since Genghis Khan, had scrambled onto a chair and commenced conducting *Sherman*. "Wild as can be," he said, though nobody heard him.

Twain had stopped at the first row of tables just below the head table—there were six vast rows altogether, Grant had counted them automatically, each one running the length of the room—and he was saying something to Bob Ingersoll, and Ingersoll too was laughing out loud. Grant sipped his coffee and recalled to mind Twain's first droll words to him that afternoon, when they had all stood together outside to review the parade. Twain had reached out his hand to Grant, but turned his head sideways to Sherman and drawled, "I first met the President back in 1870. I *know* he remembers me. I was the one who didn't ask him for a job."

"That was 'Marching Through Georgia,' " Sherman said, dropping into his seat.

Grant nodded. He had never in his life been able to tell one tune from another.

"And here comes Twain."

AT THE REPORTERS' TABLE IN THE EXTREME BACK OF THE BAN- quet hall, next to the kitchen doors, Nicholas Trist leaned forward and tried to see between two blazing chandeliers. In order to accommodate Grant's banquet the hotel had apparently knocked away one whole wall on the left of the hall to make it even bigger, and installed what seemed like a regimental band and a small village of extra tables and potted palms. From where he sat Trist could just make out the figures of Grant and Sherman at the head table two hundred feet away and raised on a platform. Both were in uniform, like three-fourths of the other men dining, and both were just now standing up to shake hands with a redheaded man about forty, wearing a full-dress evening suit with a cutaway coat.

"Grant's meat." Cadwallader jabbed his fork in the same direction. "Always burnt." A waiter was depositing slabs of roast beef in front of the two generals. Even from this distance it was evident that Grant's piece was burned coal black.

"Grant don't eat chicken," Cadwallader added. "Claims he can't eat anything that ever walked on two legs. Has his roast beef cooked till it's dry. Won't touch his meat if he sees a drop of blood."

Trist nodded and made a mental note. French readers would be delighted and appalled.

Cadwallader shaded his eyes against the chandeliers. "They called Grant a 'butcher' in the war. Some butcher, can't stand the sight of blood. That's Mark Twain the writer up there with him now—*he* fought in the Confederate Army, but just for two months. You don't like Grant."

Trist looked up in surprise.

"Right age," Cadwallader said. "Got that missing arm, got veteran written all over you. I look around, you—and maybe me—are the only two people here not having a fall-down hissy fit about being in the same room with our great General. So which one was it? Spotsylvania? the Wilderness? Cold Harbor?"

"Cold Harbor."

"Hard to forget Cold Harbor." Cadwallader poured himself more wine. "But Grant was a hero at Vicksburg," he added in a judicious tone. "Saved the country at Vicksburg."

Which was absolutely true, Trist thought as he made his way down to the front of the hall, nobody doubted Vicksburg. What interested him more right now, what would interest any reporter, was Mark Twain standing next to U. S. Grant and chattering away like a long-lost friend. Mark Twain the writer was famous all over Europe for *The Innocents Abroad*, which made hilarious fun of American ignorance, and *The Gilded Age*, which made hilarious fun of American greed. The latest book, *Tom Sawyer,* apparently didn't make fun of anything, but Trist's French editor would still be fascinated—an ex-Confederate soldier (where had he fought? get details) and the ex-commanding general of the North: a caption bobbed inevitably to mind: Never the Twain Shall Meet.

Just as he reached the top of the steps, a scowling muscle-bound man in a tuxedo stepped in front of him and blocked the way: a bodyguard for real. Nobody got near the General tonight, Trist was told, back on down, go to your seat.

The clatter of dishes and voices was deafening; the orchestra began to tune up again. Trist tried to make himself heard—General Sheridan turned and glared—the bodyguard took Trist's business card, slipped it into his pocket without looking, and stood right where he was.

Trist waited an instant longer. He had actually met Grant earlier that day as he passed into Cameron's suite for what was supposed to be a private conference—met, shaken hands, been dismissed in a minute and a half. Not even his campaign manager, evidently, could force the General to give an interview he didn't want to give. Trist moved to the right in the hope of catching Grant's eye. Directly over the head table, amid all the other flags and streamers, flapping in the smoky atmosphere like a ship's sail, floated a big black-and-white portrait that Trist hadn't seen from his distant table: U. S. GRANT——MAN OF DESTINY.

From this angle the man of destiny looked small, tired, bored. The bodyguard took a warning step toward him. Trist moved farther to his right. In a cleared space in front of the guests of honor Brobdingnagian bakers had placed a white frosted cake molded in the shape of the Confederate fortress at Vicksburg—with little cannons, little flags, little sugar soldiers. Mark Twain was just coming down another set of steps, between the cake and a bristling display of regimental shields and flags. When Trist reached him he squinted down at his card with undisguised impatience.

"I write for two French journals," Trist told him, bending forward to drown out "Tramp, Tramp, Tramp"—pouring out the flattery like syrup—"my readers would love to hear how a famous writer knows General Grant so well."

Twain had small, dark, untrustworthy eyes, and up close a

shock of carrot-red hair that was already going gray in patches. He shook his head, looked the other way to greet somebody, and told Trist no press interviews this evening, not even any whiskey—he held up his glass of water—not till after his speech. He studied Trist's sleeve.

"Veteran?" He had a slow, soft Missouri drawl.

"Yes."

"Well, come on up and see me tomorrow," he said, pocketing the card, "after breakfast, suite forty-five, down the hall from Grant."

A T TEN O'CLOCK PRECISELY (PALMER HOUSE TIME) CUMP Sherman rose to his feet, put his hands on his hips, and bellowed at crowd-stopping volume:

"Can you hear me in the middle of the hall?"

"No!"

"Then you'll have to read about it in the papers!"

There was a printed program of speakers now before each plate—the evening's star attraction was the long-winded atheist Robert Ingersoll, listed as ninth in order, certain, Trist thought with a sinking heart, to speak for an hour all by himself. Mark Twain, the single Southerner on the program, was listed last.

Sherman rapped on the table. The orchestra whinnied to a halt. The chandeliers and lights began to dim. Trist turned in his chair and saw that along the back of the room women were now filing in and standing in attentive, respectful knots next to the wall. When he turned forward again everything was deep in shadows, except for one great unwavering light focused on the head table, the first speaker opening his notes, and seated beside him, Grant.

By the third interminable oration in praise of the General, Trist could hardly sit still. He pushed away from the table and carried a bottle of brandy to the back of the hall, peering in the shadows as he went for a glimpse of Mrs. Cameron. Out training her hounds, sharpening her arrows. She was actually the widower Cameron's second wife, that much he knew, younger than Cameron by twenty years. Around other men in the hotel she was mildly flirtatious, sensationally attractive; flirtatious, intelligent, unhappy—his last adjective surprised him so much that he put down the brandy bottle and walked a few more feet along the wall. Mark Twain emerged from the darkest alcove, next to the kitchen. "Look at Grant," he whispered, pointing, "cast-iron." And down at the head table Grant's face was indeed in its famous "silent" state, which Trist had only seen in photographs: utterly blank. The orator, whoever he was, wheeled at exactly that instant and stretched out his arms dramatically toward the General, and Grant merely stared straight ahead, motionless as the room rose and cheered. "Bulletproof," Twain groaned, and went away.

At midnight there was a ten-minute intermission. In the lavatory corridor Cadwallader swayed on his feet, drunk, Trist realized, drunk and exhausted. "I *like* your new personal writer," he informed Don Cameron, who was shoving his big red-faced way back into the hall, and he gripped Trist's shoulder and gave the Senator a sweaty grin. "Veteran, well-spoken—you treat him right, you hear?"

Cameron was a bad politician, a child could see that, Trist thought, as brusque and rude as money and drink could make him; but he was also chairman of Grant's campaign committee. Even he knew enough to nod back at the little reporter and pry his mouth into a smile.

"Power of the pen," Cadwallader told Trist with a smirk. They reclaimed their seats in the banquet hall where the eighth speaker of the night had just gotten to his legs. "Grant needs every kind word in the press that Cameron can buy or borrow." He sat back heavily, slopped brandy into a water glass. "Book about Grant," he said, and leaned over confidentially. Applause and laughter were coming from scattered parts of the hall. "*My* book." Cadwallader closed his eyes, nodded. "*Not* for publication." Leaned back. "Show you sometime."

Malarial fever, Trist had learned, could rise and fall like a red-hot tide. He felt a familiar scalding flush, pushed his chair back again, and looked around the room. Mrs. Cameron was nowhere to be seen. Where was Twain? Trist passed unsteadily across the rear of the hall, stumbling like a blind man in the darkness, and found him in the farthest possible corner, at a small table by the wall. Next to him a youngish, drunkish man in a private's uniform was clutching his head between two hands.

"Vilas is good," the private whispered miserably to Twain.

Twain aimed his cigar at the speaker. "Colonel Sanderson Vilas," he muttered to Trist. "From Wisconsin, famous stump speaker and preacher."

"In Illinois," the private said, "we think Bob Ingersoll is one hell of a talker."

Vilas was a small dog-faced man whose neck and chin were lost in his high military collar. He was evidently responding to the toast "Our Gallant Leaders." Seated beside him in the spotlight, Grant kept his face clamped in an iron calm.

"Here he goes," Twain said as Vilas began to pace back and forth and pound his open hand with his fist. There was a rising shout from the crowd—

"Get up on the table! On the table!"

From the audience a blur of men suddenly surged forward, around the head table; heads, hands flashed in the spotlight, Vilas disappeared into shadows, reappeared abruptly, lifted on a wave of blue shoulders and carried right up to the top of the table, next to the imperturbable Grant. His shoes snagged on the white tablecloth, and he wobbled dangerously for a moment, straddled a plate, blinked out at the room, then, almost without a pause, he resumed his pounding oration. The hall thundered and cheered.

Lightning flashed in Trist's skull. He fumbled in his coat for a packet of medicine. A few intelligible words cut through the noise like rockets—"Grant—Heroism—Let Us Have Peace"—and then the room seemed to crash apart in applause.

"Bob can't touch *that*," the private wailed.

When Ingersoll did appear, introduced by a disheveled Sherman, he stood for a moment behind the table and looked out at the crowd. Then he grinned and pulled up a chair and climbed onto the table as well ("Now we'll *all* have to do it," Twain grumbled). He was an odd, bald figure with a high forehead and small, close-set eyes. He waited for almost a full minute, hands in pockets, audibly jingling coins. "The Volunteers," he announced, and began his speech.

Slowly, as the brandy did its work, Trist found the room growing hotter and darker. Sherman's white face became a starburst of disorder. Twain sipped water, studied Ingersoll's every gesture. The oration moved ponderously through the topic of the volunteers, how they had risked everything to defend their country, how they had entered the war certain of victory, fallen away into the bleak discouragement of the middle years—Manassas, Antietam, Fredericksburg—watched with awe as this calm man before them, the Supreme Volunteer, rose out of undeserved obscurity and took the helm.

Against his will Trist found himself straining forward, listening. As always, whenever he thought about the war, the result was a bundle of contradictions—butcher versus hero, ruined bodies versus freed slaves, a saved Union, a country to run away from.

The private from Illinois pushed the brandy toward him. You go to war because of your father, Trist suddenly thought, men always had. Ingersoll reached Gettysburg with its twenty thousand dead—the father Trist had never known had been a soldier; his stepfather had been a Jeffersonian patriot, dedicated with all his heart to the new Jeffersonian nation; as a diplomat, he had settled the Mexican War single-handedly, writing the treaty himself, and then congressional politics had done him out of a job and a pension, and he had died living on next to nothing, but still a patriot to his bones. He had driven Trist to the recruitment station in Hartford; his last political act had been to vote for Grant's second term in 1872. On the platform Grant's small, hard profile caught the light and held it. Ingersoll's high voice went on relentlessly, naming battle after bloody battle in the final year.

Trist drained his brandy. Next to him Twain scratched a note to himself in a small leather pad. Grant was a volunteer, Ingersoll told them, Sherman, Sheridan, every soul in uniform tonight— when they marched out to save their land, ready to give the last full measure of devotion, "at that sacred moment blood was water," he cried, "money was leaves, and life was only common air until one flag"—his right hand swooped and swung to the Stars and Stripes suspended above the General's head—"until *one* flag floated over a Republic *without* a master, and without a *slave!*"

Before his hand could drop, the audience was on its feet clapping and stamping and waving their napkins in a snowstorm of applause.

There were five more speakers before Twain. At intervals he turned to Trist and said something so low and fleeting that Trist could only pretend to hear. Once, in a lull, the drunken private asked if he had written out his speech, and Twain explained in his soft drawl that he never wrote things out, but instead arranged his silver and plates in a mnemonic system. A cup placed here meant such-and-such a joke, a fork turned sideways meant change the subject. "What's your toast?" the soldier asked, but Twain merely shook his head and drank his water.

By two o'clock in the morning the banquet hall was a limp haze of smoke and exhaustion. At speaker number fourteen Twain slipped away. Trist made his way back to Cadwallader's side just as Sherman rose to his feet for the last introduction.

"Cameron married his niece," Cadwallader whispered. "Sherman's."

Sherman was motioning to the top of the table. Somebody else—General Sheridan? Ingersoll?—was offering to boost Twain up, but the writer waved them both aside and stayed behind the table. Unhurried, he moved a few leftover glasses and spoons in an aimless pattern on the rumpled cloth. Then he reached into the shadows and brought out a chair and used it to climb onto the table all by himself, just to the left of the seated Grant. He pulled long and deep on his cigar and gazed about the room.

The last clatterings and clinkings faded away. "The Babies," Twain said in a leisurely tone. His voice was unremarkable, yet carried to the corners of the hall. "My toast is, 'The Babies, As They Comfort Us in Our Sorrows, Let Us Not Forget Them in Our Festivities.' "

He paused and flicked a little ash into a saucer. "I like that," he said. Another pause. "We haven't all been generals or heroes or statesmen, but when the toast works down to the babies, why, we stand on common ground." For the first time since the speeches had started, Grant actually moved his head and looked up. Twain looked down at him, utterly deadpan. "Well," he said slowly, "we've *all* been babies." Grant's beard parted in a smile.

Afterward, when he tried to remember it, Trist couldn't be sure precisely what Twain had said—they had all been babies, babies tyrannized comically even over soldiers and heroes: "You could face the death storm at Donelson and Vicksburg, and give back blow for blow, but when *he* clawed your whiskers and pulled your hair and twisted your nose, you had to take it. When *he* ordered his pap bottle, and it wasn't warm, did you talk back? Not you. You went to work and *warmed* it." By the end of the first two minutes Twain had his audience helpless with laughter, even Grant, who

was rolling about in his chair like everyone else. At the end of
every sentence he stopped and looked languidly about the room,
expressionless, while the laughter continued to build. He's routed
Grant, Trist thought, changed places with him.

Toward the end he turned his attention briefly from Grant to
Sheridan. "As long as you're in your right mind," he told the
crowd, "don't ever have twins. Twins amount to a permanent riot."

Slowly, carefully, he built to a long climax. He asked them to
picture the future rulers of the country, those who would inherit
the great flag of the Republic that Colonel Ingersoll had saluted,
when it flew fifty years hence over a nation of two hundred millions—at this very moment, Twain said, those illustrious leaders
were no more than *babies* lying in their cradles. Imagine a future
Admiral Farragut *teething*, a future *President* pulling at his tiny
tufts of hair, a future great astronomer reaching for his wet nurse.
"And in still one more cradle," he said, "somewhere under the flag,
the future illustrious Commander in Chief of the American armies
is so little burdened with his approaching grandeurs and responsi-
bilities as to be giving his whole strategic mind, at this moment, to
trying to find out some way to get his own big toe into his mouth."
The laughter died away. The crowd stirred uneasily. Grant's countenance grew blank as Twain's. The toast seemed suddenly to
hover on the brink of catastrophic insult. "An achievement,"
Twain continued, "which, meaning no disrespect, the illustrious
guest of this evening turned *his* whole attention to some fifty-six
years ago."

A kind of shuddering silence fell over the room. Twain looked
down at the table and used his shoe to move a spoon an inch to
one side. A flag rustled and snapped in a current of stale air. He
surveyed the room slowly, left to right. Raised his cigar to his lips,
took it away.

"And if the child is but a prophecy of the man"—the longest,
most agonizing pause yet; then a headlong rush of words—"there
are mighty few who will doubt that he *succeeded*."

In the detonation of laughter and cheers that followed, as
Grant actually stood to shake Twain's hand and Sherman clasped
him in a rolling, wrestling bear hug, Trist felt a grip on his arm.
"Stole my idea," Cadwallader complained thickly. "Grant in his
cradle, goddam Twain."

When Twain finally made his way past their table, heading toward the exit, still surrounded by shoulder-pounding admirers, he stopped and leaned over to grab Cadwallader's lapel. "Did you see Grant break up? Didn't I *fetch* him? Didn't I make his bones ache?" To Trist: "Didn't I nearly *kill* him?"

CHAPTER SIX

THE SECRET LIFE
OF U. S. GRANT

by Sylvanus Cadwallader

CHAPTER TWO

WELL, MEXICO MADE HIM; MEXICO WRECKED HIM.
I myself despise the whole damn hotfooted Mexican country, have from the first minute I crossed the border as a young "special correspondent," and that was not two full months after Lieutenant U. S. Grant himself marched in, in the year of decision 1846, part of old Zachary Taylor's so-called "Army of Observation."

Actually, I came to despise the state of Texas first and simply enlarged my dislike to cover Mexico too, both of them dried-up oceans of sand and thorns, under a sun so hot it seemed like a maniac slinging coals of fire. (Phil Sheridan once told me if he owned Texas and Hell, he'd live in Hell and rent out Texas.)

But Grant—Grant fell in love with every part of it. I have heard him wax almost lyrical (for Grant) over the beauty of the little Mexican town of Matamoros on the Rio Grande. He talks about the red-tiled roofs, the red and yellow flowers on the white walls, even the soft, tranquil nights, he says, full of perfume. I sometimes think the human personality is like one of those little Russian dolls, every time you open it there's another one inside. This wasn't your Grant of Cold Harbor and the Wilderness. This was the dreamy boy from Ohio popping up, who went through West Point skipping his lessons to read the romantic novels of Walter Scott and Bulwer-Lytton; Grant number one.

West Point, of course, had been his awful father's idea, not for the glory and prestige of a military career—in those old peacetime days there wasn't any—but because the education was free, and Jesse Grant never spent a dime he didn't have to.

Grant himself has told me the story more than once—home he came for Christmas in 1838, back from the latest school he'd been attending, age seventeen, and there was his father opening an official-looking blue envelope from Washington City. "Ulysses," Jesse said—nobody alive ever called him "Hiram"—"I believe you're going to receive the appointment."

"What appointment?"

"To West Point. I applied for it."

"But I won't go!"

But Jesse folded his arms and said grimly he thought he would, and Grant likes to add, dryly, *and I thought so too, if he did.*

An undistinguished time he had of it, however, hardly living up to Jesse's boasts about young 'Lyss's "genius." The only subjects he ever did well in were mathematics and drawing—an officer has to be able to see and draw the land in front of him, that was how Colonel Alexander Hamilton brought himself to George Washington's attention—and Grant did very badly indeed in French (though in Mexico he learned to speak Spanish quite well); middling in military deportment. (The cadets of Grant's era all spoke with awe of an earlier cadet who had passed through four straight years without a single demerit, Bobby Lee.) Grant hated the discipline, hated being addressed as "Animal," as all the plebes were, found the rigmarole of army customs pointless. In his first year he read in the papers that Congress was thinking of abolishing the Academy. Though not otherwise a religious person, he prayed assiduously for that to happen.

He graduated twenty-first in a class of thirty-nine and was assigned to the Infantry and posted away to St. Louis. There he passed the time drilling his troops and courting his roommate's sister. Julia Dent lived with her parents just close enough for a young second lieutenant to ride over after the day's work and linger chatting in the Missouri twilight until a disapproving father grudgingly asked him in for supper. (About West Point I will only add that in all the mathematics textbooks today the standard solution to a certain problem in analytic geometry is credited to one U. S. Grant. His famous old professor Dennis Mahan, author of a dozen books on mathematics and physics, wrote analyses of every cadet who passed through his class; Grant's "mental machine," Mahan claimed, was of the "powerful low-pressure class, which condenses its own steam and consumes its own smoke." I have no idea what he meant.)

Missouri twilight; copper-colored, flame-throwing Mexican noon. Where West Point was an episode, an interlude, Mexico was an education.

An education in injustice, first of all, because it seemed to Grant, as it did to me, that from start to finish the Mexican War was totally wrong, morally wrong, the calculated and indefensible invasion of a weak country by a stronger one, for no better reason than greed for land. One way or another, President James Knox Polk meant to "adjust" the disputed boundary between Mexico and the brand-new state of Texas and in the process simply seize all of California to the west, to make it safe for expansion and slavery. Generals who disagreed were swiftly shelved. Generals who looked as if they might become presidential rivals next election year—a lesson in politics and war not lost on Grant—found themselves out of command. While the diplomats played out their charade, Polk quietly massed his troops at Corpus Christi. And then on March 11, 1846, Zachary Taylor raised his glove and gave the order, and the American Army set out at a run for the Rio Grande.

At the first little battle of Palo Alto, the Mexicans fired their muskets at four hundred yards—might as well have fired from the moon—and discharged a few ancient, creaking cannons. (The advancing Americans stood in the dried grass and watched the cannonballs slowly bouncing and skipping toward them, then just took a step or two out of the way.) Nonetheless there were casualties. Grant wrote home to his fiancée Miss Dent that a nine-pound shot hit one Captain Page in the face, and "the under jaw is gone all the way to the windpipe and the tongue hangs down upon the throat" (a Grant love letter).

Your historians, snug in their college library, will call the Mexican War a dress rehearsal for the Civil War. But your journalists
like me will tell you it was actually the last old-fashioned war in history. The soldiers, those that were not perpetually drunk, malaria-
ridden, or pondering desertion, fought for individual glory, not for
President Polk, certainly not for the Cause. What they wanted, first
of all, was to get their names in the official reports to Washington,
second to get their names in the newspapers. Many a gift of whiskey
was I offered for a special paragraph or two in the Chicago *Times,*
concerning little local acts of heroism. And the glory did indeed rain
down—Bobby Lee, Pete Longstreet, a Mississippi colonel called
Jefferson Davis—name after name gained a brevet promotion or a
special citation in Scott's weekly report.

Not Grant's name, however. At the start of the invasion Grant
had been made quartermaster of his regiment, in charge of the
mules and the cooks and the dusty boxes of hardtack that followed
the fighting troops. Not much glory in kicking mules.

He begged for reassignment, but he was too competent at his
job, and too insignificant and unprepossessing in appearance for
his colonel to notice. As often as he could he left his braying
charges to the sutlers and raced ahead to join the battle unoffi-
cially. I claim our paths crossed once or twice—Grant says no—we
both remember the eerie sight of soldiers' corpses floating in the
Rio Grande, rolling and twitching as if they were still alive,
because the fish were already nipping their flesh. And the day at
Veracruz it was so spellbinding hot that the whole army marched
in its underwear (glory!). At Monterrey, behind a barricade, he
watched a wounded private who sat down on a boulder with his
red sticky guts spilling onto his lap, singing a psalm till he toppled
over and died.

Once, in the ironic fashion of life, the Congressman, now a
general, who had appointed Grant to West Point came galloping
by at the head of a division; two weeks later they buried him in the
sand. And once, in the battle of Mexico City, young Grant did get
his name in the reports for the commonsense feat of carrying a little Howitzer cannon up to the top of a church and bombarding the
Mexicans below.

But when the army captured Mexico City at last and the diplomats set to work, Grant was still a second lieutenant, obscure as
ever.

His comrades passed the time of the occupation in fighting duels and chasing señoritas—the Mexican girls used to come in giggling squads to the river's edge every afternoon and step out of their clothes for a bath; to an Ohio boy a vision right out of Eden—but Grant was too puritan for the one and too sensible for the other. (In 1868, in a spectacular waste of money, the Democrats hired some of Pinkerton's detectives to follow presidential candidate Grant and see if they could trap him in a bawdy scandal.) He set up a little private bakery next to his quartermaster's tent, perhaps the only profitable business he's ever run, and he wrote his weekly letter back to St. Louis. But mostly he sat in his quiet, moody way with a bottle in his hand, staring at life. The liquor started to buzz in his blood. It settled into him like a squatter into an empty house. Grant number two.

CHAPTER SEVEN

To the ladies," don Cameron said with a grimace.

He splashed champagne into a crystal flute, wiped his moustache with his hand, and looked about the room with as little good humor and grace, Trist thought, as he could possibly manage.

"Oh, don't go," said Clover Adams. And she raised one tiny palm like a traffic policeman and gestured for Trist to halt. "Do give Mr. Trist some champagne," she said to Cameron. "How often do we meet somebody who's actually been to Morocco too? Do stay, Mr. Trist, and talk to us about Morocco."

"Invite the gardener and the cook, too, why not," Cameron grumbled, and picked up the telegram the maid had placed on his table and walked over to his chair.

"Mr. and Mrs. Adams," Elizabeth Cameron informed Trist calmly, standing with her back to the window on Lafayette Square, "spent the last six months abroad."

"Dangling about every sink pit possible," said Mr. Adams in a thin, precise British accent. "We travelled not wisely, but too well." He lifted his own champagne glass with a sardonic nod to Cameron. "To the ladies, of course, and the cook and gardener too."

Trist looked at him curiously. He had only stopped by to deliver a courtesy copy of his interview with Mark Twain in Chicago three days ago—an interview now telegraphed and presumably being set in type in Paris—but he had heard the names in the anteroom and it was hard not to come in, hard not to be curious. Mr. Adams was Henry Adams, and Henry Adams was invariably identified in the press at home and abroad as the wealthy and brilliant grandson and great-grandson of Presidents, Washington City's foremost "intellectual" (to use the fashionable new word). He stood no taller than his wife, neither of them much above five feet tall Trist estimated, but where she was lively and energetic, her husband wore an air of weary, languid disapproval that made him seem even smaller. He had a round head and a high, bald, shining forehead; he kept both hands close to his chest, where his coat buttoned; the skin of his face was so soft and pink that he looked unnervingly like a baby with a beard. He had in fact once been pointed out to Trist at the beginning of the war, in the bar of Willard's Hotel, talking with Lincoln's private secretary John Hay. But then Adams had gone off with his father Charles Francis Adams to the American legation in London, Hay had gone back to the President's Palace, and Trist . . .

"We know all about *you*, Mr. Trist, from General Beale." Mrs. Adams boldly handed him a glass of champagne. "We live across the way—1607 H Street. The Senator and the General give the Square *ton*, and now here you are to give us—"

"Goddam bad news," Cameron said and stood up. "My brother-in-law," he told his wife.

"Wayne McVeagh," Adams murmured to his wife.

"Wants to change the unit-rule vote in Chicago. Make Pennsylvania the same as Maine. This is Tilden and Blaine ganging up on Grant."

"We mean to discuss Morocco, not Chicago," Clover Adams interposed firmly. "My husband and I were in Spain two months ago, Mr. Trist, pawing through Spanish archives, and for some reason now forgotten decided on impulse to press on to Africa."

Trist drank a swallow of Cameron's champagne (Cameron left the room flapping the telegram against his leg).

"Well, I don't actually know much about Morocco," Trist said. "The magazine I work for sent me to Tetuán a few times."

"*We* went to Tetuán," Clover Adams said.

"A sky so blue," Henry Adams told Elizabeth Cameron, "one can scoop it out with a spoon."

"We stayed in a Moorish house," Clover said, "kept by a Jew. I was the first American woman ever to come to Tetuán, so they carried me off to meet the Ketib's wife—very handsome woman about fifty, she had bare feet dyed the color of henna and a great grinning red-turbaned Negress who fanned her and screamed with amusement at me every three minutes. I loved Morocco, but Henry liked Spain."

"A good-natured, dirty people, the Spanish," Adams said, "always apologetic, if one doesn't somehow insult them." He turned his round head toward Trist, who wondered for a moment if he was about to be insulted. "From North Africa to Chicago, Mr. Trist—which did you find more exotic?"

"I knew he would get back to Chicago," Clover said with mock petulance. "Henry's obsessed with General Grant and the nomination."

Trist glanced at Elizabeth Cameron, still standing next to the window, with the dim gaslights of Lafayette Square behind her. The most beautiful women in the world were French. French women wore silks that clung to their skins like a kiss. They adorned their slender necks with sparkling jewels, their hair with fragrant, expensive powders. They pushed up and separated their small round breasts in a heart-stopping scoop of *décolletage*, with an engineering miracle known to corset makers as *le divorce*, because it kept asunder what would otherwise be pressed together. But he had never seen any woman, in Paris or wherever, as dazzling as Senator Donald Cameron's wife. Bad, adulterous thoughts. Poor Actaeon had died a happy man. He put his glass down on a table, beside one of Maudie's cast-off dolls. To his surprise Elizabeth Cameron picked it up and handed it back to him. "My husband will be busy answering his telegram—do have your drink, Mr. Trist."

Henry Adams was watching them both over the rim of his glass. "Not obsessed with General Grant," he said, as if there had been no interruption, "so much as bored with Europe. My wife and I are the only people we know who find America more amusing than Europe."

Clover Adams had wandered to the photograph of the train

wreck on the wall. "We saw a train wreck in England," she said, "in Shropshire. Carnage everywhere."

"Chicago, for instance," Adams said, "was a great triumph for Grant. His name is in all the papers again, his nomination is almost assured. Yet I myself think he may have come home from his world tour too soon, his candidacy may peak before the convention. Certainly he's left his enemies time to regroup. At any rate, what can be more entertaining than to watch?"

"My husband," said Clover, "knew Grant when he was President—"

"I saw him once, at his Palace. Thereafter I declined to meet him."

Trist pictured the taciturn Grant confronted with such a little engine of patrician self-amusement, and he turned to hide his smile. When he looked at Elizabeth Cameron, however, her gaze was fixed, steadily, uncritically, on Henry Adams.

"It was about somebody's hair," Clover said.

"My friend Motley"—Adams had begun by speaking to Trist, but in the course of things turned naturally to Elizabeth Cameron, so that he seemed now to be addressing her alone—"Motley was made ambassador to England, but Grant disliked him. He recalled Motley because he parted his hair in the middle."

The two women laughed. Adams began a longer story. Trist listened with only half a mind. His malaria had entered a new phase, recurring just every four or five days now and much less severely than before; but as always, drink or excess heat seemed to stir it up. He put down his glass again and moved away from the fireplace, where cut logs had been stacked by a prodigal hand. Elizabeth Cameron, still laughing, rested her fingers for a moment on Adams's arm. In the flickering light of the room her skin was soft, radiant, her eyes as pale as agates. On the other side of the fireplace poor Clover Adams looked like a small black crow.

"In fact," Adams was now saying, and as he spoke the idea suddenly occurred to Trist, in a simple, neutral, and unshakable way, that he had never met someone he disliked so much so soon—"in fact, I'm not even registered to vote, so I ought not to have *any* opinion." He made a quick, high-pitched sniffing sound that was the opposite of Don Cameron's habitual snort. "I'm merely an observer of the Great Democratic Experiment. I *will* say that, whatever he was before the war, when he became President, Grant utterly lost the distinction between right and wrong. This is, of course, the first step to success in politics."

"You were in the war, Mr. Trist," Clover Adams said. "General Beale said you wrote a book of sketches about it. He said you had a most interesting story—you resigned from Yale College in your second year to become a volunteer. Then, of course . . ." She looked sympathetically at his arm. "Did you serve under Grant?"

"I suppose everybody did," Trist replied. He was conscious of trying to appear as boorish and inarticulate as possible, to distinguish himself from Adams. "But Chicago was only the second or third time I ever saw him."

"Mr. Trist," Elizabeth Cameron interjected, surprising Trist again, "unlike most soldiers, evidently doesn't care to speak of the war."

Before Trist could say a word, the hallway door had swung open and Don Cameron walked in.

"Telegram's gone," he announced. "I've told McVeagh what to do, straight." As he passed with his small quick tread he left a sharp scent of whiskey in the air. "Dinner's almost ready," he added, and frowned over his shoulder at Trist. "Senate meets tomorrow at ten for a short session, then a Republican caucus you might want to watch."

Trist nodded and turned to go.

At that moment the black maid appeared at the double doors leading to the dining room, and half a second later the governess, with little Maudie Cameron at her side, appeared behind her.

"She *insists* on saying good night to Papa," the governess said, and Maudie skipped free with a yell and ran to her father, who stooped to kiss her.

"Our revels now are ended," murmured Clover Adams, just loud enough for Trist to hear. The maid stepped aside to reveal the dinner table, and Clover looked automatically at Henry. But her husband had already extended his arm to Elizabeth Cameron with a little sniff and a bow. From the hallway Trist heard his thin, penetrating voice. "My dear Senator, may I borrow your wife?"

CHAPTER EIGHT

THE BEST THING IN HIS INTERVIEW WITH MARK TWAIN, TRIST
thought, had nothing to do with Grant.

They had met as arranged the morning after the banquet in
Palmer House suite 45, a spacious set of rooms looking out on
State Street, and Twain (resplendent in Turkish slippers and a
deep maroon dressing gown he called his "toga") had waved his
hand airily at a breakfast table set for two. On the floor beside it,
in a sitting posture, was a life-sized cat made out of pasteboard
and tin. "The illuminated cat," he had announced, and promptly
lowered the curtains to demonstrate that the cat, painted over
with a thick coat of phosphorus, actually glowed in the dark, like
a cat of fire. "Scares away rats and mice at night," Twain had
explained, "beautiful parlor ornament in daylight"—he wanted
Trist's European readers to know that this was American ingenuity and enterprise at their finest. He, Twain, thought he would
invest fifty thousand dollars of his own money in it, make a fortune, and retire.

An irresistible first paragraph—Trist had written it out in
French for *L'Illustration* (*"chat de feu"*) and English for one of the
London newspapers that sometimes took his articles.

And the reason he thought of the illuminated cat right now, at nine-twenty-five in the morning after his evening champagne at Don Cameron's house, was that he was standing on the corner of First Street and Pennsylvania Avenue, in the shadow of the Capitol, and watching the biggest, fattest black rat he had ever seen. It was seated under a luggage wagon from the National Hotel, combing its whiskers, not glowing, but easily twice the size of the cat of fire. When the wagon lurched forward into Pennsylvania Avenue the rat gave Trist one curious, appraising glance and then raced uphill toward the Senate, as though it belonged.

As perhaps it did, Trist thought, and crossed the street in the same direction.

At the bottom of a circular carriageway he paused again to look up and admire the Capitol dome—unfinished in 1865 when he had last seen the city, which was then a vast army camp in the process of disbanding. Now the great white dome was splendidly in place, and the once cluttered and overbuilt space around the Capitol was largely cleared and landscaped, though just to the north of the Senate wing two or three stray pigs, Washington's unofficial garbage disposers, rooted in the brown grass and mud.

He made his way up past the shabby boarding houses that still lined Constitution Avenue. Inside the Capitol lobby, under the dome, he stopped beside the double-door entrance to the Senate and pulled out his watch. He could go into the visitors' gallery and observe the session—Don Cameron had arranged a permanent pass—or, better, simply meet him afterwards in the committee room that Cameron and other Grant "Stalwarts" used, next to the Supreme Court chamber. He hesitated. Whiskery men pushed around him on their way to the Senate. Clerks and secretaries threaded their way through knots of tourists. The Rotunda was crowded, noisy, poorly lit.

"You are standing, Mr. Trist, beneath perhaps the worst executed historical painting in the nation. Not to mention the least accurate."

Henry Adams's voice cut easily through the clamor of the lobby. He pointed his furled umbrella up toward the gilt-framed painting that hung just above their heads. " 'The Signing of the Declaration of Independence,' " he read. "History at its most fictitious. That's supposed to be my great-grandfather John Adams over there, but no Adams male has ever reached the middle age with so much hair. Jefferson over here"—the umbrella swung right—"was in reality quite coarsely redheaded, and entirely feline. Franklin was taller than everybody thinks. The whole thing is a fraud, of course, because the Continental Congress never did assemble for the purpose of signing the Declaration of Independence—they went to the clerk's office privately, one by one, over the space of two months—and they adopted the resolution on July second, not July fourth. Otherwise—" He spread his arms in a gesture of unruffled tribulation. Trist smiled and craned his head to look at the painting again.

"The artist, John Trumbull, was also blind in one eye. Come walk with me a little, Mr. Trist," Adams said. "As the feller says, 'I would have speech with thee.'"

I WOULD HAVE HIM TO DINNER," CLOVER ADAMS SAID. "I WOULD sit him down at the table next to anybody, if that's what you want."

Emily Beale held her teacup poised just at her lips, without tasting (though Clover Adams was known to spend a fortune on her teas), and waited delightedly for Elizabeth Cameron to reply. Emily had been away from Washington for three full months in California, which was the same as the other side of the moon, and they had only arrived home late last night, much too late to call on anybody. But today was another matter. She was not about to waste another morning without real society.

"At heart, you know, I really am a democrat," Clover continued when Elizabeth Cameron said nothing. "In my family we never make any fuss about mingling with servants"—this was true, Clover had been so friendly last year with two Irish carpenters doing work for her that she had actually gone to visit their wives, and Henry had been *furious*. "Besides," Clover said, "if Mr. Bancroft *requests* him—"

"Well, not 'request' exactly." Elizabeth put down her cup and shook her head slightly, so that a few long strands of black hair came loose from her bun, and Emily wondered for a moment (as she had, often, before) what the beautiful Elizabeth Cameron would look like if she wore her hair long and loose, down past her shoulders, like some of the women they had seen in Paris.

"He only said that the name 'Trist' was a very old name—"

"It means 'sad,' " Emily contributed, "in French."

Elizabeth smiled kindly at her. "And he does *look* sad, doesn't he?"

Emily nodded and raised the teacup back to her lips; *almost* raised her knees to her chin like a little girl. At the age of eighteen she still felt young and unformed in the company of such matrons, though Elizabeth was only twenty-two or twenty-three. Clover, of course, was forty, fifty. . . .

"Mr. Bancroft only said it was very likely he came of the Trist family that intermarried with the Jeffersons, before the war."

"Henry said the same thing. He said if he were *that* kind of Trist, he might have family papers for the Book."

"The Book," Elizabeth and Emily murmured in unison. Henry Adams had recently published a life of somebody Emily had never heard of, Albert Gallatin, who had once been Secretary of Treasury. But it was understood by everybody in Lafayette Square that Henry's *real* book was a massive, endless history of Thomas Jefferson (the Adams family enemy) and James Madison when they were presidents. He had gone all over Europe poking in archives. He disappeared most mornings into his study and wrote for hours. Emily had an impression—more than an impression, since she had once, by total accident, found two or three sheets of paper in *dialogue*—that he wrote other things as well, to amuse himself. But "the Book" was sacred.

Clover stood up to hand around a plate of seed cakes, and Emily took the opportunity to glance into the next room, where Clover had set up some of her photography apparatus. Amid the dozens of bookshelves in the sitting room—the Adamses had books the way other houses had ants—she had already hung two or three of her new photographs, including an incredibly stern portrait of her father-in-law and mother-in-law. Both disapproved, Emily knew, *thoroughly* disapproved, of Clover.

She glanced back to see Clover and Elizabeth bent side by side over the tray of cakes as Clover explained something about the recipe, which was undoubtedly her own original creation. It was a cruel contrast, there was no denying that—for all her brilliance Clover Adams was a flat, plain woman with pallid skin and a hooked nose. Next to Elizabeth she looked drab. But then, next to Elizabeth most women looked drab; drab as cabbages. (Irresistibly, Emily turned half an inch to glimpse her own profile in the windowpane.) Whatever it was that sent men weak and trembling to their knees, Elizabeth Cameron had it.

"In Europe," Emily said, taking a cake, "when he worked for Papa, Mr. Trist generally didn't eat with us." She pictured Trist as he had been in Paris and wondered if he were still clean-shaven—most of the men in America, young or old, had more facial hair than goats did. "But I think that was *his* preference, because of his arm. He went to Yale College, you know, for a little while, and he published a book of stories after the war." She ate a mouthful of very dry cake and said, as she usually did, one more thing than she should. "I thought he was handsome, but so pale he didn't look truly well."

"I fear he's given to drinking sprees à la Grant," said Clover, whose father was a doctor and who often diagnosed people quite sharply.

But the subject of Grant was one to be avoided whenever possible—Emily had been well-schooled by her father in neighborly good manners about this. While the Beales counted General and Mrs. Grant as almost their closest family friends, and the Camerons and Grants were political allies, Henry Adams's scorn for the ex-President was a Washington byword. If there was to be harmony in Lafayette Square, all you could do was bite your tongue.

"Well." Elizabeth rose and smoothed the folds of her blue overskirt. She had really the perfect figure, Emily thought, including a full and voluptuous (she chose the word with relish from her limited but specialized French vocabulary) *poitrine*. "Well, it's all a moot point. My husband is going to Scranton tomorrow. Until the June convention I doubt we'll entertain at all. If Mr. Bancroft wants to meet Mr. Trist, I can just send him around with a letter of introduction."

In the windowpane, as she too rose, Emily tried to gauge the fullness of her own *poitrine*. "It will be very nice to see Mr. Trist again," she said, and pulled her shoulders back.

CHAPTER NINE

THE CAPITOL BUILDING HAD A BASEMENT ROOM CALLED "The Hole in the Wall," one floor under the Senate, next to the steam heat boilers, which served coffee, slowly, and whiskey right away.

Henry Adams led Trist down a set of narrow wooden steps and through its padded door. A sign on the wall said MEMBERS OF CONGRESS ONLY, but the grandson and great-grandson of presidents ignored it and chose a table in a corner.

The room, little larger than a vestibule, also contained a bartender's counter, dumbwaiter, and nine or ten wooden tables. Adams pulled off his gloves and hat, gave them to a passing waiter, and held up two fingers for coffee; and then, over the clatter of plates and voices, leaned forward and explained. The speech he wanted to have with Trist concerned his unusual family name— Adams was embarked on a history of the Jefferson and Madison administrations (it would take him, he said complacently, a decade to write), and he was intrigued by the possibility that Trist was descended from the very same Pennsylvania Trists so prominent in Jefferson's last years. And if so, by the possibility of undiscovered family papers, family archives . . . Nicholas Trist II had, after all, been a diplomat of some distinction.

Trist likewise leaned forward into the clatter, not a little surprised. His father and mother had both died when he was a boy.
His father's brother had married one of Jefferson's granddaugh-
ters, Virginia Randolph, and that family had generously taken him
in, reared him, sent him off north to college, and that was all he
knew. Nicholas Trist II and his wife had both died in 1874, poor,
disappointed, patriotic. He had a stepbrother living in
Philadelphia. He himself had only visited Monticello once, many
years ago, but the Trist family proper had apparently known
Jefferson since—

"Since 1775," Adams told him, and took coffee from the waiter.
"When Jefferson boarded with the widow Mrs. Elizabeth Trist in
Philadelphia during the Second Continental Congress. My great-
grandfather knew her. You should have a Southern accent, Mr.
Trist."

"I admire the chameleon."

Adams smiled and spooned sugar unhurriedly into his coffee.
"I sometimes think," he said in his own incongruous British
accent, "that before the war—I mean the last war—America was
populated by only two or three hundred people, all of them con-
stantly tangling their feet in each other's lives. Jefferson, you
know, was once warned of a British raid on his house, led by
Colonel Banastre Tarleton, and the man who rode all night to
warn him, a kind of tidewater Paul Revere, was named Jack Jouett.
Afterwards, Jouett moved to Kentucky, where he turned out to be
the lawyer for Rachel Jackson's divorce before she married Andrew
Jackson, a divorce precipitated by the brother of Jefferson's private
secretary William Short. Jackson, of course, hired your stepfather,
or uncle rather, as his own private secretary, who had earlier married Jefferson's granddaughter. Tarleton's mistress in Paris was the
best friend of Jefferson's English mistress." He paused and arched
one eyebrow. "You're amused, Mr. Trist?"

"I hadn't thought of History as the Muse of Gossip."

"The Muse of Coincidence, in fact," Adams corrected primly.
"You're a journalist, Mr. Trist, so you deal merely in personalities.
An historian deals in scientific laws. Andrew Jackson is interesting
to the historian now only because he anticipates Grant, is in some
ways the type and forerunner of Grant. But as personalities they
have the same inarticulate, *brutal* quality, do they not?"

Trist glanced at the clock behind the counter. In thirty min-

utes or less the Senate would finish its short session, and he ought
to be upstairs again, in the committee room. Adams continued to
sip his coffee. The man sitting on his throne, Trist thought, dom-
inates the courtier who stands before him. He wanted to leave, but
stayed right where he was.

"In Boston," Adams said, "where they hated him, they still tell
stories of Jackson's visit in 1830—it was enough, apparently, merely
to be in his presence. The stiffest old New England Tories melted
when he rode by. People who knew him, even Bostonians, were
still voting for him twenty years after his death. But you know, Mr.
Trist, language is power, historical figures who are not writers,
who are mere 'personalities,' are at a great disadvantage—a generation later there are no witnesses to their quality. Posterity won-
ders what in the world made them remarkable. Look at
Washington. But Jefferson will last (and be overrated as long as he
lasts) because he wrote well. History is indeed one of the Muses,
as you say. History pardons the articulate. Jackson will be under-
rated because he wrote hardly at all."

Trist slipped a coin onto the table, but still made no move to
leave.

Adams patted his lips with a napkin. He had been, Trist knew,
a famous professor once at Harvard, a spellbinding lecturer, and
despite his absurd accent, his size, his fastidiousness, Elizabeth
Cameron had looked at him last night the way Eve must have
looked at the serpent. There was no doubt where Henry Adams's
power lay.

"I don't know of any family papers," he said, feeling less dislike
for Adams; more fear. "I can ask."

Adams finally stood and held out one arm to the waiter for his
gloves and hat. "You're anxious to be there for Don Cameron," he
said, smiling again but shaking his head. "Posterity *already* won-
ders what makes Don Cameron remarkable." He stepped around
an overflowing spittoon and led Trist out by another door.

On the broad terrace that crossed the western base of the
Capitol he stopped to wipe "spittoon evidence" from his shoe. Trist
walked to the balustrade and looked out at the busy mud-brown
diagonal of Pennsylvania Avenue down the slope of the hill to the
right, and the equally brown rectangle of the Mall, running
straight ahead until it disappeared in a low, dark Potomac fog. A
cold wind whipped gray clouds down to meet it. In the distant cen-

ter of the Mall, like an illustration for Adams's lecture on politics and posterity, sat the dirty half-finished shaft of stones about one hundred feet high, meant to be, someday, George Washington's national monument. A few cows wandered around its base. The monument had been unfinished when Trist first saw it in 1861; as far as he knew it had been untouched for thirty years.

"I'm told that in Chicago," Adams said beside him, "General Grant said not a word at his own banquet."

"Mark Twain was a better interview."

Adams lifted his little furled umbrella like a pointer. "When I met Grant socially for the one and only time, in the year 1869, I was unmarried and living in a boarding house over there." The umbrella dipped toward the shabby red roofs of First Street. "A friend of mine on Grant's staff, a man named Badeau, invited me to spend an evening with the President. We came in after dinner and took our places in a little circle of half a dozen or so intimates. Mrs. Grant strolled in and out and was pleasant—she has a pronounced squint, you may have noticed, one eye like an isosceles triangle."

In spite of himself Trist laughed.

"But Grant hardly spoke three words." Adams steered them toward a steep set of stairs, nearly hidden by thick shrubbery, that rose from the terrace up toward the Senate. "About no one man in my lifetime have opinions truly differed so widely. But as far as I can tell, Mr. Trist, whether or not he wins his third term, Grant is also going to leave posterity scratching its head. He has no power of language at all—worse than Jackson, worse than Washington, who was reserved, not mute. He can't speak, he can't write. He seems to me"—Adams paused and turned his soft, pink face blandly up to Trist—"*pre*intellectual. He should have worn skins and lived in a cave."

Trist found his emotions sliding unexpectedly from one side to the other, like a lead weight in a box. Grant was many bad things: "cave dweller" he was not.

But Adams was already going briskly up the stairs, using the umbrella now as a walking stick. "My friend on Grant's staff," he said as Trist caught up, "claimed that Grant seemed to the rest of them like some principle of intermittent physical energy." Adams's short legs took the steps two at a time. If Grant didn't speak to him, Trist thought, puffing, it was because he couldn't get a word in edgewise. "They followed him because he was successful," Adams said, "but they never knew *why* he was. They could never detect a process in his thought. They were not sure he *did* think."

At the main entrance to the rotunda lobby, Adams adjusted his muffler, stamped his feet against the cold, reminded Trist of family papers. "Another Washington specimen," he said, inclining his head. Next to a closed door Trist recognized the massive bull-necked presence of Senator Roscoe Conkling's bodyguard, pointed out to him twice the day before. "Ever since Lincoln," Adams told him, "all the ambitious politicians in Washington believe somebody's going to assassinate them. Who'd want to shoot Don Cameron?"

"It might make," Trist said, thinking aloud, "an interesting article." He looked back at Adams and added wryly, "For a journalist."

"You must send me something," Adams said, turning away, "you've actually written."

WHAT HE HAD ACTUALLY WRITTEN, TRIST THOUGHT, WAS not much. One interview with Mark Twain, Grant's unlikeliest friend, sold to two places; one news account of the banquet for a Paris daily that sometimes bought his work; one brisk summary of the Grant "boom" and the mechanics of nomination, sale pending to the same Paris daily.

Ten days after his coffee with Henry Adams he sat down at the table in his little rented parlor and pulled out a sheet of paper. *L'Illustration* took its name from the dozens of small engravings scattered throughout its news stories, and especially the portfolio of full-page engravings at the end of each issue. In Paris he had supplemented his small retainer each month by finding artists and commissioning engravings—the French were extremely fond of pictures of exotic landscapes from faraway countries, ships of all kinds, also (for some reason) bridges; he had once filled an entire portfolio with nothing but engravings of celebrated Chinese bridges. In Washington he had no artists, no supplement (plenty of bridges).

Three articles, three hundred and fifty dollars. His original expense allowance—four hundred dollars. Expected retainer next month—two hundred dollars. He slid his lucky paperweight into place to hold the paper down and wrote a column of figures for income on the right, added it up. On the left a column of figures of expenses; added. Added again. Puffed out his cheeks and sat back.

He had found a rooming house on Rhode Island Avenue, far enough away from the Capitol to be unfashionable and cheap. All his francs he had withdrawn three months ago from a *compte d'é-pargne* and used for ship's fare. The *Revue des deux mondes* would publish one long article after the Republican convention in June and pay the equivalent of five hundred dollars.

Why did you come back, Mr. Trist? Elizabeth Cameron had asked him. *Was it merely curiosity?*

Looking for bridges, he had joked. Bad metaphor. In fact, he had no idea. No real idea. He lifted the paperweight, lowered it again. In the army there had been twenty-four official categories of illness for which a soldier could be put in the hospital. Number nineteen was "homesickness." He tapped his pencil slowly against the paper, then rose and walked to the window. The ghost nerves in his shoulder tingled, as they sometimes did when he was cold. After the war he had lasted just two weeks in New Haven before he quietly packed his bag and set out to travel west. In Colorado and California he had worked at odd, roughneck jobs and written bad poems at night. In Mexico he was briefly a one-armed *caballero*. In Hawaii he branded cattle on a ranch in sight of a bubbling volcano whose lurid red fire and greasy smoke put him in mind once too often of the war. In North Africa, in Europe—it was hard to remember now; life was lived forward, he thought, but understood backward.

Under the single gas lamp at the corner of the street, snow was falling in small, swirling flakes, confetti. While he watched, three Negro men, hatless, hurried past, laughing. Then a carriage went up Rhode Island Avenue with a steady *clop-clop* of cold metal on hard dirt, a *jink-jink* of harness bells. In Paris the same dirt, same bells; different sound.

HENRY," SAID CLOVER ADAMS, BRINGING HER HORSE TO A HALT and smiling brightly down at Trist, "met Dr. Oliver Wendell Holmes in Boston last week, and *Henry* said, 'Dr. Holmes, you are intellectually the most alive man I ever knew.' And Dr.

Holmes absolutely *shouted*, 'I am, I am! From the crown of my head to the sole of my foot, I'm alive! I'm alive!' "

Trist smiled back and tried not to stare past her at Elizabeth Cameron, seated sidesaddle on her own horse a dozen yards away and not, apparently, seeing him at all.

"Happy day before New Year's, Mr. Trist."

"And to you, Mrs. Adams."

"What brings you to Lafayette Square on such a cold, cold morning? Seeking fodder for your busy pen? But Congress is adjourned."

Trist held the horse's warm muzzle with his hand while it pawed the mud. "Actually, I've just mailed off an article so remarkably dull and sober and bad that my editor will have to print it— 'Grant and the Issues: Civil Service Reform.' "

"Henry never reads anything he's written—he swears he detests his every word."

"And so I'm giving myself the day off, or the morning, or half an hour's walk." At the corner of H Street, in front of the Adamses' sprawling yellow house, Elizabeth Cameron glanced casually in their direction, then turned her attention to a shaggy Skye terrier behind the fence, yapping at a dead leaf.

"We like to go riding by the canal," Clover Adams said.

"A little isolated." Reluctantly, Trist brought his eyes back to Clover. The old Chesapeake canal ran alongside the Potomac just north of Georgetown, a beautiful stretch of river and forest, but when he had walked that way himself he had been struck by the menacing number of shacks and tramps among the trees. A great change from before the war. A greater contrast with the genteel book-and-horse world of Adamses and Camerons.

"We could hardly go the other direction," Clover told him, amused.

As if on a signal they both turned and looked in the other direction. When he had left Washington in 1865 the city still resembled what it had been almost from the beginning, an empty abstract grid of mud lanes meant to be stately avenues and ramshackle wooden structures meant to be a seat of government. Now it had pretty nearly—Twist mixed his metaphors—pulled itself up by the bootstraps. True, there were cows and pigs wandering freely out of alleys; true, only the northern half of Pennsylvania Avenue was paved (the other half was wooden blocks sunk in mud) and the dingy redbrick and white-frame buildings on either side of it were made to seem even smaller and dingier by the enormous white Roman bulk of the Capitol at the far end. But there were busy hotels, shops, saloons on both sides of the street. The sidewalks fairly bristled with telegraph poles every twenty or thirty yards, and the air overhead was almost darkened by the hundreds of black wires that ran back and forth in incredible profusion. Down the center of the avenue, where the Treasury Department jutted out, two or three elephant-hipped trolley cars were making their way between the paved and unpaved sections. Around them, all the way to the Capitol, moved wagons and carriages, and here and there a few of the funny little wooden-roofed passenger cabs called "herdics."

"I *like* Washington," Clover Adams said with a brisk nod of her head. "Washington makes me feel up-to-date. Did you know there are a hundred and forty Bell telephones already installed in this city?"

"I didn't know."

"The wires are strung alongside the telegraph lines. One of them goes straight into the President's office over there and he answers it himself. Evidently he asked Mr. Graham Bell what you should say when you pick up the instrument, and Bell recommended 'Ahoy! Ahoy!' So that's what the President says. In Boston they merely say 'Hello.'" She gave a little flick of her reins and smiled down at him. "Ahoy and good-bye, Mr. Trist."

THE NEXT TIME HE SAW HER WAS THREE DAYS LATER, ON THE sidewalk three-quarters of the way down Pennsylvania Avenue, near the set of especially dingy redbrick buildings known to locals as "Newspaper Row."

"Last night," Clover Adams told him, almost without preamble, "we were at a dinner for John Sherman, and his brother General Sherman was there and talked for hours about the war. Henry almost screamed."

Trist wore an obviously puzzled expression. From what he had seen in Chicago, Cump Sherman was a highly educated, highly entertaining talker.

"The war," Clover said, rising on her toes as if the war were rounding the corner like an omnibus, "is sometimes for Henry a great bore."

Trist kept his face a blank.

"He spent it in England," Clover said, looking somewhat vaguely around. Together they stepped away from the edge of the sidewalk and the rattle and spray of passing carriage wheels. Washington weather had turned grayer and wetter, and this side (unpaved) of the Avenue was a cold primordial slush. "Henry was his father's private secretary in London, when his father was ambassador. His brother fought in the war—like you—all his Harvard friends did. My brother did. What does Dr. Johnson say, a man who's never been a soldier will always think less of himself?"

"Dr. Johnson is a great bore," Trist said, and Clover rewarded him with one of her homely, oddly melancholy smiles.

She had come this far down Pennsylvania Avenue, she explained, in search of a new establishment called "The Boston Store," run by two men her father knew, Woodward and Lothrop. She intended to spend the whole of her father's annual Christmas cheque on rugs and lamps—"for the parlor at the yellow house, so we can ask the neighborhood in for a toot. I assume *you're* here, Mr. Trist, to send telegrams." She gestured toward the cluster of newspaper offices on the next corner, where the overhead wires were unusually tangled and thick and a big square sign for the Washington *Star* hung from a second-story window.

"In fact, I was looking for a shop that sells engravings."

"Photographs," said Clover Adams, "are much more interesting. You can't print them in a newspaper, of course. You must come and see my photographs."

They stood for a moment in awkward silence. A green-and-yellow U.S. mail wagon stopped next to a pillar box. One of the horses stretched its head down to a water trough. "This is almost the very spot," Clover said over the rattle of another passing wagon, "where I watched the Grand Parade of 1865, when Grant's army was officially dismissed from service—there was a reviewing stand over there, and the troops marched up from the Capitol, straight up Pennsylvania Avenue to the President's house." Across the street where she pointed was now, not a reviewing stand, but a nondescript wooden storefront and a signboard for Ivory Soap,

"99 44/100 PER CENT PURE." "You must have been in that very parade, Mr. Trist, when the war was over."

Trist shook his head, pulled up his collar.

"I was just a girl, not married. I spent the whole war making bandages for the Sanitary Commission—when I told my father I wanted to go to Washington to see the parade, he simply hooted." She nodded her head at the memory. "So I put on my bonnet and went forth to seek a man."

Trist found himself wondering what strange impulse had seized tiny Mrs. Adams—then or now—to travel all the way from Cambridge, Massachusetts, to see the soldiers parade, to stand on a public street fifteen years later and tell a near-stranger all about it. In a nearby shop window their cold reflections turned away from the wind. She clutched his arm like the Ancient Mariner in skirts.

"Some man," she said scornfully, "my second cousin Russell Sturgis. But he did escort three of us Boston girls on the train, and we stayed in the attic of my uncle's house on F Street. I saw Ford's Theatre and the room where Lincoln died—his pillow was still on the bed, with a dried bloodstain, and I actually leaned over and touched it because it was an historical fact, it was *real*. Then I went to the courthouse where the assassination conspirators were still being tried—my cousin Russell worshipped Lincoln and wouldn't go, but I did. Mrs. Surratt was horrible, fat, I thought how could she do it? When they hanged her later I pictured her being stuffed in her coffin like a chicken in a pan."

Trist touched her elbow to move her out of the path of two black workmen pushing a dolly down the sidewalk.

"And the next day," she said, intent on her story, ignoring the dolly, "was one of the most glorious sights I ever witnessed—it was about noon, and General Meade had just started marching the Army of the Potomac up Pennsylvania Avenue, past the reviewing stand. A band was playing 'John Brown's Body,' and all the officers' horses had beautiful floral wreaths around their necks and the officers all had one free hand filled with roses. Then suddenly—a lone horse came galloping wildly up the side of the troops, full speed, with a hatless rider—he had long golden hair like Apollo—I wrote it all in my diary—streaming in the wind."

"Custer," said Trist.

"General Custer—his horse was apparently terrified of crowds and had broken loose and started to run, but Custer wheeled it around and reared it up just over there, in front of Grant and President Johnson, holding his roses all the time, and he got his horse finally under control, and then he galloped again all the way back to his troops. The whole parade took six hours to pass, it was the biggest crowd in the history of Washington, and we never moved from this very place. Some of the regiments that marched by had only twenty or thirty men left, and their flags were just little bullet-torn rags. It was a strange feeling to be so intensely happy and triumphant because the war was over, and yet to feel like weeping."

Of the two Adamses, Trist decided, he far preferred the sweetly named Clover.

"Where *were* you, Mr. Trist, if not in the parade?"

He pulled his collar up again, unnecessarily. Looked down the street toward Newspaper Row. "About six blocks away from here," he answered. "In a hospital bed." He turned back to her and gave a lopsided smile. "Probably wrapped in one of your bandages."

"Poor Henry," she said, without any discernible irony.

CHAPTER ELEVEN

A STORY SHOULD BE ABOUT LOVE AND DEATH.

Sylvanus B. Cadwallader read his sentence over with admiration; underlined it; read it again, frowned; scratched it out; put down his pen.

Who first told him that?

Cump Sherman maybe, history's most histrionic general. He could remember one night after Vicksburg, Sherman talking about "the drama," reciting Shakespeare by the yard. Another time, not even drunk, he had declaimed entirely from memory "The Death of Little Nell" by Dickens (there was a not-so-secret affinity, Cadwallader thought, between sentimentality and slaughter). Sherman hated writers, but was fond of telling people how to write.

Or it might just as well have been that celebrity thief Mark Twain, who had his sentimental streak, God knew.

A story should be—

His pen scratched it over again. He stood up and walked to the window and stared down at State Street, three stories below his hotel, where the gas lamps were just flickering on and there was the usual entertaining mud-and-twilight confusion of wagons and horses and hatted and coated pedestrians hurrying every which direction, and storefront shutters and awnings closing and folding and three or four newsboys hawking their papers on the corners. Chicago had fourteen different newspapers, not counting the ones in German and Swedish: you could pretty well count on buying a paper whenever and wherever you felt like it.

Odd, uninvited memory: during the war, except in the thick of battle, you could pretty well count on buying a newspaper whenever you felt like it too, because as soon as the troops stopped marching and made a camp, the newsboys would magically start to appear, strolling casually right out of the piney woods, waving the New York *Herald* or the Boston *Transcript*. Did anyone remember that now?

He squinted to follow the wayward path of a man in a top hat riding his bicycle next to a canary-yellow landau with black fenders. The other thing you could count on, whether the paper was then or now, the news would be violent. The bicyclist crashed (inevitably) sideways against a fender and spun into a puddle, and the newsboys threw rocks. No blood, no news, that was the fact of the matter. What the papers brought you every day was simply vicarious gore—had that started in the war? With all those stories of battlefield casualties, severed limbs, fields of blue and gray corpses? It was certainly true that unless you were one of the privileged few who wrote just about politics, news today, twenty years after the war, still consisted of little more than coarse, brutal, completely sensational accounts of modern American mayhem. If a man was caught in a factory machine or burnt crazy by a shower of molten lead, or just beaten and robbed in the wrong part of town, then the reporter came out to write it up. For a good writer who wanted to keep his job, every pitiful groan and moan, every laceration, fracture, industrial dismemberment, was described with painterly feeling and a surgeon's vocabulary. The railroad strikes of 1877 had been like covering Shiloh.

Down on the street a crowd of pedestrians had turned on the newsboys and chased them around the corner. The bicyclist stood in the middle of the puddle wiping his hat. In San Francisco they had a new word for street thugs: "hoodlums." In Chicago the boys themselves had names for their gangs. He knew for a fact that down on the South Side there were embryo criminals who called themselves the Dead Rabbits and thought nothing of using a knife or a revolver on a perfect stranger. A gang of even younger children called themselves the Little Dead Rabbits and came out of the tenements at night to steal and sometimes kill, and a group of thieves over by the lake docks called themselves the Daybreak Boys and not one of them was over twelve years old, and every day at breakfast that was what you opened your newspaper to read about. Whatever the war had started, Cadwallader thought, it wasn't done yet.

On his writing desk, under a little shaded lamp, were three or four chapters of a "conventional" campaign biography of Grant that he had begun to write a few months ago, then abandoned. Out of curiosity, habit, he picked up the first page and read it again.

Ulysses S. Grant was born to the smell of smoke and the sound of axes ringing on wood. Easterners who moved to the banks of the Ohio River in the early 1820s often remarked that the fragrance of burning leaves and wood was just like New England, except that beside the Ohio the fires went on all year long, not just in the autumn.

That was because in those days the forests of Ohio and Kentucky still grew so thick and deep that the sun seemed to vanish in the early afternoon, lost in the endless trees overhead. No matter where you were, you walked around as if on the dark, swampy floor of a valley. Farmers cleared their land by cutting circles on the trunks of live trees, to interrupt the flow of sap, and came back in six months to chop the deadened trunks. All year long you could see a red glow at night somewhere off in the hills that meant a settler was burning timber, and the air was soft day and night with drifting ribbons of gray haze.

No blood or gore, but accurate for sure. He himself had been born and reared in Ohio, he knew exactly what Grant's boyhood would have been like.

The river first of all—it was a nice artistic touch of history that all of the Union armies Grant commanded were named after rivers, starting with the Army of the Tennessee, because any boy growing up back there, back then, would have rivers running through his soul. There was a book to be written just on American rivers—he remembered well the curiosity he'd felt moving down the Mississippi the very first time, on his way to the Mexican War, and discovering the different nature of Southern rivers, so muddy-red and slow in comparison with Northern rivers, like warm molasses spilled over clay. The Ohio was a Northern river, wide, cool, fast; in the 1820s it was covered with *life,* with travellers, immigrants, pioneers flowing west like the nation. At night you could hear the slap of keelboats and steamboats going by, the voices that carried for miles in the dark; often the flatboats had a campfire going, raised up on a little deck, a small red glow floating down the great black space, an echo, so to speak, of the distant red glow of burning timber back in the hills.

Cadwallader stretched his arms and looked at his watch. Outside, the wind was blowing harder, Chicago was lowering its big German chin and hunching its shoulders for another winter storm. He ought to hunch his shoulders himself and get back to work.

Except, of course, that he was in one of those writer's moods when he didn't feel like writing a word. He slipped his page back in its folder. The conventional Grant biography would have probably been all right, somebody would have published it; but he had given it up as pointless. Not nearly as truthful as his little secret project down in the bottom drawer of the desk, and he was writing that really just to amuse himself; he was still, despite everything that had happened, a loyal Grant man. Loyal enough.

And besides, he thought, pacing restlessly back to the window, the real story was far too big and complicated for an uneducated bumpkin scribbler like himself, and he hated to spoil it by telling it wrong. The real story was that the Civil War had completely split the nineteenth century in half, like a steel wedge in a stump, two different countries, two different times, and somebody born today—or a relative boy like that reporter Trist—would have no idea at all of life in an American river town, back when the country was raw and men like Grant were formed.

Cadwallader fumbled in his vest for a cigar. Down on the street an old man in a faded greatcoat and kepi was hobbling along past a horse trough, and it made him think of his father. His father and his grandfather. He thought of fifty generations of fathers and grandfathers, in fact, who had never travelled faster than a horse or a sail could carry them, never communicated with another person except by voice or pen; never expected to, never *dreamed* of a world much different from the one they were born into. Yet right now, if he wanted to, he could follow that old man down the street and go in an office and send a telegraphic message around the globe, in less than a minute. In certain Eastern cities you could actually talk on a wire instrument strung between two buildings. You could put fresh butchered beef in one of Gus Swift's refrigerated railroad cars and drive it from Chicago to San Francisco—two thousand miles—then take it out and eat it. There was a great story waiting for someone to tell it, not about the war, but about the reborn nation, on the other side of the war.

Somebody else. Not him. Cadwallader blew his nose on his sleeve and noticed with regret that he was now making the same fluxible morning noises that his father used to make.

He crossed over the bare floor to the chest of drawers and rummaged until he found a half-empty bottle of E. C. Booz and poured two lovely inches of it into his toothbrush mug. When he was a boy in Ripley, Ohio, the owner of the village grocery and dry-goods store kept a little oak-charred cask of whiskey on the counter, and a tin cup on a string, and any customer, man or boy, who could reach that high was welcome to refresh himself with a nip.

Cadwallader refreshed himself with a nip. He peered back at the window. The sky was louring. The wind was growing angry. Second-half-of-the-century weather.

He stood with the toothbrush mug in his hand and drank a little and thought Mark Twain was a thief and a genius; thought Grant had looked well, well and prosperous at the banquet; thought a story should be about love and whiskey.

CHAPTER TWELVE

THE SECRET LIFE
OF U. S. GRANT

by Sylvanus Cadwallader

CHAPTER THREE

LOVE, THEN. LOVE FIRST: ULYSSES AND PENELOPE.

Back in the summer of 1843—unlike him, I don't mind a bit retracing my steps—when the Mexican War was still just a rumor and a grumble on the horizon, Brevet Second Lieutenant Ulysses S. Grant, fresh out of West Point, said good-bye to his family in Ohio and took the steamboat down the Mississippi to his first official army assignment. Jefferson Barracks, Missouri, was widely considered desirable duty in those days, partly because it was set on what looked like a rich man's estate of beautiful hills and meadows next to the river, and really because the city of St. Louis was only nine miles north. This was the do-nothing peacetime army, remember. Most of the soldiers drilled and yawned and polished their buckles lackadaisically till supper, then jumped on their horses and galloped off to study St. Louis's rather fleshy and metropolitan charms.

But not Second Lieutenant Grant. Too shy. Too puritanical. Besides, even before he left West Point his mathematics teacher had pulled him aside and promised that when the first opening appeared, if Grant kept up his standards, he intended to appoint him his Assistant Professor. Much to be preferred to grunting and sweating with the infantry. Much to be preferred by somebody who didn't think he truly belonged in the army at all. Grant bought a big lined notebook, cracked open his old math primer.

But a young man of twenty-one does not live by binomial theorems alone. Grant's West Point roommate Fred Dent came through Jefferson Barracks one day on his way somewhere else and took him over to a home-cooked dinner at the family farm, not five miles away as it happened. It had the grandiose name of "White Haven," and a population of eighteen slaves, two parents, and three young daughters. And that was the end of mathematics.

The father, Colonel Dent, was no colonel, no military man at all, but he was, till the day of his death, one of Nature's prime and matchless jackasses, worse even than Jesse Grant, and that is saying a mouthful. Colonel Dent had made a small fortune before the War of 1812, cheating Indians on the frontier mainly, and then returned to his native Maryland, where he married an otherwise intelligent Englishwoman named Ellen Wrenshall. After the war, restless like everybody else, he pulled up stakes and started to wander west again; in 1817, more or less on whim, he bought 925 empty acres in Missouri, and there he settled down to amuse himself by suing his neighbors, bullying his slaves, and pretending his poor little pork-and-wheat farm was a Southern gentleman's plantation. He was all his life violently pro-slavery. I have never yet met anybody outside the family who could actually stand the old man. When Grant was in the President's Palace . . . but I jump ahead. Back in 1843 the important thing about Colonel Dent, at least to Grant, was not his politics, but his favorite daughter, Julia.

Now, of the mischievous laws that govern men and women yours truly knows just about next to nothing. There have been great men—I think of Hamilton, Franklin, Cump Sherman (especially)—who have also been perfect grinning tomcats. And there have been others who were either undersexed (Jefferson) or so utterly devoted to one woman as to defy human nature. Jackson was like that. Grant still is.

In 1843, at the age of eighteen, Julia Dent had a plump figure, small hands and feet; a bright, flirtatious way of chatter. She also had (has) a bad squint in her left eye that the idiot father said came from carrying her as a baby out of a warm bath into a cold room. Grant had first been interested, evidently, in her sixteen-year-old sister Nellie, but when Julia finally showed up, returned from a long visit to relatives, sitting on a horse like a girl who was born to the saddle, Ulysses spun like the needle on a compass and it was only Julia ever after. He proposed in a wagon, fording a stream, remarking (as the water rose up over the wheels) that she could always count on him to take care of her. And Julia responded cheerfully (water almost to her shoes) that it would be a charming thing to be engaged, secretly from her father, but married, no, not yet.

Secretly from her father, of course, because Grant was poor; a Yankee with suspected abolitionist leanings; and entirely colorless and unimpressive in appearance (the "little man with the big epaulets," Pete Longstreet used to call him).

And not yet, because she wasn't sure, she was having too much fun.

What did he see in her? Well, the physical, I guess. Grant and Julia have never gone to a meal together, not even breakfast, without his taking her arm and giving her a kiss. In the war more than once I found them sitting on a log by his tent, just holding hands. In his first term as President, Julia got up her courage and made a surgeon's appointment to have her eye fixed, and the morning she was to leave, Grant came in and kissed her hands and said he'd always loved her just the way she was, so why not unpack her suitcase and cancel the operation. She did. And, too, she is talkative, comfortable, a little inclined to frivolity—all the things Hannah Grant was *not*.

And what did she finally see in him?

Not greatness. Not glory. Not, certainly, the President's Palace one day.

Three short words, I suppose: He *needed* her.

In the Mexican War (not a writer) Grant wrote Julia every single week. He wrote her he had been terrified since childhood he would die of consumption. He wrote her he kissed every letter before he sent it, kissed her ring every day. He walked out into the blistering sun and cut flowers for her and put the petals in his envelopes. He painted watercolors of the scenery for her.

Sometimes, like a mooncalf—we are still talking about the "Butcher of Cold Harbor"—he mailed her letters with mostly blank spaces and said they expressed his love, for which no words could be found (his mother's son). I suppose there was never a younger, lonelier, sadder-eyed boy in the world than U. S. Grant in the forties and it would have taken a heart of stone to send him away.

They were married in St. Louis right after the war, after a three-year courtship, Colonel Dent complaining all the way to the altar, Jesse and Hannah Grant not even in attendance because the Dents were a slave-owning family. Then the young couple trooped off to the end of the world, known as Sackets Harbor, New York, on the frozen shores of Lake Ontario. There Julia got pregnant and set about to become a mother and Grant got so bored with army routine he couldn't stand it, and started to dream of Mexico again and those sweet brown bottles of liquor that used to console his being.

He joined the local Sons of Temperance lodge and signed the teetotal pledge. Raced his horses up and down the street. Broke his pledge. Made it again. I know witnesses who remember seeing him march in Temperance parades wearing the red-white-and-blue purity sash across his chest and the big red pin in his lapel that must have looked to the gods of rum like a bull's-eye target.

Now this was a serious matter. Never underestimate the sublime self-righteousness of the American public. All over the country men were flocking that year to join the Temperance movement—P. T. Barnum did (he was right, my old dad liked to cackle: a sucker born every minute); young Lincoln did; the man in the President's Palace this very moment, Rutherford Hayes, did, which is why the irreverent (God bless them) call his wife "Lemonade Lucy." In the army an enlisted man who drank too much could end up with his head shaved, a dishonorable discharge in his pocket, and the letters HD for "Habitual Drunkard" branded on his hip, as if he were some kind of cider-swilling maverick cow. An officer like Grant would escape the head shave and the branding iron, but lose his commission in disgrace. Julia fretted. Grant stared at the snow. Rubbed his mouth.

In the winter of 1849 Julia went back to St. Louis for her lying-in. Grant took temporary quarters by himself in Detroit. At some point while he was living there he slipped on an icy sidewalk in

front of a house and hurt his leg and sued the owner of the house
for negligence; which owner promptly defended himself in court
by declaring that if Grant and the other soldiers would only keep
sober they wouldn't fall down on the street.

The jury peered at Grant, nodded its head; awarded him the
whopping and derisory sum of . . . six cents.

There must have been some little tension, because Julia came
home briefly, then travelled back to St. Louis again with her new
baby boy and stayed away eight long months and rarely wrote, and
Grant grew quieter and quieter, watching the snow pile up.

California would be worse. California would take him down to
skin and bones. In another six months, Sackets Harbor, New York
(ice, snow, depression) would look like Paradise.

CHAPTER THIRTEEN

FOR SEVERAL YEARS AFTER THE WAR IT WAS COMMON TO SEE young men on the streets everywhere, in buildings and offices, with only one arm or leg. Most large cities had schools for teaching soldiers how to hammer and saw again, or drive a wagon or hitch a horse. In New York there had been a contest in 1866 for the best examples of "wrong-handed" penmanship, and Trist, left-handed before Cold Harbor, had actually won fourth prize (awarded by the gray-bearded old poet William Cullen Bryant, who was drunk). But now, oddly enough, Trist thought, it was uncommon to see an amputee veteran.

He put down his pencil, stretched and yawned, and walked across the newsroom to the cluster of desks by the window where Henry Lichfield West, two-handed, was balancing a mug of coffee on his stomach and leaning back in his chair. West swung a wet shoe onto the desk with a thump. "The Presidential Palace," he announced to Trist. Then he stopped to take a slurp of coffee from his mug. "Or 'White House,' to use the up-to-date term, is overrun with spiders. Head groundsman told me. Worst infestation since the days of James Buchanan. All kinds of spiders, big ones, fat ones, brown, black, purple, thousands and thousands of nasty, creeping little bugeyed pests."

"Like you." Calista Halsey sat down at the adjoining desk and uncovered a black-and-gold "Royal" typewriting machine the size of a suitcase.

West grinned up at Trist. "Tomorrow morning, if the weather clears, they're going to flush the whole building out with a fire hose. Arachnoid Armageddon. Should be a carpet of them ankle-deep in the street."

"Ugh." Calista squared a sheet of paper in the machine and poised her fingers over the keyboard.

Both men watched with interest, West because he was the senior political reporter on the Washington *Post* and assistant editor, Trist partly because he was thinking of learning to type himself, one arm or not, but mostly because Calista Halsey looked like an older, softer version, but far less dazzling, of Elizabeth Cameron.

Outside the window, far from clearing, the weather was growing worse. A freakish late-March snowstorm was sweeping a curtain of white up and down Pennsylvania Avenue. A shadowy herdic appeared to be stalled in mud. On the sidewalk, clutching his hat, a lone passerby was pressed close to the glass, evidently reading the late edition of the paper tacked to a set of plywood boards.

Trist sat down, away from the window. Inside, it was pleasantly warm and musty. A row of high wooden filing cabinets behind Calista's shoulders served as office partition and buffer against drafts. On the other side of the cabinets hung the green-shaded lamps of the composing room, where six or seven middle-aged typesetters hunched over their trays like monks in derby hats and collars. From the rear of the building, whenever somebody opened the doors to the printing annex, came the pungent smells of ink, machine oil, and newsprint.

The Washington *Post* was situated in the exact and shabby center of Newspaper Row at 339 Pennsylvania Avenue, the newest, jauntiest, most flamboyant paper in town. It had been founded in 1877, three years earlier, by a St. Louis man named Stilson K. Hutchins, who had skipped the war—nobody quite knew how— and who thought the nation's capital desperately needed a new Democratic party newspaper to rival the Republican *Star*. Hutchins's first issue had been distributed free to every congressman's desk and every government office in the city, and still was.

He claimed a circulation of fourteen thousand and actually sold, Trist thought, on a very good day about half that number.

A brass bell rang and Calista Halsey did something to the machine and looked up from her typing. "Senator Conkling's Apollo curl looked exceptionally hyacinthine today, young men. On his vast senatorial brow. If you had a yellow suit and red shoes, Henry, and hair of course, you might catch people's eyes too."

"Conkling once wore a yellow silk suit to the Senate," West told Trist. "Calista nearly fainted. Said he looked like Lord Byron."

"The last politician to wear a yellow suit in Washington was Martin Van Buren." Calista tapped two more keys, then snapped out her sheet of paper and rolled in a new one. "Although President Buchanan of the spiders used to wear a yellow frock coat, I've heard, and green trousers. He had a matching outfit made for his special friend."

"Male friend," West said with a wink at Trist. Henry West was only twenty-eight years old, bald as an egg, but he had an encyclopedic and uncensored knowledge of Washington life. In the three weeks Trist had been coming to use the *Post's* telegraph he had never yet heard the editor trumped for scandalous information.

"Well, nobody ever wrote about that." Calista's fingers began to fly again. "Nobody cared. My father worked on the old Niles *Weekly Register* back then. He said everybody just shrugged. On the other hand, a *woman's* always fair game."

" 'Mrs. Kate Chase Sprague' "—West picked up her first typed page and read aloud—" 'denied today that there was anything improper in her friendship with Senator Roscoe Conkling of New York, who is, according to Mrs. Sprague, merely one of her husband's colleagues. Mrs. Sprague further denied that she had gone alone into Senator Conkling's office for the purpose of making love.' "

The typewriter carriage hit the brass bell again and Calista flipped it back with one hand. "I'm a traitor to my sex," she said cheerfully.

I T WAS TOO WARM FOR THE SNOW TO STICK LONG TO THE ground, too cold to turn entirely to rain. Three hours later Trist stopped at the corner of Pennsylvania and Tenth and waited for a lumber wagon to sway and splash past him. He nodded to a streetwalker under a gas lamp, who showed him a toothless smile and a flash of high-topped shoe and ankle. Fifty feet farther up the slippery sidewalk he gave a coin to a beggar with a "Hungry" placard around his neck, then stamped the slush off his boots and entered Gillian's Tavern.

" 'Disillusioned,' " said Henry West, shoving a pitcher of beer along the table but not looking up. "Seven letters."

"Newspaperman." Trist sat down in the booth beside him and found an empty glass.

"You're late." West printed "cynical" in the white squares of his word puzzle. "We put it to press half an hour ago, every salacious, libelous, beautifully chosen word."

"I was collecting interplanetary mail at Willard's. Is it true Mark Twain wrote *The Gilded Age* in here?"

West raised his head with an expression of mild surprise. "Mark Twain writes everything with a typewriter now, didn't you know? Wave of the future."

"I was told he wrote it in two months one summer, at a table on the sidewalk right outside. Made fifty thousand dollars."

"They rejected another article, right? *L'Illustrate*?"

"*L'Illustration.*" Trist poured himself beer. On the street outside two derby hats and a bonnet passed by, topped like cakes with snow. Inside, the stink of cigar smoke and spittoons made his eyes hurt. In Paris there would have been a zinc counter, gay colors, tables full of ladies; no spittoons. *L'Illustration* had in fact rejected three of the last four articles Trist had sent them, as West well knew—"too *American,*" Trist's Paris editor had cabled with a sneer, as if they could be anything else—and now his arrangement with them seemed suddenly to hang by a thread. "Thirty-three hundred also beautifully chosen words, 'General Hancock the Superb, Grant's Democratic Rival.' "

"You showed me that," West said. "It was too damned good for Frenchmen—I'll get Hutchins to buy it, he wants to start a Sunday edition. You're too damned good, period. I went to the Library of Congress and looked at your book of stories."

It was Trist's turn to blink in surprise.

"And you wrote six months for the Associated Press, right? Before *Illustrate*?"

"In Paris, part-time."

"Hutchins hates the AP because they're so expensive—he steals all his foreign news from the *Star*." West waved for another pitcher of beer. "I have a proposition for you."

At one end of the bar a big waiter in shirtsleeves and apron was setting out platters of cheese. Somebody invisible began slowly to pick out notes on the house piano, one by one. "When Johnny Comes Marching Home Again."

"Hutchins has another project," West continued. "Hutchins has five or six thousand projects—he wants to publish a handbook for the election. *The Washington Post Political Manual, Election of 1880.* And he wants his name on the cover but he don't want to write it."

"A manual, like a farmer's almanac?"

"Give the man a beer." West took the pitcher from the waiter and refilled Trist's glass. "He wants a farmer's almanac for voters—graphs, statistics, party platforms, candidate statements. A brief history of presidential elections. Hutchins fancies himself a Jeffersonian. He thinks the true democratic voter is one of Nature's noble yeomen, plows in his field, reads a little Homer in Greek at dinner, and studies the facts and casts his vote rationally and theoretically. Hutchins wants to be the man who sells him the facts. It's actually not a bad idea—use the *Post*'s presses, same distribution, fifty cents a copy, corner the market, amazing nobody ever thought of it before. He wants me to find him a writer."

"I'll be back in Paris before the election."

"Forty dollars a week, part-time job. Finish in August."

"And I just find some Homeric-Jeffersonian statistics in the library and write them up?"

"Immigration, tariff, whatever the noble voter might want to know. Hutchins already has a table of contents. Pure, objective, God-fearing facts is all he needs. And if they happen to dribble mud on our leaders Grant and Conkling, so much the better."

Trist started to shake his head.

"It is," West reminded him, grinning, "a Democratic paper."

Which was so wildly and completely true that Trist couldn't help laughing. He might have the odd Jeffersonian idea, but in a town of militant partisans, Stilson Hutchins stood all alone. By his personal order the *Post* invariably referred to Republican President Hayes as "His Fraudulency" or "the bogus President"—Hutchins shared the widespread conviction that Hayes had stolen the election of 1876 from Samuel Tilden—and only two days ago he had run a headline over some presidential remarks: TWADDLE OF THE FRAUD.

"Bash Grant nicely, pass right on over to the regular staff in the fall. Stranger things have happened."

"I won't be here in the fall."

"I know, you got *der wanderlust,* Nick, you think you're a French bohemian. I think you're a *patriot manqué.*"

Trist tasted his beer and made a face. *Patriot manqué.* Patriot unaware.

"Another bug in your ear—Grant comes to town in two weeks," West said.

"Visiting General Beale."

"*Your friend* General Beale, with whom you have whiskey and tea, my dear, in the drawing room every Sunday." West ignored Trist's murmur of protest and propped himself on his elbows, red-faced and genial, bald skull gleaming in the pale blue light of the bar. "If you made like a fly on the wall, wrote up some dirt—don't shake your head—how a man who lived so long in France has scruples and morals I don't know. Wrote up something fine and factual on the side: 'Love Nest in Lafayette Square'—'Poobahs and Posture Girls.' Hutchins says 1880 is going to usher in the political millennium."

"Meaning Tilden this time."

"Or Sam Randall or Hancock the Superb—Tilden's too old and sick to make a run, I think. But in my opinion Grant don't have the thing wrapped up, not even the nomination. Whatever it looked like in Europe." West finished his beer, peered at his watch, and stood, all in one fluent American motion. "Man about a dog," he explained, swaying.

Outside, in the muddy alley behind the tavern, they stood companionably side by side and made use of the long wooden trough that the tavern had installed for its customers. Then they walked and stumbled in the dark to the Tenth Street exit, where a stray sow from one of the alley's numerous shacks had curled up in the mud, partially blocking their way. It was one of the striking features of postwar Washington that while there were houses and districts here and there of conspicuous wealth and beauty, a good part of the city's population, especially its black population, actually lived in these downtown alleys, in old canvas tents and lean-tos and scrapyard shelters that reminded Trist of the wretchedest kind of army bivouac. On the other side of the street, through a space between roofs, the white dome of the Capitol could be seen in the distance, incongruous, rising into a clearing sky.

West wrinkled his nose at the sow. "All right for money, Nick? Hutchins won't pay for a week."

"Fine."

"Good writer ought not to starve. Come by tomorrow, we'll draw up a contract, right after the mystic communion of editors." From the light of Gillian's front window he waved again, then disappeared.

Trist stood and watched the empty street a moment longer. In the nearest window, a Going-Out-of-Business dry-goods store, his darkened reflection took off its hat, wiped its brow with relief like a stage comedian; grinned faintly. "Grant's Luck," they had called it in the war—just keep on moving, never stop, see what happens, forty dollars a week. He pulled up his collar. *If* West could manage it. "Don't count your spiders before they hatch," he told the face in the window, which nodded back, soberly.

Two blocks farther north bigger, brighter globe-shaped streetlamps cast their light on pedestrians, polished carriages, well-dressed couples going in and out of restaurants. He passed Harvey's Seafood Establishment, with a glimpse between red velvet curtains of a black-and-white tessellated floor. On the next block was the gaslit marquee for Ford's New Opera House, formerly Ford's Theatre, where the latest revival of *Uncle Tom's Cabin,* complete with live bloodhounds, would just about at that moment—Trist squinted at the theater clock—have entered its last irresistible, melodramatic act. He had been told that Harriet Beecher Stowe still received $20,000 a year from royalties, but now claimed that God, not she, had actually written the book; either way, a Good Writer, not starving. At the end of the block, on the opposite side of the street, he passed the house marked by a plaque where Lincoln had been carried from the theater to die— his mind flickered back to Clover Adams and 1865, and himself far up the same street, plastered and bandaged like a one-armed ghost—and then he crossed a set of unsteady wooden planks serving as a makeshift bridge over a ditch full of sewage and snow and reached the open, windy spaces of New York Avenue.

In New York City itself there was a new apartment building located so far from everything else, on Seventy-second Street, that it was called "The Dakota." He had seen it ten days ago, on a trip with Don Cameron. Washington, in fact, had more empty spaces than New York. Washington, in fact, sometimes seemed like a whole city of empty spaces, punctuated now and then by a cluster of freestanding buildings that might have been dropped at random, straight out of the sky. He turned right, trudged alongside a huge vacant lot, a bleak rectangle of blackness surrounded by shadows and trees. Overhead, a few last flakes of snow drifted, shivering; stiff white moths. Somebody struck a match far back in the darkness and he heard menacing guttural voices.

At the corner of Fourth and Rhode Island Avenue, two or three doors down from his boarding house, Trist stopped again. He pinched the bridge of his nose and tried to calculate. Forty dollars a week, if West could pull it off . . . April, May, June. Since Christmas he had made a number of short, expensive excursions with Cameron to see the Grant nomination machine in action, twice to New York, which gobbled money like candy, once to the strange Dutch-African city of Philadelphia where his mother had been born and his grandmother had known Thomas Jefferson; and there was still Chicago and the convention to come. He blew white puffs of breath into the black air. He had seen Clover Adams twice; Elizabeth Cameron how many times? He went to Lafayette Square as often as possible, they talked, laughed, he told stories, she dazzled. *Why did you come back, Mr. Trist? Why would you ever leave again?*

Two tramps emerged from the shadows and muttered a step or two in his direction. He turned and walked up the little rise that led to his door, next to a billboard for something called "Marlowes's Electric Corsets"—how could you not love America?—fumbled for his key. Behind him, unseen but felt, stretched a whole great mysterious continent, like the curving dark presence of an immense inland ocean. In Paris he had almost forgotten it existed. In the night, in the passing winter mood, the whole scene appeared spectral, ghostlike, shrouded in snow and fog.

He didn't believe in ghosts, he decided sleepily. If there were ghosts, they were only phantom versions of all the possible selves you might have become, possible lives you might have led, had chance or war decided something different. One arm; two arms. Trist's luck. The last thought that came unbidden into his mind was of Elizabeth Cameron.

He fit his key into the lock.

CHAPTER FOURTEEN

"I HAVE LONG SINCE MADE UP MY MIND NOT TO SEEK THE acquaintance of poets"—here Henry Adams paused, sipped from his sherry glass, patted his lips with his handkerchief—"it spoils their poetry. I knew Swinburne twenty years ago and have needed twenty years to get over it."

General Beale smiled the quick, tight little grimace that meant he hadn't quite got the joke. Senator Cameron smirked. Clover Adams rose up and down on her toes. And only Emily Beale and Elizabeth Cameron truly laughed out loud. Adams lifted his chin in preparation for another witticism. Meanwhile the others began to drift away, rudely in Emily's opinion, across the drawing room and toward the food.

And to tell the truth, Emily herself was listening with only half a mind—something now about spiders and the White House—as she tried at the same time to smile, surreptitiously adjust her left shoulder strap, and also remember exactly what *Godey's Lady's Book* had said just that month about the tightness of a young lady's corset. Spiders. She leaned her head admiringly toward Adams, observing the bald spot in the center of his lacquered hair, and caught her mother's eye across the room. A tight corset, *Godey's* had pronounced, against all fashionable doctrine, will turn a young lady's nose bright red—the result of stagnation of the blood in that prominent and important feature; her mother had flung down the article in a fury, cinched up the laces herself, and marched out muttering that young ladies ought to listen to their mothers, not cheap magazines, and in her family her daughter would *always* appear properly dressed, and no, she could not pass around cigarettes at the party like a maid, her father would die.

Henry Adams had evidently changed the subject. Senator Cameron reappeared, glowering as usual, and Adams turned his wise little head—did it ever bother him and Clover to be the shortest people they knew? even Emily was taller—turned his head up to the Senator, and drawled in his Boston-Oxford accent that Standard Oil had now done everything possible for the Pennsylvania Legislature except refine it, didn't he agree? And Emily held her breath for an instant till Cameron laughed, and then the rest of them joined in, with as much relief as pleasure. In the mirror her nose looked distinctly crimson.

"I see you've invited the Press," Adams drawled, and General Beale, hovering nearby with an oyster canapé raised to his mouth, had to put it down and follow Adams's pointed gaze. Through the window, out on the muddy paths of Lafayette Square, they could all see the tall, quite handsome and romantic (so Emily thought) figure of Nicholas Trist approaching. He wore a slouch hat and dark cape over his shoulders to hide his one arm. While they watched, he stopped at the corner under a lamp for a carriage to pass. On Emily's right, Elizabeth Cameron moved away with a sudden swish of skirts.

"Met him in Europe," Emily's father said, and gulped the oyster.

"He writes about Grant," Senator Cameron added, with, for him, surprising cordiality. "Some French magazine. From what I've read, pretty damned smart."

"Oh, as to that . . ." Adams turned away after Elizabeth.

General Edward Beale had bought the nicest and most distinguished house on Lafayette Square, the old Decatur House as Washingtonians still knew it, from the far-off days when it belonged to Captain Stephen Decatur, of Tripoli War fame. And he felt obligated by his position to give more parties than he liked, Emily thought, to more people than he liked—at the last Boxing Day reception there had been so many guests, a positive "rout," that they still had a dozen unclaimed coats and muffs packed away in a third-floor closet.

Tonight, however, was calmer, her mother's idea of a quiet party: just the Adamses, Professor and Mrs. Bancroft, the Camerons, four or five people from Ohio, some of her father's business friends; and now—but before she could step into the hallway and greet Mr. Trist (in French; her mind searched helplessly for something more sophisticated than *"bonsoir"*), her brother Truxton intercepted her at the side door and hurried her off into the kitchen to help with the salads on dishes of ice that were her mother's speciality. By the time she slipped away again, Nicholas Trist was installed in the other drawing room with a plate of salad balanced before his chest, listening to Senator Cameron and two Ohioans talk about General Grant for President, who was coming next month to stay as a guest of her father.

Emily busied herself with bric-a-brac on the mantel and tried not to stare. The rules of etiquette for women, she had often complained to her mother, were irrational, vexatious, and tyrannical— the Law of the Napkin, for instance (wad or fold), the Nine Rules of Posture. Do Not Interrupt Older Men. When she was younger she had attended for six long months a Young Lady's Saturday Course in which she learned that if she met a gentleman at the foot of a flight of stairs, he was to precede her up, lest she go first and reveal her ankles; she was to avoid swaying when she played the piano; not lean her head against wallpaper, not say "You know" or "says I" or point or say "pooh." She moved a ceramic cat along the mantel and, without pointing or staring, managed to study Trist's face.

He did look, she thought, much thinner and paler than when they had met him in Paris last summer; but then, her father said he'd suffered a bout of malaria and still wasn't fully recovered. His blond hair was longer. His eyes were darker. He shifted his plate slightly, glimpsed her in the mirror, and (she ducked her head) winked.

As soon as dessert and port were served, by family tradition in the second-floor drawing room, the conversation switched, at last, from General Grant and politics. Professor Bancroft, so old he might have been made of dust, took his place in the center of the sofa, alone, the privilege of age, and cleared his throat. He raised his glass and started to discourse on the history of the house, a subject that always pleased her father, who made everybody shush and draw nearer. The very window on their right, Bancroft was saying—Emily felt her eyes begin to dull—had been cut out by Martin Van Buren when *he* lived here as Vice President, so that he could see Andrew Jackson's signals to summon him to the President's Palace. Jackson himself used to come over at night and play pinochle.

"And Thomas Jefferson, of course, dined here often." Bancroft licked his old dry lips as if at the idea. He was ancient enough, Emily thought, to have dined *with* Jefferson.

Downstairs she had brought Nicholas Trist a second plate of salad where he was talking to Elizabeth, and conversed very smoothly (*couramment*) with him in French. But there was no more chance of that *now*. Now Trist was listening to the history lecture, standing with some Ohioans at the end of the sofa, very straight and tall. He was also looking over Bancroft's white head directly toward Elizabeth Cameron standing at the other end of the sofa. While Emily watched, Elizabeth glanced at him, looked down; looked away. The best book Emily had read in years was *Vanity Fair*, where the heroine defies all rules and comes to a tragic end. The next best book had just been published, *Democracy*, in which, all the political *stuff* aside, the great idea was that opposites attract, true love is always disguised.

Elizabeth would *never* defy the rules, Emily thought, Elizabeth loved her social position, Elizabeth loved to be safe. But Nicholas Trist was handsome, serious, opposite—she looked at his poor empty sleeve, neatly folded and pinned, and thought how Desdemona had loved Othello for the dangers he had passed, and then thought of Senator Cameron and danger (a bourbon bottle!) and the idea was so ludicrous she had to pinch her nose and stifle a laugh, and Elizabeth and Nicholas Trist, who had been looking at each other again and starting to whisper, actually turned in unison to look at her, and even Professor Bancroft raised his head.

"Monticello," said Henry Adams very clearly, ignoring them all, "is presently owned by a Jew."

CHAPTER FIFTEEN

THE BOOK DEMOCRACY, WHICH SO INTRIGUED EMILY BEALE, had been published two weeks earlier by Henry Holt and Company of New York, but oddly enough with no author's name on the title page, only the curious and uninformative subtitle: *An American Novel.*

Nick Trist pushed everything else to one side on his desk and turned pages till he reached the point he had marked last night with a penciled asterisk, chapter five, in which the highly civilized Mrs. Lee goes to visit General Grant's White House:

Washington more than any other city in the world swarms with simple-minded exhibitions of human nature; men and women curiously out of place, whom it would be cruel to ridicule and ridiculous to weep over. One evening Mrs. Lee went to the President's first evening reception. She accepted Mr. French for an escort, and walked across the Square with him to join the throng that was pouring into the doors of the White House. They took their places in the line of citizens and were at last able to enter the reception-room. There Madeleine found herself before two seemingly mechanical figures, which might be wood or wax, for any sign they showed of life. These two figures were the President and his wife; they stood

stiff and awkward by the door, both their faces stripped of every sign
of intelligence, while the right hands of both extended themselves
to the column of visitors with the mechanical action of toy dolls.
Mrs. Lee for a moment began to laugh, but the laugh died on her
lips. To the President and his wife this was clearly no laughing matter. There they stood, automata, representatives of the society which
streamed past them. Madeleine seized Mr. French by the arm.

"Take me somewhere at once," said she, "where I can look at it.
Here! in the corner. I had no conception how shocking it was!"

"Gossip turned into art," Henry West said with a professional
mixture of envy and disgust. He scooped the book up and cracked
it open on a stack of election-manual papers on the side of the
desk. "You know, half of Washington's accusing the other half of
writing this. The damn thing's gone through three printings
already. They should have used asbestos instead of paper."

"I heard there was a row in New York." Trist grinned and
leaned back in his chair.

"James G. Blaine, the pride of Maine," said West, whose
knowledge of scandalous information extended well beyond
Washington, "blew up at a dinner party, said *he* was the wicked
senator in it—"

"Ratcliffe."

"—a wonderful name—Blaine swore only an intellectual or a
venomous female could have written it. The President's supposed
to be Grant, General Beale is in it, or his house anyway, the *good*
character is Luke Lamar from Mississippi. Blaine says *he* thinks
Clarence King wrote it, and he cut him dead when he saw him."

"I heard John Hay."

"Also John Hay, Henry James, *maybe* Miss Lorna Sedgewick,
maybe Miss Harriet Loring—nothing sells like a mystery. Hutchins
told you to review it, I hope?"

Trist nodded. "Give the readers what they want."

West flipped to the middle of the book and read aloud:
" '*Ratcliffe's eyes were cold, steel gray, rather small, not unpleasant
in good humor, diabolic in a passion, but worst when a little suspi-
cious; then they watch you as though you were a young rattle-snake,
to be killed when convenient.*' " He snorted. "Could be anybody."
He turned back to the first chapter: " '*For reasons which many persons thought ridiculous, Mrs. Lightfoot Lee decided to pass the win-*

ter in Washington.' " He closed the book with a snap. "For reasons which many persons think profound, I need a drink."

Trist grinned and shook his head. In two weeks' time, not counting work on *Democracy,* he had spent nine full afternoons in the dank, gloomy reading room of the Library of Congress, written four background chapters for Hutchins's election manual (the latest on "Perils of Immigration"), and done absolutely nothing for *L'Illustration.* Hutchins was pleased with his chapters, looked for more every day, and now assigned, as tidbits, little moneymaking extras like the book review, not to mention one or two stories an issue that the regular reporters were too busy to tackle. Yesterday Trist had written a paragraph about crumbling asphalt on Fourteenth Street. Tomorrow he was to do the opening of the new Thomas Cook Travel Office on Tenth Street. But today—he looked at his watch, two-twenty-five—today was his own. Today he was invited to visit Decatur House for tea, where General Grant, now visiting the Beales, might—or might not—offer an exclusive interview for European readers. At the door West gave him back the book and scowled up at the brilliant April sunshine. "Another goddam beautiful day," he said.

From the offices of the *Post* to Lafayette Square was at most a twenty-minute walk. The weather had changed completely, in fickle Washingtonian fashion, from winter-spring to summer. The low blue hills of Virginia dozed on the other side of the Potomac. A few paddle steamers and sailboats floated on the river's back, nearly motionless. Even the constant traffic of wagons, herdics, and omnibuses on the avenue itself seemed slower, lazier; Southern. He passed saloons that had thrown their doors and windows open to let the fresh air in. Several cafés were bravely setting out tables and umbrellas on the sidewalk. At Twelfth Street one of the city's numerous photograph shops had installed an open-air display of pictures—he glanced at train wrecks, actresses, Famous Race Horses and Noted Statesmen—overhead a telegraph line repairman swung contentedly in a dense black cradle of wires, looking down at the street like an amiable bearded spider.

At Lafayette Square, just past the big granite hip of the Treasury Department, Trist stopped and checked his watch, pointlessly. Looked to the left at the drowsy front porch of the White

House; the elegant redbrick town houses in facing rows on two sides of the square, the yellow Adams house on the top, a hundred yards or so away.

He opened the iron gate and sat down on the nearest bench, under an elm whose green branches hung so low they partially obscured the statue of Andy Jackson and the occasional passerby on one of the diagonal paths. He might just as well have accused himself of deliberately arriving early, lying in wait. He did; he was.

At a minute or two past three, while the bells on St. John's church were still ringing, Elizabeth Cameron stopped in front of a puddle twenty feet from his bench. She was dressed in a blue striped polonaise and a pouf bustle and a patterned scarf tossed around her shoulders with a jaunty flair. She frowned at the puddle and lifted the hem of her skirt with one hand.

"Mrs. Cameron, *bonjour*."

The hand dropped quickly, her right foot swung to the left, and she looked up at him with a perfectly gorgeous smile. "Mr. Trist."

"I thought you might be going to General Beale's for tea."

"I am, yes. My husband is already there. They had a late meal, I think, then a meeting, and I lost track of time."

"There was a wit in Paris, walking on the Champs-Élysées, knocked down by a workman who was carrying a grandfather clock. 'Why don't you wear a wristwatch,' he said, 'like everybody else?' "

She laughed and brushed back a strand of hair with one hand, and Trist took a step toward her. Her smile vanished in a flash.

"There come the Adamses," she said.

Around the corner of H Street, mounted on two brown mares, Clover and Henry Adams seemed to see them at exactly the same moment. Sidesaddle, Clover flicked her reins expertly and turned the horse in their direction.

"I thought you were Senator Don," she said with a nod and a smile to Trist when she reached the gate, "and then not."

"Quite not," said Adams, with only a nod, no smile.

Elizabeth busied herself with the muzzle of Clover's horse. "Mr. Trist is on his way to General Beale's, for tea. We happened to meet," she added unnecessarily, "just now."

"Well, tea," said Clover, "what is so nice as tea with the Beales? And to have an escort as well."

"I should have assumed," Henry Adams said dryly, "that Lafayette Square was a safe enough environs to cross without a bodyguard."

"General Grant," Trist began, "is supposed to be at the Beales'—"

"And you've come to *interview* him," Clover interrupted, "a newspaper 'scoop'—am I right?"

"He came, he saw, he had tea." Adams seemed unusually dyspeptic. He snapped his riding crop against the mare's flank, and the horse jerked her head up in surprise, snorting, and took two or three splayed steps backward into the street.

"And I *know* he's there," Clover said, bending forward and stroking her own horse's quivering neck, "because I *saw* him arrive on Sunday. From our front window. A great deal of fuss and far too many black carriages."

"Mrs. Adams sits at her window on Sunday mornings," Elizabeth Cameron explained, looking down at the horse's hoofs. "She smiles and watches the rest of us trudge to church. It's very wicked of her."

"It is," Clover agreed cheerfully. "I sit and watch funerals too, but they make me hungry. The hearses always look like bonbons on wheels."

"Grant must be planning his campaign strategy. And 'strategy' is the right word, for once, eh, Mr. Trist?" Henry Adams nudged his horse forward, inches from Trist, lifted his right hand to shade his eyes against the sun's glare, and studied the front of the Beale house through the trees. "Since the Democrats are certain to nominate General Hancock. *Duo strategoi,* what?"

"I don't know the word." Trist was standing so close that the mare's big shoulders literally pressed against his flat left shoulder. "Sorry."

"Greek," Adams said. "*Stratego* means 'general' in Greek. I thought you would know. Two presidential generals," he repeated for the ladies, with a mock sigh and a shake of his head. "And Garfield waiting in the wings, *another* general. Hancock's speeches are a wilderness of clichés, Grant scarcely speaks at all except to say, 'Let us have peace.' The whole country fights and refights the war as if it had never ended. Meanwhile the world is shifting under our feet."

"Henry is making a speech," Clover said.

"We live in the past," Adams told Elizabeth Cameron. "Heads buried in the sand."

Not for the first time Trist wondered about the Adamses' manner of speaking to each other, intimate, parallel, but neither ever quite answering or responding to what the other said. Marital geometry, he thought, parallels that don't meet.

"That's kind of a surprising complaint," he said, "for a former professor of history."

Adams smiled, a broad, charming, entirely unexpected smile that lit up his face with intelligence. "Touché, Mr. Trist," he said, and pulled his reins back as if to depart. "I see you're reading *Democracy*." He pointed the crop at Trist's pocket.

"It's very good, yes."

"I never read fiction," Adams said. Then over his shoulder as the horse swung around: "I understand you write sometimes now for the *Post*?"

Trist nodded warily.

"Not," Adams said, still smiling, "a *great* newspaper."

ONE HUNDRED YARDS AWAY, IN THE SECOND-FLOOR DRAWING room of the Decatur House, great, heroic, impassive Grant crossed in front of the Martin Van Buren window with his cup of coffee in his hand.

He smiled to himself as he sat down in General Beale's favorite chair. Great, heroic, impassive—powerful adjectives, fresh as his coffee, right out of an article in the New York *World* that very morning by John Russell Young, and Grant supposed they were meant to flatter him, or make him seem imposing and mysterious, "great" enough to attract any undecided Republican votes, "heroic" enough to overcome any third-term objections. He caught a glimpse of himself in a mirror as he sat down. The idea of writing, he assumed, was to place a grip on reality. He had never thought adjectives had much to do with reality.

"We were talking about the Mexican War," Beale said to Don Cameron, who stood by a silver coffee urn (one of Mrs. Beale's outstandingly ugly European purchases) and a porcelain china tea service so far untouched by anybody. Cameron spooned extra sugar into his cup and peered at it, as if in hope of a miracle of transubstantiation, coffee to bourbon. Grant knew the look.

"Well, I don't remember a damn thing about the Mexican War," Cameron said. "I was ten years old. But it sure as hell won't bring us any votes."

"A politically irrelevant war," Beale agreed. He puffed his cheeks and pursed his lips like a carp. Beale had recently shaved off his beard, one of the few clean-shaven men his own age that Grant knew, and up close, below his sideburns, you could see little shiny dots of whisker in the skin, like flecks of mica, where the razor had missed. Beale, of course, had run his own irrelevant side-war, so to speak, on the Mexican coast, selling contraband, buying up land, Beale and an Indian scout named Kit Carson, and he had ended up being made governor, if Grant remembered right, of a California district called San Jose.

"I once built a signal fire at San Pasquale," Beale confided, sitting down next to Grant. "Entirely and completely out of poison oak branches. Dumbest thing I ever did. Thought I had caught Pharaoh's plague. The smoke was what did it. Took me a week to get over the itch."

Grant laughed and looked affectionately over at Beale. There was something comfortable and comforting about a man of your own generation. A wealthy man, too, he thought, as he took in the newly remodeled elegance of Beale's house, with its floral tapestries and its teakwood cabinets and display cases and fine Louis Tiffany lamps, and its splendid view of Lafayette Square and, just in one corner, the President's Palace, where Grant had once lived; and might live again.

"Now we ought to talk about the convention. Two months is not a long time off." Businesslike, impatient, Cameron spread some of his papers across the quilted ottoman in front of his chair. He started to go over the delegations again briskly, who was for whom, state by state. Like a commanding general, Grant thought, and smiled again, inwardly. Outwardly, he was sure, nobody could have told that his mind was elsewhere, lazily turning over thoughts, memories, making similes. His mental process, he believed, resembled an old Missouri farmer digging at a stump, slowly prying it up from the dirt, excavating his idea. There were two parts to the world. There was the outward world of mass and line, force and counterforce, noun and verb, that the eye took in and the body felt. And there was the world inside the closed blank sphere of his mind, a kind of fragile white eggshell of consciousness through which he could see, but dimly; dimly. He knew he seemed silent, impassive; he knew other people mistook that for strength.

Cameron asked him a question about the Illinois delegation and Elihu Washburne, but because he hadn't quite heard the question he simply sat in his chair with his cup of coffee and said nothing. Cameron fidgeted. Beale looked out the window and waved. The clock on the mantel ticked. Abruptly Cameron went on to his next sheet of paper.

CHAPTER SIXTEEN

THE SECRET LIFE
OF U. S. GRANT

by Sylvanus Cadwallader

CHAPTER FOUR

BENJAMIN LOUIS EULALIE DE BONNEVILLE—NAME LIKE sweet French brandy, fairly curls around your flat American tongue, does it not?

Eulalie de Bonneville was born in Paris in 1796—an eighteenth-century man by the skin of his teeth. His family fled Napoleon for the New World shortly after his birth, and the boy, without much schooling or influence, somehow ended up at West Point, class of 1815; somehow after that was assigned, despite manifest incompetence, to lead an exploring party through fur-trap and Indian country, up the Columbia River to Hudson's Bay, object: Fort Vancouver.

Never mind that he got so completely lost that he never managed to find Vancouver; or that he got lost again in the next few years, repeatedly, in the Cascade Mountains and then the Rockies, and only emerged into dim mediocrity when he fought alongside

Scott in the Valley of Mexico. Bonneville had the comic French touch for strutting self-display. He refused to wear military head-gear, sported instead an enormous stiff white beaver stovepipe hat that made him look tall and imposing, not short and bald; he sought out newspaper reporters to write about his supposed adventures, including the nostalgic rumor that he was secretly the illegitimate son of the Marquis de Lafayette. That fat-bottomed New York–Dutch journalist Washington Irving swallowed his story whole and wrote a book that made our Frenchman famous. Last time I looked, a grateful and gullible nation had even named some arid, godforsaken stretch of scrub desert after him, out near the Great Salt Lake.

But in the year 1852 Bonneville was still in the army, not on the maps, a flap-jowled, petulant little infantry lieutenant colonel; and much to his disgust and dismay one fine day in the spring of that pleasant year he was put in charge of the U.S. Fourth Infantry, Sackets Harbor, New York, and ordered to take it at once across the Isthmus of Panama and up the Pacific coast to California.

Now this was welcome news to Lieutenant Grant. California was in the grip of a gold-and-land rush such as never had been seen, the place was one great big golden throbbing nerve, and the army was frantically needed to keep the Indians and displaced Mexicans calm and maintain a semblance of general order. Opportunities for promotion here. And if not promotion, numer-ous soldiers sent to California had already dropped out of rank, bought a pickax and a pan, and struck it rich, and as long as I have known Grant he has entertained the fantasy that sooner or later he too will stub his toe on a rock or scratch at some dirt and like-wise strike it rich.

Add to that the fact that life at Sackets Harbor had become as blank as a bowl of water.

The drawback was that Julia was in the family way again and she and the baby boy couldn't go with him. And the second draw-back was that Colonel Bonneville for unknown reasons took an instant, permanent, and querulous dislike to Grant and tried to have him demoted from his regimental quartermaster post. (Flamboyant people, Sherman excepted, often don't like Grant.) The other officers protested: Grant was quiet and inconspicuous but he got his job done. Bonneville waved his hand airily, Frenchily. All right, then let the quartermaster work out how to transport seven hundred soldiers and a hundred or so wives and children on a steamship built for three hundred and fifty, let the quartermaster manage the trip.

The quartermaster built a set of clever berths and bunks on the outer decks, measured and paced and sawed and hammered and actually squeezed them all aboard. Bonneville snorted, disappeared into his own private cabin. On July 5th, the U.S. Fourth Infantry cruised out of New York harbor and set off down the Atlantic toward the Gulf of Mexico.

I happened one day at City Point, Virginia, summer of 1864, to make the acquaintance of the former captain of that little paddle steamer, an elderly party named J. Finley Schenck, then employed on the army hospital ships that crawled up and down the James. Schenck remembered that Quartermaster Grant, if you ever got past the diffidence and shyness, was a thoughtful but high-strung man; talkative, not phlegmatic. Everything to do with the voyage devolved on him. Schenck wrote it up in a note for me—"Most conscientious. Grant never went to bed before three in the morning, after he had seen to everybody's needs. He paced the decks and soothed people's nerves; he smoked cigars eternally. I told him the first day if he needed a drink to stop by my cabin anytime. Every night after that, after I turned in, I would hear him, once or twice, sometimes more, open the door and walk softly over the floor, so as not to disturb me; then I would hear the clink of a glass and a gurgle and he would walk softly back."

They docked at a town called Aspinwall, on the Gulf side of the Isthmus, July 13th, and stepped down the gangplank into a green, wet, and scummy hell. I have a copy somewhere of Dante's *Inferno*, translated by H. W. Longfellow, about which chiefly I remember that I was surprised that Dante thought Hades was going to be as cold as ice, not hot as . . . Panama, I suppose. Nobody who hasn't been there can imagine the heat, the dripping orange flame-colored sky, the daily equatorial rain that hits your bare skin like drops of scalding oil—they get twelve *feet* of rain a year in that part of Panama. The sidewalks in Aspinwall were all eight inches under water. You waded through mud and slime, mosquitoes, sandflies, snakes—the town was built on a stinking marsh where the railroad construction crews had hauled loose fill—up to the edge of the jungle. There the great but unfinished Panama Railroad waited, steaming and sweating, for its passengers.

Bonneville was no help. Took off his high beaver hat, wiped his jowls; climbed in the nearest railroad carriage and waited. Quartermaster Grant got them all out of Aspinwall without incident, twenty-five miles of rickety one-track vertigo, up the Chagres River to the end of the line. At a little town named Barancos they clambered into a fleet of dugout canoes, *bungoes,* poled by naked Indians and Negroes. At an even smaller town upriver called Gorgona, most of the able-bodied troops swung out of their *bungoes* and said good-bye to the civilians. According to the War Department's plan the soldiers were to march twenty-five miles or so, straight from there to the Pacific and Panama City and a waiting troopship. Wives and children were to travel farther upstream to the village of Cruces, where the army had arranged for mules to carry them and the regiment's surplus equipment down an easier path to Panama City.

What the army hadn't foreseen was the absence of actual mules in Cruces.

Or the presence of cholera.

Here is what happens when you take sick with cholera.

First comes the diarrhea that wrings you out like a filthy rag. Then vomiting, violent and constant. After that, cramps begin in the legs and torture their way up to the belly. Then a thirst like burning sand starts in your throat. Your skin turns blue toward the end, your voice gives way to a hoarse, gagging croak that the medics call "vox cholerica." Healthy on Monday, sick on Tuesday; dead and buried Wednesday.

The promised mules of Cruces had all been hired away earlier, free-market style, at inflated prices to California-bound miners coming through first. The best that Grant could do was to round up what few beasts remained, at double the authorized prices, and find some native bearers who would carry boxes or sling canvas hammocks between their shoulders for the weakest women and children. And even this took time. The army buried some of their number right at Cruces. At the end of a week, when everybody and everything that could be hired was hired, Grant gathered them all at the edge of the village. One hundred and twenty guards, women, children. They started off single file, heading west.

A two-day trip, normally. In July, a walking, sweltering, endless nightmare. The jungle crowded in like a hot green blanket. The sides of the path, one-mule wide, were on fire with flowers.

Monkeys and parrots screeched and chattered overhead in the coconut palms. Where there was water it was covered with thick gray slime—Grant warned them not to touch it, told them to drink the colonel's wine or nothing, but such was the heat that few listened. When the Americans stopped for the night they would wearily watch the native cooks chewing sugarcane, then spitting into a pot for sweetener. Rains came daily. Cholera victims would suddenly slide off their mules or tumble from their hammocks. Sometimes they buried their dead in the mire, in the roots and blossoms tangled along the foot of the path. Sometimes the native bearers would simply fling them back across the donkeys, or roll them like logs into a hammock.

More than a third of the party died before they reached Panama City—of twenty children, only three survived—and many more died soon after that. The idiot Colonel Bonneville had already hustled all his people aboard the troopship, even the ones who were showing sick. Grant and the regimental doctor were horrified, and Grant hurried back to shore, where he leased (unauthorized) the unused hulk of an abandoned clipper ship out in the harbor. The shore authorities had by now quarantined the Americans, so Grant and the regimental doctor carried the sick and dying over to the hospital ship in dinghies and then organized shifts of volunteers to tend them. Bonneville thought this was an excess of authority and threatened the doctor with court-martial (ignored).

Grant supervised the move and the fumigation of the troopship. He somehow also talked more medical supplies out of the Panamanians. And every other day for two weeks he took his turn with the other volunteers nursing the sick in their beds. An unexpected image: the Butcher of Cold Harbor sits down on a stool next to a dying soldier, feeds him his meal with a spoon, tenderly wipes his lips with a cloth.

On the fifth of August the survivors heard the anchor chains rattle up, and the nicely named ship, the *Golden Gate,* set sail for California.

Now flip the coin over.

From the tropical rainforests and cholera plagues of Panama, move north, above the forty-five-degree latitude line, all the way up to the present-day border of Washington State and Oregon. If you have an old map, slide your finger to the rugged little village of Portland, five or six hundred dreary souls perched on a bare hill looking down at the fast-moving, iron-gray Columbia River (no shiny green jungle scum here, no dugout *bungoes;* just salmon and fog, fog and rain).

Fifteen or twenty miles farther north, stop at Fort Vancouver, the biggest army outpost in all the Northwest, a dozen makeshift buildings behind a wooden stockade and a fifty-foot watchtower with holes for cannon they don't have; beyond the stockade, impenetrable spruce and fir woods, silent and dark as a cave. When Grant walks out on his porch in the early morning, a tin cup of coffee in his hands against the chill, his boots clump on rough wood planks. In the distance a horse neighs. Nothing else stirs. Down by the river a waterfowl slaps its wings a few times, then the silence drifts back like the fog.

Actually, Grant and the *Golden Gate* stopped first in San Francisco, for medical supplies, and Grant went ashore on leave for twenty-four hours to what was then, in the middle of the Gold Rush, without a doubt the closest thing to Babylon or Babel the planet had to offer.

In 1848 San Francisco enjoyed a quiet population of under twenty thousand people, mostly fishermen and timber traders. Then, over on a fork of the American River, a laborer named James Marshall bent down one afternoon and started to pick up gold nuggets, so they claimed, as big as a baby's head. A year later there were a hundred thousand people in San Francisco, from every nation on earth, and Mars and Venus as well. In 1852, when Quartermaster Grant stretched his legs out on the Long Wharf, the city had been burnt down and rebuilt three times already, each time gaudier and grander than before, and people said it had reached a quarter million at least, with no sign of stopping.

The single day he was there Grant strolled along the docks and admired the polyglot *bagnios* and brothels and gold assay offices set up right among the ships. He took a carriage ride out past the hills the Chinese coolies were digging up and dragging down for landfill, all the way to the sand dunes that made up the western shore of the city. He won forty dollars in a faro house and spent the better part of it on drinks and a meal in one of those splendiferous and gaudy gold-blown hotels on Market Street, and if friends are to be believed, almost quit the military then and there—I say it again and again, nobody ever believes it. He looks like the mildest, quietest little man in the world, no mystery about him, no steam coming out of his ears like Sherman, no show-off ways like "Old Brains" Halleck or that insane Young Napoleon George McClellan (about to turn up again one page later)—but Grant is a nervous, volatile person, *inside*. And outside, he craves excitement. Give him a plague to fight or an isthmus to cross—but routine bores him. Monotony drives him back in his shell.

What he got in Fort Vancouver was monotony squared. A room in a two-story house next to the wood-fence stockade. A quartermaster's office with barrels for chairs and unpainted walls and order forms and account books and military purchase manuals. One lumpish day after the other of gray skies and gray rain and humdrum routine.

And he handled it about as badly as a man could do.

Once at City Point late in the war I remember watching from my tent while Grant and Lincoln tried to settle some matter of routine paperwork, about which neither of them was ever much good. Grant stood there emptying his coat pockets one after the other, each one a worse rat's nest of crumpled papers and flimsies, while he tried to find his document. Meantime Lincoln had pulled off his old black stovepipe hat and was holding it up to look inside, where *he* filed *his* papers.

"From the kitchen where I worked," Grant's old Vancouver cook, a lady named Sheffield, wrote me, "I could see him every day walking back and forth on the porch, smoking and thinking for hours at a time, or else he would order his horse and ride till sundown by himself in the woods."

He had his own liquor cabinet now. Or when that ran dry, he would stroll over to the officers' mess. He was what in the army was known as a "four-finger" drinker—he held his glass in his fist, said fill it up to the fourth finger, no water ever ("Do you think I'm a camel?"—army joke as old as Julius Caesar).

When the mails finally caught up in late October he learned that Julia had given birth in July to another baby boy and named him U. S. Grant, Jr. This spurred him on for a time—he leased some bottomland by the river and planted twenty acres of potatoes, aiming to sell them next spring down in San Francisco and make a fortune, but the river flooded, the potatoes spoiled; he went part-share in a shipload of ice for that same thirsty city, ice melted. He bought some hogs, was swindled; went partners in a billiard house, till the manager ran away with the cash.

ONE OF THE FEW DUTIES THE QUARTERMASTER HAD AT FORT Vancouver was to outfit surveying parties on their way north, toward Indian country.

I hear his defenders say, well, Grant never drank *on duty*, never let drink interfere with his *work*. Well, yes, he did. Early spring, here comes that poker-assed s.o.b. Captain George McClellan (same as later commanded the Army of the Potomac till Lincoln fired him and took on Grant), leading a survey party inland. And Grant chose his arrival as the time to go on one of his longer sprees, so bad that Captain McClellan fumed and ranted and officially complained (and ten years later tattle-taled to Lincoln).

Loneliness had come down on Grant like a hammer. He carried Julia's letters wrapped in a bundle under his coat and took them out to read while he wiped his nose and held his bottle. Mrs. Sheffield remembers his pathetic hungry lope down to the mailboat, his hangdog look when he came back empty-handed. Once she was chattering away about something and Grant abruptly pulled out his latest letter, showed her the last page where Julia had made a pencil trace outline of a baby's hand, then walked away trembling, tears in his eyes.

Back in Shakespeare's day the actors used to try an experiment from time to time—present a play one night as a tragedy; next night, exact same play presented as a comedy—it was all in the tone of voice.

Grant's tone of voice here is what has always bothered me— too much sniffling, too much self-pity. Other men in the West had been away from home longer, had just as much humdrum and disappointment to swallow. (Down in San Francisco about this time Sherman, working as a banker, went totally bust.) Grant couldn't afford to send for Julia because he kept losing money instead of making it, and that was his own fault, and he felt forsaken and lost and he couldn't figure out how to live in the woods without her. Same man who had marched through Panama and cholera like a cast-iron angel.

At the end of a year, news arrived informally of his promotion to captain. He was ordered to leave the comfort of Fort Vancouver and report two hundred miles down the coast at Fort Humboldt, California, which wasn't a fort at all, just two understrength infantry companies huddled on a mudflat at the edge of a dense pine forest, commanded by a man named Robert Buchanan, who had once been Grant's commanding officer back in Missouri and didn't (another one) like him a bit.

Fort Humboldt lay three miles from the city of Eureka—Westerners will name two planks in the road a "city"—which had a seasonal lumber mill, a few scattered houses, and exactly one place of business, called Ryan's Store. People in Eureka remember seeing Grant tumble off the boardwalk by Ryan's Store, tipsy. They recall he was sick a good deal with migraine headaches, and when he was not, he would sit by the stove in Ryan's, near the long-handled wooden dipper and the whiskey barrel, and tell long stories about the Mexican War and read his letters.

Julia wrote to say she wouldn't go to California at all if she had to cross at Panama. Colonel Dent bragged that the two little boys were growing up at his house to be "true Dents." Grant's father wrote that Julia wouldn't bring the grandsons to Ohio to visit and rarely answered their letters (Julia rarely answers anybody's letters).

The comic tone just wasn't in Grant. Four months into his tour at Fort Humboldt he showed up one day at the paymaster's table so drunk he couldn't count, and Colonel Buchanan hauled him in and gave him a choice: court-martial or dismissal.

On April 11, 1854, his formal letter of promotion to captain arrived. He wrote the Secretary of War a letter saying he accepted the promotion. Then he pulled out a second sheet of paper: "I very respectfully tender my resignation."

He wrote Julia he had received a "leave of absence." At San Francisco he was penniless and had to sleep on a sofa in the harbormaster's office till a free military ticket on a ship could be found, and then on June first "Useless" Grant started for home again, thirty-two years old and broke and no matter what he thought, still not even halfway down to rock bottom.

PART TWO

VOX HUMBUG

CHICAGO

May–June 1880

EXTRACTS FROM A REPORTER'S NOTEBOOK
—NICHOLAS P. TRIST, *June 1880*

"Interview in Chicago with John Corson Smith,
Union veteran"

The Seventh Illinois Infantry Regiment was mustered into service on June 28, 1861, in Springfield. We were mostly a bunch of ignorant farm boys, so wild and undisciplined that the first colonel assigned to us in the recruiting camp couldn't stand it and up and vanished.

Two Illinois Congressmen came out for the swearing-in ceremony, Logan and McClernand, and of course being politicians both had to get on their legs and make speeches. McClernand talked for an hour about God and Country. Logan talked even longer, and I tell you, that man was a spellbinder, he orated like a wizard. By the time Logan finished he had us farm boys whipped up to such a patriotic sweat and frenzy we were ready to grab our bayonets and rifles on the spot and make a dash for Richmond.

Then Logan held out his arm in a big flourish and said, "Men, allow me to present to you your new commander, Colonel U. S. Grant!"

The regiment started to whoop and carry on and slap each other on the back, everybody bellowing, "Grant! Grant! Give us a speech—Grant!"

But Grant stepped forward without a word and just stood there waiting. And it slowly began to dawn on a few of us that this was a new world and a new kind of war. It wasn't going to be won in the old Andy Jackson style by the commander who rode out in front of his troops and waved his sword for a charge. Not by speeches either. After a while the noise and uproar died down and the room got perfectly silent. Then Grant merely said, "Men, go to your quarters."

We looked at each other, then back at him. Then we turned around and did what he said.

CHAPTER ONE

"CUMP SHERMAN," CADWALLADER SAID, POINTING HIS CIGAR, "has *presence*. Look at him."

The young reporters obediently turned their heads and observed, through the barroom grill of the Grand Pacific Hotel of Chicago, the tall, ferocious, and thoroughly present figure of General William Tecumseh Sherman, Grant's right hand in the war, the Scourge of Georgia. As was his custom, Sherman was bare-headed to display his brilliant crown of red hair, but he wore a dark blue full-dress uniform with gold braid, gold stripes, and he looked every inch what he was, commander-in-chief of the U.S. Army.

"Grant don't have it," Cadwallader said. "Sometimes you think he *deliberately* makes himself inconspicuous. Grant goes into a room of people, he just disappears, you don't ever notice him. First time Secretary of War Stanton met him, he come on a special train to Indianapolis in '63, walked right up to Ed Kittoe, who was a doctor on Grant's staff, and said, 'Why, General Grant, how are you? I'd know you anywhere, you look so much like your photographs!' Grant was standing over to one side, slouched-like, chewing his cigar, kind of amused. Didn't say a word, just smiled. I was there," Cadwallader added, though in fact he wasn't.

The reporters looked at him, looked back at Sherman, who was surrounded in the lobby now by dozens of noisy backslapping well-wishers and admirers, including two or three young ladies in tight pastel dresses, not backslappers, who did not appear, if appearances were correct, to be anybody's wives.

"Come to see his brother, I guess," said a skinny young reporter from some twice-a-week newspaper in Maine.

"Why don't you go ask him?" Cadwallader said with a grin, and all the other young reporters laughed and picked up their glasses again, because, young as they were, even they knew better than to walk up uninvited to Sherman, whose hatred of all reporters, young and old, was a national fact. "He foams at the mouth at the mere sight of a newspaper reporter," somebody had written the other day in the New York *World*. "He actually *snaps* at them." Back in the war, when a bursting Confederate shell killed three reporters at Vicksburg, somebody had run and told Sherman and he had just nodded his head with that amoral, half-animal little grin that was one of his secrets with women and said, "Good. Now we'll have news from Hell for breakfast." Of course, he had his reasons back then. That same New York *World* had gone on for weeks and weeks in 1862 about his supposed nervous breakdown and mental collapse and almost got Sherman kicked out of the army, till Halleck, who always liked him, stepped in. But Sherman had ever been friendly to Cadwallader. Gave him one of his nicest quotations one day just before the elections of 1864, when Lincoln looked likely to lose and Sherman was fulminating against democracy and all its misguided principles, which had got us, he thought, into this war in the first place. *"Vox populi, vox humbug,"* Sherman had said, and watched to make sure Cadwallader wrote it down correctly.

Out in the lobby he was now moving through a dense mass of people toward the staircase and his brother John's second-floor campaign headquarters (suite 268, worth a pint of E.C.B. two days ago; now everybody knew it).

"Are *you* going to interview General Sherman?" one of the other young men asked, respectfully.

"Already saw him," Cadwallader replied. He finished his glass of bourbon that they had been kind enough to buy him and gathered his bundle of out-of-town newspapers. "Saw him at the train station last night. Passing through on his way to St. Louis, he is."

"Does he think his brother has a chance?"

Cadwallader folded the papers into a bulky package and tucked it under his arm. In fact, he *had* bumped into Cump Sherman last night, and Sherman thought like everybody else that his younger brother John, who was a fine, outstanding Secretary of Treasury but not a politician, didn't have a Chinaman's chance on the convention floor next week. But Sherman said he didn't want to be quoted, and Cadwallader knew when he meant it.

"General Sherman stays out of politics completely, you know that."

Now Cadwallader was halfway to the door and the packed swarm of agitated sightseers and hangers-on and flunkies in the lobby that a political convention always attracted like demented ants to a sugar spill. But one of the young reporters evidently had drunk more than Cadwallader would have thought, because he swayed a little and raised his voice to be heard over the hubbub.

"You ought to go down to Galena, Caddy, interview Grant, that's what. *That's* a story."

"Well, he won't come up to Chicago, you're right."

"Damn shame how he treated you after the war, Caddy."

Cadwallader merely nodded and closed down his face a little (like Grant) and went on out.

On La Salle Street the sun was shining and hot, just the way late May ought to be, and the streets were full of traffic and more convention hangers-on and about seven thousand yards of banners and bunting on every window and storefront from the Grand Pacific to Exposition Hall. Cadwallader hunched his papers tighter under his arm and started to walk in the opposite direction, toward the lake.

At two or three intersections he paused to watch some of the marching brass bands that were out on the streets, practicing, raising hell by weaving between streetcars and carriages, scaring the horses. Somebody had told him there were more than twenty such bands in town already, and most of them weren't officially attached to any candidate, so they just went in and out of the hotel lobbies whenever they felt like it, on a lark, and played patriotic songs and collected tips and drinks and generally contributed to the *vox humbug*. God bless our Cump, he thought, and sat down on a bench just above the sandy strip of beach at the corner of Michigan and Fourth.

Usually it was windy by the lake in the afternoon, but May had been so hot the winds had never really got into a Chicago rhythm. Today it was blistery and still as a steam bath. Cadwallader loosened his collar and took off his coat and opened the first of his papers. He always read the New York *Times,* though he thought the prose was so dry and bad it sounded like a woodchuck gnawing a sausage. And he read the New York *Tribune,* since he was ostensibly one of their correspondents. But this afternoon the first paper he pulled out of his stack was the Washington *Post,* whose owner was a maniac but had a good eye for writers.

He put his coat on top of the other papers. A barge full of something black and smelly was hovering offshore, under a cloud of flapping white seagulls, and there were toy boats and paddle-steamers and more barges farther away on the horizon, busy as a city street. Down at the water's edge a woman with a white parasol stood holding her little girl's hand and looking out. Nobody ever stands the other way, Cadwallader thought, with their backs to the water, staring at the land. He wondered if that were a profound observation. Decided not.

The Washington *Post* devoted the left-hand side of its front page to more or less factual political news, the right-hand side to sensational cases of rape or murder, preferably both. Page two contained numerous nasty, sneering pro-Democrat editorial paragraphs, almost all written, as everybody knew, by Stilson Hutchins, and two full columns of patent-medicine advertisements and bits and pieces of miscellaneous and local news. There was one running story on the back, been there for weeks, about a White House clerk named Chapman who seduced female job applicants in his office and was, the *Post* gleefully pointed out every day, a Republican appointee. There was also a very funny series about the awful Washington water supply and the four different colors of Washington drinking water, depending on the daily state of contamination of the Potomac. Cadwallader believed he could recognize a reporter's work by his style, and he was next to certain the clever story about water was the work of the clever one-armed young veteran, Nicholas Trist.

He chuckled through Chapman's latest denial, then went to the front page to see what they said about the convention, although it was still two days till the opening gavel and most papers weren't doing anything but describing the carnival atmosphere and the dead-certain third nomination of U. S. Grant. He knew Trist was writing part-time now for the *Post*. And sure enough, on page one, column three, his eye went straight to a short political bulletin, with the initials "N.T." at the end (next to a column that had a typical *Post* headline: BUTCHERED BY HIS BETTER HALF).

But Trist's was a quick, concise, completely original and serious story. Nineteen of the forty-two members of the Pennsylvania Republican delegation, supposedly under Don Cameron's iron rule, were secretly ready to bolt from Grant and throw their support, after the first ballot, to James A. Garfield. Unlike most reporters, Trist was sure enough of his facts to name names. The rebels, he wrote, were led by a Philadelphia banker named Wharton and a professor of medieval history named Henry Lea.

Cadwallader's first thought was that professors had no business at all in politics—that consummate little snob Henry Adams had tried to meddle in the election of 1872, with pathetic results— professors were not a competent class, professors couldn't cross the street together safely. His second thought was that Don Cameron was going to holler like a stuck pig.

T EN BLOCKS AWAY AND FOUR HOURS LATER, THE VERY SAME image occurred to Trist. A stuck pig in a poke.

He leaned against a corridor wall in the gallery level of Exposition Hall and watched as Don Cameron, porcine of bulk and violently red of cheek, jerked his cigar from his mouth and turned to shout at one of his aides.

Trist was too far away to hear what Cameron said, and the corridor was too crowded for him to move closer. Downstairs, in the main auditorium, an orchestra was tuning up for the evening's concert, and to add to the din, outside on the street a peripatetic brass band was coincidentally marching by. He considered for a moment trying to push his way up to Cameron's side. But half the Pennsylvania delegation seemed to have jammed themselves into the narrow corridor, and the crisis of the Philadelphia banker and the nineteen Garfield defectors was evidently going to be dealt with in private—so a furious and beleaguered Cameron had informed him earlier. No further story was likely that night. Trist wiped his brow, turned around, and collided gently with the Senator's wife.

"Mr. Trist."

"I do apologize—I wasn't looking."

"My husband—" She broke off as Cameron abruptly spun on his heel and disappeared into a door beneath a banner with Grant's famous slogan of 1868: LET US HAVE PEACE.

"I think," she said, and they were now both pushed to one side by yet another squadron of hats, elbows, cigars hurrying down the corridor. Elizabeth Cameron held on to her hat with one hand and braced herself with the other. "I think," she said wryly, "I've just lost my husband."

The orchestra downstairs could suddenly be heard quite clearly: "Go Tell Aunt Rhody."

"Well, I could try and find him for you," Trist said, but doubtfully. The corridor was busier than ever, the door to the traitorous Pennsylvania delegation had by now been slammed emphatically shut. By unspoken agreement they both edged closer to the stairs.

"It's a pity. We were supposed to go to the concert"—Elizabeth held up two green pasteboard tickets and made a rueful "best-laid plans" kind of face. "But now—"

The pause hung in the air. Trist cleared his throat. "If you'd like an escort," he said.

She cocked her head in a way that Emily Beale might have called flirtatious. "No stories to file, Mr. Trist? No meetings, deadlines?"

"Everything done, shipshape."

"I thought journalists worked till *all* hours, Mr. Trist."

"My motto is 'Don't Get It Right—Get It Written.' "

She laughed and held out her arm. "I haven't seen you for weeks, Mr. Trist," she said.

A T THE BOTTOM OF THE STAIRS THEY EMERGED INTO THE WIDER, calmer passageway that ringed the great open space of the convention auditorium. Trist looked at her tickets and turned to the right. "I would have been lost in two minutes," she murmured.

He knew what she meant. He had already written a description of the building for the *Post*—the largest amphitheater in Chicago, maybe in the country, able to hold ten thousand people on the main floor, another four or five thousand in the balconies and galleries. Workmen had been busy for a week installing flags and banners, an enormous canvas screen painted to be an American flag had been draped from floor to ceiling at one end, and since this morning they had added wooden arches and trellises along the walls, potted evergreen trees, and numerous giant oil portraits of Republican worthies behind the speaker's platform, including Lincoln, Grant, Hayes, Conkling, and even, benign and smiling in one corner, Don Cameron. To test the acoustics, a patriotic concert had been scheduled for that night and the Chicago Symphonia installed, Trist was amused to notice, right beneath the portrait of Grant, who was known to dislike every form of music. On the central platform the orchestra finished tuning up with a whinny of violins and a brass burst of trumpets.

An usher led them down a long sloping aisle, then stood aside to show them their seats. Trist put the ticket stubs in his pocket, pulled his hand out again, and fumbled for change. Elizabeth Cameron waited beside him, unconcerned.

In Washington, he thought, they always met in somebody's house, somebody's safe little drawing room or parlor. Here—he found himself suddenly tongue-tied, awkward as a schoolboy. They sat down side by side, leg by skirt on their wooden chairs.

He muttered something pedantic and stupid—in Europe they didn't number the selections in a printed musical program, as the new practice was in America. The first time he'd heard someone call a song a "number," he'd been as puzzled as Rip Van Winkle.

Elizabeth smiled and whispered "droll Mr. Trist," but just at that moment the bandleader strode to the front and bowed, and then the auditorium lights went down.

The first few selections were all sentimental favorites, each one greeted with applause—"Annie Laurie," "Greensleeves," "There Is a Happy Land," "Finnegan's Wake." In the heat of the room, in the dark, Trist was acutely conscious of Elizabeth Cameron inches away. The curves of her face caught and held what light there was. Her hair spilled in dark curls onto her shoulders. He inhaled a scent from her skin of soap and lemon verbena. When he moved in his seat her skirt yielded softly to his hip and leg.

At the first interval they stood and looked about irresolutely.

"It's terribly hot, Mr. Trist—perhaps?"

Numerous small black boys were selling flavored ices from trays around their necks, but they were all confined to an area next to an outside exit. By the time they had reached the nearest of them, and Trist had fumbled again in his pocket for change, the bandleader was back on his podium again, clapping his hands for silence.

"Our next selection," he called out in a booming voice, "is in honor of our brave boys."

"War songs," Elizabeth whispered. The gas-jet lights around them began to fade. In the growing darkness neither of them took a step.

"Back in the great and terrible Battle of the Wilderness," the bandleader said. A spotlight bathed him in a garish yellow light. Trist put his unfinished ice on an empty stool. "May 1864," the bandleader said. "A certain brigade of the Ninth Corps had just broken the Rebel line and started forward, when the threat of a flank attack threw them all back in disorder. After a desperate retreat, the brigade re-formed and turned to face the enemy, but the prevailing mood was one of despair. Just at this moment a soldier in the Forty-fifth Pennsylvania launched into song."

The first few notes were unmistakable. Behind the bandleader a solitary young man rose into the spotlight and began to sing in a sweet, clear tenor:

"We'll rally round the flag,
Boys, we'll rally once again,
Shouting the Battle-cry of Freedom!"

"And his words were picked up by the others, and soon the entire brigade was singing the defiant chorus and charging back again into the heroic fray—join in with us! Sing!"

The crowd came to its feet with a roar and a cheer and the huge auditorium rocked with sound:

"The Union forever!
Hurrah boys, hurrah!
Down with the traitor, up with the star,
While we rally round the flag, boys, rally once again,
Shouting the Battle-cry of Freedom!"

Behind them two of the ices boys flung open a door to the sidewalk outside. Instantly, without thinking, Trist turned and walked

toward it—in a moment he was on the street, under a hot gas
lamp, wiping his brow with his handkerchief. When he looked up,
Elizabeth Cameron was standing a few feet away, studying him
with a curious gaze.

"You're not nostalgic, Mr. Trist," she said, "for the war. I've
noticed before."

"Touch of malaria," he muttered. "Comes back sometimes."
He felt the handkerchief, sopping wet. "I tend to agree with your
Uncle Cump."

" 'War is pure hell,' " she quoted.

"Pardon your language," Trist said and was rewarded with an
utterly dazzling smile.

"Do you want to go back in?"

"Actually, Mrs. Cameron, I don't feel much like a musical person. Not really. Not tonight."

Around them on the street and brick sidewalks it was as if the
convention had taken over the city. There were men and women
walking, laughing on the sidewalks, in the street—some carried
banners and badges, next to the entrance more little boys had
gathered with trays of ices, and through the door, from the interi-
or of the Hall, came the martial thump of drums. It was the
women, Trist thought, who were the great surprise. Women
seemed to be everywhere, escorted, unescorted, amused, part of
the show. In the Palmer House Hotel, opposite "Grant for
President" headquarters, a Women's Suffrage committee had
opened a booth. In front of them right now three women in bus-
tles and hats with dyed feathers came giggling out of a side door,
a restaurant, unattended. It was not quite so odd, he thought,
today, tonight, to be standing in a city street with somebody else's
wife.

Elizabeth Cameron had already turned and started toward the
brighter lights of the State Street intersection.

"I have only a girl's perspective," she said as he caught up.
They stopped at a corner and watched Roman candles pulse and
flutter up over rooftops, green and red puffs, blocks away; neither
of them mentioned Don Cameron somewhere in the vast bulk of
brick and masonry behind them. "When I was not quite twelve my
uncle invited me on a four-month trip to the Yellowstone River in
Montana—he was inspecting army camps and we rode horseback
and slept in tents all the way."

"Rugged country." Trist took her elbow and steered her out of the path of whooping Republican delegates marching six abreast and shouting "Blaine of Maine" slogans. Away from the lakefront, Chicago was a city of endless wooden tenements, soot, overloaded wagons, its streets were forever littered with boxes and crates, it had a raw, brutal un-Washingtonian feel to it, of commerce and hard weather and life perpetually in motion. But tonight in the heat and high spirits of the convention, dense with promenaders, dazzling with lights, it seemed as gay and pleasure-bound as Venice. The Blaine delegates thrust them aside, into an arched doorway, where they were pressed so close together for a moment that their shoulders and arms touched and recoiled with an electric shock.

They pushed back into the street.

Near the entrance to the Palmer House they slowed to a breathless stop in the darkness, fifty yards or so from the torchlit portico of the hotel. Elizabeth Cameron leaned against a solitary sycamore tree, planted against all odds in a square of the sidewalk, and fanned herself with one hand.

"Not quite the Montana wilderness," Trist said, nodding at the tree.

Her hair was in loose curls around her neck; in the flickering light of the torches her cheeks were flushed. Don Cameron is an ass, Trist thought. Because of the clatter of horses and carriages in front of the Palmer House he had to lean in and ask her to repeat what she had said.

"Several years ago"—another pause while a wagon rumbled by—"several years ago I went back, after . . . a disappointment."

"To Montana?"

"My married sister Mary and I." She turned, straightened her dress; wrinkled her nose at the pungent aromas of horse sweat, smoke, burning kerosene somewhere. Chicago after all, not Venice. "My brother-in-law Colonel Miles was leading troops against the Indians, on the Tongue River, and we stayed in his headquarters, which was actually nothing but a log cabin with a flat tin roof in the middle of the woods. Most glamorous, Mr. Trist—I loved every minute. We went about with an armed escort, we saw Indian braves in full war regalia, and once we came up just at the end of a skirmish the troopers had fought with some of Sitting Bull's stragglers. We went to Sioux powwows, we camped with the Crow Indians—Colonel Miles said we'd been where no white woman had ever gone before."

"You were very adventurous," Trist said, and meant it.

"Well, it was wonderful, the most exciting time of my life. Colonel Miles invites me to come back, but of course, now—" She shrugged.

There were two Elizabeth Camerons, Trist thought. One was a cool, formal, married woman, older and stiffer than her twenty-four years. But that woman was back in Washington, in the overfastidious world of Henry Adams. This Elizabeth had a wide, sensuous tilt to her mouth, her skin was flushed and prickly, as if with heat, her voice so low that it was scarcely more than a murmur.

"But that wasn't at all what you saw," she said, "I suppose, at the Wilderness, Cold Harbor, those places you couldn't hear them sing about. We were just girls, my sister and I, tourists. What you saw was what my uncle saw."

Trist was silent.

"There was one curious episode," she said, so close now that her dress brushed against his arm, he could smell her scent again. "On that second trip to Montana I wasn't yet married—Mary and I travelled on a steamer up the Missouri from Sioux City, and the name of the boat oddly enough was the *Senator Don Cameron*."

"An omen," Trist said.

"Do you think so?"

He held his hand up to her face and slowly bent forward and kissed her. She sighed deep in her throat and pressed against him, and for a long moment the city moved in circles around them, rattling, clattering, a distant background of wobbling lights and dizzy motion. He kissed her lips, neck, his hand went to her breast. She moaned and cupped it with her own, and he tasted salt, honey. She trembled and moved against him harder.

"Come back to my room."

"*No!*" She pulled back, then came forward again and kissed him again with her whole mouth and body and whispered, "My aunt will be waiting," and then before he could take a step she was hurrying up the sidewalk, into the light, head down. A liveried doorman from the Palmer House moved toward her, raising his hat.

WHY, THE *DON CAMERON* SANK," CADWALLADER SAID. "THAT was four years ago at least—hit a snag in the river above Sioux City, went down like a box of rocks. Another boat came by and rescued everybody—the *William T. Sherman* as a matter of fact—but the *Don* was gone. Two of the Sherman girls were on it, Lizzie and Mary, I think, made all the papers, and of course Lizzie *married* him next year, didn't learn a thing. What the hell makes you ask about that?"

"Just reading." Trist looked down and shuffled his notes one-handed like a card shark. "Old clippings."

"Well, the real Don Cameron's about to sink too, take my word." Cadwallader picked up his pencil and nodded in the direction of Cameron at the other end of the room. Trist picked up his own pencil. In the main auditorium of Exposition Hall, reporters were scheduled tomorrow to have special reserved tables and chairs just under the speaker's platform, in the center of the hall. But here, in what was essentially only a peripheral meeting room, the press was shoved together at the rear, backs to the wall, a good ninety feet from the long mahogany conference table where Don Cameron and the rest of the Republican National Committee officers were in the process of taking their seats.

"Where's Henry West?" Cadwallader asked out of the corner of his mouth.

"Sick. Mumps."

"So they sent you instead, man with the inside track to Cameron, very nice. Stilson Hutchins is an idiot, but he's no fool."

"Chandler's here," Trist said.

"Fiat nox," Cadwallader said; snorted; wrote "Let there be bull-shit" on his pad.

Trist shifted in his chair and leaned forward. In the last few days he had devoted considerable energy to getting the players straight, the stakes right. Every national newspaper and magazine had already conceded the presidential nomination to Grant, and the National Committee had actually ordered "Grant for President" posters and badges, but the anti-third-term forces were putting up a stubborn struggle. Former Senator William E. Chandler was chief spokesman for perennial candidate James G. Blaine of Maine, the still-indignant villain of *Democracy,* and Chandler was attending an otherwise routine preliminary com-mittee meeting for the sole purpose—everybody in Chicago knew it—of defeating Don Cameron in a crucial vote. The issue was the so-called "unit voting rule" of the convention, according to which states voted by blocs instead of by individual delegates, and Grant's whole strategy depended on it: With the unit rule gone, dissenting delegates like the nineteen from Pennsylvania might be recognized on the floor and cast their votes for somebody other than Grant. And from all indications, the heavy-handed Cameron was about to lose the battle to keep it.

Whatever Trist had learned so far, however, was inconsequen-tial compared to Cadwallader's intimate knowledge of names and personalities. While the committee went about its preliminary business—a steady, remorseless series of victories for Chandler—Cadwallader kept up a muttered running commentary that had most of the reporters chuckling into their notebooks. Moments before the final vote of the day, which would not only eliminate the unit rule but also depose Don Cameron from the committee itself, Cadwallader turned around ostentatiously.

"There's 'Lord Roscoe,' " he said, loud enough to stop conver-sation all over the room. "Come to watch his horse get beat."

At the rear, Senator Roscoe Conkling of New York, Grant's other campaign manager, always dramatic, always arrogant, had suddenly appeared in the doorway like Banquo's ghost. He made no move to speak or step inside. Instead he folded his arms across his massive chest and stared scornfully down the aisle. Cameron grimaced and shook his head. William Chandler stared back at Conkling defiantly, then rapped his gavel for the vote. Conkling vanished again into the corridor. Around the long committee table hands slowly began to rise.

"Chandler wins by nine," Cadwallader said a moment before the total was announced. "Grant's in trouble. Let's go see Senator Don."

By the time they reached the corridor outside the meeting room Cameron was pushing his way furiously through a knot of hangers-on and sympathizers, marching as fast as he could toward the Pennsylvania office where Trist had seen him last night. When he spotted Trist he walked quickly up.

"Mr. Trist," he said. He paused, jammed his fists in his coat pockets, and for a split second Trist thought that last night was about to explode in his face, that somehow Elizabeth— Guilt made him stand up straight and square his shoulders. Cameron looked bigger, redder-faced than ever.

"Mr. Trist, you published an interview with me a while ago in which I said I was for Grant and had no second choice, and that I knew he would be nominated by acclamation on the first ballot."

"I remember."

"Just print that same interview over and over again and keep on printing it till everybody knows that Grant's nomination and election, no matter what's happened today, are as sure as tomorrow's sunrise."

Cadwallader had come up with a broken-off bit of toothpick, which he now stuck in the corner of his mouth like a rustic bit of straw. "What about Washburne, Senator? The way I figure, if Washburne don't drop out and give his votes to Grant, then you don't have any real chance at all."

"Tell your friend," Cameron said to Trist, "that he's a goddam moron." And turned on his heel.

When Trist looked back, Cadwallader was chuckling with undisguised satisfaction. He put his arm through Trist's. "Buy a moron a drink," he said.

ONE OF THE GREAT CURIOSITIES OF THE CONVENTION TO
Trist—no one in Europe, he thought, could have believed
it—was the large number of black delegates in attendance. Most
were from the South. Some were members of Congress. One, the
former slave Frederick Douglass of Washington, was scheduled to
address the convention. And another, Blanche K. Bruce of
Mississippi, was being seriously proposed in certain quarters as a
vice-presidential candidate.

"And every man jack," Cadwallader said as they sat down at
their restaurant table three drinks and two hours later, "has a lily-
white 'minder,' keep 'em out of trouble, watch their votes, you can
count on it."

"I interviewed Bruce." Trist picked up a printed leather-bound
menu and winced at the prices. The Great Northwestern
Steakhouse was Cadwallader's choice, but not, he had made plain,
his treat.

"And I saw that story." Cadwallader glanced indifferently at
the menu, turned in his chair to survey the room. "You were too
damn gullible. Blanche Bruce is a sop to New England. Most self-
righteous place on earth, New England. Slavery's gone, but up in
Massachusetts they still vote the abolition ticket out of sheer
lunatic fanaticism. There comes John Sherman."

Trist wrote "chicken and rice" on his order slip, the cheapest
thing on the list, and the easiest to eat with one hand, then looked
up to follow Cadwallader's gaze. The Great Northwestern was the
biggest restaurant in Chicago, and by far the most popular with
the convention. Characteristically, Cadwallader had chosen a
table next to the door with a view of everybody in the room, coming and going. Secretary of Treasury John Sherman was indeed
standing at the double-curtained entrance, shoulders and hair still
wet from the rain, waiting stiffly in front of the maitre d'. When
he bent forward to listen to something, Trist saw that he was
accompanied by his wife, and then, behind her, dressed in a stun-
ning pale blue evening gown with jeweled tiara, his niece.

"Lizzie Cameron," Cadwallader said, chewing a breadstick.

John Sherman waved at Cadwallader, nodded to half a dozen
other men. Somebody stood up to shake his hand. A booth of

diners far in the back broke into applause. Elizabeth Cameron looked straight ahead, chin high. Did she see him? *Would* she see him? In another moment the procession had disappeared around a corner, into a private room.

Cadwallader, as he might have expected, was a rapid drinker, greedy eater. He ordered oyster stew as a first course. A bearded waiter in both tuxedo and full-length white apron—with an effort Trist put Elizabeth Cameron out of his mind and made a mental note for *L'Illustration*—ladled it from a huge steaming tureen into a china bowl the size of a derby hat. Then fish; then slices of both pork and beef, mountains of white potatoes covered with redeye gravy and also (another mental note) grated cheese. The waiters knew Cadwallader. They came at a steady pace, heels clicking like ponies on the tessellated marble floors. Trist poked at his chicken, watched the never-ending stream of chattering delegates and wives going back and forth. At the end of the pie and whiskey course Cadwallader belched softly, signalled for the check; pushed back his chair.

"Contrast," he said, rising with a little wobble. "Secret of great prose. Show you something."

Outside the rain had stopped for the moment. In the early-evening darkness State Street smelled fresh, newly washed. Cadwallader walked slightly ahead, slightly unsteadily, and in answer to Trist's question merely repeated, "Show you something."

They entered the Palmer House Hotel by a side door. Cadwallader stopped in the middle of the corridor to drink two swallows from a hammered brass flask, then led Trist down one hall, down another, past the barbershop, which was still open, catering to a lonely unshorn Western delegate. At a double door marked only "Storage" he greeted by name a watchman sitting on a stool and offered him a pull at his flask.

"Going up on Friday," Cadwallader told Trist when the watchman had let them in and turned on the two wall-mounted gas lamps. "Supposed to go up last week, but they had hell's own problem with some kind of switch."

It was a fair-sized room, crowded with surplus hotel equipment: stacked chairs and tables, boxes of linen, broken sets of trays and dishes. Along the right-hand wall were a large black metal box shaped like a Dutch oven, a tangle of copper-colored wires, and what appeared to be several dozen two-by-four six-foot-

long planks studded with oversized gas-lamp bulbs, but on closer
inspection had no gas-pipe fitting and no on-and-off cock.

"Secret of prose," Cadwallader said, "is contrast. You write
well, Trist, damn nice for all that time in France, but you keep
missing your chances. Point about Blanche Bruce ain't that he's
coal-black. Point is, he's coal-black in a room full of white
reporters and white manipulators, *starched*-white Massachusetts
abolitionists. Point about Roscoe Conkling ain't that he looks like
a bird of paradise that's wandered into a country barnyard—
although that's contrast—point is, U. S. Grant is the quietest,
dullest, most self-effacing little brown rooster in the barn, but look
how his chosen number-one campaign spokesman is Conkling—
what does that tell you about Grant? What does it tell you about
Conkling?"

Cadwallader pulled one of the chairs off its stack and sat
down. He wiped sweat from his brow with a handkerchief, then
used the handkerchief to clean the mouth of his flask.

"These are Brush arc lights," he said.

"Electric lamps." Trist stooped to look at them with new
curiosity.

"Not Edison's," Cadwallader said. Thomas Edison had invented a highly publicized electric lamp and J. P. Morgan had
recently announced he was going to finance it, but Edison had
many serious rivals. Trist had read of whole city blocks in the
Midwest being illuminated by Charles F. Brush's arc-lamp system,
first in Cleveland, last month in Wabash, Indiana, while Edison
was apparently still testing and refining.

"Company's going to put them up in the Palmer House lobby,
spell out 'U. S. Grant' behind the registration desk. Then probably do it again in Cincinnati for one of the Democrats." Cadwallader put away his flask and stretched out his left hand to
touch the nearest lamp. In his black-and-white houndstooth
jacket, his unshined shoes, his battered old slouch hat, he looked
more like a carnival pitchman down on his luck than a writer, a
friend of cabinet officers and hotel watchmen—contrast, Trist
thought wryly—but there was no mistaking the boozy sincerity in
his voice. "This is the real story," he said, stroking the glass bulb,
"what's being unleashed by people like Brush and Edison. It won't
matter a plugged nickel who they finally nominate here. Those
old boys are living in the past—they can't think of anything but

Civil War generals. World stopped for them in '65, started for everybody else."

"I was in the war," Trist said. He pulled out a chair for himself and straddled it, facing Cadwallader. An insane conversation, in a half-dark storage closet.

"You're the younger generation. Besides, you didn't think the Civil War was the number one high and bright point of your life, did you? You were at Cold Harbor. Buried your arm there. Then you saw the mess they made *after* the war. What did Emerson say? Generation of young men with knives in their brains. You're pretty clever, friend Trist. But you're a watcher like me, not a doer."

"You're a drunk watcher."

Cadwallader grinned and poked the glass bulb harder with his finger. *"Fiat booze,"* he said.

"Is Grant going to win?"

"Think of a whole city," Cadwallader said. "Think of Chicago or New York lit up at night from one end to the other, like a hundred thousand angels come down to earth at the flick of a switch." He pushed an unconnected lever with a snap. "Keep your eye on Washburne," he said.

CHAPTER THREE

THE NEXT TWO DAYS PASSED IN A BLUR OF INACTIVITY—A phrase Trist rather liked, but Hutchins irritably edited out. Still, it was accurate enough, he thought, as a description of the massive, epic tedium inside Exposition Hall.

Outside the Hall on opening day—contrast—the streets were choked, hot, clear weather had returned, and enterprising boys set up stands on one corner, hawking "Blaine lemonade." New York Stalwarts for Grant marched about, six abreast like a drill team. Volunteers handed out free banners and badges—Red for Sherman; Red, White, and Blue for Grant—walking canes, even umbrellas. The first delegates crowding up on Wednesday morning already showed signs of wear and tear. Many had arrived in Chicago two and three days early, and they were bleary-eyed from hours without sleep, hours of arguing in hotel lobbies, waiting in endless lines for food, beds, even drink. At the entrance to the Hall there was still more waiting in line as guards bent officiously and inspected each credential.

Once inside, the wilting delegates faced a badly ventilated hot-house jammed with narrow row after row of straight-backed wooden chairs (ten thousand seats, no cushions). At eleven o'clock on Wednesday the mayor of Chicago and a legion of minor party officials began their welcoming speeches. A few privileged characters like Conkling roamed the Hall at will, but most of the ten thousand sat bumpishly and listened, fanning themselves, drinking yet more lemonade from the Negro boys with trays.

In the afternoon, welcoming speeches gave way to reports from committees. Fewer delegates kept to their seats. Some slept. Some stretched out on leather settees that had mysteriously appeared along one wall, under the portrait of Rutherford B. Hayes. Trist sat at the reporters' table just below the speakers' raised podium and scribbled long, unprintable descriptions of the Hall, which he tore up, started again. At three o'clock a reporter from the New York *Tribune* held up a hand-lettered sign announcing that the temperature inside the room was 96 degrees.

In the evening he attended John Sherman's "hospitality suite," now moved to the Palmer House—no sign yet of electric lamps— and caught another glimpse of Elizabeth Cameron, passing from one room to the next; but when he made his way around the bowl of "Sherman punch" and tried to reach her, his way was blocked by the swirling skirts of "Sherman ladies," and a moment later she was gone.

On Thursday morning the day dawned even hotter. By ten o'clock the convention had entered into the drawn-out business of certifying delegations, but so acid with sarcasm and bad temper was the atmosphere that Conkling rose to suggest, sensibly, they adjourn till evening and cooler temperatures. It was inadvertently the first—and stupidest possible—test of Grant's delegate strength. Out of dislike for Lord Roscoe's imperious manner or out of sheer inertia, the anti-Grant forces combined to defeat the motion, and the convention remained in pointless, droning, steaming session until seven-thirty in the evening, when a Blaine man, stripped to sweat-soaked shirtsleeves, finally moved for adjournment.

I N GALENA THE NEXT AFTERNOON, FRIDAY, ROCKING GENTLY IN his chair on his front porch, Grant accepted first the cup of fresh coffee that the colored maid brought out, then the sheaf of new telegrams that his son Jesse laid carefully on his lap.

It was hot in Galena, hot for June, and the paved stretch of street just below the house was shimmering up white worms of heat, so that it was even hotter up where Grant was, on top of the hill. His own fault, he thought, because of course when he had come back to Washington in '65, after Appomattox, and they had asked him about running for President, all he wanted, he'd said, was to go home and be mayor of Galena and fix up the sidewalk on the street by his house. Week later he had a new house, gift from the city, with a brand-new sidewalk.

He opened the first telegram in the stack and read it without expression. Conkling had lost another round in the unit-rule voting battle. Cameron thought Garfield had done himself some good with a speech. He shuffled methodically through the rest. Blaine was losing ground. John Sherman's strength was beginning to fail. Elihu Washburne still insisted on having his name put in nomination as a favorite son of Illinois, which meant thirty-five or forty votes lost on the first ballot anyway. Washburne was loyal to Grant, no question of that, Cameron wrote, but Washburne was old and vain and hankered for the honor of nomination too.

Grant sipped his coffee and listened to the lazy rattle of horses' hoofs and wagon harnesses down on High Street. Galena was really not much more than a series of ascending shelves and bluffs running east and west from the Mississippi, cut in two by the river, but higher by far over on the northwest side where the cheaper houses were. From the porch of his old house Grant used to look down eighty or ninety wooden steps to West Street, or if the day was clear he could look over roofs and steeples and see a few distant steamboats or sails on the river. Back of the old house was a cemetery, headstones right up against his fence, which had made Julia uneasy and superstitious when they first moved in, back in 1860. On the opposite bank of the river, where he was now, stood the nicer houses, some of them actual two- and three-story white-columned mansions that made people think of Vicksburg and Natchez, though this was Illinois.

Grant took another sip of the coffee and watched a fat brown chicken hawk circling over the street. In the fifties Galena had bet its future on the steamboat, not the railroad, and it probably had fewer people now than it did thirty years ago, thanks to that. About the dullest, sorriest little town he had ever seen, to tell the truth.

He put down the cup and tugged at the points of his vest. Funny kind of loyalty. Washburne was from Galena too. Grant had made Washburne ambassador to Paris his first term in the

White House, because Washburne's wife was French and he
thought Washburne would like it. Anybody would thank him, trading Galena for Paris, he supposed, any day of the month.

"Do you want to go downtown, Pa?" Jesse rapped on the windowsill for the maid to come and take his cup.

Grant nodded and put on his hat. About four o'clock in the
afternoon was when the out-of-town newspapers arrived in
Galena, and there might be a few more telegrams too, at the
Western Union office.

"Do you remember when we moved here, Jesse?"

"You worked in Grandpa's leather store."

"Anything else?"

Jesse just shrugged and started on down the steps ahead of
him. Grant knew what the boy really remembered: the war. From
just before Vicksburg on, he'd kept either Jesse or Fred around
headquarters, living right in his tent with him, as often as Julia
would let one go—read later that was an ancient tradition, traced
all the way back to the Greeks and Persians—the commander of
an army always liked to keep a son with him on the field of battle
if he could. Near Vicksburg little Fred had even been wounded
slightly in the leg by a stray Rebel bullet, something neither father
nor son ever bothered to tell Julia. Probably another tradition.
What Jesse obviously didn't remember was their evening ritual in
Galena *before* the war, which never varied. When Grant came up
the wooden steps home every night from the store, three-year-old
Jesse would always be waiting for him in the parlor, and every time
he greeted his father with the same words: "Mister, do you want to
fight?" And Grant would reply—he could remember the very formula—"Well, I'm a man of peace, but I'll not be hectored by a person of your size." And then they would wrestle and caper and roll
all over the floor till Grant would give up, flat on his back, and
Jesse would run tell Julia he'd won again.

At the bottom of the steps some of the neighbor men were
waiting to tip their hats and fall in with him for a few blocks. He
listened to their chatter, as if from a distance. Mike Lebron was
there, who used to have a jewelry store across Main Street from
the Grant leather store, and he was evidently in a reminiscing
mood as well, because right off he started telling the others, "I was
just recalling, General, how you came to Chetlain's grocery store
one night not long after you'd moved to Galena."

"Moved from St. Louis," Grant said.

"It was a chilly night and some of the lawyers had come in to take a drink or two from the barrel and sit by the stove and one of them said to you, 'Stranger here, ain't you?' And you said, 'Yes.' And the lawyer said, 'Travelled far to get here?' And you said, 'Far enough.' "

Grant remembered the story now, but of course he let Lebron finish it up his own way.

"Then the lawyer said, 'Look pretty rough, look as though you might have travelled through hell.'

" 'I have.'

" 'Well, how did you find things down there?'

" 'Oh, much the same as in Galena—lawyers nearest the fire.' "

Lebron laughed hardest because he had told the story, but the others laughed too, and even Jesse, who had graduated just the year before from the Columbia Law School, chuckled.

They turned down Ninth Street toward the river and Lebron started some other story, but this time Grant didn't pay any real attention. There was the smell of moving water and wet rope and wet boards coming up from the wharves. His mind turned far off, toward Chicago. He started to think hard about Elihu Washburne and what to do about ingratitude.

CHAPTER FOUR

O N SATURDAY, JUNE 5TH, THE OPENING PRAYER WAS DELIV-
ered punctually at nine A.M., but Exposition Hall was barely one-
quarter full at that hour, and those few yawning delegates present
seemed more hollow-eyed and weary than ever.

Trist observed them sympathetically from his chair at the
reporters' table. The convention had sat for sixteen straight hours
the day before, its third official day in session, and yet so far not
one single name had been placed in nomination for President.
Worse, the printed program for the day listed only more resolu-
tions and reports, not a syllable about nominations.

He propped himself awkwardly on his elbow, over a cup of coffee—"Blaine Coffee" or "Sherman Java," he couldn't remember—
and listened sleepily to the first of the scheduled credentials reso-
lutions. That morning, just after sunrise, he had tramped through
the empty streets to the Western Union office in the Grand Pacific
Hotel and telegraphed a short paragraph that he knew would
please Hutchins. Thanks to a marathon session yesterday a serious anti-Grant rumor had begun to make its indignant rounds—
Roscoe Conkling and Don Cameron were said to be forcing votes
on every individual credential and resolution, for the sole purpose
of prolonging the convention into another week. Lord Roscoe

apparently believed that many delegates couldn't sustain the expense of staying in Chicago over a long period; his calculation was that they would very soon be in a mood to stampede for Grant, before their railroad tickets expired.

At ten-fifteen, while yet another delegation went through its individual report, district by district, Trist followed an Alabama delegate he had befriended down from Exposition Hall to Union Station. There he listened while the delegate pleaded with the stationmaster to extend the validity of all railroad tickets to three days after the end of the convention. The stationmaster had a telephone instrument in his office. As Trist and the delegate drank more coffee in the cavernous old waiting room he rang up each of the railroad companies in turn and received their approval. At eleven-thirty, from the station itself, Trist telegraphed an addendum to his story—an exclusive now, putting the *Post* ahead even of the New York *Tribune*—and returned to the convention just in time to see it adjourn for lunch.

At two o'clock the gavel rapped again. The delegates took their seats. Cadwallader slipped into the chair next to Trist and spat, accurately, into the brass spittoon on the floor between them.

"Once saw an Indian chief come into the Palmer House lobby," he said. Over their heads the chairman of the convention, Senator George F. Hoar of Massachusetts, announced that the clerk would now read the report of the party platform committee. "Beautiful manners. Took one look at that fine oriental carpet on the floor, spat on his hand instead." Trist grimaced and laughed at the same time. "But *not* the one he used for shaking," Cadwallader said. "Exquisite manners. This is the crucial day, you watch."

But the platform yielded no crises, no surprises of any sort. It denounced the Democrats and Chinese immigration. It was silent, as expected, on the subject of civil service reform, though that was one of Rutherford Hayes's few known passions. "Conkling calls it 'snivel service reform,' " Cadwallader informed the reporters' table, whose resulting guffaws brought a reprimanding rap of the gavel down from Senator Hoar.

On the convention floor somebody offered an amendment asking that reform of civil service be "thorough, radical, and complete." A delegate from Texas rose in immediate and angry opposition. "Texas has had quite enough of the civil service," he said to growing laughter. "What are we up here for? I mean that members of the

Republican party are entitled to government jobs, and if we're victorious, why, by God we'll have them."

At six o'clock the convention adjourned again for dinner—one
hour only, Hoar warned as the room stood and stretched and
shook itself awake.

In the crowded Sherman hospitality suite, now moved again
from the Palmer House to a set of rented rooms upstairs in the
Hall, Trist took a cup of coffee—eating with one hand would be
impossible—and stood with his back pressed against the wall. His
Alabama delegate emerged briefly from the crush of people to tell
him that Conkling had done this sort of thing before—in the '76
convention at Cincinnati, after Ingersoll had made a powerful
speech for Blaine, somebody (and it had to be Conkling) had
secretly turned off the gas supply and plunged the house into
darkness. Another delegate showed Trist the afternoon Chicago
Record featuring his own railroad ticket story reprinted from the
Post and credited to him. With his fifth cup of coffee of the day
(served in a Sherman souvenir ceramic cup) came another rumor,
that Hoar had decided to press on that evening to the nominations, no matter how long it took, no matter how much Conkling
stalled. And as if to confirm it, candidate Sherman himself
climbed on a chair and urged them all first to have another drink,
and second, to hold fast.

"My niece says you live in Paris." Mrs. John Sherman clutched
a copy of the Chicago *Record* in one hand and her niece's arm in
the other. Around them a few supporters were making prepara-
tions to return to the floor, but most were still gathered happily
beside the long buffet. "The City of Light," Mrs. Sherman
explained. She was constructed, as Trist's father used to say, along
American lines. She was tall, even taller than her husband, with
her gray hair stacked in a kind of Empire bun, broad-shouldered,
generous-figured, ample-hipped. She wore an expensive dress of
gunmetal gray, cut low at the bodice to show off an ivory brooch
the size of the souvenir coffee cup, and next to her Elizabeth
Cameron looked as slender and willowy as a girl. Mrs. Sherman
patted her niece's arm. "She speaks excellent French herself. She
was schooled in Boston." This seemed not precise enough. "On
Mount Vernon Street."

Trist put down his cup and bowed respectfully to Mount
Vernon Street.

"But I suppose you miss Paris terribly now." Mrs. Sherman was politely sad on his account. "Especially in this dreadful Chicago heat."

"Well, I have to go back for good in the fall," Trist said, "so I haven't really thought so much about it."

"In the fall?"

"After the election."

"Mr. Trist," said Elizabeth Cameron, bending forward to make herself heard over shouts of "Sherman Forever," "has come here as a French magazine correspondent, just to write about the campaign."

"Ah. I thought you were with one of our newspapers." Mrs. Sherman was a candidate's wife. French correspondents had no role to play in holding fast. She looked at his empty sleeve. Her smile faded to a pinpoint. She nodded once, rudely, and turned away.

"Don't ask me to speak French," Elizabeth told Trist.

"No."

"She's my uncle's wife. I'm very fond of my uncle."

"You're a Sherman," Trist said, "of course."

"You should have seen me in Montana, in my wild Indian war dress."

"I can picture you now."

Elizabeth looked quickly to the right, toward her aunt, and the color rushed to her cheeks. Impulse, desire rose like a flame in Trist's throat. As the crowd swirled, bumped, jostled around them, he reached his hand forward and touched her waist. Her chin came up, her mouth opened. His hand moved lower, to her hip— he couldn't believe that no one saw, no one was watching—she took half a step closer. Loud applause broke out near the door, where Sherman was raising both arms in a victory clench. "Sunday." Her voice was hoarse, rasping, her face still turned away in profile. "Sunday, Centennial Park, noon, meet me." She turned to follow her aunt, took two steps, and then turned back. "I hate it when they condescend to you," she whispered.

A T THE REPORTERS' TABLE A MAN FROM THE NEW YORK *HERALD* was passing around a set of old clippings. The galleries and balconies were packed now to capacity. Somebody had suspended a new "James G. Blaine" banner between two pillars directly in front of Trist; a Blaine band in the rear of the Hall was playing an exuberant version of "Wait for the Wagon." In the special section of the balcony just to the right, reserved for dignitaries' wives, a number of ladies sat with souvenir umbrellas inexplicably open.

"Seen the clippings?" Cadwallader dropped into the chair on his left. Trist shook his head. "You're red as a beet. Fellow covers Conkling in New York, brought his scrapbook, all his stories about Conkling and Kate Chase Sprague."

There were four reporters' tables just beneath the speaker's podium. Cadwallader's pencil pointed at a pasty-faced man in green tweed at the farthest one. "You ever hear about Conkling and Kate Sprague in Rhode Island?"

Trist shook his head again, knowing that Cadwallader was about to tell him.

"Conkling went to pay a visit to her two years ago. The little drunk husband was supposed to be away on a trip. But he comes home late that night, unexpected. Next morning goes downstairs, there's Conkling sitting at the breakfast table, reading the paper. Sprague grabs his shotgun, Conkling takes off like a rabbit. The *Herald* ran the story for weeks, never cost Lord Roscoe a vote." He stirred a cup of something brown with his pencil. "Ruined Kate Sprague," he said.

At seven-thirty-five, as the Blaine band marched away into the corridors, the convention wearily came to order again, and the clerk began to read the final, amended platform.

At nine o'clock, platform read and voted, Trist made his way upstairs to the telegraph room and sent a short, uninspired report to the *Post*.

And at ten o'clock, at last, Hoar's gavel rapped briskly three times and the clerk announced that the floor was open for nominations.

The crowd stirred. In some corners it came visibly awake. Delegates sat up straight. Cigars were extinguished. The Blaine band played a few separate discordant notes. Blaine would be the first man named, and everyone knew that Blaine, who had come very close to stealing the nomination from Rutherford Hayes four years ago, wanted Robert Ingersoll to give the nominating speech again, but his campaign manager had just decided on the spur of the moment that Ingersoll's increasingly notorious atheism would spoil the good effect of his oratory. (Ingersoll had recently held up to a New York audience a greenback dollar bill, which promised to pay the bearer in gold or silver, and shouted, "I know that my Redeemer liveth!") Instead, Ingersoll now mounted the speakers' platform waving a red shawl while the unannounced official nominator walked head down, with a hangdog look, to the podium.

"James P. Joy," Trist muttered, glad to be able to tell Cadwallader something.

"Detroit businessman," Cadwallader said. "Millionaire. Hopeless speaker."

And in fact Joy began to speak in a dull, barely audible, certainly joyless voice. He apologized for taking up the convention's time. He regretted that he had been chosen to give the speech, since he thought his words would benefit the candidate but little. He said that Michigan was a safe state for the party and would vote Republican no matter who was the nominee. Finally, glancing nervously at the clock, he declared it was his pleasure to present the name of James S. Blaine.

Ingersoll lowered his shawl in disgust. In the Maine delegation half a dozen men came to their feet, shaking their fists—"James G. Blaine, you fool!"

When the shouts and music had died down, Hoar rapped for order. Senator William Windom of Minnesota was nominated next, to perfunctory cheers. Then a long pause followed. The Blaine band had already skulked out of the Hall, but a new and bigger band could be seen gathering behind the last row of chairs. Some delegates were on their feet, expectant. The low rumble of background talk and whisper and rustling cloth and scraping chairs that had come to seem part of the air itself now slowly died away.

John A. Logan was senator from Illinois, yet another Civil War general. In 1868, when Grant had received 650 of 650 convention votes, Logan had nominated him for his first term as President. His shock of white hair was caricatured by every political cartoonist in Chicago and instantly familiar to every delegate in the Hall. Now he made his way at a steady pace down the aisle from the Illinois delegation; mounted the steps; spoke right away without introduction or notes: "In the name of our loyal citizens, soldiers, and sailors—in the name of loyalty, of liberty, of humanity and justice I nominate Ulysses S. Grant for President!"

A stupendous cheer exploded over his last words, drowning out even the band. In the aisles, on the balconies, Grant Stalwarts roared in a swirling chaos of streamers and confetti. On the railing above Hoar's platform a young woman dressed in red, white, and blue sang, unheard, at the top of her lungs, as friends clutched her ankles to keep her from falling. Trist sat hunched at his table while the wave of sound rolled and broke over his head, watching a group of men in the balconies open and release umbrella after umbrella, thinking the French would never believe a word of it. He glanced over once at Cadwallader, who was sitting back, lighting a cigar. He squinted up toward the galleries to see if Elizabeth Cameron was there. His mind made a curious leap toward the book he had been reading, *Democracy.* This was it, he thought, this was the unreal democratic thing itself.

Logan had long since disappeared from the podium. As the crowd noticed, its cheers began to fade, little by little, into individual shouts, then murmurs, then a low, tense, nearly palpable silence. Could this be all? Was this the whole of the nomination? The band lowered its instruments. Here and there someone cleared his throat or coughed.

From the second row of the New York delegation now emerged the splendid figure of Roscoe Conkling. He was dressed in a coat of deep, rich burgundy, a yellow cravat, crisp blue trousers. His red hair was curled around his brow, his red beard was combed and thrust forward, bristling with virility. He walked slowly, confidently toward the riser that led to the reporters' tables. At a gesture one reporter stood and offered his chair. Conkling braced his hand on the man's back and vaulted from chair to table in a single motion. The vast silence of the Hall grew deeper still, a drawn breath, held. Every eye was on him. He looked to the left, the right. And then at the moment of absolute maximum suspense his clear voice suddenly burst out:

> "And when asked what State he hails from,
>   Our sole reply shall be,
> He hails from Appomattox,
>   And its famous apple tree!"

The roar that followed was total bedlam, a tumult of noise that went on twice as long as before, till Conkling himself finally held up his arms imperiously. The delegates fell panting back into their chairs.

"The need that presses upon this convention," he cried in the same ringing tones, "is of a candidate who can carry doubtful states both North and South. And believing that he, more surely than any other man, can carry New York against any opponent, and can carry not only the North, but several States of the South, New York is for *Ulysses S. Grant.* Never defeated in peace or in war, his name is the most illustrious borne by living man!"

The Hall was now entirely under Conkling's spell. He raised his arms again for quiet, then launched into a long, detailed account of Grant's career, the hero's relentless, unparalleled drive toward military victory, his magnanimous terms of peace to Lee, his service in Reconstruction, his great courage in 1875 in vetoing the inflation bill, wherein, as the present prosperity showed, he had been exactly right. The criticism of corruption in Grant's administration he dismissed with a sneer: "We have nothing to explain away. We have no apologies to make. The shafts and arrows have all been aimed at him, and they lie broken and harmless at his feet."

And as for the objection that a third presidential term was unprecedented—"Having tried Grant twice and found him faithful, we are told that we must not, even after an interval of years, trust him again. Who dares—who *dares* to put fetters on that free choice and judgment which is the *birthright* of the American people?"

And had he stopped right there, Trist thought, he could have called for a vote on the spot. But Lord Roscoe went on a moment too long, he turned his sneers directly and sharply against the Blaine and Sherman forces, and then against the self-declared "independents" of the party—"charlatans, jayhawkers, tramps, and guerrillas"—who hesitated to join at once with Grant, and as he spoke those same independents could be seen all over the Hall hardening, crossing their arms, growing cold.

The peroration was splendid, masterfully delivered. At the end of it yet another twenty minutes of unrestrained bedlam swept over the building—the reporter from the New York *Times* shook his head in rueful amazement and showed his first sentence to Trist: *Today the friends of Grant threw away sobriety and became like boys once more.* Too bad about "sobriety," Trist thought, pondering his own report, which would have to be telegraphed to the *Post* in a matter of hours. He watched as exuberant Stalwarts lifted Conkling from their table and swept him on their shoulders back to the New York delegation. Had he learned that jumping-on-the-table trick from Mark Twain last fall, Trist wondered, and the excruciating sense of pause and timing? He scribbled a note for his own first sentence: *Not since Samuel L. Clemens climbed up on a Chicago table and brought the house down* . . .

Around him, other reporters folded their notes and slipped down into the aisles, heading toward the telegraph room. Trist wrote a sentence or two more and then swung down to the floor himself. He had just pushed through confetti ankle deep to the rear of the Hall when something—a voice, a subtle change in the hum and clamor of the crowd—made him stop. Down on the raised platform, even as the Grant demonstration was still trailing away, James Garfield had started to speak. Trist pulled out his notebook again and bumped elbows, he was flabbergasted to see, with Roscoe Conkling himself.

"I have witnessed the extraordinary scenes of this convention with deep solicitude," Garfield said. His voice had a classicist's pitch and precision. "As I sat in my seat and witnessed this demonstration, this assemblage seemed to me a human ocean tossed in tempest." Beside Trist, Conkling grunted. "But I remember that it is not the billows but the calm level of the sea from which all heights and depths are measured. Gentlemen of the convention, your present temper may not mark the healthful pulse of our people. When your enthusiasm has passed, we shall find below the storm and passion a calmer level of public opinion."

"Calm," Trist wrote twice.

"This makes me seasick," Conkling muttered to Trist and watched to be sure he wrote it down. Then he marched out into the corridors.

On the platform Garfield continued doggedly on, calling for a candidate who could heal the breach in party unity—not increase it—someone who might draw together the votes of the whole country.

He spoke for nearly fifteen minutes by Trist's watch, a gray, sensible, modest figure preaching reason, and not until the last minute did Trist realize that this was in fact the official nominating speech for John Sherman, because Garfield, by accident or design or treachery, made no actual reference whatsoever to his candidate's name until his final sentence; and because every word he uttered about conciliation and calm applied, demonstrably and preeminently, to himself.

"And so," he concluded, gazing imperturbably at the now placid human ocean seated before him, "I do not present him as a better Republican or a better man than thousands of others that we honor; but I present him for your deliberate and favorable consideration. I nominate *John Sherman of Ohio*."

Trist held up his watch again. It was past one-thirty in the morning. The last candidate on the schedule was Elihu Washburne, Grant's old friend, who had no chance whatsoever, everybody knew it, of winning the nomination. Stilson Hutchins would be tearing his hair out in clumps—Trist looked at the sheet of paper where he had written his first sentence, wadded it into a ball.

At an empty chair in the very last row he made a prop of his knees and started again: *A "dark horse" appeared tonight in the closing minutes of the race—James A. Garfield has nominated himself for President.*

By return telegraph Hutchins replied: BULLFEATHERS. HAVE REWRITTEN LEAD: "GRANT NOMINATION IN SIGHT."

CHAPTER FIVE

ELIHU B. WASHBURNE OPENED HIS GOLD WATCH AND PEERED at the spidery hands, which showed quarter past six in the morning.

"Come right back here, one hour," he told the little Irish driver, immigrant, probably illegal.

"Cold and wet, boss." Black teeth made an apologetic flash in a pucker of doughy white flesh. "Need to be *sure* you're coming back."

Washburne had never taken a drink of liquor in his life, which accounted, some people said, for his lifelong irritability. He slapped two silver coins hard on the driver's bench, then looked significantly at the little round blue-and-white Chicago Hackney license badge dangling from the carriage roof. "I am Congressman Elihu Washburne," he hissed so furiously that the driver actually seemed to shrink inside his coat. "I am paying a breakfast call in this hotel." Washburne jerked his head at the painted sign, barely visible through the drizzle, ANGSTROM'S ROOMS, not strictly speaking a hotel, but nobody was going to tell him that. "I will come out at seven-fifteen precisely and you will take me to the goddam Palmer House Hotel."

He clambered down, adjusted his collar, and, because he had

once been ambassador to France, appointed by U. S. Grant, and therefore thought of himself as a diplomat, added "Thank you."

Inside the boarding house he stamped his shoes on a mat and proceeded to a musty, sparely furnished chamber that passed as Angstrom's dining room. Washburne's wife was French, but Washburne himself had been born and reared in the rough north woods of Maine, and his heritage—as anybody could tell by a glance at his bulk and scowl—was German. He sat down at John Russell Young's table, grunted a Teutonic good-morning, and without another word forked a massive slice of boiled Virginia ham onto a spare plate. Then some fried potatoes and gravy. Then poured himself a cup of black coffee.

"Sherman's gone," Young told him. "Blaine too."

Washburne nodded and speared a potato. He hated being told things he already knew, but as a politician and diplomat that was how he spent most of his time. John Sherman, of course, had left for the train station last night directly after the nominating speeches had begun. James G. Blaine had left a little earlier. Both were presumably in Washington now, observing the unwritten Republican rule that candidates keep away from a convention once the balloting starts. Washburne thought it was an odd rule, and as favorite son and official Illinois delegate he had decided to honor it in the breach.

"How was Galena?" he asked, going right to the point.

"Hot." Young poured a little more coffee into Washburne's cup and looked suspiciously around the empty room, as if to be sure nobody was listening. Like every newspaper reporter Washburne had ever known, Young had a tiresome kind of theatrical streak. At six-thirty on a Sunday morning there wasn't going to be anybody up, or anybody awake enough to care what they were saying.

"Hot for June," Young elaborated, smacking his lips as if he were now an old Illinois farmer. "But the General looked fit and cool."

"Well, is he coming or ain't he?" It was too early in the morning to beat around the bush. Washburne looked down and saw that there was nothing left of the ham on his plate except a sweet ivory rind of fat.

"Mrs. Grant would certainly like it."

Washburne sucked up the rind of white fat like a string of spaghetti.

"She is a very tense lady at the moment, Congressman."

"That's because"—Washburne swallowed the fat and licked his fingers—"she wants to be First Lady again. What does *he* want?"

"Calm as if in a battle," Young said. "Telegrams piling up, neighbors hanging off the porch. He just sits there and smokes his cigars."

"My best count is three hundred and six," Washburne told him. "That's over seventy votes short."

"Senator Cameron quoted the very same number."

"Well?"

Young narrowed his eyes and hitched his chair closer to the table, obviously relishing his role as political conspirator. Don Cameron hadn't trusted the public telegraph, and so had asked the reporter to deliver his message privately, but not before Washburne had got wind of it and had to be included. If Grant would come up to Chicago Sunday night or Monday morning and just *show* himself on the convention floor, a stampede of votes was sure to follow. No delegate could resist the flesh and blood sight of him, that was the theory, and it was probably right.

"Well, he said he would rather cut off his right hand."

"And Julia heard him?"

"She said, 'Don't you *want* the nomination, Victor?'—that's her pet name for him, 'Victor.'" Washburne drummed the table with his fingers. Something else he already knew. "And the General said, 'Since my name is up, I would rather be nominated, but I won't do anything to push it along.' And Mrs. Grant carried on and on about cabals and Garfield"—Young hesitated—"and you, and finally the General said, 'Julia, I am amazed at you' and left the room."

"That can't be all." Washburne rapped his cup with a spoon and when a sleepy black face appeared at the door, he pointed at his empty plate.

"Well, he wrote Senator Cameron a letter. He says if it seems as though he won't be nominated after all, his friends should withdraw his name."

Washburne looked at his watch.

"And Mrs. Grant said confidentially when I was leaving, to tell Senator Cameron *not* to withdraw his name, ever." Young finished his coffee and bobbed his head two or three times and sat back and didn't say anything else. Washburne recognized the moment.

Reporters were worse than politicians with their *quid pro quo,* and Young, who might have a bad case of Grant hero worship, wasn't any fool. Clearly, he hadn't seen Cameron yet today, and clearly what he would like in exchange for these little communications was an exclusive word or two about Washburne's personal motives and intentions in the convention, because Washburne had, as everybody understood, between twenty-five and thirty favorite-son votes for himself, and Washburne also had a thousand reasons to be grateful to Grant for kindnesses received. Why wouldn't he just send his votes over to Grant right now and start the stampede himself? Washburne listened to the growing silence between them. He was an old man now, he thought, and politically obscure. Gratitude was not the same as loyalty. There was a cynical French saying: "Something in our best friend's misfortune does not altogether displease us." He could help Grant, he guessed. But he wouldn't.

CHAPTER SIX

WASHINGTON POST *June 3, 1880.*

DEMOCRACY: AN AMERICAN NOVEL

BY "ANONYMOUS."

Henry Holt & Co., New York. $1.00.

Who wrote *Democracy?*

If you take the book simply as a *roman à clef,* a mischievous portrait of present-day Washington society life, this is an entertaining and interesting question, and there is no doubt that trying to guess his (or her) name has been a favorite dinner table pastime from Capitol Hill to Lafayette Square.

And yet beneath its local and topical interest, *Democracy* is a serious story of a woman forced to choose between two men, one a powerful but corrupt Senator, the other a veteran of the Civil War, now a mild but ineffectual lawyer in Washington. The woman herself, Mrs. Madeleine Lightfoot Lee, is a wealthy widow who has come to the Capital with the idea of putting her own hand, the author says in an impressive image, on "the massive machinery of society." Mrs. Lee is, in other words, "bent on getting to the heart of the great American mystery of democracy and government. What she wished to see, she thought, was the clash of interests, the interests of 40 millions of people and a whole continent . . . What she wanted was POWER."

The author, whoever it is, deserves much credit for opening a genuine debate on the place of give-and-take in democratic government as opposed to high and unyielding principles and ideals that may be admirable but fail to accomplish useful work. Much credit also for a finely observant (and malicious) wit: the President and his wife are thinly disguised portraits of General and Mrs. Grant: "they stood stiff and awkward by the door, both their faces stripped of every sign of intelligence, while the right hands of both extended themselves to the column of visitors with the mechanical action of toy dolls." The corrupt Senator (James G. Blaine?) rises to flattery "like a two-hundred-pound salmon to a fly."

And finally, the heroine Madeleine Lee is a compelling portrait (not, so far, identified as anyone real) who combines wit and energy with an almost self-destructive weakness. When she lost both her husband and her child, her sister tells the lawyer, "Madeleine was excessively violent and wanted to kill herself, and I never heard anyone rave as she did about religion and resignation and God."

The romantic plot, it must be said, resolves itself intelligently. The style is polished and bright, reminding one of Trollope for literary excellence. But the curious and even contemptuous detachment of the narrator's voice, elegant but aloof and mournful, may strike some readers as a flaw. No wonder, perhaps, the author chooses to remain unknown. It is a voice that seems to shrink back from life, impotent. It makes the strangest possible contrast with the passion of its fascinating heroine.

—BY NICHOLAS TRIST

"No need to wait for me, thank you," Elizabeth Cameron said, "thank you very much." She folded the clipping into her leather pocket book and stepped down from the carriage.

"Yes, ma'am. You sure you all right here, ma'am? By you-self?"

The driver was a black man well over sixty, with a face as wrinkled as a walnut and a jagged white knife scar that ran from his ear to his jaw. Back in Ohio she would have found him frightening. She would never have walked boldly up to his hackney, all on her own.

"I tell you what, ma'am. I'm going to wait just over there, take a rest, if you change your mind." He pointed his whip handle toward a clump of wet sycamores at the farthest edge of the park; tipped his hat; clattered away.

Elizabeth adjusted the strings of her bonnet and looked around at the wide expanse of grass. Centennial Park was divided from the lake and the beach by Michigan Avenue. At one end, through the restless gray curtain of drizzle, you could see the upper floors and roofs of the commercial district—a giant American flag marked the Grand Pacific Hotel—and at the other end a little rise of lawn led to a knoll framed by still more dark sycamores.

She looked down to be sure that her pocket book was snapped shut, then started along the pathway toward the knoll. The pocket book contained a tablet and pencil, a watch on a ribbon, some money, the clipping from the Washington *Post*. Shouts reached her from the other side of the knoll. She slowed her pace.

It was a very clever book review. She was foolish—*foolish*—to clip it out. The romantic plot resolves itself intelligently, yes. Yes. No.

Uphill she walked more slowly still. Two tramps in soggy clothes passed in the other direction and squinted closely at her, but said not a word. Along another path several women appeared, carrying rolled umbrellas and wicker picnic baskets and apparently trying to herd six or seven little boys, every one of whom was carrying either a wooden bat or a white leather Base-ball. Shouts reached her from the other side of the knoll.

She had seen a great deal of Base-ball in her life, Elizabeth thought, and once or twice, when she was with her brother-in-law Colonel Miles in Montana, she had even been allowed to play, or at least to *bat* at the ball when some of the soldiers pitched it. Soldiers had played the game all the way through the war, her brother-in-law said, sometimes right on a battlefield where there were still unburied corpses and wounded men—her mind veered suddenly toward Nicholas Trist, and she brought it back with an effort of sheer will. When he was President, she made herself remember, General Grant had liked to stroll down to the South Lawn of the White House in the afternoons, and at the makeshift diamond the local Washington boys had laid out the President would pick up a bat and stand there, cigar in his mouth, and hit the ball as the boys threw it. Just like her.

She stopped in the middle of the path. She was flirtatious, she knew it, she admitted it, the vital fascinating heroine was a flirt, a tease, she had kissed other men, she had kissed men even in her own house, even—but never, *never* had she made an actual rendezvous. And Nicholas Trist was not a man to be content with a meeting and another kiss. He was a serious man, with serious needs, that was his appeal. Nicholas Trist had a look of hunger, she thought, and hard intelligence, his wound had made him both hard and vulnerable. Which was nonsense, sentimental nonsense, but true. Every person, she thought, has an outside and an inside, and the two can be hopelessly different. Outside she was flirtatious, charming, men loved to be near her. Inside—inside, she was a jumble of fear and uncertainty, stupidity. In love, she thought, in physical love, a man had to make himself hard, a woman had to make herself soft to receive him.

Under a tree at the very top of the knoll she stopped again. Down below was the roof of the Base-ball stadium where the professional Chicago team was playing Cincinnati, that much she knew from the papers. The part of the field that she could see beyond the roof was still muddy, half shrouded in cool mist, but a few players stood with their hands on their hips in the grass. Another was lining up bats beside a bench.

To meet him she would have to descend the hill and pass the grandstands and the ticket gate and go along the park to the little pond she had described in her note to him. Descend the hill, shatter everything. *Facilis descensus Averni*, one of Henry Adams's favorite sayings: Easy the way down to disaster. Soft little Henry Adams.

Her face had grown hot and flushed, despite the chill in the air. She looked back at the trees safe behind her and the road, the gray sheet of glass in the distance that was the lake. Her pulse was pounding in her wrist so hard that she tucked her right hand into her armpit to stop it. When she was a girl she and her sister Mary had giggled at the names of the parts of their bodies. "Nipples" was funny, so was "armpit" or "breast" or "loin" or, worst of all, "cunny." But there was nothing to laugh at now, now that she was a woman. She could feel her nipples stiff and tender against the smooth fabric of her corset. She could feel her loins literally ache. He would have a hotel nearby, a private room. Her husband was a heavy man, she thought, he smelled of bourbon, hair oil, meat. His weight crushed her breath. Elizabeth took a single step downhill. Her pulse pounded till she trembled. She took another step, a quick shallow breath; then gave a little strangled sigh like a cry of pain and turned on the path and hurried back to her carriage.

WHEN MONDAY MORNING DAWNED, HOT AND CLEAR AGAIN, the convention hive came back to life. Long before nine o'clock the cramped streets around Exposition Hall were jammed and buzzing with thousands and thousands of delegates hurrying forward, eager to get inside after the long, free day of Sunday and take their seats and finally, at last, begin to vote.

At the entrance doors, as they massed and waited to show their credentials, rumors flew. Grant had withdrawn. Grant was in Chicago. Henry Cabot Lodge had called on Garfield and asked permission to nominate him, if Grant and Blaine should deadlock. Garfield had accepted. Garfield had refused. The only rumor gaining general credence was that a delegation from Kansas had offered to place Roscoe Conkling's name in nomination if Grant would withdraw, and Conkling had pulled himself up to his full magnificent height, looked scornfully down his nose, and announced that any man who would desert his chief hardly merited election.

"All this ding-dong about Washburne," a Pennsylvania delegate told Trist in the reporters' room outside the main auditorium—"do the arithmetic!"

No need, Trist thought—every person in the Hall seemed to

have a pad of paper, a column of figures. His delegate tore off a sheet of calculations and thrust it in his hand. "Grant on the first." His voice was already hoarse. "Put that in your pipe and smoke it."

At half past eight the building was filled to capacity, heaving and buzzing with excitement. Trist pushed his way into the telegraph room with two more last-minute paragraphs for Hutchins, only to find it a blue chaos of cigar smoke, frustrated men, crumpled flimsies. Storms in the North and East had brought down every telegraph wire linking Chicago and New York and Washington. Blaine and Sherman were cut off from their managers, half the Eastern delegations were adrift without instructions.

He sat down at a desk where somebody had knocked a telegraph printer over and left it humming and shaking there like a black metallic electrical insect. Aimlessly he felt in his pocket for the sheet of calculations, found it, found the three separate handwritten notes that had been delivered at slightly hysterical intervals to his hotel Sunday, by an increasingly bemused messenger. The calculations he wadded up and threw on the floor with all the other scraps of paper and garbage; the notes he took out and read again slowly.

Two-thirty p.m. I'm so sorry, please forgive me. I just couldn't come. EC.

Four o'clock. I went to the park and could see you waiting at the pond, but we should never have begun, please understand. EC.

Seven-thirty, Grand Pacific Hotel. We mustn't meet in Washington, please don't come to us in Lafayette Square, please, EC. Please.

He braced himself with his hand on the desk and stood up awkwardly. Then he dropped the three pieces of paper one by one in front of a janitor's broom.

At nine o'clock promptly the session began. A hasty prayer, a two-minute litany of protocol reminders and announcements. Gavel, gavel. Applause. Alabama's chairman shot to his feet.

The states were to be polled individually, alphabetically, reading their breakdown of votes while the clerk at a desk beside Senator Hoar dipped his pen, wrote, dipped again as fast as he could.

At nine-forty-five Conkling stepped into the aisle to give New York's totals. Typically, he paused until the low background hum had faded into silence, then in a studied, insolent drawl announced, "Two New York delegates are *said* to be for Sherman, seventeen are *said* to be for Blaine. Fifty-one *are* for Grant."

The Hall crackled with nervous laughter, but Trist, doing his arithmetic, noted for the first time how much the loss of the unit-rule vote had cost the Grant camp. Nineteen more votes from New York, plus Washburne's elusive twenty to thirty—if Conkling and Cameron had prevailed last week, Grant would be only twenty votes away from nomination. Pennsylvania rose. Twenty-three of its votes defected to Blaine, three to Sherman, one to Garfield. When the West Virginia chairman stood, he tipped his hat mockingly to Conkling and shouted across the Hall: "One delegate is *said* to be for Grant. Eight are *known* to be for Blaine!" At the end of the first ballot Grant had 304 votes—75 short—Blaine had 284, Sherman 93, Washburne 30, Garfield 1. Trist joined the crush outside the telegraph room, but the wires in the East were still down. He took a cup of Sherman coffee in a waxed cardboard mug back to his table, looked up at the galleries in vain for Elizabeth Cameron, settled back for ballot number two.

The second round changed nothing. At eleven A.M. Grant received one more vote, 305 now, Blaine two fewer, Garfield his solitary mark from a Pennsylvania delegate who sat with his arms stubbornly crossed, staring straight ahead.

The long morning wore into afternoon; a one-hour recess; voting again. A telegraph line to New York came back into service, but none to Washington, Philadelphia, Boston, and in any case there was nothing to report. At ten P.M. the convention took its twenty-eighth and last ballot of the evening. The totals were almost precisely what they had been on the first.

In the corridor outside the Pennsylvania office Trist fell into step with Don Cameron, who scarcely glanced at him but did at least mutter his name. The ideal journalist, Trist thought, was part hound, part leech. He matched Cameron stride for stride, down the back stairs, out into the alley where the Senators, committee chairmen, and various other convention dignitaries had a private rank of carriages and hackneys waiting. Cameron climbed into his personal four-seater landau and shifted around to face the front like an old bear in a leather cave. Trist climbed in after him and pulled the door shut. Cameron raised his head with a snap. "What the hell do you think *you're* doing?"

Trist gripped the passenger strap next to the window. The landau started forward with the crack of a whip and swayed out into Michigan Avenue like a bouncing black ball.

"There's a delegate I know," Trist said over the clop of hooves and the rattle of the windows. "He works for the Illinois Central, and he told me General Grant got on the train secretly this afternoon in Galena, headed north."

Michigan Avenue was by now a tangled canyon of horses and wheels. Men and women leaving Exposition Hall were streaming across it in all directions, between carriages, in the gutters, up and down the middle of the street. From the elevated landau window the sidewalk looked like a riptide of hats and shoulders. A passing streetlamp lit up Cameron's big red brick of a face.

"Well, he's going to Madison, Wisconsin," Cameron said. "Been scheduled for months for the Grand Old Army reunion dinner."

"The trains go direct from Galena to Madison," Trist said.

Cameron struck a match.

"If he's stopped in Chicago tonight," Trist said, "Senator Cameron would know. If he's planning to show his face at the convention tomorrow, his campaign manager would be the *first* to know."

Cameron snorted. The tip of his cigar glowed in the dark like a coal.

"The telegraph line is open to Washington now," Trist said. "I can sell an exclusive to the *Post* and the wire services; it'll be in every paper in Chicago tomorrow—you can have the convention hall packed to the rafters."

Cameron exhaled smoke and assumed the conspicuously insincere frown of a politician calculating. "Not a goddam word for publication," he said, "unless I tell you different."

At a three-story brick house just one block away from the lake the carriage wheeled over flying gravel, then mud, then clattered to a stop in a courtyard in the rear.

Inside the house Cameron motioned Trist toward a side par-

lor. Trist took a seat by a window with a silhouetted view of a railroad line, on stilts, that ran between the beach and the first row
of lakefront houses. He listened to murmurs from across the hall,
stood up to inspect a bookshelf. Twenty-four iron-black volumes
of classic English poets, as alike as bars in a cage. He picked up
John Dryden, put him back. An Irish maid came in to offer him
cakes and coffee, and when she left he waited two minutes, then
pulled the door open and stepped into the hall.

The house belonged to a friend of the Grants, that much was
clear, which made sense because it was impossible to imagine the
General, in the middle of the convention, simply driving up to a
Chicago hotel and quietly taking a room for the night. Through
the closed door the murmurs were more distinct. Trist recognized
Cameron's baritone grumble, a woman's voice, two other men.

As he hesitated, hand on the knob, thinking Cameron would
have his head, the door suddenly swung open and revealed Mrs.
Julia Grant, turning sideways in a noisy rustle of wide skirts and
bustle. She halted instantly at the sight of Trist, then managed a
thin, unwelcoming smile before disappearing up the stairs.

"What the *hell* do you think you're doing?" Cameron blocked
the door.

"Let him come in," said an unexcited voice in the parlor.

Trist stepped into a room more or less the twin of the one he
had just left; same view of the lake and the railroad, same horse-
hair sofa, red plush chairs. There was a matching bookshelf, but
filled with china bric-a-brac, not poets, and standing beside it and
switching his cigar to shake hands was U. S. Grant.

It was only the second or third time Trist had actually seen his
former commander up close—Chicago in November had hardly
counted, a few quick words on the run—and just as before, his
reaction was one of vague disappointment. The General was of
average height, about five feet eight, average weight. His shoulders
were stooped. He was carelessly dressed in an old frock coat, shiny
at the elbows, and a black necktie. The beard was full and unevenly
trimmed, the hair ordinary brown with streaks of gray. When you
came into Andrew Jackson's presence, Trist's stepfather used to say,
it was like an electric shock to the system—bone, flesh, *lightning*—
Jackson's secret of leadership was that he conveyed a sensation of
raw physical force (with a touch of backwoodsman's pure lunacy)
that made most men back away in something like fear. Grant shook

hands and sat mildly down in one of the red plush chairs; picked up his porcelain coffee cup, crossed his legs like a farmer on his porch.

"Nicholas Trist," Cameron said belatedly. A lanky middle-aged man on the sofa, presumably the owner of the house, stood up and also held out his hand.

"You write for a French magazine," Grant said. "I remember we met in Chicago. There was a fine French journalist named Clemenceau in Washington after the war. Best reporter in the city. Now he's a politician."

"I write for the Washington *Post* now, as regards the convention."

"The Washington *Post*," said Grant, "is not much impressed with me."

"No, sir."

"They enjoy my malapropisms," Grant told Cameron. "Once I said it was a pleasure to be received so warmly at a certain reception, the *Post* went on for a month about being *received* at an occasion for *receiving*."

"Trist is new to the *Post*," Cameron said, which was, Trist figured, about as far in the direction of an endorsement as Cameron was likely to go.

"Well, I don't have a statement for you, Mr. Trist."

In retrospect it could have been Grant's calm, imperturbable tone, or the sight of him so close, or simply fifteen years of more or less suppressed memory. "Goddammit," Trist said in a flat, cold voice.

Cameron had been pouring a tumblerful of something at a sideboard. Now he turned around slowly, glass in hand.

"I don't care two cents about a statement," Trist said. "The first time I ever saw you was in the Wilderness campaign."

Grant put his cigar to his mouth, recrossed his legs.

"I missed the 'Bloody Angle,'" Trist said. "But I was in the next regiment to Emory Upton's at Cold Harbor."

A train rattled by outside. The man on the sofa said, "Oh, dear" very softly.

"June third, 1864," Grant said.

"Twenty-first Connecticut Infantry. Sixth Corps."

"That would have been Colonel Birney's regiment, I guess." Grant sat in his chair and looked steadily up at Trist. "Artillery barrage for five minutes to soften up the line. You started your assault at half past four in the morning, if Birney followed my orders, and I'm sure he did."

"There was a pasture six hundred yards wide that we had to cross, and a ravine and gun emplacements that none of the commanding generals had bothered to scout when they ordered the attack. Lee's men were entrenched behind them at the other end of the pasture."

Grant said nothing.

"We actually reached the trenches, some of us, but then we were driven back to the middle of the pasture and slaughtered like lambs. One of my sergeants back in the third wave said when the Rebels fired it was a burst of flame two miles long, he said it sounded like the judgment trump of the Almighty. I was a captain and I had forty-four men when I started, and six when it was over."

"You think I owe you something," Grant said, with no inflection whatsoever in his voice.

"No, sir."

"Go wait in the carriage, Trist," Cameron said.

"I think," Trist said, and stopped. "I have no idea what I think," he said. His shirt, he realized, was soaked with sweat. In the mirror behind the sideboard he observed with curiosity that his empty left sleeve had come unpinned and his own brown hair had streaks of gray as well, or else the mirror was flawed.

Grant drew at his cigar, expressionless.

"Lost his arm at Cold Harbor," Cameron said, to Trist's enormous surprise, and added what he could not possibly have known, but did. "Had to lie out in a field, in a pile of corpses, for a day and night before the doctors found him. Got a brigade citation for bravery." He looked at Trist. "My wife took some newspapers out of the library."

Grant said nothing. Cameron put one hand on Trist's right shoulder and began to steer him toward the door.

"I will tell you, Mr. Trist," Grant said, "for publication if you like. I don't intend to go to the convention tomorrow morning."

"Then," Trist heard himself say, "there goes your nomination."

Grant sat in his chair, blank and silent as a wall.

In the carriage Trist slouched against the seat with his head back, rolling gently with the motion of the wheels. They passed the big crenelated Chicago water tower, entered a park. He held his watch up to the wavering light of a streetlamp and saw that it was already well past midnight. On the opposite seat Cameron pulled out a flask and unscrewed it.

"Is he likely to change his mind?" Trist asked.

"Grant don't really want to be President," Cameron said wearily, last surprise of the night. "If they make him President, it just means that they forgive him."

O N THE TWENTY-NINTH BALLOT, WHICH WAS THE FIRST BALLOT of Tuesday morning, it looked for a moment as if Secretary Sherman had begun to gather strength. From 93 votes, his high point on Monday, he rose unexpectedly to 116. Grant stayed steady at 305, Blaine at 278, and Washburne slightly increased to 35. But for all practical purposes nothing had changed.

On the thirtieth ballot Sherman reached 120 votes; delegates here and there began to speak seriously of a real Sherman break-through. But on the thirty-first, he lost ground; by the thirty-third he was plainly slipping away.

At noon the convention recessed to take its lunch and digest its staggering ration of rumors and gossip. In an alley outside the Hall, next to a billboard advertising next week's attraction (a giant mechanical "taffy pull" on the auditorium floor, powered by steam engines) Trist and Cadwallader ate fried chicken from a stall and drank Blaine lemonade. Cadwallader, who had been up at dawn, going from delegation to delegation, reported that the newest scheme from the anti-Grant side was something called the "Wisconsin Plan."

"Which is, of course," he said through a mouthful of chicken—they moved away from the crowd, to the side of the stall—"a *Pennsylvania* idea. Idea is, when they reach a deadlock Wisconsin will suddenly swing all its votes to Garfield, as a com-promise candidate. Next ballot, Indiana acts like it's inspired, does the same thing, and presumably everybody else that's still awake and sick of voting jumps on the bandwagon. Pennsylvania man named Wharton Baker thought it up, made Cameron go through the roof this morning at breakfast." He wiped his mouth with his sleeve and looked up between the buildings at a hot sky the color of hammered pewter. "Mrs. Cameron left town already, you hear that? Late Sunday night, took a train. Damned odd."

Trist put his uneaten chicken on the wooden counter next to the stall and rubbed his face.

"Which makes this correspondent wonder." Cadwallader picked up Trist's discarded chicken and stuck it in his jacket pocket. "What the hell they think constitutes a deadlock?"

"Is thirty-three ballots the record?"

"In 1801," Cadwallader said, with the air of a man remembering a bad taste, "the House of Representatives went through thirty-six ballots for President. Finally elected Jefferson over Burr."

"You were there."

Cadwallader grinned. "I would have voted for Burr. Better copy."

On the thirty-fourth ballot, the governor of Wisconsin stood to announce that sixteen of its twenty votes were now to be cast for Garfield. The Hall went silent. Garfield himself instantly stood and waved his rolled-up tally sheet at the podium. "I challenge that vote! The announcement contains votes for me. No man has a right, without the consent of the person named, to vote for someone in this convention. Such consent I have not given!"

Yet even before the last sentence the chairman was hammering his gavel, drowning out Garfield's voice. The speaker was out of order, not recognized by the chair. Garfield sat down abruptly.

Trist made his way across the floor toward the Ohio delegation. Garfield was sitting rigidly, hands on knees, but behind him the governor was passing a telegram from delegate to delegate. Sherman had wired new instructions from Washington—if defeat of Grant were possible, he released Ohio from himself and appealed for Garfield as a compromise. Trist knelt beside Garfield while the Hall grew noisier and noisier and the thirty-fifth ballot began.

"Senator," he said, "there's been at least one vote for you on every ballot—why suddenly object?" Garfield's reply might have been Greek or Latin, because not a word was audible over the sudden roar from Indiana, which announced through a megaphone that all twenty-seven of its votes went for him.

At the center of the Hall, Roscoe Conkling could be seen standing, surrounded by clamoring delegates. Trist recognized a senator from Nevada, somebody from Illinois, Virginia. Anybody would guess what they were asking: Would Conkling throw New York behind Blaine just to stop Garfield? But Conkling's cold, defiant profile made the question pointless.

"New York casts its votes *exactly* as before," Conkling informed the chairman.

Now Garfield pushed his way to the governor. "Cast *my* vote for Sherman," he said, and looked around to be sure Trist was listening. "Do *not* desert Sherman." The governor shoved the telegram into Garfield's hands and clambered up on a chair. "Ohio casts all forty-three votes," he cried, "for *James A. Garfield!*"

Even in the uproar that followed, Garfield kept an expressionless face. He motioned Trist closer. "I wish you would say this is no act of mine," he said. "I wish you would say I've done everything possible for Sherman."

On the thirty-sixth and final ballot Garfield received 399 votes and the nomination. Grant received 306. At the reporters' table Cadwallader leaned toward Trist. "You know the headline now?"

" 'Garfield Wins.' "

Cadwallader shook his head, and for an instant all that Trist could see was a strange, disconnected look on his face, weary as Don Cameron's, impossible to read. " 'Grant Loses,' " Cadwallader said.

PART THREE

FROM
THE
NOTEBOOK
OF
N. P. TRIST

1883–1884

EXTRACTS FROM A REPORTER'S NOTEBOOK
1883–1884

You have asked me to write you confidentially. I will now say what
I have never breathed. *Grant is a drunkard.* His wife has been
with him for months only to use her influence in keeping him
sober. He tries to let liquor alone but he cannot resist the
temptation always. When he came to Memphis he left his wife at
La Grange & for several days after getting here was beastly drunk,
utterly incapable of doing anything. Quimby and I took him in
charge, watching him day & night & keeping liquor away from
him & we telegraphed to his wife and brought her on to take care
of him.

—BRIG. GEN. C. S. HAMILTON
Feb. 11, 1863

The soldiers observe him coming and rising to their feet gather
on each side of the way to see him pass—they do not salute him,
they only watch him with a certain sort of familiar reverence. His
abstract air is not so great while he thus moves along as to prevent
his seeing everything without apparently looking at it. A plain blue
suit, without scarf, sword or trappings of any sort, save the double-
starred shoulder straps . . . a square-cut face whose lines and con-
tour indicate extreme endurance and determination, complete the

external appearance of this small man, as one sees him passing along, turning and chewing restlessly the end of his unlighted cigar.

NEW YORK *TIMES*,
June 21, 1863

General Grant seemed the most bashful man I ever encountered. When I came in, the room was wreathed in heavy cigar smoke and the table where he was writing was stacked high with military papers. He got up in a hurry, tried to shove half a dozen chairs at once forward for me, took his cigar out of his mouth and his hat off his head and then replaced them both without knowing that he was doing it and asked what he could do for me, ma'am.

—MRS. MARY LIVERMORE
nurse, Vicksburg, July 4, 1863

Grant made what looked like a snap judgment one day on some supply orders. The quartermaster pointed out that this would cost a good deal of money and asked whether Grant was sure he was right.

"No, I am not," Grant replied, "but in war anything is better than indecision. *We must decide.* If I am wrong we shall soon find it out and can do the other thing. But *not to decide* wastes both time and money and may ruin everything."

—COLONEL JAMES F. RUSLING
Nashville

I met Grant in Willard's Hotel. Obviously the man was no gentleman; he had no gait, no station, no manner. He was smoking a cigar and he had rather the look of a man who did, or once did, take a little too much to drink. He was an ordinary, scrubby looking man with a slightly seedy look as if he was out of office on half pay. Later in the week I saw Lincoln in his office and found him no better. Such a shapeless mass of writhing ugliness as slouched about the President's chair you never saw or imagined. Grant and Lincoln get on very well.

—RICHARD HENRY DANA, JR.

Once he sat on the ground writing a dispatch in a fort just captured from the enemy. A shell burst immediately over him, but his hand never shook and he kept on writing. "Ulysses don't scare worth a damn," said a soldier nearby.

—ADAM BADEAU
military aide

While he was passing a spot near the roadside where there were a number of wounded, one of them who was lying close to the road-side, seemed to attract his special attention. The man's face was beardless; he was evidently young; his countenance was strikingly handsome. The blood was flowing from a wound in his breast, the froth about his mouth was tinged with red, and his wandering, staring eyes gave unmistakable evidence of approaching death. Just then a young staff-officer dashed by at full gallop, and as his horse's hoofs struck a puddle in the road, a mass of black mud was splashed in the wounded man's face. The general, whose eyes were at that moment turned upon the youth, was visibly affected. He reined in his horse, and seeing from a motion he made that he was intending to dismount to bestow some care upon the young man, I sprang from my horse, ran to the side of the soldier, wiped his face with my handkerchief, spoke to him, and examined his wound; but in a few minutes the unmistakable death-rattle was heard, and I found that he had breathed his last. I said to the general, who was watching the scene intently, "The poor fellow is dead," remounted my horse, and the party rode on. The chief had turned round twice to look after the officer who had splashed the mud and who had passed rapidly on, as if he wished to take him to task for his care-lessness. There was a painfully sad look upon the general's face, and he did not speak for some time.

—COLONEL HORACE PORTER
Wilderness campaign

Grant is certainly a very extraordinary man. He does not look it and might well pass for a dumpy and slouchy little subaltern, very fond of smoking. They say his mouth shows character. It may be, but it is so covered with beard that no one can vouch for it. He sits a horse well, but in walking he leans forward and toddles. Such being his appearance, however, I do not think that any intelligent person could watch him, even from such a distance as mine, without con-cluding that he is a remarkable man. He handles those around him so quietly and well, he is cool and quiet, he is a man of the most exquisite judgment and tact.

—CAPTAIN CHARLES FRANCIS ADAMS
to his brother Henry Adams

On the subject of assassination, Bismarck expressed indignation at those who had caused Lincoln's death. "All you can do with such people," said the General quietly, "is kill them." "Precisely so," answered the prince.

—JOHN RUSSELL YOUNG
Around the World with Grant

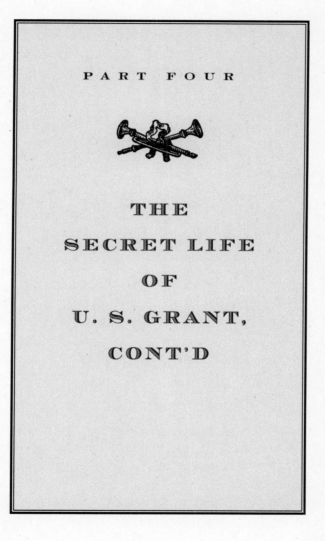

PART FOUR

THE
SECRET LIFE
OF
U. S. GRANT,
CONT'D

CHAPTER ONE

THE SECRET LIFE
OF U. S. GRANT

by Sylvanus Cadwallader

CHAPTER FIVE

BACK IN THE EARLY DAYS OF THE WAR, FEBRUARY 1862 IN fact, when Grant was laying siege to Fort Donelson, Tennessee, it happened by an odd coincidence that the commander of the Confederate troops inside the fort was an old, old friend, Simon Bolivar Buckner. Buckner had been at West Point with Grant, one year behind, and fought with him in Mexico at the battle of Churubusco. He was an unflamboyant but practical-minded general, competent enough to see that at Donelson he was completely surrounded and cut off from help. So on February 16, after three days of miserable, go-nowhere fighting, Buckner sent over a reasonably cordial letter, considering the circumstances, full of fine Southern rhetorical flourishes and asking what might be his old comrade's terms for armistice.

Grant rubbed his jaw and thought about it for awhile, and then rode off to get the advice of the elderly gent who was his second in command—also (as it happened) the former commandant of West Point when both Grant and Buckner were students—who instantly flung the letter down on the ground and growled, "No terms for any damned *Rebels!*" Which sentiment Grant revised somewhat in one of the most beautifully concise little communications any soldier since Julius Caesar has ever written:

> *Yours of this date proposing Armistice and appointment of*
> *Commissioners to settle terms of capitulation is just received.*
> *No terms except unconditional and immediate surrender can*
> *be accepted. I propose to move immediately upon your works.*
>
> Your obt. svt.
U. S. Grant
Brig. Gen.

Buckner (no literary critic) grumbled that this was harsh to an old classmate and friend. Grant made no comment. But after he received his prisoners and signed all the military forms, he took Buckner quietly aside and pulled out his wallet and asked if Buckner needed any money to see him home. Nobody but Buckner observed the gesture. Nobody but Buckner *would* have understood.

Fact was, the last time the two had met was just about eight years earlier, when Grant was not a victorious general, not a general at all, not even a soldier. In midsummer 1854, having drunk himself right out of the army in California, Grant had stepped off the Panama steamer in New York City absolutely penniless. He wanted to check into a hotel and write his father for money, but the hotel clerk, sizing up his man, said cash in advance was required. Grant wandered out into the streets, hopeless, and somewhere along Broadway, at an army recruiting office, spotted his old friend Buckner, who (sizing him up as well) said he wouldn't give him cash (which would likely be spent on drink), but he would guarantee his hotel bill and all his meals; and gratefully, humbly, soberly, Grant sat down to wait for a letter from home.

Not coincidence at Donelson, I guess, as much as Greek tragedy reversal. Or just old red Mars giggling and laughing up his sleeve.

Jesse Grant hadn't giggled much when he got his son's letter. First thing he did, as if Ulysses were a schoolboy in trouble with his teacher, was to write the Secretary of War and ask if the army couldn't overlook the lad's hasty resignation. Grant, he wrote, hadn't really known what he was doing. The Secretary wrote right back—more Greek reversal—resignation already accepted, matter closed, Yours truly, Jefferson Davis, Sec. of War.

There never was any question, evidently, of Grant's going back to the tannery. Jesse was too humiliated by having a disgraced down-and-out son around, and Grant still clung to his youthful vow never to work at curing hides again. But Julia owned outright, in her name, some sixty acres of hilly wooded land near her father's house in St. Louis, and these Grant eventually decided he would turn into a farm.

Colonel Dent was not much happier than Jesse Grant about his son-in-law's failure. Still, Julia was his favorite daughter. The old man advanced the couple the money to buy seeds and tools, and rocked on his porch and watched.

For the first few months Grant set to work like a man possessed. Cleared fields, sold cordwood in St. Louis, started to build a two-story log cabin for Julia and the two little boys (he named it "Hardscrabble" in a dig at Colonel Dent's pretensions). But as anybody at all could have predicted, nothing prospered.

He was too easy on the slaves, for one thing—they belonged to Julia and were supposed to work in the fields, but Grant could never bring himself to drive them hard. Neighbors shook their heads when he paid free Negroes for extra labor (*over*paid them, by local standards) and talked about setting his own people free as soon as he was able.

Not a popular position in Missouri in the late fifties. Colonel Dent was far from the only pro-slavery man in the state. Just up the way in the Kansas Territory a crazed abolitionist named John Brown, soon to be heard from again, murdered five slave-holder settlers one day, and instantly hundreds and hundreds of armed Missouri vigilantes swarmed across the border to try and hunt him down—Grant's kind of loose talk was only bringing a crisis closer (curiously enough, old Jesse Grant had gone to school with John Brown and remembered his playmate fondly).

Day by day Grant's debts increased. When the crops came in poor he took to selling his cordwood in town himself. One day General William Harney, who had been a colonel back in the Mexican War, came riding down a St. Louis street in a brand-new gold-trimmed uniform. Harney stopped beside a wagon and looked over at the driver, a shabby man in a faded blue army overcoat.

Looked again.

"Why, Grant, what in blazes are you doing here?"

Grant scraped his muddy boot on the buckboard. "Well, General. I'm hauling wood."

Harney took him into a restaurant and bought him a meal.

Cump Sherman passed through town, likewise out of the army. He had been a banker in San Francisco till the bank went bust, and now he too was stone broke, on his way back to Ohio to work for his father-in-law. "I'm a dead cock in the pit," he told Grant, and moved on.

General Edward Beale, who had known Grant back in California, ran into him one day outside the Planters Hotel and asked him to come inside and have supper.

Grant gestured at his filthy coat and boots and said he wasn't dressed.

"Oh, that don't matter," Beale said, taking his arm, "not in the least."

But it mattered to others. The officers out at Jefferson Barracks took to looking the other way when Grant came by with his wood. Colonel Dent's prosperous friends and neighbors would cross the street rather than speak to him. Jesse Grant sent a few stingy checks, but the farm kept gobbling everything up. Two days before Christmas 1858, Grant walked into a St. Louis pawnshop and handed over his gold hunting watch and chain so he could buy a few presents for Julia and the babies (three of them now, a fourth on the way). His health began to fail—a boyhood asthma came back, along with the shaking ague, courtesy of Panama—and the neighbors started to whisper that Captain Grant was taking to drink again.

In the fall of that same year he gave up on Hardscrabble and moved the family into a rented house in the poor section of the city for twenty-five dollars a month. Colonel Dent made one last effort and persuaded a friend named Harry Boggs to set his son-in-law up as a real estate salesman and rent collector. But Grant was too softhearted to press anybody with a hard-luck story for rent, and too shy and diffident ever to sell a house.

Worse, he slept late many days, out of bad health or just plain temperament (even in the war Grant liked his sleep). Sometimes he would go up the street and waste time chatting with another merchant, William Moffett, who had a red-haired brother-in-law, steamboat pilot, liked to sleep late too. One afternoon the brother-in-law sat down at Moffett's piano and made up a song about himself:

> Samuel Clemens! The gray dawn is breaking,
> The cow from the back gate her exit is making,—
> The howl of the housemaid is heard in the hall;
> What, Samuel Clemens? Slumbering still!

Mark Twain says that this was the first time they ever met; Grant just shakes his head and says he don't remember.

In any case, Boggs had had enough. He fired Grant and turned him out of the office. For a few weeks hope fluttered—Grant applied for the job of County Engineer and thought that as a graduate of West Point, with a degree in engineering, he stood a good chance. But slavery politics entered into every part of government now, especially in Missouri. The board of appointments was anti-slavery. The son-in-law of Colonel Dent was presumed to share the old man's pro-slavery politics. The job went to somebody else.

Grant pulled his hat down lower over his eyes and sat morose and listless in his rented room. Maybe, as rumor said, he opened a bottle or two when he could. People who knew him then remember he wandered downtown sometimes from office to office, just asking about jobs, looking haunted, shabbier than ever. In December 1859 they hanged his father's old boyhood friend John Brown, who went to the gallows saying, "The crimes of this guilty land will never be purged away but with blood." Grant was too down and broke almost to notice. He got a month's worth of work as a customs house clerk, but the superintendent died and the politicians swept him out again.

By February 1860, two years exactly before Fort Donelson, he was living on borrowed money, from those few friends of Julia's who would still take a little pity on the family. He had no job, no prospects, not even—for the first time in his life—a horse. Jesse Grant, fuming and disappointed and sitting on his tannery wealth, hadn't spoken to his son for months, but Grant had nowhere else to turn. Halfway through the spring, thirty-eight years old, he swallowed what was left of his pride. He scraped up train fare from somebody and went to Ohio to ask the old man for help. Anything at all, work, charity. Down to the bottom at last. Unconditional surrender. At about which excellent time, the war gods started to chuckle.

PART FIVE

ESTHER

———

WASHINGTON

AND

NEW YORK

March–December 1884

EXTRACT FROM A REPORTER'S NOTEBOOK, 1884

From Esther: A Novel, *Chapter One*

"Miss Esther Dudley is one of the most marked American types I ever saw."

"What are the signs of the most marked American type you ever saw?" asked Hazard.

"In the first place, she has a bad figure, which she makes answer for a good one. She is too slight, too thin; she looks fragile, willowy, as the cheap novels call it, as though you could break her in halves like a switch. She dresses to suit her figure and sometimes overdoes it. Her features are imperfect. Except her ears, her voice, and her eyes which have a sort of brown depth like a trout brook, she has no very good points."

"Then why do you hesitate?" asked Strong, who was not entirely pleased with this cool estimate of her cousin's person.

"Miss Dudley interests me," replied the painter. "I want to know what she can make of life. She gives one the idea of a lightly-sparred yacht in mid-ocean; unexpected; you ask yourself what the devil she is doing there. She sails gaily along, though there is no land in sight and plenty of rough weather coming. She never read a book, I believe, in her life. She tries to paint, but she is only a second rate amateur and will never be anything more. . . ."

To the surprise of nearly everyone who knew him, Henry Adams had actually bought a typewriting machine, late in the year 1883.

Not for his personal correspondence, of course. There a quill pen was still required by courtesy and decorum, and not for the first draft of any really serious work such as his History. And not, certainly, for the purposes of his friend Henry James, who didn't manipulate the instrument himself, but did send his manuscripts out now to a public stenographer's office to be "typed."

"It's been the ruin of poor Harry," Adams declared with a quick little grimace of satisfaction. "Thanks to the stenographer he can revise his novels effortlessly, over and over, and every draft is apparently more complicated and convoluted than the one before. Some of his sentences begin to seem to me like the whorl in a seashell, one long dizzy spiral. A literary historian might say his 'style' has been completely changed by technology. So you're back, eh, Mr. Trist?" As if Trist had merely stepped around the corner. "From Paris, is it? Or London now?"

"London now, for several years." Trist acknowledged his backness with a handshake. "Miss Beale said you would be through with your work for the day."

Adams turned his whiskery little terrier smile on Emily Beale. "She knows our routine by heart, Miss Beale does. My wife and I ride in Rock Creek from nine to eleven every morning, I write until four."

"Then you serve," said Emily, bending to inspect the typewriting machine, which was resting disassembled on a black lacquered Hitchcock chair beside the fireplace, "the most expensive and delicious teas in Washington. Naturally, I'm not supposed to drink them."

"Our Miss Beale has been unwell of late," Adams told Trist.

"Our Miss Beale is under orders to return straight home and rest." She poked one finger delicately at the keyboard. "Did you break it, Mr. Adams, like a cowboy riding his horse?"

Trist laughed. Adams kept a straight face. "I would prefer another analogy. Perhaps Beethoven pounding his piano, Miss Beale."

"Miss Beale apologizes."

"It is merely," Adams said fastidiously, "due to be cleaned."

Emily Beale had in fact been very sick. For nearly half of the year 1883, she had been confined to an invalid's room in a New York residential hotel, where surgeons and doctors visited daily and treated her, painfully, for what she would only describe in her letters to Trist as "female complaints." She looked gray, thin, washed out; far older than her twenty-one years. She stayed a few moments longer, bantering with Adams, but the fatigue in her eyes was unmistakable and at quarter to four she left.

Adams closed the door behind her; returned to the parlor and rubbed his hands together awkwardly. "You were never here before, I think."

"Never inside. Often passed by."

"Let me ring," Adams said, "for some of our expensive tea." He moved toward a servants' bellpull. Trist watched him automatically, for a moment, then let his glance stray. He'd once interviewed a French police detective who had described to him the best way to examine a strange room: divide the space in front of you into quadrants, proceed left to right, low to high, focus on the single most important object. The parlor of 1607 H Street was a long, well-lit, hopelessly cluttered collection of . . . *possessions*. The furniture was a mixture of odd pine hand-me-downs from

New England and beautifully crafted French antiques. The carpet on which he stood was a Shiraz, others lay scattered in oriental profusion: Cashmere, Kurdistan, Bokhara. Every mantel and shelf held bric-a-brac, porcelains, Japanese and Chinese vases. Trist had been in enough Parisian *salons* to recognize some of the paintings: sketches by Watteau, Tiepolo, Rembrandt, Raphael. A watercolor above a leather chair was surely by Turner. The single most important object in the room was a large drawing over the fireplace representing the mad king Nebuchadnezzar, from the Old Testament, crouching on his hands and knees in a field and eating grass. The single most curious fact was that every chair and sofa had had its legs sawed down almost to the floor, to match the scale of their diminutive possessors.

"My wife," Adams said when tea had been presented, hecatombs of cake and sugar offered, "is in her room writing a letter to her father, which filial duty she performs every Sunday at eleven, the hour of worship, but yesterday we were for once engaged. Her father," he added, studying Trist over the rim of his teacup, "who art in Boston. We never did embark on our Jeffersonian business, Mr. Trist."

"No, I went off to Chicago to the convention, and then home."

"And now you're back, for the same melancholy reason."

Trist shook his head. He tasted the tea—thought his stepfather had been right as usual, all tea is muck—and considered for the first time that he really was back, that he really had crossed the Atlantic again, drifted to Washington as before, settled down (far down) in an American chair in an American home, just as if four years had never passed. He had landed at Baltimore only yesterday, taken a room at the Willard this morning. "Reason I'm here," he said, and realized that he disliked Adams's droll, ironic cock of the head as much as ever, "my stepbrother died last year, and I found in some of his papers a whole set of Jefferson's letters to Mrs. Trist, from Paris."

"So you aren't reporting the Republican high jinks for our French—or English—friends this time around. But of course, there's hardly any suspense, is there? Grant is sick with pneumonia, Blaine is certain to be the presidential nominee, and the poor Democrats will win at last with Mr. Cleveland."

This was so succinct, and accurate, that Trist could do no

more than nod in agreement. The maid had placed the table for his cup on his left; he reached awkwardly across his knees (what kind of person cut *every* chair down to his own size?) and chest.

"And you can't have voyaged so far just to offer me—so kindly—your manuscripts?"

"Mr. Trist," said Clover, bounding into the room like a ball, surrounded by a whirling, yapping blur of little dogs—"Possum! Boojum! Marquis! Down, you canine wretches—Mr. Trist, *quel plaisir*, welcome! General Beale, your second greatest admirer— Emily is first—told me all about it. Henry"—still bouncing on her toes, practically flying from handshake to teacup to chair, she waved him back to his seat, held her cup chin high with both hands while dogs scrambled back and forth on her lap. "Mr. Trist is a famous journalist now, Henry, he writes *travel* books, there was a splendid one last year about Egypt—Henry never reads travel books I'm afraid—you look very well, Mr. Trist, older, wiser, stouter, I like your completely clean-shaven style. Bit more gray in the hair, I think, yes. Emily says you've come back to write a book about the Virginia battlefields, and, what is most exciting to me, you're going to tour them with a *photographer*! Have I got all that right?"

"Battlefields, yes, gray hair. Famous, no."

"Oh, don't be modest, Mr. Trist, modesty is the most boring of virtues. I'm a photographer myself. If Henry would allow it, we'd decorate this room from top to bottom with my pictures. As it is, we make do with mad Babylonian kings and landscapes. Of course Henry wants your letters."

"Of course I do," said Adams after a moment.

In the reception hall, tea finished, dogs banished out of sight, Trist paused to shrug on his coat and button it one-handed at the collar, cape-style. Behind him Adams murmured a polite good-bye and disappeared, presumably to his study. At the window Clover lifted the corner of a lace curtain, peered, shivered.

"*Another* book," she said, turning brightly back to him. From a side table she held up a mottled gray cover for Trist to see. *Esther: A Novel.*

" 'By Frances Snow Compton,' " he read.

"Whoever *she* is." Clover replaced it on the table. "Henry leaves improving books here, where I'll see them coming in, as one of his subtle little instructions for me to read it. Married life, as no doubt you'll find out one day, Mr. Trist, is a series of unspoken communications, like red Indians with their smoke signals. Put on your hat and I'll walk outside and show you a sight."

She led the way across the porch and down the steps to the sidewalk, where she turned abruptly to the left. Trist followed slowly, still adjusting his coat. The March afternoon was cloudy, chill. Straight across Lafayette Square, behind a filigree of bare branches, the White House stared back at him. Halfway along a row of handsome redbrick facades, Don Cameron's house looked quiet and deserted, except for a tradesman's wagon parked in front. Trist hadn't seen Elizabeth Cameron either for all those years, not since Chicago, not since— It was inevitable that he would run into her now, sooner or later; it wouldn't make the slightest difference. He hadn't crossed the ocean to see her. He was older, wiser, stouter; dazzleproof. Clover Adams waved him forward.

"This," she announced as they reached the corner of H and Sixteenth Streets, "is our new purchase." She nodded her bonnet at the empty lot in front of them, an L-shaped expanse of stumps and mud that stretched from the shrubbery beside the Adams house halfway up the block. "It belonged to our landlord Mr. Corcoran—"

"Of the famous art collection," Trist said.

"Exactly the man. Dull as a bedbug. Former Confederate sympathizer. Spent the war in Europe. *He* was going to build an apartment house here, which wouldn't do, of course, all the world staring in our windows, but Henry and his friend John Hay dug in their pockets and bought the whole whacking property and divided it in two. John Hay doesn't mind the church, so he gets the corner half." Together they looked at the facing columns and steeple of St. John's Episcopal Church on the other side of Sixteenth Street. "I couldn't *bear* it, all that piety *leaking* out every Sunday. We've hired the same architect to build us adjoining houses, one of Henry's Harvard friends named Richardson. Very fat, dresses in a cowl like a monk. I hope you're not religious, Mr. Trist. I come from a family of ministers and Transcendentalists, but somehow it doesn't take. My evangelical cousin Russell Sturgis said the other day he would only hire a Christian gardener, so I told him *I* would advertise for an agnostic one."

"Did you?"

She shook her head. "I'm too cowardly. But I do like the story about Mrs. William Travers, who told her husband on Christmas Day she thought their home life should be sweeter and holier. So she hung up in their parlor an illuminated text, 'God Bless Our House.' Mr. Travers read it and said he felt regenerated. Next day, going into her dining room, Mrs. Travers practically reeled to the floor when she saw *another* text he had just put up: 'God Damn Our Cook.' "

She joined in his laughter, but the wings of her bonnet hid her face so completely in shadow that for a moment the effect was oddly ghostlike, disturbing. Trist made motions of leaving.

"A rather daring assignment." Clover put her hand on his arm. "Revisiting your old battlefields, writing about the war." The bonnet nodded at his left shoulder. "Do you think of it, Mr. Trist— what was Lincoln's phrase?—as going over 'consecrated ground'?"

It had never occurred to her husband, Trist thought, to see a human connection between his book and his past. Clover Adams, for all her bounce and wit, was an acutely sensitive woman. "I have no idea, Mrs. Adams," he said truthfully, "what I think of the war. I never have."

"Or the battlefields or the generals?"

"Them too."

"I was amused," she murmured, and he caught a glimpse of the parchment white of her face in the bonnet, "in my grim New England way, by the fact that they put wounded soldiers in office buildings and churches here in Washington, but wounded generals they put in the old lunatic asylum at Dupont Circle." She lifted her tiny hand and moved it back and forth in a kind of waggish blessing. "You must come and see us often, Mr. Trist."

"A PRIZE INVITATION," SAID HENRY WEST, SOMEWHERE UP ahead in the dark. "Of course, she's loony. Her whole family in Boston is loony, religious fanatics half of them, other half in the nuthouse. One of her aunts took poison, famous case. I think baby girl Mrs. Adams even found the body."

The sun was not yet risen on the morning after his Adams tea, and the air in front of him was cold, dark, full of blurred smells from the nearby Potomac. Trist walked carefully just behind West on the frozen grass of the National Mall, between carelessly stacked piles of lumber and what, when he scraped his ankle and West held up his lantern, turned out to be two massive rows of marble building blocks.

"But there's no doubt the Adamses are the social center of Washington," West said over his shoulder, "loony or not. Or 'Washington village,' as Adams calls it. *Which* they manage by being so goddam exclusive they squeak. Won't go to the White House, even when the President asks them for dinner. Snub Senators, skewer Congressmen. Adams says Senators are like hogs and you have to hit them on the snout with a stick. When Oscar Wilde was here last year, came with their writer friend Henry James, Mrs. Adams absolutely refused to meet him and told everybody"—a mincing falsetto—" 'I try to keep far away from thieves and noodles.' "

Trist laughed, scraped his ankle again, and stopped. A few stray snowflakes drifted around his face like long, wet feathers. Other lanterns could be seen up ahead, bobbing in the air. Men's voices floated downhill. The slow tap-tap of a hammer came from the right, where the lantern's beams revealed a bare dirt path and still more piles of lumber.

"Up here." West gripped Trist by the elbow and steered him up a slippery hillock of grass and mud. "You go there for Sunday dinner, write up a few notes under the table. *Voilà*, a *Post* exclusive, 'At Home with the Insufferable Adamses.' "

Trist shook his head. Pointless in the dark. "I like her," he said.

West snorted. "I wish there was a Hippocratic oath for reporters. 'First, Do all the harm you can.' "

"Are we there yet?"

"Hold your horses."

It was always amazing, Trist thought, how fast the sun rose. Already the sky in the east was beginning to glow a soft yellow-white, and a dark rim of trees and rooftops was showing across the horizon. In another hour or two the sun would have dried the grass and burned away the damp haze and the brief March snow would amount to no more than puddles, slivers of coppery water in the mud, Washington would present its usual early-spring panorama of pale green and brown. But for the moment, in the long gray suspension of the dawn, they could have been anywhere—Paris, by the slapping Seine. Boston. Chicago. He blew in his cupped hand for warmth. Possibly not Hawaii.

"We go in here." West held up the lantern, but lowered his head to pass under a network of wooden scaffolding. To his left now was an open door and, just growing visible in the milky light, what appeared to be a ship's prow made out of stone.

They stepped inside. Blacker, colder; another lantern, hanging from a beam overhead, pulled wooden steps out of the darkness. With a grunt, West started to climb.

"Remember your catechism?"

The railing was on the left-hand side. Trist held on awkwardly, arm stretched across his chest. "Eight hundred ninety-eight steps. Five hundred eighty-seven feet."

"*When* they finish." West swung the lantern out to show the rough surface of the stone walls on either side of the steps. "*If* they finish."

Twenty feet up the steps had begun to narrow claustrophobically, and at the same time to zigzag back and forth as they rose. West's lantern clattered around a corner and vanished. "Washington's Monument," his disembodied voice called down, wheezing. "Father of his goddam country. Thirty-six years' parturition—you didn't think I knew that word. You're a good sport, Trist."

"You're a lousy climber, West."

From time to time they passed a window slit on the outside wall, and each would pause to peer out at the rapidly dawning sky. It was the only time to see it, Henry West had insisted last night, three large beers into their reunion at Gillian's Tavern. It was his favorite view in the world, and thanks to the *Post*'s ceaselessly boosting coverage of the monument's progress, he, West, was friendly with all the construction workers, including one cordially corrupt young foreman, who was glad to allow him "on site," as they put it, any time, day or night.

The lantern faded around another corner, leaving Trist in a pleasant musty darkness that smelled of stone dust and cut wood. He stumbled and clutched the handrail; one-armed man, he thought, in the country of the blind. He turned the next zigzag and felt a sudden push of cool, fresh air. You could do the same thing in Paris, he remembered, climb the inside steps to the top of Notre Dame or Saint-Sulpice, though not at dawn, and look out at the medieval rooftops and cramped black alleys below, a gargoyle's-eye view of the Old World. But when he rounded the last corner here and stepped up to the open platform at the end of the stairs, it was not the Old World but the New he saw before him, and bald, unsentimental Henry West, cap off for some reason, leaning against the stone rampart and looking due east toward the great white dome of the Capitol, caught now in the sheer radiance of the rising sun, while all below them the streets and buildings of the city were still faintly gray, unresolved, coming into focus, and the smooth, broad back of the Potomac wound off to the right, like the river of Time itself, disappearing into the blue-green Virginia horizon of the past.

"Absolutely," West said, "fucking glorious."

"*Vaut le voyage.*"

"Worth the trip."

"How high are we?"

West leaned a little farther out. "Four hundred feet, more or less." He shifted his weight, and the wooden platform under them rocked unsteadily. On the Mall below they could just make out a few shadowy workmen tramping uphill.

"Now when I was a boy"—West stopped to strike a match against the stone—"I called this the 'hour of work.' " He waved the match under a cigar. "Because my father always got up before sunrise to light the fire in the kitchen, and I could hear him from my bed, rattling pans and closing doors, and I used to think when I get big that's what I'll do too, get up before everybody else in the world, bring everything to life." He exhaled smoke with a long sigh and rested both elbows on the rampart. "No dome on the Capitol when you were a soldier boy."

Trist shook his head. "They didn't finish the dome till the end of the war."

"At Cold Harbor," West said, "you attacked just about this time of day, I think."

Trist looked off to the right, where a sailboat was shaking out canvas on the river. A seagull coasted in front of them, fell away.

"Four-thirty in the morning," he said. "Those were the General's orders. It was darker than this."

West blew a smoke ring that flattened in the breeze and became a feather, a snowflake. "Well, what you have, my friend, is one brilliant idea—book of pious battlefield engravings, a little patriotic narration, some interviews with the just and unjust alike, as Lucy Hayes used to say. Twenty-year anniversary of the Wilderness campaign and the end of the war. Nostalgia fever. I tell you, ever since Sherman published his *Memoirs,* we can't get enough of anniversaries and reminiscences, fight the goddam war all over again."

Trist walked along the platform until he was facing due north, toward the White House and Lafayette Square. Henry Adams's house he could identify by the two vacant lots to one side, and St. John's church on the corner. Elizabeth Cameron's house was lost in shadow.

"I grew up in Pennsylvania," West said, joining him. "Had an aunt lived near Gettysburg. When I went to visit as a boy you could still plow up a skull sometimes or a set of bones. My aunt told me that after the battle, for weeks, when it rained the ground would turn swampy and soft and there would be hands and arms and legs just sticking up out of the fields, like somebody had planted them."

"Well, they had a bumper crop at Gettysburg," Trist said. "I wasn't there."

West nodded. "Joined in late '63, am I right? Not long before Grant took command?" When Trist didn't answer he went on, carefully holding out his cigar and studying the ash as he spoke. "Know the single most important decision a writer makes?"

Trist turned his head.

"The most important decision a writer makes," West said firmly, "is which person you write in, first or third."

Trist turned all the way now to look at him. After four years West was, if anything, balder than ever. Permanent wrinkles had started to line his forehead and scalp, giving his head the appearance of a rumpled corduroy rug. While Trist watched he pulled his old cloth cap from his coat pocket and put it on again. In a window of the White House, through the gray air, there suddenly appeared the unmistakable yellow glow of an Edison electric bulb.

"Read your first two chapters last night," West said.

"Draft chapters."

"Draft chapters. Smooth as a baby's bottom."

"All a writer ever asks," Trist said, now genuinely curious about where West was going, "is total, complete, unconditional praise. Henry Adams," he added for some reason, "told me yesterday he just tosses his sentences up in the air and they land on their feet like cats."

"Well, the fact is," West said, "with all due unconditional praise, you write pretty dry about the war. Facts, figures, dates—big fence to keep the reader out."

"European readers," Trist began, and it was in his mind to argue, to explain that the project, his own idea, dreamed up in a bare brown patch of London winter, was meant to be translated and sold all over Europe, where the Civil War (and Grant) still exerted as much fascination as ever; his old magazine *L'Illustration* was paying part of the costs, the London *Times* the rest, and the *Post* had already tentatively agreed to run Sunday installments at home. But West knew all of that. Second most important decision: A writer doesn't argue or explain.

"First person," Trist said.

"What you want to do"—West stood up straighter, worked his hands—"is turn it into a *personal* tour, if you get what I mean— veteran goes back to his old battlefields twenty years later, revisits his past, sees his old self, old comrades. You can tell us what it was like to lose old Buster there." Unlike most people, who never referred at all to his arm one way or the other, West was capable of being cheerfully, crudely direct. "Tell us what the war was *like*. All these generals writing memoirs now, it's 'Fourth Encalibrated Diocletian Regiment, Ninth Army, Tenth Division' or else 'enfilade and scarpis won the day'—nothing comes alive, nothing *dies*. You want to write it up straight, detailed, make it the real thing, reality."

By now the sun had cleared the eastern trees, a low orange disk gathering speed, beating dents in the iron-gray surface of the river. Telegraph wires floated in long silver nets above the streets. The air was filled with rising birds. Trist narrowed his eyes against the glare.

"Tell you a secret," Henry West said, and grinned. "That anonymous novel you liked so much when you were here, did a review for Hutchins?"

"*Democracy.*"

"They say Clover Adams wrote it."

CHAPTER THREE

EVERY MORNING OF THE WORKDAY WEEK, MONDAY TO FRI-
day, Ulysses S. Grant, banker and broker, observed a little private
ritual at his desk.

On the green blotter, next to the framed photograph of Julia,
stood a handsome glass jar, picked up somewhere on his travels in
India, brass-trimmed on the bottom and topped with a polished
conical lid; and inside the jar, no matter how early or late Grant
arrived at the office, were invariably twenty-five fresh, fine new
Havana cigars. These were the gift of Ferdinand Ward, "the Young
Napoleon of Finance" and executive partner of Grant & Ward,
Inc., which Ward personally counted out and placed in the jar and
which Grant then, for some reason he had never bothered to ana-
lyze, always counted out again for himself.

Two days after Trist climbed to the top of the unfinished
Washington Monument, a hundred and seventy-five miles to the
north at Number 2 Wall Street, Grant sat down heavily in his
chair, hitched up the knees of his trousers, and as usual counted
his cigars. Twenty-five. He glanced at his clock and picked out the
first of what his son Buck called "the day's fruits." Then lit it with
an extra-long wooden match, inhaled the finest smoke in the
world, and leaned back.

Buck's voice he could actually hear now, or thought he could, downstairs on the first floor where Grant & Ward had their main offices. On the second floor, where he sat, there was of course nothing but storage closets and his own private suite, whose letters on the ground-glass door said not "Grant & Ward," but "Mexican Southern Railroad Company," an entirely separate and unsalaried (and so far unprofitable) venture, but one close to his heart, a pure expression, as several admiring newspaper articles had put it, of Grant's lifelong friendship for the Mexican people.

Friendship for the Mexicans he had in abundance; actual work, he acknowledged, not much. Negotiations for land and rights-of-way, not to mention heavy construction equipment, not to mention Spanish-speaking engineers, certainly not to mention some unrecorded financial transactions with members of the Mexican government—none of these things proceeded very quickly in the best of times, or even lately, in the doldrums of March, proceeded at all. *Harper's Weekly* had just last month warned its readers that Mexican railway stock was an exceedingly risky investment. Luckily, Grant thought, he had no need for a Mexican profit. Or for advice from *Harper's Weekly.* He swivelled the other way, to look at his wall of books and paintings and the beautifully constructed club leather chair for visitors that Ward had presented him the day they signed their partnership agreement.

In 1861, at Cairo, Illinois, he remembered, he had taken up his first executive office in a bank. It had been the Citizens Bank of Cairo, confiscated from the citizens for army headquarters in the Illinois-Kentucky Department, and he had arrived there September 4, 1861, as brigadier general in command, thanks to Elihu Washburne, who had finally convinced the War Department in Washington that an old West Pointer might still be of use. Nobody in the building had looked up or paid the slightest attention when Grant walked through the door—he had never in his life, he thought, had the knack of catching people's eye—and the colonel in temporary charge had actually threatened to arrest him for an imposter. But when they got all *that* straightened out, Grant had quietly set up shop behind one of the tellers' counters and started in to work. Just like now.

He smiled to himself and tapped cigar ash into a silver tray that Julia had bought for him at Bloomingdale's store. Not quite like now. No Bloomingdale's in Cairo, Illinois, then, not much of anything in fact except mosquitoes the size of rats, and green canal mud everywhere from the levees that the Confederates had broken up before they left—along the riverfront and even in the lower streets of the town there had been a peculiarly unpleasant mixture of rank water and pestilence, dead mules floating by, and pigs, and unfriendly secesh locals staring at the Union soldiers and muttering threats. What was it Cadwallader had written in his paper?—*"If the angel Gabriel should alight in Cairo the natives would steal his trumpet before he could blow it."* Well, not in a bank.

At ten-fifteen the first of his appointments was due to show up, and indeed a little past ten-thirty Nathaniel Wilson Lyon, who had been a skinny redheaded cavalry colonel in the early years of the war, finally did make his appearance, not all that late for New York. Grant greeted him warmly, noted the absence now of red hair and the presence of considerable fleshy padding, and offered him coffee and a cigar. Lyon sat back in the splendid club chair and just plain grinned like a boy.

"Prosperous times, General!" he exclaimed.

Grant lit first Lyon's cigar, then his own. "Well," he said modestly. "Prosperous enough, I guess."

Lyon made a loud pshawing sound like a wet thumb on a hot stove and waved blue Havana smoke away from his eyes. He had been travelling in Europe the past six months, as Grant might recall, but hadn't he read in the London *Times,* the day before he sailed home, that Grant & Ward now had a rating of fifteen *millions* of dollars?

Pretty close to it, Grant agreed.

And wasn't that about as spectacular and prosperous a rise as Wall Street had *ever* seen? In less than a year? And wasn't it a damned good thing, Lyon said, practically bouncing around in his chair, restless and excitable like all good cavalry soldiers, to see the greatest man in the country truly and properly rewarded at last for his selfless service?

There was a good deal more in this vein, and Grant, who was used to it, sat there and listened and nodded with a fixed, polite smile on his face, but in truth paid very little attention. The presiding genius of Grant & Ward was Ward—everybody in New York City was aware of that. Grant had brought his name and all of his capital to the partnership, but Ward alone had the responsibility for investing the money and Ward alone paid out the monthly dividends, and it was simply wonderful to see how well he did it. The only condition Grant had made was that there be no trading in federal government contracts, no improper use of influence for profit; otherwise, Ward had a free hand, and such was his golden touch, inside a year most of Grant's family had invested *their* savings too, and now dozens and dozens of old army men like Lyon were also depositing sums of money in their former commander's firm and collecting dividends at twenty, twenty-five, even thirty percent per annum. And Lyon was partly right at least—after so many years of failed businesses and backbreaking debt—Grant's mind went back to Galena, to the little hardscrabble cabin he had built by himself in St. Louis—after so many years of that, it was a d——d good thing at last to succeed. He pressed a small electric button on his desk and stood up to refill his visitor's cup of coffee.

The electric bell was for Ward, of course, and not two minutes passed before there was a knock on the door and then the young executive partner poked his head inside. Another two minutes for introductions and pleasantries before Grant got right down to business.

"Colonel Lyon invested fifty thousand dollars with us last summer, Mr. Ward."

"Before you got so sick, General Grant." Ward took the big manila paper envelope Grant handed him and glanced at the notation on the side. "The General," he told Lyon, "had a very rough bout with pneumonia last December."

"The General," Lyon said, basking in reflected glory, "is as tough as they come."

"Can we bring the Colonel up to date on his money?"

Ward studied the envelope again. Slick black hair, clean-shaven. Dressed extremely well in fine blue suits and English cravats—Grant never paid much attention to his own clothes, but he had a sharp eye, he believed, for other people's dress. Sherman said Ward reminded him of Uriah Heep, and since Grant had just finished reading *David Copperfield* aloud to Julia, he caught the allusion all right, but rejected the meaning. He watched Ward snap the envelope under his arm and say he'd be right back.

Lyon wanted to talk politics while he was gone—the perfidy of Blaine, the disgrace of having ex-Confederate generals in Congress, gobbling up federal money like pigs at a trough. Grant was used to this, too, and listened calmly without hearing much, and when Ward walked back in with the envelope still tucked under his arm and a folded check in his hand, he stood up again in pleasurable anticipation.

"We have so many clients," Ward said, holding out the check. "It took me a minute to find your records, Colonel. Here's the original investment plus nine months' dividends."

Lyon, Grant knew, owned a string of three or four hardware and dry-goods stores in southern Ohio; at his level he was a shrewd, experienced businessman, just as he had been a shrewd, hard-to-fool cavalry commander. He put on his reading glasses, then unfolded the check, then looked up at Grant with a whistle. "Ninety-seven thousand dollars!"

"March comes in like a Lyon," Grant said, enjoying the play on words.

"We try to take good care of the General's special friends," Ward said.

Lyon tapped the check against the center of his palm; looked at Ward; looked at Grant. "Well, I'd be a goddam fool to desert my old general now," he said, and the boyish grin came back again, bigger than ever, making him look (this time Grant was glad to think of his own allusion) like Huckleberry Finn in the book *Tom Sawyer,* all he needed was a straw between his teeth and a fishing pole in his hand. "You take this check, Mr. Ward," he said, "and reinvest the whole kit and caboodle, every dime, every solitary dime!"

When they were both gone Grant took a last sip of coffee and walked around the corner of his desk. There, slipped into the edge of the blotter next to the cigars, Ward had also left his personal dividend check for March, which Grant opened and smoothed on the blotter. Three thousand dollars. Paid like clockwork every month, along with numerous bonuses and special distributions. Without counting Julia's investment in the firm, or Buck's or Fred's, he himself was now worth, he calculated, a clear one million, eight hundred thousand dollars.

He replaced the check on the blotter and continued on to the window behind the desk, where he parted the velvet curtain slightly and looked down at the splendid, busy intersection of Broadway and Wall Street.

One reason he and Lincoln had gotten on so well, he thought, was that both of them believed in Fate. Grant, of course, had taken his belief from his mother. Where Lincoln had imbibed it Grant never knew, but more than once the two of them had stood in the mud at City Point, Virginia, in the winter of '64, and talked about the mysterious movements of Fate and Necessity that had chosen them each for his role in the great and bloody national drama. And more than once Lincoln had told him that when the war ended, he, Lincoln, ended too. The single consolation Grant had for Lincoln's death was that he knew that Lincoln would have understood it as the wise and irresistible disposition of Fate; Fate and its higher purposes.

Down on Broadway there was a fine tangle of horsecars and wheels and axles going on now. Some of the drivers had hopped down into the middle of the street and rolled up their sleeves, ready to fight. Irish, he thought, catching the faint hubbub of their voices through the glass. Or Italians. Hard to know at this distance. Italians lived uptown in squalid tenements, ten to a room, shouting, singing, never silent for a minute. The Irish drank.

He walked back to the desk for a new cigar, number four of the day, and looked down at the check again; felt his mood lighten. Whatever else it had in mind, Fate, he thought wryly, striking his match, inhaling deeply, had evidently decided that he, Grant, was going to end his days as a very rich man.

What he and Lincoln had in common, Grant thought, was an infinite capacity for loneliness.

CHAPTER FOUR

"Now," said Henry West, well launched on a mono-
logue, "people claim he just gets drunk on millionaires. Before the
war he needed whiskey. *During* the war he needed whiskey. But
after, when he was in the White House, he apparently stopped
drinking—cold stopped, just like that. Hasn't touched a drop in
years. So the irony is, he was almost brought down as President by
the Whiskey Ring."

Trist shaded his eyes with his hand and came to a halt at the
curb. Not long after he had left Washington for Paris the *Post* had
moved its offices from 331 Pennsylvania Avenue to a new building
at the corner of Tenth and D. Next door Hutchins had constructed a second building to house the National Electric Light
Company, which he partly owned and whose first act apparently
had been to install overpoweringly bright electric streetlamps at
each corner of the intersection. It was seven o'clock at night just
now, but looked like mid-August noon on the planet Edison. A
similar set of lights illuminated the west front of the Capitol, a
faint but lurid glow now over the rooftops behind them. The two
men blinked in the glare, waited for a horsecar to rattle by, then
crossed to Tenth.

"But then again, you weren't here when he was President."
West made it sound vaguely like an accusation.

"No. Leading a life of pleasure in the Old World."

"Well, the Whiskey Ring came at the end of Grant's second
term. Some of the internal-revenue supervisors out west got in
league with the local whiskey distillers and pocketed all the taxes.
The Chief Clerk of the Treasury went to jail, and Grant's little
brother Orvil almost did. They indicted his private secretary, too,
General Babcock, noble veteran like yourself. But Grant wrote a
testimonial letter and the jury let him off."

"I only remember Black Friday."

"My favorite." West nodded approval. They passed a streetwalker stranded like a mermaid in a pool of electric light. "Much
gaudier than the Whiskey Ring. And the poor old Crédit Mobilier
was just a bunch of crooked bookkeepers. Your modern up-to-date
voter has to be a connoisseur of corruption. That's the new
Pension Building over there, ugliest pile of bricks in Washington.
The only thing wrong with it, Phil Sheridan claims, is they made
it fireproof."

Trist laughed, and they crossed the next street. Grant and his
scandals. Out of sheer force of habit he started to dredge up
details. Crédit Mobilier was railroads and bribery. Black Friday
had been the day in September of '69 when Jay Gould and Jim Fisk
tried to corner the gold market in New York. Apparently they'd
thought Grant was simply too dull and slow-witted to stop them,
and afterward most journalists, predisposed to admire the sharp-
witted and the larcenous, had decided they were absolutely right.
Henry Adams had written a savage and much reprinted article
about Grant's incompetence.

"But, you know, Grant"—Trist halted on the sidewalk and
looked up in wonder at the newest product of American technology, the electric billboard, where Edison's great invention was
illuminating a brilliantly colored green-and-yellow jar of *Heinz's
Pickles*—57 *Varieties!* Why in the world would he defend Grant?
"In fact, Grant was innocent every time, wasn't he? It was the people around him who were dishonest. As far as I remember, he
actually outsmarted Fisk and Gould. He went over to the Treasury
and released government gold on the market when they didn't
expect it, and Black Friday turned out to be a fizzle."

"Shouldn't have been consorting—lovely word—with known

millionaires, that's what started all his troubles. Something about being so poor and inept at business before the war, and Papa Grant being so good at it—all those tycoons just licked him up and down like a sucker. Still do. Jim Fisk owned a beautiful sailing yacht back then, and each stateroom had its own canary, and each canary was named after one of Fisk's pals. So there was the canary John D. Rockefeller, the canary J. P. Morgan, the canary Leland Stanford, and also, you will not be amazed to learn, the canary General Grant."

They stopped again while Trist adjusted his collar. He needed one of the new snap buttons for his coat, West had informed him earlier, and another set for his shoes. Latest thing in fashion, invented by a one-armed veteran just like Trist.

"I don't believe," Trist objected, "the canaries."

West shrugged; grinned.

"And I thought about *Democracy* all week and I still don't see Mrs. Adams in it either."

West's shrug came a little more slowly. "Well, that's what everybody says. She's witty. She's got the sharpest tongue in the city—it's a woman's book—feline, all those little asides about fashion and marriage. I know a guy in Henry Holt's, the publisher, swears she wrote it."

Trist opened his mouth to object, couldn't think of a logical objection. *Democracy* was in its twelfth phenomenal printing, sixth translation, an international success; librarians routinely catalogued it under John Hay or Clarence King. It was a brilliant novel, and it belonged to her world for sure. But whatever else she was, bright, sensitive little Clover Adams was not an anonymous person.

"Well, I'll ask her when I see her," he said, and Henry West snorted.

At Gillian's Tavern they went, not to a booth, but straight to the long mahogany bar itself, where Trist ordered only the mildest lager beer, since he was indeed walking on from the tavern to Henry Adams's house for a "quiet *soirée*," as Clover Adams had put it in her note (not anonymous). But the bar was crowded from one end to the other, a phalanx of shoulders and hats and foul-smelling cigars at rakish angles, and they quickly moved back to their accustomed corner in the rear.

For all his casual irreverence, West had a bulldog kind of stubbornness. They drank a few moments in companionable silence, then he leaned forward and poked Trist in the ribs with a finger.

"I spend half my day talking about U. S. Grant," he grumbled, "like back then, and he ain't even running for *nomination* now."

"Most famous man in the world."

"Fact is, you can't decide whether Grant was corrupt or incompetent until you decide how smart you think he is."

"Henry Adams swears he doesn't think at all, he's 'preintellectual.' "

West laughed into his beer and then wiped his dripping moustaches with a sleeve. "You tell me how a man can lead an army of five hundred thousand men and defeat Bobby Lee and *not* think."

Trist shook his head and finished his beer. A hovering waiter started to come forward, but Trist waved him away. It was too early to leave for the Adamses', he thought, too late to have another drink. Henry West was now identifying the drinkers at the bar as either Congressmen or pimps by the slouch of their backs. Newspaper Row was situated in the middle of the Washington district that had been known in the war as Hooker's Division, because General Joe Hooker seemed to have enlisted as many whores as soldiers at his headquarters there. Trist's mind moved in a series of elliptical skips that reminded him of his woozy malarial fever days—whores, pimps, "hookers"—in Paris the most expensive courtesans were known as *grandes horizontales,* in Colorado after the war he had seen a sign in a Chinese brothel: "10¢ Lookee, 25¢ Feelee, 50¢ Doee." Beside him West said something droll and unprintable about Congressmen with hands in their pockets. The canary Nick Trist. First person. His mind began another wild skip of association, which he stopped in midflight, by sheer force of will.

Twenty minutes later he paid his hackney driver and descended awkwardly to the sidewalk in front of 1607 H Street. Then stopped and listened for a moment to the sound of barking dogs coming down from the second-floor windows. He squinted at his watch.

"Goddam kennel in there," said Don Cameron's voice behind him. "What the hell do they call them?"

"Boojum," said Elizabeth Cameron, "Marquis, Possum."

"It's Trist." Cameron leaned forward and stared. The march of electric streetlamps had not yet reached Lafayette Square, so Trist was unable to see clearly how much Elizabeth blushed, or how much his own hand shook as they greeted, nodded, smiled. Inside the house, while he was still awkwardly unfastening his coat, she disappeared at once—"First thing women do," said Cameron, pulling out a cigar, then glowering at it. "They spend two hours getting ready for a party, then they arrive and right away they go upstairs to do their face. Can't smoke here, dammit."

"You look well, Senator."

Cameron's face, in Henry Adams's softly lit hallway, was redder and beefier than ever. He wore his hair long now, curled around his collar Western-style, and when he smiled (grimaced) one incisor was missing. But otherwise he was the same vaguely menacing, highly physical presence he had always been.

"Well, *you* look," Cameron began, but before he could say another word Clover Adams was at his side, rising on her toes, smiling her homely crow's smile, touching each of them by the arm. "Come inside, drink, *boire*"—she pulled them into the parlor where tea had been served to Trist three days before, and in another minute Trist found himself standing next to the fireplace and the portrait of mad Nebuchadnezzar, holding a glass of champagne. In front of him a stooped and gray-bearded man he recognized as the historian Professor Bancroft advanced; took Trist's glass of champagne from him, shook his hand in greeting, gave back the glass. "George Bancroft," he said. "Mrs. Bancroft." A white-haired woman peered around his shoulder like a mouse. "Met you at Beale's three years ago."

"The historian's memory," said his wife proudly. "My dear," she added, clutching Clover's arm as she passed, "you have more beautiful *things* in this house every day. I dislike auctions very much, but I mean to go to yours after you die."

Clover stood for a moment, modest, blushing, uncharacteristically silent—write *Democracy*? That most unblushing, ironic of books? Trist dismissed the idea on the spot. Clover rose on her toes and gestured toward an open door. "Henry's in the dining room," she said, "supervising the food. We eat buffet-style tonight because General Sherman is coming—yes!—but we don't know when, he's on the train from New York."

Both Bancrofts had something to say about trains, New York, unpunctual generals. Trist listened politely, glanced as often as he could around the room. It was a party of thirty people at least, few of whom he recognized. Young Emily Beale, looking unwell still, sat in a chair while her father stood with one hand protectively on her shoulder. Don Cameron glowered in his best party manner at a small, highly moustached man with bright eyes and a German accent, identified later as the more or less famous civil service reformer Carl Schurz. Others appeared to be senators, neighbors, a few members of the German diplomatic legation. In the British fashion the Adamses made no effort to introduce anyone.

"Who is that couple?" Trist boldly asked Clover Adams as she came up to him again. She frowned and touched his arm. "Mr. and Mrs. Schuyler," she murmured. In the dining room, just visible from where they stood, Henry Adams's bald white pate bobbed like a cork between two taller, stouter guests. "Mr. Schuyler works in the State Department library," Clover said. "He helps Henry sometimes with research. Very dull man. His wife is even worse. *Never* gossips. For social purposes I prefer—don't you, Mr. Trist?—the vicious and the frivolous."

Trist laughed out loud, turned to place his empty glass on a tray, and found himself in mid-laugh face-to-face at last with Elizabeth Cameron.

"Well, you two," said Clover beside him, "old pards." She gave one more bounce, a pat on Trist's arm, and headed toward the unvicious Schuylers.

"Mr. Trist," said Elizabeth Cameron, "again."

Whatever he had rehearsed or imagined or thought of beforehand to say, whatever he had remembered of her black hair, the curve of her throat, or the curl of her lip—all of it flew out of his head in an instant. He felt the flush steal across his face, burning. Just as he knew she would, Elizabeth Cameron burst in his mind like a star.

"The proverbial bad penny," he replied in a voice unsurprisingly thick. "I just keep turning up."

"Mrs. Adams," Elizabeth said, looking toward Clover now on the other side of the room—abruptly she changed her mind about the sentence. "I was just back there in the study with Mr. Adams. He was showing me some old manuscripts. He's hard at work on his *History*, he says."

"Well, he was hard at work on it when I was here three years ago."

"Was it so long, Mr. Trist?"

"Two and a half years since Chicago."

"Chicago," she murmured, and reached down to the tray for a glass of champagne. "How silly of you to stay away so long."

It was foolish to say, as people did, that looks never mattered. There were beautiful women who locked their hips and rounded their shoulders forward, as if they were determined to hate themselves, and Trist had known some of these in Paris. There were women, especially in America, who were nervous, warm, quick to smile, quick to touch, who nonetheless carried their bodies as if they were fortresses, to be stormed and defended. And there were beautiful women, sometimes, who came bearing themselves like a gift, a Renaissance Quattrocento painting, like light made flesh.

He had the illusion of seeing her at a distance, through a window from the street. He must have asked her how life in Washington was, though he couldn't remember doing it, because she was suddenly telling him at pleasant, too-great length about an addition they had made to their home in Lafayette Square, how Maudie hated her school, how all the Senator's grown-up children disliked her. And she must have asked him in turn about his travels, because, while Henry Adams's white face passed back and forth three times in the mirror, he heard himself describing the battlefields book and then the move from Paris to London, where society was duller but business was better.

"So restless," she said. "Even in Europe, American men are always so restless."

In the dining room Henry Adams was now bowing to them both, crooking a finger at Elizabeth.

She hesitated, lifting her chin, pursing her mouth in a gesture Trist could have sketched from memory. "Mine host."

"I didn't think," Trist said, not believing that he was actually going to say it, "that I would ever see you again, after Chicago."

She leaned forward, so close that Trist could see the swell of her breasts under the soft blue silk of her dress, the faint black hairs on her neck.

"There is always more order to life than we think, Mr. Trist," she murmured, turning away, but her hand on his arm as she turned was like a spark to his skin.

General Sherman was late, hungry, stupendously dramatic. He came through the front door and into the cluttered Adams house like a redheaded bombshell, one hour and thirty goddam minutes late, as he announced, spreading his arms, cursing the trains, dropping a muddy cloak from his shoulders to the carpet as every face in the house turned toward him.

"Jupiter Pluvius reigns!" he cried, and shook his hands to show how wet they were. As if on cue, lightning cracked, a thunderclap rolled over the roof, and ladies (and Mr. Schuyler) shrieked, and then for the next two tumultuous hours Sherman transformed the house into a theater of personality. If Mars himself had blazed into the fragile porcelain world of the Adamses the effect could have hardly been less shattering. Sherman gathered a drink in each hand, marched from lady to lady introducing himself with a bow and a leer, paused to wrap both arms (not spilling a drop) around his niece in greeting, winked over her shoulder first at Trist, then at Henry Adams, who literally recoiled three steps toward his books. In the second parlor, while one of the ladies played muted but martial chords on a piano, he recited passages from Dickens, Shakespeare. Studying Trist's empty sleeve, he launched into a series of war stories, each one wilder and funnier than the last. The week before they took Vicksburg, he told General Beale, who stood beaming with an arm around his daughter Emily, the engineers were experimenting with tunnels and explosives. One day they blew up a Rebel hill—no damage, except a nigger cook who was standing nearby was thrown ninety feet in the air like a flying black duck, still holding his spoon, and landed on his feet unhurt on the Union side, where he was promptly hired as a cook by Grant.

"Where did you lose it?" Sherman aimed a ferocious eye at Trist's arm.

"Cold Harbor."

"Bugger the Rebs," Sherman said, and refilled Trist's glass. "When I was in Georgia somebody wrote me a seriously crazy letter—could have been Mark Twain, craziest man I know—said, 'General, why not fill all your shells and bullets with *snuff*? When they explode, the Confederates will be *sneezing* so hard your people can just walk up and take 'em!' Somebody else said, The war could be over in a week, just make all the Union bayonets one foot longer than the Confederate ones, they'll never be able to touch you."

"Show us, General," said Clover Adams, who seemed, unlike

her husband, charmed and enthralled by so much martial energy, "how you marched through Georgia."

Sherman grinned. The Adams servants had set up two long tables of food in the dining room, and another smaller table nearby. From one of the long tables Sherman gathered spoons, knives, a handful of tiny salt and pepper shakers. "Rebels," he said, lining the pepper shakers up around a soup bowl. "Atlanta. Us. Joe Hood's troops." In loud, snapping commands, as if the little spoons and shakers would jump to life and start to march, he maneuvered them left, right, around the defenseless, bewildered bowl. Somebody handed him a candle. Sherman swung it fluttering above Atlanta, leaving a trail of smoke in the air. Clover pushed a teacup forward to represent McPherson. Sherman showed his yellow teeth in a wolf's smile.

"You remember what Jeff Davis said when we started?"

Clover shook her head. To Trist's surprise it was Henry Adams's patrician drawl that answered. "He said you would meet the same fate as Napoleon when he invaded Russia."

"And Grant," said Sherman, cackling, "said, 'Who's going to furnish all that Moscow snow in Georgia?'" He drove his little army forward, calling out names of battles, set the bowl rocking, said, "Aaaah! Jonesboro!" and suddenly *swept* the Rebel shakers off the tablecloth with a pudding knife and a clatter—"next stop, *Charleston!*"

"Oh, dessert first," murmured Henry Adams.

On the porch afterwards, as the guests put on their raincoats and tested umbrellas, Sherman lit a cigar in defiance of Jupiter Pluvius.

"Mr. Trist," said Clover against the steady tattoo of raindrops on the porch roof. As if by signal they all moved closer to the rail and peered over into the darkness at the Hay-Adams empty lot, presumably now a field of mud. At the other end of Lafayette Square, in the civilized and uneasy glow of its gas streetlamps, the White House looked like a watery canvas backdrop. "Mr. Trist," Clover repeated, "is writing a new travel book about the battlefields of the war, the ones you can visit now as a tourist, a kind of Baedeker-history. He starts out tomorrow for Manassas."

"Well, I read your book on Egypt," Sherman said, "brilliant. Better than John Russell Young."

"You should go with him, General, bring your knives and forks."

The cigar was a cheerful burning dot in the wet darkness. "Can't. Going back to New York tomorrow night, dinner with Grant and Ham Fish, his old Secretary of State." Trist felt his arm gripped by fingers like iron. "But take the ladies with you, Trist, why not? Make an excursion out of it—Mrs. Adams here knows all about the war." A carriage clattered up H Street and its swinging lantern caught first Sherman's fierce red hair and beard, and then Elizabeth Cameron standing next to her uncle. Sherman wrapped a long arm around her shoulder and almost pushed her forward into Trist. "And Lizzie—you should have seen Lizzie when she was a girl, out in Wyoming, Trooper Lizzie Sherman that was—take Lizzie too!"

CHAPTER FIVE

THE BATTLE OF THE WILDERNESS BEGAN IN THE EARLY spring of 1864, shortly after Lincoln summoned Grant to the east, intending, as the whole country knew, to present him, first, with a third star for his shoulders, lieutenant general, a rank unprecedented since George Washington and Winfield Scott; and, second, with supreme command of all the scattered Union armies, east and west, five hundred thousand men.

Grant's modesty, of course, was already legend by then, and his trip to Washington did nothing to diminish it. When he travelled up from Tennessee for the official ceremony of his promotion, the general-in-chief-elect simply took a cab from the train to Willard's Hotel, entered unannounced through a side door, and strolled up to the desk with no other escort than his twelve-year-old son Fred.

"Help you?" the clerk said, picking his teeth with a pencil stub. Grant had on a tattered blue private's coat with two stars, badly faded, sewn on one stooped shoulder only; a black felt hat with a scruffy gold braid; down-at-the-heel muddy boots. Two-star generals were a dime a dozen in Washington, of course. The clerk at Willard's could have thrown his pencil into the bar and hit one, any hour of the day.

"We'd like a room," Grant said, "for the two of us."

The clerk yawned. "Hotel's full. Nothing left but a little up-stairs loft, one bed, no window. And you'll have to wait till four for that."

"Then that's what I'll have to do," Grant replied. The clerk shoved the registration book across the desk, and Grant picked up a pen and wrote his name in his usual scrawl: *U. S. Grant & Son, Galena, Illinois.*

He pushed the book back across the desk, and the clerk turned it around to read. Without the slightest change of expression, he said, "You'll have the Presidential Suite, General Grant. We'll take you up right now."

When Simon Cameron came by that night to escort him to the White House, Grant objected that he didn't have an invitation, and Cameron had to assure him that it was just the Lincolns' weekly reception and anybody at all could attend. They walked together from Willard's and went inside to the Blue Room. Cameron said he thought Grant could go straight over to the President, Grant said, "No," that was all, and took his place in the reception line to wait his turn. But Secretary of State Seward saw him first and started shouting, "Here is General Grant! Grant is here!" And instantly there was such a rush of people from every corner just to look at him and shake his hand that wily old Seward made him climb up on top of a sofa, and stand there, so people could have a better view. By the time he finally was rescued by Lincoln, he was sweating profusely and looking as unhappy as a cornered cat, and his very first words to the President were, "For God's sake, get me out of this show business!"

Not long after that, he vanished from Washington into the bivouac headquarters of the Army of the Potomac. Then he quite literally vanished into the forty-square-mile barrier of gloomy scrub oak and pine and undergrowth and trackless vegetative anarchy that lay between Richmond and Washington and that, in fact, was called simply "The Wilderness" by locals. On the other side of it, swinging toward him like a fist, was Bobby Lee's army.

The Battle of the Wilderness took place from May 5 to May 7, 1864. It was a victory of a kind for Lee—though he lost at least 7,000 men—because Grant's losses for the same two days were somewhere in excess of 17,500 men, and after both sides had pulled back slightly to catch their breaths Grant was still bogged down in the smoking, splintered nightmare forest, exactly where

McClellan and Burnside and Joe Hooker had been stopped in years before. North and South, in the field and in Washington as well, everybody who could read or hear expected Grant to turn tail just like the others—just like Joe Hooker one year ago to the day— and skulk back to Washington in defeat.

But for several months, ever since Grant had taken command, the Army of the Potomac had been feeling a change in its nature. Discipline was tighter. Organization was clearer. After three long years of inept and horrible leadership, men said, business was beginning to be meant.

About midnight May 12 the Union soldiers in General Warren's V Corps were trudging along in unspeakable weariness on a crowded, smoky road, part charred forest, under a pale, drooping moon. Suddenly their officers began to clatter their scabbards and shout: "Give way to the right, move to the right!" And then going past them at a quick, jingling trot came a few staff officers bending forward in their saddles to keep up with the big black horse in the lead, and on it, recognizable everywhere by the stars on his old blue coat and his eternal cigar, rode Grant, and, almost at the same moment they saw Grant, the troops likewise saw that he was going, not north in retreat, but *south,* at the head of the column, to fight again. For once the Army of the Potomac broke into spontaneous cheer, so loud and long that Grant's big horse reared and pranced and the little stoop-shouldered rider had to wrestle it around and down, and then he quickly issued orders that there was to be no noise in case the Rebels heard, and he put his spurs to work again and disappeared.

That much Trist remembered well, because he had only just been transferred to Warren's V Corps two weeks before, and as he stood on a pleasant windswept knoll a little south of Chancellorsville twenty years later he could almost point out the very spot to Clover Adams and the rest of her assembled party.

He hadn't intended at all for the day to turn into a lecture tour. Clover, Elizabeth Cameron, the Beales, two or three couples whose names he never quite got had gone the afternoon before to the Shenandoah Valley to see the Luray Caverns ("lighted, Mr. Trist, with electric lamps," Clover said happily, the truest apostle of technology among them). From there they had taken the train to Fredericksburg, hired a team of carriages, and despite a lowering sky and a feel of cold, hard weather in the air, had come on to meet him at Little Brock Hill. To the right, halfway down the slope, his photographer was still struggling with a cartload of equipment, helped and hindered in about equal measure by the two Negro boys from town he had hired as assistants.

"And from there," Clover said, "you pushed down this other road to the Bloody Angle."

"Spotsylvania Court House," Trist agreed. "May ninth to May twelfth." For the excursion today Clover had come equipped with a set of enormous old leather military binoculars that had belonged, she said, to her father, and these she now used to scan the thick forest below. Some fifty or sixty yards away, where the ruined shell of the Little Brock Hill farmhouse served as a kind of tourist battlefield headquarters, General Beale and his wife had set up folding chairs for themselves and Emily. Other guests wandered among the rusting cannons and caissons and assorted old wagon frames and wheels and shell casings local residents had halfheartedly gathered together. Nobody else had been curious enough to climb up to the exposed summit of the knoll, except Elizabeth Cameron, who now stood next to Clover, holding her bonnet down with one hand and her skirt with the other, carefully avoiding, Trist thought, his eyes.

"Well, it was Grant's 'war of attrition,' " Clover said. She nodded decisively, so that her own black bonnet flapped like a pair of crow's wings in the wind. "Butcher Grant, wearing down the South by sheer force of numbers. Appalling way to wage a war."

Trist started to object, then simply nodded. He led her a few steps farther around the path and indicated a line of swaying willows off in the distance that marked where Warren's troops had ended up next morning, after Grant had turned them south. It was a generally accepted fact that in the Wilderness campaign Grant had indeed proceeded with all the finesse of a muscle-bound giant, straight ahead, mulishly, against the foxlike intelligence of Lee, and that his only strategy had been to overpower Lee by superior resources, not by generalship. It was amazing, Trist thought, how much they had talked in those days about the mystery of Grant, how he ate a breakfast of cucumbers and bread, how he had his staff aide present him every morning with twenty-four fresh cigars, how he used a flint-and-steel lighter with a long wick to light those cigars in the wind—no detail was too trivial, too uninteresting about the man who was leading them, as the newspapers invariably put it, into the Shadow of Death. And of course everybody from the newspapers right up to Lincoln and Clover Adams had got it wrong—Grant never meant to wear Lee down by attrition. His whole strategy was to bring Lee out from behind his defenses into the open to fight, and Lee's whole strategy was to dodge and deny, but Grant had prevented that by the most brilliant series of flanking movements in modern history, and Lee was forced to engage and the two giants fell locked together through the long spring and summer of '64, crashing and rolling southward toward Richmond. Whatever else you wanted to say about him, thirteen months after Grant was put in charge the war was over.

"You tell a vivid story, Mr. Trist," said Elizabeth Cameron, standing quite close beside him now. Down the side of the hill the others were beginning to pack up their parasols and chairs and look around for the carriages. "But it's not very personal, is it? Not much about you."

"Editor friend of mine said the same thing."

"You left Yale College to enlist, I think." Clover lowered her binoculars and frowned at the sky. "Rain."

"And did you ever see General Grant again," Elizabeth asked, "in the war?" Clover put away her giant binoculars and turned to leave. Trist buttoned the collar of his coat.

"I saw your uncle and Grant once, outside a tent. And a few days after Spotsylvania Court House we were marching past a railroad siding and Grant was sitting by himself on a flatcar, gnawing a piece of ham bone. The company ahead of us gave a cheer and he just waved the bone and kept right on eating."

Elizabeth laughed and then looked around, startled, as a flash of lightning cut across the northern horizon. A moment later thunder rolled and grumbled over them.

"God's artillery, Mr. Trist!" Clover called gaily from far down the path. At the bottom of the hill the hired carriages were already lined up and people were hurriedly climbing in. Lightning crackled again. The photographer hauled his cart around a bend in the road and vanished.

"My dress," said Elizabeth, and she bent to pull the bottom half of her skirt free from a low patch of briars. Trist knelt on the edge of the path beside her. The skirt was a heavy cotton fabric, thoroughly tangled. He tugged gently, working the briars free one by one, but before he could get to his feet again the first rain had reached the knoll and the wind was blowing it into their faces in a blinding veil.

"This way!" Elizabeth bunched her skirt in her fists and started to the left. Trist glanced the other way, saw the last of the carriages backing, turning. A clap of thunder broke directly over their heads: the whole hilltop seemed to whirl and dip and the full roaring force of the storm came up.

The red clay paths that crisscrossed the knoll turned instantly to mud. Elizabeth slipped and cried out. Trist caught her hand. She staggered ahead, bearing left and downhill. Overhead the sky was literally, everywhere, black. In front of them the forest, colors running like a soaked painting, offered the only possible shelter— they cut directly down across the grass, through another patch of briars and tall weeds, and two minutes later, panting and shaking, stumbled into a grove of windswept oaks.

"Not much here!" Elizabeth's voice could barely be heard over the lash of the rain. Her hair was flattened onto her cheeks and neck, her heavy dress sagged and clung. Trist stepped from under their tree to look for the carriages, but all he could see was a blur of rain and wind, not a carriage or a horse in sight. He splashed back to the oak and wiped his face. "This way," Elizabeth said.

At the bottom of yet another little hill they came to a wide, swollen creek, thirty feet across at least and spilling rapidly out beyond its banks.

"Did you bring a canoe, Mr. Trist?"

"In my other coat."

"The road's probably just past those trees. But I think every-body's gone by now. They won't even miss us till they reach the sta-tion." She made a face and shook her hands out as if to dry them, then drew them back and shivered.

"I see a barn over there," Trist said.

THE BARN SAT AT THE NARROW END OF AN OVERGROWN LANE, between two bending stands of dark pine. It had evidently been abandoned years ago, but used occasionally since by tramps or hunters, because a faint trail could be discerned across the weeds to the door and an old patchwork blanket hung nailed to one of the windows. Trist ran skidding and sliding through the rain, yanked the latch open for Elizabeth, then ducked inside himself.

There was one large open space, fitfully illuminated by gaps between planks; two or three animal stalls in a corner; a loft, a ladder, a wooden roof with splits and cracks everywhere that let in dozens of steady, rattling trickles of rain.

Elizabeth stopped three feet inside the door and looked at the leaking roof; then turned back to stare at the black sky and the wind-whipped trees on the other side of the lane.

"It looks," she said with another shiver, "as if it's going to rain all week."

Trist poked among the harnesses and boxes on the far wall.

"If we'd been in Washington," she said, beginning to wring out one sleeve of her jacket, "Clover Adams would have known the storm was coming to the very minute. She gets the Weather Service forecast delivered to her house every morning."

"There's an old blanket over here," Trist said doubtfully.

Elizabeth peered at the saddle blanket he held up for her inspection; shook her head. He watched her in silhouette against the murky light of the open door.

"Or I suppose *you* should have known about the weather, Mr. Trist, the canny old soldier." She slipped the jacket completely off and squeezed more water onto the floor. "And of course you ought to have known these woods too, so we didn't get lost like Hansel and Gretel in a monsoon."

He laughed and took off his own coat, then gave it to her. "This may be a little drier, Miss Gretel."

"You *did* fight here?"

He walked over to the door and squinted at the blustery landscape. Pines, scrub oaks, snarled undergrowth. Long gray clumps of Spanish moss were strung out flat in the wind like flags or old men's beards. A low, rumbling sky poured rain down in a constant blistering hiss. He had in fact marched and fought and ate and slept for nearly three weeks all over these woods, but trees and brush had grown up in different patterns now, and that was twenty years ago, almost exactly.

"I wish *I* could have fought," Elizabeth Cameron said. She wrapped his coat loosely around her shoulders and came to stand beside him. "I've always heard there were women who joined the army and passed for men and actually fought in the ranks. I would've done it in a flash."

Trist ran his hand through his wet hair and looked down at the wet cloth clinging to her hips and breasts and thought that in fact Elizabeth Cameron could never in her life have passed for a man; thought also that that was probably not a thing to say just now. After a moment she turned and walked back into the shadows of the barn.

"It's three-thirty by my watch," she said two minutes later.

He heard the sound of boards being moved, a clatter of old pots or harnesses. He stretched his arm and flexed his fingers and noted that his own shirt was soaked through and clinging to his skin. When he reached her, back in the driest corner under the loft, she had shaken out two musty blankets, cleaner than the one he'd found, and set up a rusty kerosene lantern on a sawhorse.

"Like Robinson Crusoe in his cave," she said, holding the

lantern so he could hear the gurgle of kerosene in the base. "There's a flint-and-steel too."

"Puts the Palmer House to shame. *Bien trouvé.*" He knelt and pinched the oily lantern wick another inch higher, then placed the flint under the heel of his shoe to hold it fast. Dry straw made a miniature faggot. He scraped the steel five or six times as hard as he could against the flint: a shower of sparks jumped into the straw. Then he bent and blew them into a tiny flame, and this he held to the wick of the lantern, where it caught and flared.

"You do everything with just one hand." Elizabeth sat down heavily on the straw facing him. "And you never talk about it or complain. You never even ask for help. I could have held the flint for you."

He was silent, listening to the rain.

"You've cut your wrist." She reached forward and held up his hand, so that both of them could see the thin red gash bleeding raggedly into his muddy cuff. She gripped his wrist with her left hand and began to wipe the blood away with a damp corner of her blouse. He shifted to brace the hand on the sawhorse and felt the small circular motion of her chest against his shoulder. His pulse began to thump. Slowly he became aware of the stiffened tip of her breast, and almost at the same moment she stopped and sat back.

"Not exactly a case for the ambulance," she murmured.

"But it's my writing hand."

She laughed and rested her chin on her knees. After a moment she said, "Is this where . . . it happened?"

"No." He looked down and opened and closed his fist. "Cold Harbor was just about three weeks after the Wilderness. June third, and fifty miles south of here, almost to Richmond."

She sat quietly in the darkness. Half her face was lit by the flickering lantern, a soft, radiant oval of white against a backdrop of restless shadows. The first time he had ever seen her, he thought, the day he had clownishly blundered into her dressing room, she had also been soft, radiant, sheathed in light. Her skirt rustled as she moved her legs. He leaned farther back until his head touched the wood.

"After the war," he said, "I used to make a little mental list of 'accomplished amputees,' as I called it. My hero was Major John

Wesley Powell. He went down the Colorado River in a rowboat and mapped the Grand Canyon. And there was O. O. Howard, who lost an arm at Seven Pines but still commanded the Army of the Tennessee at Atlanta, under your uncle. And Ulric Dahlgren, minus one leg, a brilliant cavalry officer. The best of all was a Confederate enlisted man, I never learned his name, lost *both* arms in the Wilderness. When he went home to North Carolina, he had no money, no hope, no future. He told his wife to hitch the plow harness around his shoulders and guide him, and up and down the fields he walked, plowing ground. I was twenty-two years old. An arm or a leg here or there, I told myself, it wasn't a brain, it wasn't a heart."

He got to his feet and walked to the open door. The rain was falling, if anything, faster than before. He stepped into it and stood for a moment with his face to the sky, feeling the wind and water, then he wiped his mouth with his sleeve and came back in.

Elizabeth was still sitting in the same position. He eased his back against the wall again. "Oddly enough," he said, "if I hadn't been an officer I might not have lost it. The surgeons always treated the officers first, then the enlisted men. But the field hospitals were so bloody and dirty, often the privates who were just left alone out in the ambulance wagons did better."

Thunder rumbled far off in the distance, but still strong enough to make the barn roof shake, and a three-second gust of wind sent a new cascade of water pouring down past the door. Her hair was wet and long and the scent of it reached him even in the darkness. He felt his blood pound in his veins like a drum. He felt rather than saw Elizabeth stretch out a tentative hand and touch the cuff of the empty sleeve that hung from his left shoulder. "In Chicago," she said, "I was afraid you would think I didn't come to the park because of this."

"No."

She touched his shoulder, then the flat plane of his chest. Her fingers found a button, skin. The wick of the lantern flared in a sudden draft, and light seemed to blow hard against the glass, the walls. Her face drifted behind a veil of shadows. He saw the curved outlines of her cheek, throat, white on black. He bent forward and kissed her lips. He murmured in French, English; cursed in French the acreage of clothes a fashionable lady wore. "Hold this," she giggled, "and *this*." The wet cloth fell away from her breasts in a sweet whisper. When he kissed her nipples the wind groaned. When he touched her waist the wind said his name, and then light and shadow arched their backs and turned together. His hand touched her thigh and parted a sea of petticoats, stroking gently upward till he reached bare flesh, and he thought as she held out her arms and drew him in that poor befuddled Actaeon himself never went to his doom with such a cry of pleasure.

AFTERWARDS THEY SAT SIDE BY SIDE WITH THE BLANKET around their shoulders and watched the chill rain as it pelted the grass and weeds outside.

"Now a better planner, of course," Trist said, pulling her closer, "a *French* lover would have had a bottle of wine and a basket of food stashed away in the straw."

She shook her head and smiled. "No wine, thank you very much, monsieur." She used one finger to trace the outline of his jaw. At the door of the barn a brown-and-white rabbit hopped into the light and stood on its back legs. "I see enough," she said in a faintly weary tone, "of bottles of wine and liquor."

"Senator Don."

"Senator Don," she agreed softly. "The Pennsylvanian sponge." She let her finger drift down his jaw to the underside of his chin; scratched a bristle of beard where the razor had missed. "I have never," she said, "understood men." She shifted under the blanket and brought her little gold watch out to see. Trist read it over her shoulder. Half past four. The rain was lighter now. The wind had almost stopped. "I don't suppose," Elizabeth said as she stood up, "that Clover Adams or Emily Beale has told you the scandalous story that I was once engaged to somebody else, secretly, before the ever-thirsty Senator."

Trist watched her reach behind her back to do something complex and sibylline with hooks and clasps. "Not a word."

"His name was Joe Russell, and I was seventeen and he was twenty, and I was about as desperately in love as a girl could be, and we plighted our troth in a rather sweet and innocent Ohio way, and then my mother and father went—what would be the French expression for stark-staring-out-of-their-heads with puritan horror?"

"You would have to use English."

"Yes. They said Joe Russell *drank* and he wouldn't be a suitable husband, and besides—and here we came to the point—he was as poor as a church mouse and likely to stay that way."

"Whereas the Senator—"

"My uncle John Sherman already had his eye on the Senator. He was a widower. He had older children, but the famous Maudie was still just a baby. He had an enormous fortune. The family *controls* Pennsylvania politics and Uncle John had thought of that too—they laid down the law to me in Ohio and then shipped me off to Washington for a season of dancing and twirling in front of the gentleman's eyes—I felt like a slave girl at a genteel auction, or a sacrificial lamb—and before very long we were engaged and married and the lamb was in the Senator's private railroad car on our first night of wedded bliss, and of course he staggered in drunk and heavy and—" She turned swiftly and kissed him, full on the lips. "He was not a French lover," she said.

"I'm sorry."

"I cried all day before the wedding, and my mother came in and slapped my face. The only one ever on my side was Uncle Cump. I remember at a reception in Washington—it was at General Beale's house, Decatur House—and I was standing with a group of blighted Camerons and Uncle Cump came striding through the door in his full-dress general's uniform, looking as angry as Mars, and he walked right up to me without speaking to anybody else at all, and he glowered left and right at all the Camerons and said in a voice you could hear across the street, 'Permit me to say, my dear, that I wholly *disapprove!*' Then he spun on his heel and marched out again."

At the door of the barn they stopped and she held out her palm to test the rain. "When we get to the Fredericksburg station," she said briskly, "tell them we stayed in a farmer's house with his wife and family."

CHAPTER SEVEN

THE RABBIT IN THE BARN PUT TRIST IN MIND OF AN EPISODE
the autumn before the Wilderness—he couldn't remember the
date or the place exactly, somewhere in late '63 along the Maryland
border, a pitched battle for a field and a hill. There were five or six
infantry regiments on each side, two or three of them with heavy
artillery attached, and the noise of the cannons and muskets was,
as always, terrifying, apocalyptic. The ground and trees shook, and
at eye level the air itself seemed to burst into flames, catch fire,
and turn into smoke—and then, suddenly, unbelievably, out of the
burrows hidden beneath the trampled grass and along the road-
side, hundreds and hundreds of tiny rabbits came running and
hopping across the battlefield, crazed with fright. And more amazing still, they ran for protection, not to the woods or the road, but
directly toward the soldiers. Trist and his men were lying down on
the hump of a cleared ridge, firing at dug-in Rebels seventy yards
away, and the rabbits simply swarmed all over them and huddled
under their legs and arms, nestled trembling in their coat flaps,
pockets, against their belts and under their chins. For five or ten
minutes at least the troops on both sides held their fire and
watched, or stroked the rabbits' ears and bellies, and comforted

them. Finally some idiot in one regiment or another began to fire again, and everything reexploded back to normal.

First person.

Trist put down his pen and read his paragraph over; then folded it once with his elbow and placed it in his thick manuscript notebook. When the knock on the door sounded, he had already drawn out another sheet of paper and picked up his pen, and Elizabeth Cameron, closing the door quickly behind her, leaned her back against it, cocked her head in her new spring bonnet, and smiled.

"A writer not tearing his hair and gnashing his teeth," she teased. "Stop the presses."

She pulled off the floppy bonnet with an easy, practiced motion and tossed it to the floor as she crossed the room, and together they swayed, spun, fell laughing onto the bed. She was, in Washington, in the more or less civilized setting of his rented room, with real mattress, pillows, clean sheets, even more uninhibited a lover than before. She pushed him aside and sat up, then unfastened catches front and rear, twisted, wriggled her dress from her shoulders and rolled under the covers. When she sat astride him and lowered her breast to his mouth she murmured "Sweet, sweet" and then "yes" and at the last moment, shuddering, "Love, love, *love*."

"A noisy girl," she said later, holding the sheets demurely to her chin.

Trist poured tea from the little pot he kept on a kerosene burner (strictly illegal) and carried her cup back to bed.

"It's your Sherman side. The wild woman of Wyoming."

"Say that three times," she said and kissed him. While he was back at the burner pouring a second cup for himself, she added, "My Uncle Cump is notorious that way, you know."

"I drink more tea in Washington," Trist told her, "than I ever do in London."

"Uncle Cump has dozens of women, in towns all over the country. They write him notes at his hotel after he gives a speech, and they pursue him like demon lovers—one of them's a sculptress right here in Washington—that's where he went after Mrs. Adams's dinner—and I think the old-time generals actually trade the ladies around among themselves, even with the Confederates.

After all, they all went to West Point together, a thousand years ago."

"Your Uncle Cump is married," Trist said as he sat down on the edge of the bed.

"Ah."

"And about as inconspicuous as a comet."

"Ah again." She let the sheet drop a few inches, leaned forward. Her fingers traced a slow line from his naked stomach to the top of his thigh; lower. "We are not alone, Mr. Trist," she whispered.

At ten minutes to five she looked at her watch, gave a little yelp, and hurried out of the bed. "Dinner at Mrs. Adams's house," she said, gathering dress, bonnet, shoes, white silk items he couldn't quite, from the bed, classify or describe. "A command appearance, because their famous Boston architect is here this week and Clover means to have him show the plans and a wooden model *and,* if the weather holds take us over the site. 'My modest mausoleum,' she calls it. So there'll be Clover, Henry, the Beales, the Bancrofts, two or three of their tame Senators."

"You will charm them with your hat." Trist stretched his arm and placed the bonnet upside down on her hair. She tugged the laces together under her chin, stared at him, then made a face and crossed her eyes.

At the door she stood in front of the mirror and smoothed her skirt.

Trist touched her cheek gently. "In Chicago," he said, "you were so fearful."

She looked down at her shoes, up at the mirror. "That was three years ago," she said in the brisk voice he had heard before. She smoothed her skirt again. "And I'm still fearful."

"We're very careful."

She studied her mouth in the mirror; rubbed a spot on her cheek. "When he has enough whiskey in him, my husband is a very jealous man. He hates it when I have lunch with any of the Sherman men. Or tea with Henry Adams."

"And me?"

She stood back from the mirror and tied the laces of her bonnet in a quick, decisive bow. "I don't think he sees you," she replied, "actually. You're not wealthy, you don't have a house or a carriage or belong to a club or own a state, you don't write books he would ever read."

"We live in different worlds," Trist said, and hated the stiffness in his own voice, but Elizabeth seemed scarcely to hear.

"Yes," she said, and opened the door. "Yes."

CHAPTER EIGHT

E LIZABETH CAMERON WAS NEVER, EVER GOING TO CHANGE.
This was Emily Beale's view, and Emily Beale was twenty-one years old—almost twenty-two—and experienced in the ways of the world.

She watched Mr. Trist balance his teacup and saucer with his sad one hand and listen, nodding, to Clover Adams's description of the recent "Architectural Visitation" and all its delays and outrages. On the other side of the Adamses' parlor Henry and Elizabeth sat chatting cozily side by side on the sofa; but Elizabeth's eye kept straying to Trist, from time to time Elizabeth turned or twisted her shoulders on the sofa almost as if to show her torso and present herself.

In Paris two years earlier, Emily knew, Elizabeth had gotten herself into a peck of trouble. It was one thing to be madly flirtatious in Washington, where the men lived just for politics. But in Paris, while Senator Don was travelling around Europe on government business, Elizabeth had beguiled a Russian prince-in-exile named Orloff, who invited her one day to a *rendezvous* in a private room in the rue Royale, and when Elizabeth had refused to grant what Emily's mother always called "the last favor," Orloff had flung her into the corridor half naked, and it had taken the embassy itself to hush up the scandal, from the French *and* Senator Don. Elizabeth needed men, Emily thought, as Elizabeth gazed an instant too long at Mr. Trist, the way a cat needed birds. But Elizabeth needed safety and social position—and money— even more, and that was something *else* that wouldn't change.

"Emily, dear, come back to earth." Clover Adams put her cup on the table and beckoned Emily to follow her into the "studio." With a last glance at Henry and Elizabeth, curled up now on the sofa like a pair of gossiping sisters, he carefully braced his one hand on the chair arm and stood. Poor, Emily thought, Mr. Trist.

The "studio" was, in fact, only a kind of glorified storage room for Clover's chemicals and cameras—the new house, whose foundations they could see through the window, bright and cheerful in the April sunshine, would have a special room designed just for photography. Some of her less elaborate equipment, Clover explained to the two of them, she kept upstairs in her bedroom, the rest down here. She pulled out albums and folders from a set of overcrowded shelves as fast as her hands could fly. There was a notebook in which she wrote, in a large and loopy hard-to-read script, the particulars for each photograph she had taken since 1882: date, subject, exposure, light conditions, chemicals mixed for development. She riffled its pages and thrust it back. There was another notebook of short "aesthetic" observations—the nature of shadows, the difficulty with indoor photography—and there were, of course, wrapped individually in clean white tissue paper, like big white teeth, Clover said, the photographs themselves.

The first that she handed to Trist was of her parents-in-law in Massachusetts, the redoubtable Charles Francis and Abigail Adams, staring at the camera (or photographer, Trist thought) with ill-concealed dislike.

"This is *my* father," she said, and unwrapped a portrait of an elderly man in a derby hat and handsomely tailored country coat and trousers, sitting on a carriage behind a horse.

"A doctor," Emily Beale remarked, in the wary voice, Trist thought, of one much acquainted with doctors.

"An ophthalmologist, in fact." Clover took back the photograph and studied it a moment before rewrapping. "He was a volunteer surgeon at Gettysburg. He wrote me wonderful letters about the troops when he was caring for them—I was still at

Professor Agassiz's school for girls in Cambridge—but that was the first time he had actually practiced medicine since my mother's death. He went out of sheer duty and humanity. She died of tuberculosis, you know; I was only five. Then *her* mother died not long after that, and my Aunt Sturgis before I was twelve, and my Uncle Hooper—sometimes I think, my dear Emily, Boston is just one big charnel house. Henry and I have made up our minds that when we die we'll be buried right here and not shipped back to Boston like canned terrapin."

Trist guessed that Emily might profit from a change of topic. He reached for a photograph.

"That is our Neo-Agnostic Architect Richardson on an earlier visit, Mr. Trist. You see the monk's cowl he wears, I don't exaggerate."

Emily had rather boldly unwrapped the photograph of Dr. Hooper again. "You do look alike, you two," she said wistfully. General Beale was a tall, strapping man, athletic of build, square of shoulder; he didn't in the least resemble his now invalid daughter.

Clover was pleased, rose on her toes. "My sister claims it's ridiculous any man and woman should be so like one another as we are. My father raised me from a girl. I've written him every Sunday of my life since I was married. Twelve years this month."

There were dozens of other photographs of relatives, houses, the Adams family retreat at Beverly Farms north of Boston. The earliest picture was of Henry in the stateroom of a Nile River steamer, reading a book on their wedding journey to Egypt. In another, Clover had posed her three Skye terriers around a child's doll table, in a tea party. The last one, taken evidently just a week or so earlier, showed their friend John Hay standing before their fireplace and holding, with a curious proprietary expression on his face, a copy of the French translation of the novel *Democracy*. "People do say," Clover observed with perfect blandness, "that he wrote it, of course."

After which, Emily Beale pleaded fatigue and returned to her home to rest, and Clover and Henry and Elizabeth and Trist sat down, awkward somehow, in the parlor again, beneath the portrait of demented King Nebuchadnezzar. But the second round of tea had scarcely been poured when a servant hurried in to announce that Mrs. Bancroft had a crisis in her garden and wished to see the ladies, and in a matter of moments, in a flutter of disappearing coats, hats, parasols, Trist found himself alone with Henry.

Not precisely, he thought, a consummation devoutly to be wished by either of them. His host, ironic at all times, had been for some minutes now both prickly and ironic. "I must remember to thank you for your Jefferson letters," he said now to Trist, and added, "Not much use to the historian, I fear."

"Ah. Sorry."

"They're merely personal," said Adams.

"Too bad I couldn't offer you something better." Trist crossed his legs, glanced at the clock. "A photograph of him, say, like Mrs. Adams's photographs."

Adams regarded him for a moment from his tiny chair, then put down his cup. "You cared for her photographs, did you?"

"They seem charming to me, artistic even."

"I don't see photography in terms of art." Adams said it bluntly. "Journalism, a hobby perhaps. My wife's talent seems to me quite ordinary. Perhaps you would like to come into my study and see what I mean."

The study lay at the end of a whitewashed corridor and was almost as cluttered as the parlor. Three walls were covered floor to ceiling with shelves of books; even the window seat behind the desk had a foot-high stack of books and journals; two more stacks seemed to hold down corners of the carpet. The desk was disorderly, but in a way that Trist recognized as a writer's working confusion. Above the fireplace hung a pen-and-ink drawing, signed by William Blake, which portrayed, on inspection, Ezekiel mourning his dead wife.

"Wedding present," Adams said, nodding at the drawing, "from Frank Palgrave in London, man who did the *Golden Treasury of Poetry.* Peculiar taste for a wedding gift, no? yes?" He pushed aside the novel *Esther,* which Trist had last seen in the Adams hallway. "These are your Jefferson letters, which I *will* hold on to a little longer, if you don't mind. *These* are pages from my chapter attempting—already one falls back on the old vocabulary—a *sketch* of Thomas Jefferson's quite impossibly feline character. I'd be grateful if you took it to your home and read them over, for errors. Professor Bancroft does this for me, often, but since you have perhaps the great advantage of having heard, at second hand of course, family anecdotes, perhaps—? In any case, you'll see that I pursue the *motif* of painting, not photography, as the only art that might do justice to Jefferson's, what would I say? His semitransparent shadows?"

"A very nice phrase." Trist took the pages with an odd sense that Adams had asked him in for something more.

"This is what I've managed so far." Adams held up two richly bound red leather books, one in each hand, but made no move to offer them to Trist. "I've had my first two volumes of the *History* privately printed in New York, and bound as you see. Six copies in all. I intend to send them to a few friends for comment or, possibly, pleasure."

"But you mean to publish them too, of course, in the regular way?"

Adams replaced one of the volumes on his shelf; opened the other on his desk and spread it flat. But he didn't turn it around for Trist to read, or step aside so that Trist could see the opened pages. "I care very little for publication, in fact, Mr. Trist." He tilted his bald head and smiled a small, pinched smile. "Shocking notion to a journalist, no doubt. Yet I'm almost entirely content to write my books, show them to one or two trusted friends, and for the rest—what do I care really? I never bring a book into the world without a sense of shame. Indeed, to say that I detest my own writing is a mild expression."

Trist could only make a feeble murmur of protest.

"You are now a reporter again for the Washington *Post,* I understand? Lizzie Cameron told me."

Trist folded the sheets of paper with Adams's "sketch" of Jefferson and placed them in his jacket pocket. "I always miscalculate expenses, I suppose." The thought occurred to him that Henry Adams, born to wealth and privilege, had probably never calculated expenses of any kind, at all. "My battlefields book is going to need more time. I have to revisit some of the sites. The photographer is costly. So I've signed on with the *Post* as a kind of temporary special correspondent, yes."

Adams opened the door to the parlor and held out his stiff arm like a miniature butler. "I never read the *Post.* I am, despite your friends Senator Cameron and General Grant, a Republican to my core. Although perhaps this year, if Cleveland is nominated, I may, for once, deviate."

"I'm going to New York next week. I'll tell you what I learn about Cleveland."

"Travel, Mr. Trist," said Adams as he closed the door behind them, "even to New York, is one of the two great consolations of life. I see the ladies returning *en force*. We should sit down and finish our tea."

But Trist was beginning to catch the rhythm of Adams's habitually ironic, habitually self-deprecating voice. "What is the other consolation then?"

"The first five or ten years of a happy marriage," Adams replied as he sat down and picked up his cup. "I hear their rustle-rustle at the door, Mr. Trist."

CHAPTER NINE

Mark Twain liked to invite himself to lunch with General Grant about once a month. Or in any case, as often as he could come down from his palatial home in Hartford to New York City and turn himself loose, as he said, on an unsuspecting metropolis.

The lunches were not elaborate affairs. Usually Twain simply called at the offices of Grant & Ward at 2 Wall Street and the General sent out for sandwiches and coffee and the two of them dined in shirtsleeves at his desk. Each smoked two or three companionable cigars. Twain reported on the progress of his latest investments—he was going to start a publishing company, he had invented a children's board game for learning English history, also a self-pasting scrapbook and a new kind of grape-pruning shears, he was sponsoring a Connecticut genius named Paige (wonderful, prophetic name), who had invented a revolutionary typesetting machine for books. Grant listened and puffed and laconically reported in turn that Ferdinand Ward was also a genius and Grant & Ward were still setting Wall Street records, though the Mexican railroad project was as far as ever from reality. Sometimes they talked politics—the mugwump Twain supported the Democrat Grover Cleveland—Grant remained a loyal Republican. Sometimes, too, they talked about the war; and on that subject, if no other, Grant usually held forth at length and the former Confederate private listened.

These facts and more Trist learned from Twain himself at a table in the bar of Delmonico's Restaurant on Madison Square, in the late afternoon of April 28, following (Twain carefully explained) only the second such lunch of the year.

"Missed January, of course," he said, "because the General still had his pneumonia, and then February—" He paused to tap cigar ash into a sterling-silver ashtray placed at his elbow by Charles Delmonico himself, and at precisely that moment somebody at the bar called, "Hey, Mark!" Twain (was it Twain or Clemens?) gave a world-weary sigh, patted Trist on the shoulder, and got to his feet, and Trist leaned back and watched him work his way down the row of barstools, shaking hands like a politician, with a word or a joke or a waggish wag of his red head for every hanger-on in the room.

They had run into each other by chance in the offices of the *Century* magazine, where Twain (it was surely Twain), with a politician's memory, had instantly recalled Chicago, their interview, the illuminated cat ("not prospering," he confided glumly). Everybody in the magazine had known Twain—no surprise—but so had people in the streets as they walked to Delmonico's, even the hackney drivers and the newsboys standing in the sunshine by the Union Hotel, who likewise waved their hands and shouted, "Hey, Mark!" As writers went, Trist thought with more than a twinge of envy, the forty-eight-year-old author of *Tom Sawyer* and *The Innocents Abroad* had achieved an astonishing level of popular celebrity.

But far more surprising was the fascination Twain himself revealed for *other* celebrities. When he returned to the table and picked up his Scotch old-fashioned again, he quickly reverted to the subject of Grant and their intimate lunches, then to the various financiers, playwrights, actors, tycoons, dignitaries of every stripe that he, Twain, personally knew, knew *of*, *intended* to know.

"Your Henry Adams, for example," he said, "exclusive fellow?"

"Well, retiring, quiet."

"He and John Hay—I know John Hay pretty well—and Clarence King, they all have a secret club. The 'Five of Hearts,' because their wives are in it too."

"I didn't know."

"And Edison—you say you're going down to New Jersey to see him tomorrow?"

Trist nodded. Henry West had originally sent him to New York to write a story for the *Post* on Governor Grover Cleveland, whose public admission of having fathered an illegitimate child was rapidly becoming the kind of campaign issue the *Post* delighted in; but then he had telegraphed that morning to ask Trist to stay on and write a feature about Thomas Alva Edison and his Menlo Park laboratory for the Sunday edition.

"I might come down with you," Twain said in his slow Missouri drawl. "Like to meet him."

But in the end it was not so much literary or even electrical celebrity that seemed to matter to Twain—by degrees he brought the conversation back to Grant and the war and the phenomenon above all of what he called the "self-invented" man, that strange American ability to be two completely different people in one lifetime. Sam Grant had been a total failure, did Trist know that? Before the war he was a *nothing,* a nobody, ordinary and obscure. The truth was—Twain lowered his voice to a whisper—he *did* drink, before the war. Maybe even once or twice *during* the war. And yet in the fiery crucible of battle Grant had actually created a whole new self—a second nature—Sam Grant was a flop, U. S. Grant turned out to possess the mysterious powers of a giant.

"Odd how you both have the same first name," Trist observed as they parted at the restaurant door. "Sam Grant, Sam Clemens."

"Noticed it myself," Twain agreed.

"Except almost nobody calls you 'Sam.'"

Twain nodded. "Howells does. My wife calls me 'Youth.' Sometimes Grant's wife calls him 'Victor.'" He raised one hand to wave to a passing admirer on the sunlit sidewalk. "*I'm* a self-invented man, too, you know. Respectable Old Sam Clemens blushes to his eyebrows when he thinks of that terrible ruffian Twain."

There was something so comical and outrageous in Twain's deadpan drawl and hangdog wag of his head that Trist burst out laughing.

Twain watched him complacently. "You can live a small life, Trist," he said, and paused to puff at his cigar, "or a big one."

IN THE WAR THE GUNPOWDER USED IN MUSKETS AND RIFLES always left long tattered sheets of greasy black smoke hanging in the air, a foul, sticky smear that clung tenaciously to the hair and skin. In a matter of minutes it would deposit a black film on every soldier's face and hands, so that sometimes a charging line of infantry looked bizarrely like a row of poorly made-up actors in a minstrel show.

Trist glanced at one of the murky alleys that opened into this part of lower Broadway, and the pair of dirty-faced newsboys standing at its mouth, hawking their papers, and he thought of the smoke in the war, and then by a natural logic of other black things: the coffee beans that every soldier had carried in his knapsack and ground with his musket butt on a stone and often ate raw, out of his hand. The "war paint" some troops made by breaking open cartridge papers and rubbing their cheeks with black powder. "Shadow soup," which certain army cooks were said to fix by boiling water with the shadow of a chicken over it (add salt and serve). The secret of prose is contrast, Cadwallader had told him back in Chicago. Like so much else that Cadwallader said it was badly overstated and still probably true. At the far end of Broadway Trist could already see the brilliant white glow of a string of Edison

electrical streetlamps, not orange-tinted like the ones in
Washington, but intensely, purely white, so painfully bright that
the rest of the city around them looked, by contrast, infernally
black.

He crossed to the east side of Broadway, dodging between two
horse-drawn omnibuses rattling at frantic New York speed in
opposite directions, and came up beside yet another alley, where a
pale girl no more than ten or twelve stood holding a wooden board
with boutonnieres of artificial red flowers. Ten cents. He bought
one and let her pin it to his collar, a solemn, wordless exchange.
Despite the hour—automatically he looked up at one of the big
clocks set on a high iron pedestal, still faintly luminous at seven-
thirty in the evening. Despite the hour, he thought, the sidewalks
were jammed with busy, fast-moving crowds of pedestrians and
shoppers, the streets with traffic. Every doorway or alley mouth
held somebody peddling something. Beggars in old flat blue army
caps crouched on the curb, men in glossy top hats hurried east
and west, up and down, the whole long street surged and heaved
with restless "electrical" energy.

He stepped up his pace, turned to the left again, and caught a
whiff of the Fulton fish market. The Edison lights grew even
brighter. Warehouses and offices began to replace the shops and
restaurants of the Broadway district. The streets were filled now
with workers, finished for the day, streaming toward the enormous
new Brooklyn Bridge above Fulton Street. In Washington—contrast—at this time of night there would be only scattered taxis and
private carriages and a few stray clerks or black servants out on the
street, a sleepy, small-town atmosphere compared to the push and
shove of New York.

A stray thought crossed his mind, as if at an angle. If he were
Henry Adams and rich enough to live in luxury anywhere in the
world, why of all places would he choose Washington? Placid,
pleasant, undemanding Washington?

He turned left again at Nassau Street and almost stopped in
the middle of the sidewalk to shade his eyes.

You *must* go back to New York, Edison had said at the end of
their interview yesterday in New Jersey (a man accustomed to giving orders) and see my installation at the Pearl Street station. And
Henry West, by return telegraph, had not only agreed but insisted.

Trist had told Henry Adams the plain truth. He had indeed

miscalculated his expenses, especially photography and travel, and he was more and more dependent on his part-time income from the *Post*. And besides, he had already written one long feature on Edison—in 1881, at the Exposition d'Électricité in Paris, Edison had swept every prize and award the French could think to offer, and Trist had covered half the pages of *L'Illustration* one month with Edisonian lore and information, though of course Edison's lieutenants, not the great man himself, had made the trip to Paris.

Go to 257 Pearl Street, he had been instructed. Show them this note. Go straight on down into the basement.

Contrast. The Paris Exposition had been held in the vast Palais d'Industrie next to the Tuileries gardens, an enormous steel-and-glass structure that housed not only room after room of newly invented electrical devices but also—this was France, after all—numerous exhibits of a purely irrational and decorative nature. The entrance hall had been given over to a full-sized reproduction of a Normandy lighthouse, three stories tall, with a revolving electric lamp at the top and an artificial seacoast at the bottom made up of rocks, waterfalls, waves, sailboats, and three or four electrical "canoes" that circled the lighthouse base. In the exhibit rooms proper, under a fully inflated dirigible airship, complete with electric propeller, you could see Edison's phonographs, his improved telephones, his strings of dazzling electric lamps, whose circuits a lady or gentleman could adjust at will by the touch of a switch. If you chose, you could also pick up the telephone and hear a voice ten blocks away at the Opéra begin to sing, or (at another booth) connect yourself to the Comédie-Française, where an actor politely asked whether you preferred to hear him recite Molière or Racine.

But the Pearl Street headquarters of the Edison Electric Company in Manhattan was a grimy old warehouse *sans poésie,* reinforced by heavy timbers and steel, that housed workshops and toolrooms on the upper floors and six gigantic subterranean dynamo engines, each supported in turn by a wilderness of cables, wires, pipes, coal bins, and water pumps. Not a lighthouse or dirigible in sight. Edison had contracted to furnish electrical power, including light, to a square-mile area bounded by Spruce, Wall, Nassau, and Pearl Streets, and to replace the gas lamps in every single building with his own electrical ones, and it was, as far as Trist could tell, his genius at organization as much as invention that had made the experiment succeed. The dynamo rooms were deafening and filthy, but they supplied the power. The gas lines under the cobblestone streets had been uncovered and next to them workmen had simply buried parallel insulated pipes of bundled electrical wires, and every building in the district had been given a free supply of patented carbonized lamps (a dollar a bulb to replace) which fit in the old gas fixtures. When you climbed back out of the dynamo rooms and looked down Pearl Street to the west, the effect was a fairyland—streets brilliantly clear and lit, window after window glowing with pure white light, the stars themselves eclipsed by Edison.

Trist toured the workshops and dynamos with a guide, examined the wall-length charts that showed the location of all the wires and meters in lower Manhattan, and finally emerged on the street again at a little past nine.

He walked west to 23 Wall Street and looked, for no good reason, at the redbrick offices of J. P. Morgan, who had prophetically underwritten Edison's company; then started north again, past City Hall Square, past the Ladies' Mile of clothing shops on Broadway, dark now but thronged with thousands and thousands of shoppers during daylight and next, he was told, on General Edison's list of targets for illumination.

At the Hoffman House on Fifth Avenue he went inside and found a booth as far as possible from the long, loud bar. He drank two beers and scribbled his notes on a tablet. Then he put his pencil down, leaned his head back against the booth, and looked very carefully at nothing at all, nothing whatsoever.

Elizabeth Cameron—his mind started, stopped; stalled. Of the mysterious laws that govern men and women he was still, he thought, at the ripe old age of thirty-nine largely ignorant. What Edison should invent was a machine to turn off desire, to make husbands vanish, shower one-armed adulterous lovers with wealth, station—for the first time in weeks he felt a throb of pain in his nonexistent left arm—with symmetry.

Some sort of cheer went up in one of the private rooms toward the rear. He pushed his empty beer glass aside and pocketed his notebook. Mark Twain had told him the Hoffman House was the largest saloon in New York. It was surely the noisiest. The booths and tables were dimly lit (gas, not electricity) and stank of spittoons and smoke. Over the bar was a string of elegant crystal gasoliers, and under them a fifty-foot-long painting showed end-less sepia-colored nudes peering through bushes at the double-deep row of gentlemen drinking as fast as they could and peering right back. It was a splendid painting; he would buy it for his rooms in Washington. A black-aproned waiter with sideburns down to his jaw paused to help with his coat. "Ladies upstairs, sir," he muttered in Trist's ear. "In the back of the cigar store two doors down. Ladies everywhere."

The night was cold for early May. He pulled his collar closer and hurried up the sidewalk to Forty-first Street, where patrons from the National Theater spilled onto the sidewalk in a rich dark wave of furs and top hats, and horses and carriages jammed together from curb to curb, filling the air with voices and bells and the clatter of horses' hoofs.

In a momentary irony of great city-small world he caught a glimpse of Cump Sherman, of all people, the General's unmistak-able red beard blazing from a carriage window. Then the traffic shifted, a whip cracked, and Sherman was gone.

At Forty-fifth Street he turned into the modest little hotel that Henry West, with an eye on the *Post*'s travel budget, had chosen for him. He trudged upstairs to the fourth floor, briefly considered going back out for another beer (ladies everywhere), but looked at his watch, calculated (accurately) how much money he had already spent in New York, and sat down instead on the edge of the bed.

No electricity this far uptown, though both J. P. Morgan's and William Vanderbilt's mansions on Fifth Avenue were said to have private Edison systems. Trist adjusted the lamp on the wall to reduce the faint, cloying scent of gas and opened his book.

He had seen the novel *Esther* twice in Henry Adams's house, and out of curiosity had bought a copy himself at a bookshop on Broadway that afternoon. The *Post* paid five dollars extra for "filler" reviews that could take up space in the slow Sunday edi-tion, or the *Century* magazine might run it for three dollars more. When the bellboy knocked on the door with his telegram Trist was just beginning chapter two; drowsy, half-asleep, he carried the yel-low envelope back to the lamp and turned up the gas, because Western Union printing, as always, was dim.

RUMORS GRANT AND WARD BUST STOP STAY IN
NEW YORK TILL TUESDAY STOP WEST.

CHAPTER ELEVEN

Afterwards, CADWALLADER, THOUGH NO LONGER WRITING regularly for the *Herald* or any other newspaper, pieced the story together this way.

On Sunday, May 4, Ferdinand Ward appeared unexpectedly in the late afternoon at Grant's house on East Sixty-sixth Street. "Buck" Grant (so called because he had been born in Ohio, the "Buckeye State"; a certified idiot) showed him into the parlor and skeetered off to find his father. When the General came in and sat down and spread his hands on his knees expectantly, Ward, as charming and silver-tongued as ever, smiled with his eyes and his teeth and said the firm had come to a little bump in the road.

Father and son cocked their heads like a pair of dim-witted puppies.

Fact was, Ward said, the Marine National Bank was experiencing difficulties.

"What's that got to do with us?" asked Buck.

Ward was patient, of course. He explained that the Marine Bank held some six hundred and fifty thousand dollars of Grant & Ward money on deposit. But yesterday, Saturday, the City of New York, which also banked there, had withdrawn three hundred thousand dollars to pay off bonds; this left the bank rather badly short of cash. If there were another large withdrawal in the next few days, the bank would be hard pressed to pay, and Grant & Ward—he gave them a Pearl Street smile—would be . . . crippled.

The General was as calm and direct as if he were taking a sub-ordinate's report at Vicksburg. "What do you want us to do?"

Ward liked directness. It was how he did business himself, he said. What they should do was, among the three of them, raise three hundred thousand dollars as a loan and deposit it right away in the Marine Bank, where one of their special partners, Jim Fish, was president. He, Ward, was sure he could raise a hundred and fifty thousand. Now if the General and Buck could do the same, why, it would be a loan for one day only, Monday. The bank would haul in its creditors and pay them back without fail on Tuesday.

"But," said Buck, "this is Sunday."

Ward had noticed that.

"Where in the world could we find a loan like that on *Sunday*?"

Ward continued to smile and nod his head and drink the glass of sweet sherry Grant's old black manservant had brought him on a polished tray.

About an hour later—Grant's house is conspicuous, people watch it off and on all day long, to catch a glimpse of him—about an hour later Grant himself came down the front steps, limping. He had slipped on the ice beside these very steps back in December and hurt his leg, and now and then still walks with a cane. The house itself is an ugly four-story redbrick affair that he purchased three years earlier, in 1881, and furnished lavishly with so many mementos and souvenirs of the war that visitors often think they've wandered by mistake into a military museum. The money for the house itself had come from a hundred-thousand-dollar trust fund raised by the owner of the Philadelphia *Ledger* after Grant lost his try for a third presidential nomination. The chief subscribers to the trust were millionaires like J. P. Morgan, who thought Grant had been a wonderful President and deplored the fact that ex-Presidents didn't receive a government pension. (In New York a second trust fund was soon established, two hundred and fifty thousand dollars this time, and its chief subscribers were the rail-road scoundrel Jay Gould and William Henry Vanderbilt, who remarked *apropos* to the *Times* that "Grant is one of Us.")

Now he could have called for his carriage, of course, or even a public taxi, but for some reason the General hobbled on his own power down the street to Fifth Avenue; hesitated for a time on the corner, then turned south. A group of small boys followed him silently right down to number 640, which occupies, as everybody knows, the entire block between Fifty-first and Fifty-second Streets. One of Vanderbilt's Irish stablehands came out and chased the boys away with a whip, cursing.

Inside the house, William Henry V. bestrode his leather chair like a paunchy colossus. He watched Grant lower himself into another chair on the other side of the fireplace and hand his hat and scarf to the butler; then he arranged his fat little Vanderbilt hands on the arms of his chair and listened.

Grant has always possessed a remarkable memory. He now repeated Ward's information just about word for word, arrived at the sum of one hundred fifty thousand dollars, and stopped.

The other thing that everybody knows about him, besides his address, is that William Vanderbilt is as cranky and unpleasant as fifty million dollars can make you. When Grant was finished, he pursed his lips and frowned and flipped one pink hand over, like a chop on a grill. "Well, I don't care anything about the Marine Bank," he said. "It can fail. And as for Grant & Ward—I wouldn't lend it a dime." Grant sat in his chair and didn't move a muscle. "But I'll lend *you* a hundred and fifty thousand dollars," Vanderbilt said. "Personally, a loan from me to you."

He picked up a silver bell and rang for his checkbook.

"I'll pay you back on Tuesday without fail," Grant said.

William Henry grunted.

As it turned out, Ward was waiting at Sixty-sixth Street when Grant returned. No luck on his side getting that loan. How had the General fared? Grant, who had once gone bankrupt trusting people in the real estate business and later surrounded himself, unknowingly of course, with swindlers in the White House, reached in his pocket for Vanderbilt's check. I will deposit it myself, Ward told him over another sweet sherry, first thing tomorrow morning.

WHICH, NATURALLY, HE DIDN'T DO." TRIST WATCHED WITH awed fascination as Cadwallader shoveled scrambled eggs into his mouth with one hand, toast with the other. Two hands, he thought, not always an advantage.

"Cashed it himself," Cadwallader said indistinctly and wiped a massive glob of golden egg from his chin. "Bank went bust, Grant & Ward went bust—you wrote that part up very nice, I saw the *Post* every morning."

"But I missed the whole Sunday visit to Vanderbilt, the silver bell, the check."

"Oh, hell, everybody did." Cadwallader was nonchalant. He mopped up the last of the egg with the last of the toast and sat back, gently belching. One of the Willard Hotel's legion of green-jacketed waiters sprang to his side with a silver-plated coffeepot in hand. "Grant's gardener is an old Michigan sergeant I knew back in the war. Vanderbilt has two thirsty veterans on his downstairs staff. Don't pay them worth a damn. Can't afford it, ha."

"And you got the cashier at the firm too," Trist said. Because, though he looked twenty years older and seriously dissipated and unfocused, Cadwallader had written a special article for the New York *Herald* three days ago in which he described, with surprisingly sympathetic and eloquent prose, the scene at Grant & Ward the day the General learned he was totally bankrupt again at age sixty-two. According to Cadwallader, Grant had come to the offices late Tuesday morning in a hansom cab, after the Vanderbilt loan on Sunday, unaware that two hours earlier that same morning the Marine Bank had closed its doors and lowered its great iron shutters down to the sidewalk. The crowd of angry men gathered at its Wall Street entrance grew louder and angrier. They made their way up the street to the Broadway intersection, and by the time the General arrived there were so many of them that the police had also gathered, as if to control a mob. The crowd parted long enough to allow Grant to go inside; but inside was no better. The corridors and first-floor offices were jammed with more depositors and creditors, banging on counters, waving certificates, shouting, clamoring for their money.

Buck was waiting at the back, coatless, not even wearing a tie. He was enough like his father at least to give the facts succinctly and simply: "Ward has fled," he told the General. "Nobody can find our securities."

And Grant was still Grant. He said nothing whatsoever. He absorbed the news, limped on over to the elevator, and rode up to his second-floor office. All day long people came and went with further details, but the great central fact was that all the money, every cent, was gone. The Philadelphia trust fund, whose surplus he had put in Grant & Ward. The money Buck and his father-in-law had invested. The savings of every single member of the Grant family. The investments of all the old soldiers and comrades who had sent the General their pension checks and savings books. Every solitary penny gone.

At the end of the afternoon George Spencer, the cashier, came into Grant's office and told him that Buck had finally located the firm's securities, locked in a third-floor cabinet, but they were now utterly worthless, and Ward had also made off with Vanderbilt's personal check.

"Spencer," said Grant, "how has that man deceived us all in this manner?"

Spencer shook his head, looked down at the piles of ledger books on Grant's desk. The old West Point mathematician had evidently been trying to work out where the firm's sixteen *million* dollars in listed assets could have vanished. "I have made it a rule of life," Grant told Spencer, "to trust a man long after other people gave him up." He paused. Spencer may have thought of the stories of Grant's military loyalty to his White House subordinates, no matter how much his enemies attacked them. Or maybe the stories of Grant's own down-and-out years in St. Louis, begging former colleagues to buy his firewood. "I learned that rule in the war," Grant said. "But I don't see how I can trust another human being again."

Spencer gathered up the useless ledger books and left the room. At the door he stopped and looked back. He saw U. S. Grant slowly bury his head in his hands and his shoulders start to heave. And not many men, if any, have ever seen a sight like that.

"Called Roscoe Conkling in the next day," Cadwallader said, lighting a foul cigar.

Trist nodded. *That* he *had* reported. Conkling, having resigned in a fit of pique from the Senate, was now a prominent lawyer in New York; but even Lord Roscoe could do nothing to help his old candidate and President. Ferdinand Ward had been running what was called in Wall Street parlance a "bucket shop"—he took the money and tossed the contracts and orders in a bucket—paying dividends out of the original cash deposits, using the rest to maintain a splendid mansion in Brooklyn, a stable of thoroughbreds, a huge country estate in Connecticut.

"You know he once coined a word?" Cadwallader tapped cigar ash onto the remains of his scrambled eggs and looked around at the big half-empty dining room of the Willard. "Grant did. When he was President he used to stroll over here with his bodyguard of a night and smoke a cigar or two, and he said all those lawyers and smooth talkers waiting by the potted palms to hoist a glass with a congressman, they ought to be called 'lobbyists.'"

"Is there anything," Trist said, leaning back and contemplating Cadwallader's lined face, his rumpled houndstooth jacket, his genial air of having just stepped off a racetrack, "you don't know about Grant?"

"I know something about everything. Service at Willard's Hotel."

"Service at Willard's Hotel."

"Look at them poised in their thousands, ready to pour me coffee. Used to be terrible service, till a few years back a California congressman got fed up and shot a waiter dead on the spot, improved things something wonderful. Hence the expression 'stiffing the waiter.'"

Trist grinned, not believing a word of it (though later he learned it was all true), and Cadwallader tapped ash on his plate. "Pay the bill, my dear, and walk me safely to the street."

On Pennsylvania Avenue he pulled out a dog-eared address book, which he proceeded to consult in the middle of the sidewalk. He had quit the Chicago *Times* two years ago, he said, and taken a state government post in Michigan, dealing (unclearly) with insurance and veterans' pensions, and his trip to Washington was mostly concerned with that.

"You get tired of writing," he told Trist and snapped his address book shut. "You just plain run out of words. Use 'em up. I had a little project, a book I started—which way is Louisiana Avenue? I used to know this town."

Trist pointed toward the Capitol. Cadwallader took him by the arm and started to shuffle, and Trist was suddenly reminded of his stepfather's last, failing years, and then of boys in the war, and then of limping Grant again, the wounded giant, and as if he were reading his mind Cadwallader shook his head as they walked and said, "Well, the humiliation is pretty bad, I should think—half the country believes he stole that money, the rest just say poor old *inept* Grant, broke again. He went home that Tuesday, you know, emptied his wallet on the table, and Julia's purse, counted his money on hand. A hundred and eighty dollars, all he had left in the world. Now he's got to do something to put food on the table for his family, poor devil." He stopped again in the middle of the sidewalk, indifferent to the pedestrians around him. "You're good enough company, Trist, and not that bad a writer, but I never can tell whether you admire Grant or hate him."

Trist blinked in surprise and said nothing.

"He clipped your wing at Cold Harbor." Cadwallader nodded at the empty sleeve.

For one ridiculous moment Trist looked at the sleeve as well, as if to confirm that it was empty. "I used to think the newspapers were right," he said slowly, "that Grant was just a butcher."

"And then you got to know newspapermen," Cadwallader said sardonically.

"And then I got older. I think if they had assassinated Grant instead of Lincoln, we would have lost the war. I don't hate him."

"Well, you can feel sorry for him anyway," Cadwallader said. "I do. Had everything the country could offer—general, president, millionaire—and lost it. Bust. Now he's all the way back to hardscrabble. That girl over there seems to know you."

Trist turned and saw Elizabeth Cameron standing beside her carriage on the other side of Fourteenth Street, gloved hand raised in greeting. Cadwallader reached into the limitless pockets of his disreputable jacket and came up with a gold-plated toothpick. He grinned around it like an alligator. "Senator Cameron's pretty young wife," he said.

Themes of 1884 came early, unseasonably mild and inviting. Toward the end of May, Trist counted out his savings on the table, Grant-fashion, stared a long blank time at the dusty pyramid of notes and photographs on his desk; then abruptly applied for a two-month leave of absence from the *Post*. Since his March trip to Fredericksburg and the Spotsylvania Court House, he had actually written nothing, nothing at all, not one syllable or page of the promised book on battlefields—he glanced at the calendar beside the basin on the shelf—due now in three weeks.

"How does it feel to produce a book?" Elizabeth Cameron had demanded of him one afternoon, propping herself up on her elbow and admiring what he had taken to calling the Leaning Tower of Notes.

"Like giving birth to a grand piano," Trist answered, and she had laughed and called him back to bed, and that night he had read the account of Ulysses and the sirens in a schoolboy's Homer he had bought at a sale. Ulysses, he thought, glumly poking at his scant pages; a step up from poor old baffled Actaeon.

Three days after Trist began his leave, Don Cameron took his family away to Pennsylvania for the summer; shortly after that, Henry and Clover Adams likewise retired to their seaside house in

Massachusetts, to be near Clover's father; Congress stumbled to the end of its session, President Chester A. Arthur wandered back to New York City for a rest; and Ulysses—Ulysses, Trist thought with another glance at the battered Greek textbook, took to the road.

The hired photographer had long since handed over his battlefield photographs and disappeared. Trist was to make a preliminary selection, and these would be winnowed down in turn by his editors in London and then delivered to the engravers for reproduction. All that was needed now was one good push, one good look at the landscape again, a last hundred pages or so of narration and captions.

He began by travelling north to Gettysburg, less than an hour's carriage ride from the Camerons, where he paced restlessly through the military cemetery and looked about at the scattered monuments and weathered bronze tablets that various regiments, Southern and Northern alike, had erected here and there in the bare fields. No one could tell him exactly where Lincoln had stood to give his speech. No one could tell him how to write a chapter that was anything more than the desiccated facts, figures, dates that Henry West had warned against—*"The battle of Gettysburg was fought on July 1, 2, and 3, 1863; to see where Pickett's gallant charge was beaten back, the visitor should walk one mile south on Cemetery Ridge, turn to the right at the marker."* He wadded up sheets of paper and threw them in his wake like bobbing corks.

From Gettysburg he took a train south to Antietam. He unfolded his maps and notebooks again and worked out where the famous bloody cornfield had been, where the swarm of bees had comically stopped the battle, where incompetent McClellan had stood on a hill with his hand in his tunic like Little Napoleon and watched his lambs march off to slaughter, six thousand of them in a day.

Trist hadn't fought at Antietam. He had still been an almost-boy sitting in a classroom in Connecticut. Nor had he fought at Ball's Bluff farther down the river toward Washington, or the Second Bull Run or Chancellorsville, and somehow, as if that mattered, everything he wrote now grew stiffer and stiffer, more and more lifeless. Dust flowed from his pen.

On a cloudless hot afternoon near Manassas Creek, two weeks into the trip, he sat on a rock and watched for an hour while an

old man and his grandson walked from one end of the battlefield
to the other, maps in hand. Now and then they paused and drew
on the ground with their sticks, or looked across with wary expres-
sions to a dark stand of timber on the east, as if Jeb Stuart's cavalry might still come charging at any second out of the shadows.
But there were only field hawks circling in the sky, an occasional
misguided rabbit that peered from the brush. On the main road,
carriages bound for Washington hurried by in the heat, their
spoked wheels turning in the strange backward blur of something
going forward too fast.

Trist tried to remember anecdotes. In a lull between the
Wilderness and Spotsylvania Court House, one of the artillery
companies had fixed up a local good-natured dog with a can tied
to his collar, and the dog trotted cheerfully back and forth all day
between Rebel and Union lines, carrying packs of cards and clean
socks and clothing one way, tobacco and cured beef the other.
Once—Trist was there and witnessed it himself—the skirmish
lines were close enough that the soldiers traded insults with each
other between shots, and one Connecticut boy grew so angry and
personal with his Confederate counterpart that both finally flung
down their rifles in a blazing, sputtering fury and came out in a
clearing together, and all the firing for hundreds of yards just
stopped while those two boys went at each other with their fists,
and when they were finished (a draw, both with bloody noses and
black eyes) they withdrew to their lines and started shooting to kill
again.

At the Rapidan River below Manassas, on impulse, he crossed
a little bridge and entered the Wilderness forest on foot, just as he
had in the spring of 1864. In the tangled brush and second-growth
pine that grew right up to the edge of the road, untouched or
cleared for twenty years, he found broken wagon wheels, bones,
bits of skull, rusted canisters. When they had begun to fight, when
Lee's army had come screaming in like banshees on Grant's flank:
so thick and terrible was the gunfire that the trees, the brush, the
very leaves and grass on the ground burst into flames. The whole
battlefield burned like tinder. Fire running out of control would
reach the dead and wounded lying underfoot, heat would make
the cartridges in their belts explode, dead bodies would jerk and
roll about with the explosions, men with broken legs or backs,

crawling through the flames, would scream as their own ammunition blew holes in their flesh. At night, in an impenetrable black smoke, they could hear men crying for water, or mercy, or a bullet, and then the flames would start up again and drown their pleas.

At Spotsylvania Court House, scene of the infamous Bloody Angle, the 21st Connecticut had been held in reserve and not fought. Afterwards they were transferred to General Wright's VI Corps and ordered south toward Jericho Mill. Trist scribbled a note; all those biblical battlefields mixed with the most American possible names: Jericho Mill, Shiloh, Chicamauga, Pamunkey River. But he could make no pattern or sense of it. At Hanover he stayed overnight in a wretched Virginia tavern, sharing a bed with two other travellers, though they were youthful and prosperous and headed north, as if to another country.

The next morning he sat in the empty tavern long after breakfast was over, notebooks open, and wrote six pages; tore them up in the afternoon. Late in the day he hitched a ride to Mechanicsville in a farmer's wagon. He walked the last few miles of the trip with a borrowed lantern, so that it was almost midnight when he reached Cold Harbor.

He had never intended to come back, he thought. Never consciously meant to write a word about it. There were fine, parklike cemeteries at Gettysburg and Antietam, groomed and tended like weeping gardens; battlefield guides and museums at Bull Run and Richmond and half a dozen other consecrated sites. But nobody visited Cold Harbor. Nobody erected monuments there.

Nobody, in fact, could even explain the name, because the place was twelve miles from the nearest body of water, the Chickahominy River, and not, by any standards, cold. It was a traditional English name for a stagecoach rest, somebody had told him, or perhaps a corruption of "cool arbor," since the plains around it were bare and hot; but near the crossroads and the little white clapboard church that had actually survived the battle, there were a few stands of sheltering pines, and far back of the battle lines, where the generals had pitched their tents, a pleasant grove of oak.

He spent the night in another roadside tavern, sitting on a bench by the fireplace because all the beds were taken, listening to the rain outside. Early in the morning, without breakfast, without his notebook, he walked up Cold Harbor Road in the soft gray light of the dawn.

The rain had stopped an hour or so before, leaving the promise of heat. His shoes splashed in a puddle. Out of sight, over a low, dark ridge, a rooster crowed, and the sound carried far and clear. Sarcastic crows answered somewhere, and then the whole drifting, out-of-focus landscape was mute.

If time were a forking path, he thought, a series of choices instead of whatever irrevocable thing it is, he or his ghost or his younger self could turn here, go one step backwards. As he moved down the road he would be able to feel the straps of his cartridge belts biting his shoulder again, the weight of the rifle on both his arms. He passed the hollow spot on the left where the Connecticut troops had crouched in the mud, waiting for the artillery signal to begin. Ahead, no more than two or three hundred yards, easy range for a rifle, a zigzag line of raw earth had marked the Confederate trenches, which nobody on the Union side had yet scouted out or studied, because incompetent officers had marched them all in the wrong direction the night before. So General Grant's quite brilliant plan for attack had been delayed for twenty-four hours while Bobby Lee's ragamuffin soldiers dug themselves an unassailable line of works that nonetheless Grant had ordered them to storm and charge and overrun.

You can wait a lifetime on a line of battle. You see with supernatural clarity every flag and guidon, hear every broken note of the military bands tuning up far to the rear, every tap of the drums whirring low and steady behind you, building and building like a lighted fuse of sound.

At four-twenty-five, orderlies and grooms could be seen going back down the road with riderless horses, a sign that regimental and brigade commanders intended to go in with them on foot. A soldier nearby wrote his name on a scrap of dirty paper, then pinned it to his shirt. Somewhere back by the clapboard church General Meade, in charge of the battle that day, looked at the hands of his watch and nodded to an aide and a signal flag went up and a lone brass trumpet sounded.

For a split second it is possible to think that destruction looks exactly like creation—a gigantic roar of pure and inconceivable volume, a flash of light two miles long, like the first moment of the first morning of the universe, and then the trenches were dotted with thousands of black slouch hats and glittering musket barrels and a long blinding sheet of flames ran from one horizon to the other, and the charging army before it burst into smoke and blood.

He found a few of the trenches and rifle pits where the Confederate troops had waited, but most of the zigzag line had been filled in now by twenty summers of leaves and dirt. The big plain where he and his troops had stood up and run forward to their fates like men leaning into a rainstorm was still not plowed or cultivated. No trees grew anywhere around it. Everything was flat and bare as a table. He had no anecdotes here, not where he was shot, not how he had fallen. Once or twice he thought he had stumbled upon the very place, but who could be sure? Seven thousand Northern soldiers had been killed or wounded in the first twenty minutes of Cold Harbor. They had covered the ground two and three deep in every direction, and for the next two days Rebel gunfire, merciless in victory, had kept the ambulances and rescue teams away while the wounded, dead, and dying lay in a great blue and red carpet under the boiling sun, waiting for the generals to agree to a cease-fire. He would never understand the minds of generals. He had used up all his words for Cold Harbor.

At midday a colored boy who must have been watching him brought out a wooden kitchen chair and a piece of bread and a gourd of water, and he gave the boy a dollar and sat on the chair, bareheaded, feeling the hot sun on his face, and the long afternoon passed slowly on, time itself passed, like pages in a book turned by the breeze.

W ELL, MEADE LOST IT, OF COURSE."

Emily Beale's young man was named John Roll McLean, and he was a handsome barrel-chested person in his middle thirties, with straw-blond hair and fine blue eyes and the irritating quality, Trist thought, of somehow being an expert on the Civil War, although he like Henry Adams had never served a moment in it. He was also the sole owner, publisher, and editor of the powerful Cincinnati *Inquirer,* the "Voice of the Middle West," and therefore a potential source of income to Trist, and therefore an individual to whom, no matter how irritating, one listened with respect.

"General Meade," young McLean repeated firmly, "was just as incompetent as all the rest—McClellan, Pope, Hooker—"

Emily stopped behind his chair, rumpled the straw-blond hair, and sang in a cheerful soprano,

> *"Joe Hooker is our leader.*
> *He takes his whiskey strong."*

McLean grinned and raised his left hand to hers and continued his recital. "Burnside, Butler—the Army of the Potomac was run by the most *incompetent* generals. Wouldn't you agree with that,

Trist? If Meade had attacked when Grant gave the order, June second instead of June third, the war would have ended on the spot.
Am I right? Same thing two weeks later. Grant crosses the James
River and outflanks Lee, and then Warren and Wright and all the
rest can't figure out how to attack in time. But bad as they were,
Grant never quit, Grant never stopped fighting. I like to say Grant
willed the army to move, just the way Lincoln willed the Union to
stay together. We ran a series of articles in the *Inquirer*, 'Great
Generals of the Century,' starting with Napoleon and Andy
Jackson, and everybody agreed that the greatest of all was Grant."

Magical words, of course, in the Beale household. As they sat
down to lunch in the second-floor dining room, pleasantly cool for
Washington in late September, General Beale ostentatiously
cleared his throat and read a personal letter from Grant with all
the latest news. The Grant family had spent the summer, as
always, in a borrowed seaside cottage at Long Branch, New Jersey,
although the General was still suffering from the sore throat that
had started with his pneumonia. The scoundrel Ward had been
arrested for fraud, along with the president of the Marine Bank,
and would come to trial next year. Vanderbilt had generously
offered to forgive his $150,000 debt, but Grant had insisted he take
as payment all of his military souvenirs and memorabilia, and
these the admiring millionaire had now donated to the Smithsonian Institution.

General Beale paused to look out the window across Lafayette
Square, as if to the Smithsonian, but all Trist could see was the
still-unfinished white shaft of the Washington Monument rising
above the trees.

"Well, but how in the world," McLean said, turning back to his
soup, "how in the world does he *live* if Ward stole all his money
and he don't have a job or a government pension?"

"Friends," said Mrs. Beale somewhat tartly.

"He received," General Beale explained, "a generous check in
the mail from an old soldier in upstate New York. Soldier said the
enclosed money was a loan 'on account of my share for services
ending in April, 1865.' "

"Other people have helped," Emily said with a sidelong glance
at her father. "General Grant sold everything he had, even his
horses that he loved so much, and his wife now does all the cook-
ing and housework."

"Going to write articles about the war," General Beale said, snapping Grant's letter open again, "for the *Century* magazine— you write for them sometimes, don't you, Trist?—first one to be about Shiloh. Then Vicksburg and Chattanooga."

"Well, nobody could touch him as a general, of course." McLean began to carve a vast slice of chicken for himself. "Monstrous fine poultry," he muttered. "But I've hired and fired a hundred reporters, and I'm damned if I think Grant's a writer."

AFTERWARDS, BECAUSE THE DAY WAS STILL COOL AND PLEAS-ant, General Beale led everyone down H Street to a handsome redbrick enclosure, walled off from city traffic, and they all inspected his stables, including the two blooded mares that Henry and Clover Adams boarded with them while they were gone for the summer.

"And what, in fact, do you hear of the Adamses?" Trist asked as he and Emily held out a pair of monstrous fine carrots.

"Well, Elizabeth Cameron spent July with them at Beverly Farms," Emily replied. Emily was now completely recovered from her illness of the previous year. Emily had, in fact, metamorphosed into a bright, pretty, and thoroughly grown-up young woman. A young woman much too good, Trist thought paternally, for John McLean. "Of course, Clover was so preoccupied with her father, who isn't well, you know, he's a kind of invalid, Elizabeth mainly visited with Henry."

"Ah." Trist held out a carrot to Henry's horse, which showed her teeth and turned away with an equine sneer.

"Then," said Emily, "Henry went to New York on business, and there they were again, the Camerons."

"The Senator too?"

"Maybe just Elizabeth."

"Ah," said Trist, "again."

As they strolled back toward Decatur House, McLean detached himself from General Beale, busy talking with his head groom, and fell back with Trist and the ladies.

"I thought you were just a reporter," he told Trist, "but now I hear you write books too."

"A sideline, to pay the rent."

"Mr. Trist," corrected Mrs. Beale, "has published *several* books of history and travel and personal impressions all put together, he's much too modest. He wrote one about travelling in the south of France, and one about Egypt, and one last year about Paris in the Second Empire. We met him years ago"—she gave a proprietary nod toward Trist—"in Paris, and now here he is, writing a new one." And she proceeded to give a brisk and impressively accurate summary of the battlefields book.

"Not fiction?" McLean asked.

"No."

"You ought to try fiction. The best war books are fiction. Look at Thackeray, look at Tourgée."

"I knew a fiction writer in Paris," Trist said, "a novelist, who had a wonderful way of writing." They had reached the corner of Lafayette Square, where both houses and trees seemed dappled in a lazy golden light. American light, Trist thought, looking across to the construction site of Henry Adams's new house, a brick shell of astonishing bulk and ugliness. "He had the idea"—Trist turned back to McLean and found himself faintly startled to see Emily smiling up at the publisher, her arm in his—"the *ideal,* really, that a book ought to feel as if the author had written it all at once, in a single blow, so that it seems organic and not mechanical."

"That's the way you make good horseshoes," said General Beale, his mind apparently still on his stables. "All in one blow."

"So my friend devised what he calls the Thirty-Day Draft— when he writes a book he completes the first draft in thirty days exactly, and each day he gets up at exactly the same time, puts on exactly the same clothes, has the same breakfast, walks the same route to his office, has the same lunch, dinner—everything he does is an unbroken repetition of Day One till he finishes his book."

"Whom the gods would destroy," declared Mrs. Beale more briskly than ever, leading them back into the house for tea, "they first make authors."

On the steps of the house Trist held the door for Emily. She stopped and smiled up at him—a girl of smiles and songs today, he thought—and they paused to look back companionably together at the quiet square.

"Henry Adams has taken *ten years* to write his *History,*" she said, "and he's not finished *yet.*"

"He changes his clothes too often."

She laughed easily—a girl of laughter too—and held out her ring to be admired again. "You told me you were going to write a review of that book *Esther*. So I actually went and read it myself, and I've been looking for your review all summer."

Trist propped himself against the open door and looked down at her curiously. From inside the house someone called to them to hurry in. "Well, I didn't know what to write about it," he said finally, not quite truthfully. "It's a very strange book."

"It is a book," said Emily, suddenly somber and showing her mother's talent for precise summary, "about a homely young woman with an invalid father and her friend, a younger, very beautiful and charming woman, and how the homely woman is filled with despair and doubt because her friend is so lovely."

"Yes."

Emily's smile had now completely vanished. "It made me think," she said, "of Clover Adams and Elizabeth Cameron."

PART SIX

GENERAL GRANT

AND

PRIVATE TWAIN

———

WASHINGTON

AND

NEW YORK

Fall 1884–Winter 1885

EXTRACT FROM A REPORTER'S NOTEBOOK, 1885

General Grant began to write despatches, and I arose to go, but resumed my seat as he said, "Sit still." My attention was soon attracted to the manner in which he went to work at his correspondence. At this time, as throughout his later career, he wrote nearly all his documents with his own hand, and seldom dictated to anyone even the most unimportant despatch. His work was performed swiftly and uninterruptedly, but without any marked display of nervous energy. His thoughts flowed as freely from his mind as the ink from his pen; he was never at a loss for an expression, and seldom interlined a word or made a material correction. He sat with his head bent low over the table, and when he had occasion to step to another table or desk to get a paper he wanted, he would glide rapidly across the room without straightening himself, and return to his seat with his body still bent over at about the same angle at which he had been sitting when he left his chair. Upon this occasion he tossed the sheets across the table as he finished them, leaving them in the wildest disorder. When he had completed the despatch, he gathered up the scattered sheets, read them over rapidly, and arranged them in their proper order.

—COLONEL HORACE PORTER

Wilderness campaign

CHAPTER ONE

ESTHER WAS, IN FACT, A FAR STRANGER BOOK THAN EMILY Beale's summary suggested. In the first place, there was no author called Frances Snow Compton, as far as Trist could discover. In New York City, where he now had acquaintances at two or three publishing houses, nobody had ever heard of her. At the *Century* magazine, Compton was completely unknown. And as for the novel itself, the heroine Esther Dudley was a young woman in her late twenties, and Frances Snow Compton evidently hated her— *"She has a bad figure,"* the first chapter said by way of introduction. *"She is too slight, too thin; she looks fragile, willowy, as the cheap novels call it, as though you could break her in halves like a switch."*

Trist put down the book and pondered the idea of an author who wants to break her heroine in halves.

In his notebook he had jotted down dozens of other references to Esther's homely appearance—she was short, gloomy; dressed badly: *"Why, Esther,"* drawls one of the men when she appears in a new robe, *"take care, or one of these days you will be handsome."*

Nor is she particularly intelligent: *"Her mind is as irregular as her face,"* remarks a friend. She is only a *"second rate amateur"* painter, hopeless compared to a male artist. *"Esther,"* observes the author, *"like most women, was timid, and wanted to be told when she could be bold with perfect safety."*

By contrast, the ingénue, young Catherine Brooke, just arrived in New York from the West, is quick and bright and *"fresh as a summer morning, pretty as a fawn."* All the men in the book are in love with Catherine. Frances Snow Compton herself is enraptured— *"No one could resist her hazel eyes and the elegant curve of her neck,"* she trills when Miss Brooke steps onto the stage; *"her pure complexion had the transparency of a Colorado sunrise."*

Bilge, Trist thought, and stood up and tossed the book onto his desk. Bilge and syrup, enough to make you gag. Henry West hadn't wanted Trist's review for the *Post,* pointing out that he'd never seen an advertisement anywhere for the book or heard of the author. As far as West knew, nobody in the world but Trist and Henry Adams had ever bought a copy.

And Emily Beale, of course. It was the character of Esther, Emily had said, who first made her think of Clover—homely, fragile Esther with her bad figure, devoted to her invalid father, deeply vexed in a vaguely Bostonian way about matters of duty and religion. Esther was a sad black frump, Emily thought, next to the pretty fawn Catherine; just like Clover and Elizabeth.

Trist picked up the novel again and opened it to the last chapter. Wooden characters, turgid prose, nothing at all resembling the wit of *Democracy.* Early on in the book Esther becomes engaged to the pompous clergyman named Hazard, but the only discernible theme in their long-winded romance is that marriage is a stultifying prison—*"As for bringing about a marriage,"* says Esther's sharptongued aunt, *"I would almost rather bring about a murder."*

In the end, poor unattractive Esther loses everything—her beloved invalid father dies, her "second rate" art comes to naught, her fiancé deserts her. *"I loathe and despise myself,"* she whimpers, and Frances Snow Compton, licking her chops, leaves her creation standing miserable and alone at the edge of Niagara Falls.

She should have just pushed her over, Trist decided irritably. Or made her jump. But Compton lacked the authorial nerve, he supposed; or the imagination; or the publisher had interfered at the last moment. It was an angry, frustrated book, there was no denying that; a book that somehow, obliquely but deliberately, sought to cause pain.

Who had written it?

TWO HUNDRED MILES AWAY ON EAST SIXTY-SIXTH STREET, AT almost precisely the same moment, Julia Grant came into her husband's study on the second floor and handed him a yellowing slip of notepaper that she had found while she was sorting her letters.

The date in the corner, he saw, was May 22, 1875, the last year of his second term in the President's Palace.

> Dear Ulys,
> How many years ago today is it that we were engaged? Just such a warm day as this was it not? Julia.

She had given it to a servant to carry to him, and on the bottom he had written two lines in pencil and sent it back:

> Thirty-one years ago. I was so frightened however that I do not remember whether it was warm or snowing. Ulys.

Grant read it over now and looked up with a wry little shake of his head. Julia leaned down, kissed him, smiled.

That evening, in the sitting room, remarkably bare and uncomfortable since it had been stripped clean of military souvenirs, she laughingly repeated to their guests the story of the "warm day or snowing" note. And then by a kind of leap of association she went on to describe the equally hot day last June when the General hurt himself. "What he *did*," she said, "was bite into a peach—"

"It happened at lunch," Grant explained.

"And then he bounced up from the table in terrible pain and walked around the room as if he'd been stung—"

"I thought there was an insect in it," Grant told them, and Elizabeth Cameron frowned and nodded with such a charming look of sympathy that he added as an aside to her, not Don Cameron, who wouldn't care in the least, that the peach was his favorite fruit.

"Well, I hope you saw a doctor," Elizabeth Cameron told him.

"He saw Dr. Da Costa, from Philadelphia." Julia stood and smoothed her skirt like a nervous bride and started to pass around the plate of chewy after-dinner cakes that she had cooked herself, just as she had cooked the whole meal for the four of them, pork chops, beans, potatoes, stewed tomatoes, everything the General liked, most of which he hadn't touched. "He comes to Long Branch every summer, and he examined the General's throat—"

"Right there on the porch," Grant said, amused at the memory of the dapper little Philadelphia doctor shading his eyes against the bright June sunlight and telling Grant to open wide, while carriages and horses were going by on the street not twenty yards away.

"*He* said the General should go to his regular New York doctor, Dr. Barker."

"But Barker was in Europe all summer, so I haven't got around to it yet. And besides"—Grant looked up at Don Cameron, who had refused Julia's cakes and was now at the sideboard helping himself to some brandy in the unceremonious fashion of an old friend. "Besides, I've been busy, as you may know."

"Heard about it," Cameron said.

"You've become a *writing man*," Elizabeth said in her lively way. "*Three* magazine articles about the war. We saw them announced in the papers."

"Well, truly just two and a half." Of late Grant had developed what he could only describe as a kind of second self or presence in his head that appeared to listen to everything he said and then comment on it. Now, for instance, he heard himself speaking, but inside his consciousness he was remembering how his Secretary of State Hamilton Fish used to tease him for being the most scrupulous and honest man in the world in regard to fact. "One and a half, really. The *Century* magazine asked me to write a few things about the war, and with everything that's happened"—he shrugged stoically, Julia looked down at the floor—"I thought I would."

"How much do they pay you?" Cameron was blunt as usual.

"Five hundred dollars an article."

"Not nearly enough."

"That's what Mark Twain said."

"Tell them about Mr. Johnson, Ulys," said Julia, settling back in her chair, and Grant smiled at the prompting because in all the shock of Grant & Ward and the loss of money and the relentless accusations of theft, in all that humiliating "come-down" as his old mother would have said, Julia never stopped thinking of him first, what would please him and lift his spirits. He glanced for a moment at Cameron and his pretty young wife, on opposite sides of the room, and then, to please Julia, he told them all about Johnson.

"Professor" Johnson, he had actually taken to calling him, although he couldn't be thirty years old. Tactful man, sweet-natured. As the Camerons knew, the *Century* intended to run a yearlong series of articles called "Battles and Leaders of the War" and then make a book of them. Grant was to start the series off with an article about Shiloh—they paid him money in advance; it went straight to the grocer's bill—and so he had got out all his old records and letters and sent them a clear four-page essay not all that different from his official report in April 1862, to tell the truth. And two weeks later young editor Johnson showed up at Long Branch smiling and shaking hands all around and sitting on the porch with lemonade in his hand and the folded pages of the article in his pocket, and Grant had known at once there was trouble.

At Shiloh, General, Johnson said casually when all the small talk was done, you were much criticized for not entrenching against Johnston's troops.

Well, yes, Grant admitted; he had made a mistake, and he went on to explain about entrenching as a tactic and how they had only come to see how important it was in the Wilderness, he and Lee at about the same time.

Shiloh was, to that point in the war, the bloodiest battle ever fought on the North American continent, Johnson suggested.

And Grant had told him, sipping lemonade, such is the contrast between the times of a man's life, that on the Sunday night after the first day's battle he had been sitting on the ground at Shiloh, on the mud in fact, nursing a sore ankle; but it was raining so hard that around midnight he limped over to a log cabin about a mile away for shelter. Except, the cabin was being used as an improvised hospital, and it was full of wounded men stretched out on the floor, dozens and dozens of them, moaning and screaming with pain, and there was a farmer's bushel basket of amputated limbs in the doorway and surgeons covered with so much blood they looked like cardinals of the church, cutting away on a kitchen door they used as a table. Grant had sent those men into battle, his orders were responsible, and there must have been four or five thousand Union casualties, that day alone. "But I couldn't stand the sight of all that pain," he confessed to Johnson, "I just couldn't endure it, and I went back out into the rain instead and spent the night under a tree."

And the battle next day? Johnson asked.

So fierce, Grant told him, he saw at one time what he had never seen before or since: swarms of musket bullets in flight, overhead and visible to the naked eye, like buzzing insects.

And *then*, Grant explained to the Camerons, Johnson finally pulled out his article and said *that* kind of thing was what his readers wanted, and could the General just go over his pages one more time?

"He became your literary tutor!" Elizabeth Cameron declared with a charming little clap of her hands.

"Well, what I wrote at first," Grant said, "was pretty bad."

"He told Ulys," Julia was proud, "he had never seen somebody work so hard and learn so fast."

"And now I've just about decided to write a whole book about my experiences in the war and let the *Century* publish it."

"How much for the book?" Cameron had finished his drink and was standing with his hands in his pockets, a sure sign that he was impatient to go.

"I have a meeting tomorrow," Grant told him, "and then I guess I'll find out." And the inner voice reminded him that right after the meeting with Johnson he was to see his doctor at last and have his throat examined again, because the soreness now was such, as Don Cameron had remarked after dinner, the General hadn't touched a cigar all night, and that was not for reasons of economy alone.

At the door Elizabeth Cameron was telling Julia, at female length, about her summer away from Washington, and Grant was standing by, docile husband, when he heard the name Henry Adams and looked up quickly. One of the things people said about Grant, he knew, was that he possessed a remarkable memory, which he supposed was true, and another was that if provoked, though outwardly calm and nerveless, he could be a ferocious hater.

"Henry Adams the journalist," he said flatly.

Elizabeth Cameron smiled. "Our neighbor in Lafayette Square."

"I met Adams once when I was President," Grant said. "Came

over after dinner one night with Badeau." Badeau was his former aide, who was even now upstairs helping to arrange the material for the book. "Sneered at me, sneered at Julia."

"Oh," said Elizabeth Cameron, flushing. "Oh, surely not."

"Wrote all sorts of magazine articles attacking me in the White House, after Black Friday he said I was just a pathetic old soldier out of my depth. When my son Buck was at Harvard he took a course in history from Adams, and Adams failed him. Only course Buck ever failed in his life, pettiest thing I ever heard of."

"Oh, dear."

"But that's all right." Grant smiled and felt at last in his pocket for a cigar. "Now I'm a writer too."

THE NEXT MORNING, OCTOBER 22, GRANT WENT TO THE OFFICES of the *Century* for a brief, inconclusive meeting with Johnson and Johnson's boss, a middle-aged man named Richard Watson Gilder, who was eager to sign a contract but still more eager to talk about the way his artillery unit had taken the wrong road in July '63 and marched northwest instead of southeast and thereby, somehow, missed the entire Battle of Gettysburg.

When Gilder had finished, it became, in an obvious but unspoken kind of fashion, Grant's turn to tell a story. And as it happened, that very morning he had been working with Badeau on some of the records from Kentucky and Tennessee in 1862, after Shiloh, and so the name Braxton Bragg was already in his mind.

"Confederate general," Gilder informed young Johnson, nodding sagely. "Good man."

Grant sipped the coffee the *Century* had provided, felt a little sting in his throat but nothing terrible, and thought, as he began to talk, that here was U. S. Grant, "Silent" Grant, in his old age metamorphosed into a *raconteur*! What would that peerless chatterbox Mark Twain think?

"Bragg," he said, and noticed that five or six other men, some young, some old, had stopped at the office door and were leaning in to listen. "Bragg was a West Pointer. He fought in the Mexican War when I did. He was always a good soldier, but he was far and away the most argumentative and litigious man I've ever known. Before the war he was serving as a company commander in somebody's division, and also, because we were shorthanded, as the company supply officer as well. One day as company commander he decided to order new rifles for his troops and he passed his requisition slip on to the supply officer, who was, of course, himself."

Gilder was already hissing with suppressed laughter, Grant observed, but then, veterans of a certain age found everything about the war and the army interesting and entertaining, and meanwhile Johnson was proudly smiling up at the faces in the doorway, as if to show off his discovery.

"Well, as company supply officer," Grant said, "Bragg denied his own request as company commander. So on one side of the sheet of paper he wrote his endorsement and approval and on the other side he wrote his denial."

Everybody leaned forward expectantly. Grant thought of Mark Twain again, Mark Twain's advice—always draw out your punch line as long as possible, make them *wait* on the edge of their chairs. Grant picked up his coffee cup again; and sipped; and paused.

"And so next day Bragg walked straight across the parade ground to the colonel of his division and gave him the paper and asked for a resolution of the matter. 'My God,' said the colonel, 'you've quarreled with every other officer in the whole army, Bragg, and now' "—longest possible pause—" 'you're quarreling with yourself!' "

Afterwards everybody congratulated the General for his story, and Gilder said it was *exactly* what they wanted in the magazine articles and the book memoirs to follow, but they thought it would be better to draw up a separate contract for the book, and unfortunately that would take the lawyers about a month, if Grant didn't mind.

Which he didn't. He had recently sold two small houses in St. Louis that Julia had inherited from her father, and so there was a little money to last through Christmas at least, and he was sure that Johnson and Gilder meant to do well by him, though even as that idea rose up in his mind he remembered Ferdinand Ward for a harsh, bitter instant and how far trust in somebody's goodwill had taken him *then*.

At one o'clock, not having eaten a lunch, he arrived at Dr. Barker's office on Fifth Avenue for his promised consultation. Brisk, brief, thoroughly professional—Dr. Barker was waiting at the door. Grant loosened his collar, removed his coat and tie.

How long had he felt the pain in his throat?

Since June, the episode of the peach.

And it was still sore now?

To tell the truth, in the excitement of writing—learning to write—the pain had either gone away or subsided greatly during the summer. But since he'd been back in New York it kept him awake at night, it made him cough in the day, his whole neck— Grant looked at the ceiling and searched for a word—*throbbed*.

Barker examined his mouth for a while, thumped his chest, studied for some reason his ears; then wrote on a card and told him to go that day, that very afternoon, six blocks over to the office of Dr. John H. Douglas, who was a specialist in throats.

On the street again, Grant hesitated. He read the address card over two or three times as he stood on the sidewalk and people streamed around him. Barker's manner was always brisk and professional, alarming to many patients. Somebody said, passing by him, "Hello, General," and Grant tipped his black silk top hat, gravely, and finally started to walk.

Dr. Douglas the General already knew fairly well, from the war. And where Barker was dour and foxy in complexion and wore his sideburns fluffed out like a pair of bushy red spinnakers, Douglas was a more comfortable man to be with, mild and white-haired, with a good full beard like Grant's own. Barker hadn't been in the army, but Douglas had served with the Sanitary Commission—they had actually met on the march to Fort Donelson, Grant's first great victory, in '62—and Douglas had been at Shiloh and later the Wilderness, in charge of field hospitals for the Army of the Potomac. What he always remembered about Dr. Douglas was his pet remedy for the scurvy, which afflicted more soldiers on long marches than you would like to think: sauerkraut and pickles, prescribed and requisitioned by the barrel.

At Douglas's office a nurse was already holding the door open when he arrived—on the desk he saw a telephone, which Barker had in his office too, of course—and the nurse led him past a bench full of waiting patients into an examination room, and there, for the second time that day, he took off his shirt and tie and sat like an old beaver in his undershirt and trousers on a doctor's chair.

The first thing Douglas had noticed, the doctor said, when he came in, was that Grant was limping down the hall. "Can't be your throat causing *that*," he commented pleasantly and sat down opposite.

"I fell on the sidewalk just before Christmas," Grant told him, "right in front of my house." Barker had been the first doctor in the United States to use a hypodermic needle—learned about them in Europe—and Douglas was just as up-to-date. While they bantered quietly about the condition of sidewalks on East Sixty-sixth Street, the doctor pulled out an elaborate system of linked mirrors from a drawer, all of them about the size of a quarter, and started to look in Grant's throat.

"You hurt that same leg in New Orleans. After Vicksburg, if I remember. Fell off a horse." Douglas put a wooden tongue depressor gently on Grant's lips. Outside on Fifth Avenue—Grant could see the reflection in another mirror strapped to the doctor's forehead—carriages and buses floated by, a garment-company wagon seemed stuck in traffic, but it was all strangely noiseless, taking place in miniature, like some remote and mysterious version of ordinary life. "You ought to fall on the other leg sometime," Douglas said, moving his instruments around, "give every limb its chance."

Grant started to smile, as far as he could with all that hardware in his mouth, but at that same moment Douglas stiffened a little, somebody else might never have noticed, and the instruments and mirrors stopped right where they were.

It was still warm for late October. Out on the street, in a leafy yellow sunshine, you could see deliverymen in their cloth caps and big shoes unloading crates and wearing just short sleeves instead of a coat. On the wallpaper of the examination room a fat black fly crawled lazily sideways, also silent.

"I'm going to give you a prescription," Douglas said slowly.

"Sauerkraut and pickles?"

Douglas didn't smile back. He stretched his arm over to a white enamel tray for another of his miniature mirrors, this one on a metal stem like a child's lollipop.

"Muriate of cocaine," he said. "It should bring you relief from the pain. And I'm going to swab the area with Iodoform, which clears up congestion."

He held out the little mirror and Grant could see on its concave surface a reflection of the other mirror in Douglas's hand, and see as well that the trouble wasn't his throat at all. It was the root of the tongue that was red and inflamed, with hard white scales scattered all over the right side. On the top of his mouth, where the hard palate joined soft tissue, three small dark red warts hung straight down like stalactites; like segments of the claw of a crab.

Douglas pulled the mirror back.

"Is it cancer?"

Douglas unstrapped the mirror from his forehead and laid it on the tray. Then he lined up the interlocking system of mirrors beside it. Then he drew a prescription tablet from his pocket, and a pencil, and for a moment he held the pencil poised, as if he were about to write. "General, the disease is serious, epithelial in character, and sometimes capable of being cured."

"I see."

"The epithelium is the tissue that lines a membranous surface." Douglas nodded once, not at Grant but at something unseen on the floor, on the wall. He began to write his prescription.

Grant reached slowly for his coat and his tie. In the war, he thought, certain kinds of bullet wounds were always fatal, even if they didn't seem so bad at first. You would see men shot in the stomach—not bleeding much, able to stand—but they would look down at their bellies and hold them, and then look up at you, and they knew; both of you knew. Sometimes you would say to encourage them, It's all right, you'll be all right, you might be cured; but you never believed it, nobody ever believed it. Outside on Fifth Avenue the garment wagon had got unstuck and was moving nicely along with the rest of the traffic, bouncing horses, swaying cabs, some boys on bicycles, a signboard man on wobbly stilts. But even with the mirrors put away there was no sound, everybody and everything moved in utmost silence, as though something in the construction of the building or the position of the observer kept normal life at a distance. "We won't tell Julia," Grant said.

CHAPTER TWO

IT WAS TEN FULL DAYS AFTER HER RETURN FROM PENNSYLVANIA and New York before Elizabeth Cameron came to Trist's rooms on Vermont Avenue. And even then, the meeting was hasty, awkward, not at all (Trist thought as he splashed cold water on his face) satisfactory.

Of the mysterious laws that govern men and women, he concluded, he actually now knew less than before. Marriage, of course, had never been a possibility, not for a moment. *She* understood it perfectly, the Sherman in her relished the game, the pleasure. The Cameron kept her cautious. *He* was the one writing love letters at his desk, and one-armed sonnets, tearing them up, staring all day at moonish, mawkish daydreams. In French romantic geometry, the perfect figure was the triangle, the most stable thing on earth, until the woman changed her mind. What Trist wanted to be was Parisian, cool and indifferent. What he was turning out to be was earnest, American.

The next day he saw her hurrying down Pennsylvania Avenue toward the Capitol in a carriage with Henry Adams.

"My husband," said Clover Adams in a distracted manner, "spends *all* his spare time with Elizabeth Cameron. And Senator Don, too, of course." She steadied the wooden legs of her camera tripod and adjusted a brass lever. "Elizabeth's young and charm-ing." Clover pushed the brass lever into place with a snap. "And beautiful, as any fool can see. And that's what you men like, I know. Henry and John Hay always talk to each other about the 'beauties' of the new social season when they think I don't hear them." She paused to straighten the big camera on top of the tri-pod and shake out its black felt hood. "But Elizabeth is intelligent, and her house is really a kind of political *salon*—she was quoted the other day in the New York *Herald* about Grover Cleveland and Blaine. Though I'm afraid she's drawn a blank in poor Don. Duller and drunker every minute. In any case, there is Henry *chez* Cameron day and night. And meanwhile here I am spending all *my* time—"

"With a handsome one-armed reporter," Trist said.

"I was going to say, in cemeteries." Clover showed him for an instant her sweet, homely smile, then disappeared at once under the hood of the camera. Clover always wears her bonnet tied very tight under her chin, Emily Beale had once remarked to Trist, and she pushes it forward in such a way that it really conceals her face; and in all the hundreds and hundreds of photographs she's taken and collected at 1607 H Street, the only one of *her* has her face in a shadow, completely obscured.

Under the hood Clover moved the camera a few inches to her right, so that the long row of tombstones in Arlington Cemetery seemed to approach her lens at an angle, not straight on.

"I've been out here to photograph this plot three times," she said in a muffled voice. "I still haven't got it right."

"You're very dedicated."

"I'm very morbid. Hand me the first plate, Mr. Trist, don't touch its center, please."

Trist stooped to the large wooden box of equipment he had helped her haul to the end of the row. He took the first dark glass photographic plate and held it out between two fingers, and Clover's hand came out from under the hood and disappeared again. Trist walked a few steps uphill. Arlington Cemetery had a remarkably beautiful view across the Potomac, toward the White House and the National Mall and the still-rising Washington Monument, whose square top was clearly visible here through the laurel trees; from higher up, at the empty Lee mansion, you could also see the Capitol dome and the great brown curve of the

Potomac southward toward Mount Vernon. But down in the little valley where Clover had chosen to set her photograph, what the eye took in was not a dreamy, somewhat romantic landscape. There were over sixteen thousand Union soldiers buried here— two thousand of them were unknown by name and had been gathered together in a large granite tomb by the mansion. The rest lay in parallel rows of small white headstones that stretched along the hillside, down into the shaded valley, up again and over into a flat, level field of trimmed and dying grass, so endless and dramatic a sight that it seemed as if Cadmus must have reversed his myth somehow and sown living men to come up dragon's teeth.

"Have you ever thought of publishing your photographs?" he asked out loud.

"Shall I wait until those horses are past?" She pulled her head out from the hood to stare down the ranks of tombstones toward a gravel path where a young woman and a somewhat older man were riding slowly by on two chestnut-colored horses. "Yes," she answered. "One of the editors at the *Century* magazine saw my photograph of Professor Bancroft and asked if they could reproduce an engraving of it, and Henry might write a paragraph or two of caption to explain the professor's work."

"It's a fine portrait." Trist tried to remember the photograph from his tour of the collection with Emily Beale.

"Henry said no, of course. What could be more vulgar? 'My wife doesn't appear in magazines,' he wrote them."

"Ah."

"I'm sure Henry was right. I'm sorry you've abandoned *your* book, Mr. Trist." Clover lifted the edge of the hood and prepared to duck under once more. "It was a splendid idea, I thought."

"It was turning into a gigantic history of the war," he said, taking another step or two uphill. "And the publisher didn't like it and I wasn't the man to write it." But the couple on horseback had now passed behind a screen of tall hedges and Clover had gone back under her hood without hearing him.

"If you time it for forty-five seconds, please," she commanded in the same muffled voice, and Trist pulled out his watch.

A breeze stirred the trees and moved down the long slope like an invisible hand, smoothing the grass.

"What will you do now?"

"Stay at the *Post* a while longer—I like the editor I work for,

Henry West. Then go back to Europe, I suppose." He took another step and tried to see what it was that she saw in the rows and rows of tombstones, the odd, off-center angle, but nothing occurred to him, no profound idea or thought. *The silent majority,* Homer had called the dead.

"Beautiful," said Clover under the hood. "Perfect."

Afterwards they strolled, at her suggestion, through the Lee mansion, which dominated the whole enormous cemetery, and though Trist found it a dull and melancholy place—the Lees had been driven away from it in the earliest days of the war, everything had been stripped bare, first by soldiers, then by tourists—Clover insisted on going into each empty, gloomy, cobweb-covered room and looking about. At the front hall on their way out she stopped to sign the cheap little cardboard-bound guestbook that someone had placed on a desk by the door, the single piece of furniture left in the house. "It reminds me," she said, "of our house going up next door, nothing but walls and a wooden roof." In a firm hand she wrote *Mrs. Marian Hooper Adams & friend.* "An empty shell is much the same, no matter who owns it."

"Oh, but your new house is going to be—" Trist opened the front door, searched for a word.

"Impossibly ugly," Clover said. "Tomblike. No need to flatter, Mr. Trist. Richardson designed Trinity Church in Boston and certain massive classroom buildings at Harvard that people admire, but he's not an architect of *houses,* not on a human scale, not for me at least. Henry *adores* his work—I dread it."

At times, Trist thought, Clover spoke to him, and as far as he could tell, to him alone, in a personal, revealing, entirely unironic way. She never spoke this way in front of Henry. His arm, Trist thought, evoked, not her sympathy, but identification. Because for all her brilliant wit and intelligence, you couldn't be long around Clover Adams without understanding that she, too, was missing a part of herself.

"Did you ever read a book called *Esther?*" she asked abruptly two minutes later, not entirely to his surprise. They had stopped again on the edge of the wide brick porch, and she rose on her toes and looked straight up at him.

Trist cleared his throat. "Well, yes. Actually, I saw it on your hallway table in the spring, and I was curious and bought a copy."

"Do you know the author?"

"Frances Snow Compton. A woman of mystery, evidently."

Clover started to say something more; closed her mouth, shook her head.

At her carriage, parked behind the house, while the Negro driver loaded her photographic equipment, she strolled away to the nearest row of winding headstones, and appeared to be reading names at random. When she came back she said briskly but calmly, "You're a friend of the arts, Mr. Trist, I think. Let me take your photograph someday soon, for my collection."

"Well, if I can have one of you in return," Trist said gallantly, trying to cheer her up again.

But Clover had already regained her irony if not her cheer. Behind the black crow's wings of her bonnet she smiled faintly and touched his arm. "I would only break the camera, Mr. Trist."

IN THE LATE SUMMER AND FALL OF THAT YEAR, AS WORK ON HIS book slowed to a halt, Trist had written articles from time to time about the yammering, bad-tempered presidential contest raging between James G. Blaine of Maine, Grant's old nemesis from the 1880 convention, and the fat, popular, but scandal-bedeviled New York governor Grover S. Cleveland. Six or seven times at least West had sent him hurrying north on a late express to cover a speech by Cleveland for the *Post*, or a predicted eruption of temper by Blaine, caught in a vicious struggle against the "mugwump" rebels in his own camp who loudly and vigorously preferred Cleveland's progressive views on civil service reform to Blaine's notorious personal dishonesty.

Once, Trist managed to pry a quotation out of Roscoe Conkling himself, now a private attorney, which was picked up and published in newspapers all over the country (and brought him a small bonus check from Stilson Hutchins himself). Catching the acerbic old warrior on the sidewalk outside his New York office, Trist had bluntly asked Conkling if he planned to campaign for his fellow Republican Blaine. Conkling had stroked his red beard and smiled beatifically. "My friend, you have been misinformed. I have given up criminal law."

A week before the election Trist had attended a New York meeting where one of Blaine's Presbyterian supporters, in the candidate's own smiling presence, had denounced the "Three Rs" of the Democratic party, "Rum, Romanism, and Rebellion." Unlike most of the weary audience, Trist recognized that with a single disastrous alliterative phrase, Blaine had just lost every Irish Catholic vote in the state of New York. (Was there a politician alive who could resist alliteration?) When he telegraphed his report the *Post* was ecstatic, the mugwumps noisily jubilant; through Henry West, Hutchins made it known that Trist was a crown prince, he could write for the Washington *Post*, under his own byline, for just as long as he liked.

Four days later, exactly two weeks after the photographic visit to Arlington Cemetery, the reform Democrat Grover Cleveland was finally elected President by the extremely narrow margin of just over a hundred thousand votes out of nine and a half million cast; and one week after *that*, though he was a lifelong Republican, the reformer Henry Adams decided to throw a celebration party.

"WE'RE DELIGHTED TO SEE YOU, MR. TRIST," SAID ADAMS, opening the door himself and not looking especially delighted. He ushered Trist into the hallway. It was a Boston kind of celebration, Trist decided at once. Adams wore a tiny "Cleveland" badge on his black formal coat, but otherwise his manner was as coolly superior as ever, his patrician speech as arch and fluent. "Come in, come in—coat this way, hat over there. Were you at the victory parade last night, Mr. Trist? They marched right through Lafayette Square, thousands of *hoi polloi*—we kept candles in our windows as a sign of grace—I actually went outside and mingled for ten minutes. Do you know, in Jefferson's and Jackson's time the streets would have been absolutely mobbed with drunken voters and casks of whiskey? Men would have carried Old Hickory brooms to sweep the rascals out. Last night was comparatively sober, although our flowers were trampled, and somebody broke down John Hay's scaffolds."

At the parlor entrance Adams stopped, waved a diminutive but lordly hand. "You'll know many people—the Bancrofts, some necessary Congressmen, Mrs. Cameron—Senator Don, being no mugwump, alas, couldn't bring himself to celebrate. My wife is by the punch bowl, at the fireplace, talking with the ladies. At every word, of course, a reputation dies."

He gave a little tight-lipped smile and bow and turned back to the door. Trist made his way over the gorgeous rugs, between knots of milling guests, to the celebration punch bowl, where Clover greeted him warmly, rising on her toes and shaking his hand, and Elizabeth Cameron, by their agreed-on policy, merely smiled politely and murmured his name.

"We are speaking of books," announced white-haired old Mrs. Bancroft over the noise of the room, "and here you are, an author."

"Because," said Clover, "I've just received in the mail a gift, a book of privately printed poems by Dr. Mitchell of Philadelphia, and he advises me to thank him *before* reading it, as most of his friends have done."

"You know so many authors," Elizabeth said. Without meeting his eyes she handed Trist a cup of pinkish punch liberally sprinkled with floating raisins.

"Not my idea, Mr. Trist." Clover followed his doubtful gaze. "The cook is a tyrant, I believe she has a brother in the raisin business. But no, I find no advantage in knowing authors. Present company excepted, of course." She bobbed like a cheerful little doll on a spring. She couldn't have possibly been more different, Trist thought with some relief, from the day at Arlington, the *Esther*-like moment of despair. "I've told my husband," she said brightly, "I shall have to give up reading if he brings home any more authors. I can't read a word of Matthew Arnold's, now I've met him."

"Do you really know Matthew Arnold?" Trist heard the boyish awe in his voice and blushed; but then, Matthew Arnold, he believed, was one of the great poets of the time, an Olympian.

"I re-ally do," answered Clover in a teasing mock-British accent that made Mrs. Bancroft guffaw. "He came here last winter on a speaking tour, he has dreadful table manners, and condescends to all Americans."

"British snob," muttered Mrs. Bancroft.

"You also know Henry James," Elizabeth prompted.

"For a hundred years. *He* came here two years ago with that unspeakable noodle Oscar Wilde."

"Hosscar Wilde," repeated Mrs. Bancroft.

"I refused to meet him. He went everywhere in a brown plush tunic with a yellow sunflower pinned over his heart. When Henry James told him he was homesick for London, Wilde said, 'Re-ally?

You care for *places*? The *world* is *my* home.' I saw Mr. James often, but not his friend Oscar."

"I've just finished reading *The Portrait of a Lady*," Elizabeth said.

"Did you like it?" Trist asked.

"It was," Elizabeth said with a charming moue, "awfully *long*."

Clover bounced on her toes again, almost shaking with nervous energy. "Henry James," she said, a brilliant smile lighting up her homely face, "always chews, I think, more than he bites off."

At dinner Trist found himself seated beside a congressman from Louisiana named Carrington, a veteran, as it turned out, of the Confederate Army, who talked at length about the war, his political career since Reconstruction, the battles he and Trist might have fought against each other. At the other end of the table, next to Henry Adams, in a low-cut Parisian gown of rich emerald green that set off her eyes and her upswept hair, Elizabeth Cameron beamed, glowed, radiated pure feminine delight in his company, and Adams responded with such obvious flirtatious pleasure that once or twice Trist looked down toward Clover in near embarrassment. But if Elizabeth was beautiful and her husband flirtatious, Clover seemed to take no notice. Host and hostess, separated by twenty feet of glittering silver and china, chatted away in rapid-fire fashion, high-pitched Boston voices, dominating everyone around them, each oblivious to the other.

When they adjourned after dinner to the parlor again, there was port, brandy, and champagne, and still more guests began to arrive, postprandial, as Adams explained, but not unwelcome.

At one point, crowded into a second parlor opened just for the occasion, Trist overheard Clover behind him, talking with some of the new arrivals. Her manner, if anything, was more energetic than ever, yet also, to Trist's ear, now curiously strained and frayed. She was telling a joke, an elaborate story—Mrs. Harriet Beecher Stowe on the vulgarity of New Yorkers, a concert she had attended, a particularly tender and hushed moment in the music—then a penetrating nasal voice: "I always cook mine in vinegar."

Her guests laughed, tiny Clover bobbed on her spring, but when she turned and started to walk past Trist her unguarded face was empty.

In an alcove off the passage to Clover's darkroom, where he

had retreated for air, Trist encountered Adams himself returning from some hostly errand. Trist stepped aside to let him pass, but Adams was in no hurry, in a mood, in fact, to stop and talk. "A quiet celebration," he said, gesturing toward the noisy party in the next room. "Just right. I can't feel the slightest sympathy for the defeated viper Blaine, can you, Mr. Trist?"

Trist had drunk far more champagne than he intended. "I've always heard that Blaine was Senator Ratcliffe in the book," he said impulsively.

"*Democracy*?" A surprised look, an ironic tilt of the tiny Adams's head.

"*Democracy*, yes. Can you believe, Mr. Adams, that it's still in print, five years later?"

"There is no accounting for literary taste. *C'est la vie sportive*, Mr. Trist." A little pause, a further tilt of the head, as if he were seeing Trist for the first time. "Do you know," he said slowly, "I've even heard the absurd rumor that my wife is the author of that novel."

"And she's not?"

"My wife," replied Adams with a smile, "couldn't write for publication if she tried."

"Ah." Trist stood up straighter, abruptly sober.

"I'm sorry Senator Cameron didn't come tonight," Adams said over the rising noise from the other rooms and a clatter of dishes from the nearby kitchen. "Did I tell you how friendly we are now, Mr. Trist? I'm like a tame cat around his house. We disagree on presidential politics, naturally, but otherwise Don and I stroll from room to room with our arms about each other's necks, chatting happily." Another pause, a sip of his own champagne. "I should prefer to accompany Mrs. Don in that attitude, of course, but he insists on my loving him for his own sake."

Trist murmured something, anything. Adams looked past him into the parlor, where Emily Beale had just entered with her publisher fiancé John Roll McLean. "Tedious young man." Adams put his glass on a shelf and frowned in McLean's direction. From an open door the smell of Clover's photographic chemicals made him wrinkle his nose. "Poor Emily. I see you met Carrington at dinner, the veteran bore?"

"He said we almost met, in fact, in '64."

"With your prehistoric friend Grant." In the parlor Elizabeth

Cameron was embracing Emily, smiling at McLean. Trist drew in his breath and felt his face flush hot and cold at the same time. Under the pinned-up sleeve his left shoulder began to ache. "Who's started to write a book of memoirs," Adams added. "Or so I read in the daily press." He tugged at the points of his little stiff black vest, as if to face down the daily press. "Now he'll see what a battle really is, yes, Mr. Trist? Blank page versus brain, not for the weak or the faint, not for mere generals."

Elizabeth Cameron was slowly turning in their direction. Her eyes slipped past Trist, she made a motion with her glass toward Adams. "*La Doña* calls," Adams said, and started to move away, then hesitated, and in a gesture remarkably like his wife's, put a tentative, almost gentle hand on Trist's arm. "My conceit, Mr. Trist," he said softly, "you understand, is due not to my admiration of myself, but my contempt for everyone else."

And suddenly Trist had had enough—enough irony, archness, the hothouse atmosphere of too many bodies and books, too much talk. He hurried into the parlor past a startled Elizabeth. Emily Beale called his name. In the hallway he fumbled for his hat and coat, thrust a coin into the servant's hand, and stepped outside into the mild November night.

Behind him voices rose and fell. He walked to the edge of the porch and gripped the stair railing with what he knew Emily Beale called his sad one hand. Over his shoulder he could see dark party-going silhouettes against a white curtain. Ahead of him lay the gaslit vacancy of Lafayette Square. He took a deep breath and let the night shadows fall into place. Through a partially opened window he heard Henry Adams again, urbane as a glacier. "I sometimes think," he was saying, "my wife is my oldest piece of furniture."

CHAPTER THREE

SYLVANUS B. CADWALLADER COUGHED ONCE AS HARD AS HE could, a sharp explosive sound like a man punching a paper sack, and then examined the contents of his handkerchief with a thoughtful eye. Not consumption, he decided. Not influenza either. He wadded the sticky rag into a ball and dropped it into his pocket and looked out the window at the acres and acres of snow on brown dirt that was all you ever really saw from November on in the Badger State. He felt pretty sure it was killing him.

He sighed and crossed the room with an old man's shuffle to the inefficient Franklin stove his landlord had reluctantly installed two weeks before, but it was badly set up, poorly ventilated, and was probably killing him too. What he would do, he thought, was move to California, the way Grant always talked about doing—and Lincoln, too, for that matter; Lincoln always said he wanted to see the Pacific Ocean before he died—move to California, eat oranges every day for breakfast, rustle cattle, learn to swim.

He sat down and reached over the hot plate and took the little cup of camomile tea that, against his better judgment, he was going to drink this morning instead of E. C. Booz. What he needed, what any human being who had lived his whole life in Wisconsin and Illinois needed at the age of fifty-eight, was simply to be warm. He had read in the New York *Times* the other day that two or three workers had been injured trying to install Edison lights in that city, and one of the rival electric companies in Pennsylvania had promptly said that Edison's electric circuits were too dangerous for public use and would probably kill the family dog, and somebody in *Edison's* camp had fired back that you could probably use the *other* company's electric circuits to execute prisoners in jail, just stick them in a chair and turn on the current. At least, Cadwallader thought, it would be a *warm* way to go, and fast.

He picked up the *Times* he had bought last night but hadn't read yet, and saw that there was another little paragraph on the front page about General Grant's ill health, attributed as usual to the shock his system had received when Ferdinand Ward had fleeced and pauperized him. It was amazing to Cadwallader how closely the New York papers watched Grant's every move, you would think the goddam war was still on. Every morning at eleven, they reported now, for medical treatment the General walked from his house on East Sixty-sixth Street to the Fifth Avenue offices of noted throat specialist John H. Douglas, walked presumably to save the carfare, no thanks to Ward, because Cadwallader well knew that ever since he had hurt his leg falling off a horse in New Orleans in 1863 Grant didn't really care to walk anywhere at all if he could help it.

Fell off his horse, Cadwallader remembered, because he was drunk.

He put the *Times* aside without reading more. If he went to his desk by the window and opened the bottom drawer, he would find his manuscript on Grant, and no doubt he had written something about the New Orleans episode; he had written two or three chapters, he knew, about Grant's toots and benders during the war. Cadwallader sipped his camomile tea and made a face.

The *worst* bender Grant had ever gone on, he thought, was during the Vicksburg siege in 1863, when he had suddenly drunk himself pie-eyed one night and jumped on a borrowed horse (name of "Kangaroo") and galloped off into the woods whooping and waving his hat like a madman. Cadwallader had actually followed him on another horse, and he almost caught up once or twice—but drunk or sober U. S. Grant may have been the best horseback rider the U.S. Army ever saw—and he finally found the

General nearly two full hours later passed out by the side of the road, next to a bayou. Cadwallader had sent one of the soldiers for an ambulance and got Grant back to his headquarters more or less unseen, where his teetotal aide Colonel Rawlins was meanwhile throwing a fit and cursing the air bright blue, and Grant just stepped out of the ambulance wagon, fresh as a rose, nodded to one and all, and strolled off to his tent for bed.

Another time Rawlins issued strictest orders against *any* whiskey in camp, fearing a toot coming on. But one of the Sanitary Commission doctors snuck a bottle of rye into his tent and invited Cadwallader in to share a drop. They had just poured a tin cup full of it and set it on a cracker box to admire when the doctor heard footsteps outside. "Oh, Christ, it's Rawlins," he muttered. But in fact it was Grant who stuck his head in. Without one word he reached between them, picked up the cup and drained it, then wiped his mouth dry with his sleeve and disappeared.

Cadwallader wiped the tea from his own mouth and thought it sounded like Grant could use a cup or two of the oil of gladness right now, if the *Times* could be believed.

He put down the cup and looked at his desk again. He wasn't going to publish his goddam book, he thought. There had been a long spell after the war, right through the 1880 Chicago convention, when he was mad at Grant, when he thought Grant as President had been unfair to Rawlins, who was a gifted, selfless man, and ungrateful to Cadwallader too, who could have written up a story or two about Grant's drinking anytime he wanted—the New York *Herald* would have paid a fortune. But Cadwallader thought then—and thought so now—that U. S. Grant was the only Union general capable of winning the war against Bobby Lee; thought Grant was a mysterious man, weak and lazy in many ways, but with a core of integrity, patriotism—a *hero,* Cadwallader thought, pulling out his filthy handkerchief again; a hero then, and nothing but a sick old man right now.

On the same day halfway across the country, in weather almost as bad as Wisconsin's, only rain not snow, at 10:45 P.M. Mark Twain stepped out the back door of Chickering Hall on West Fifty-fourth Street, New York City, and pulled up his coat collar with a scowl.

He had just finished giving a joint lecture with George Washington Cable ("The Twins of Genius") to a lackluster audi-

ence, and he was, as so often happened on these tours, in a perfectly terrible temper. For one thing, he dreaded the coming
weekend, when he would have to stay an entire extra day in
Pittsburgh because Cable insisted on respecting the churchly
injunction against Sunday travel. That very morning Twain had
written his friend Howells that Cable had taught him to abhor the
Sabbath-day and hunt up new and troublesome ways to dishonor
it. And for another thing, his New York hotel was dreary and
uncomfortable, and he likewise abhorred and despised a bad
hotel. And for a *third* thing, he had lost his umbrella, stolen no
doubt by a boy he had noticed that night in the backstage dressing rooms. Twain squinted up at the dark sky and the falling rain
and considered taking out an advertisement in the newspaper,
five dollars' reward for the umbrella, two hundred dollars for the
boy's remains.

The idea put him in a better humor. He held out his hand to
test the rain and then started up the sidewalk.

Three blocks farther on, as he later remembered it, in the
midst of a watery black gulf between streetlamps, two dim figures
suddenly stepped out of another doorway and began to walk just
ahead of him in the same direction. He heard one of them say to
the other, like a pair of Orphic prophets sent down from above to
change his life, "Did I tell you Grant has finally promised to give
us his memoirs? He means to start writing this month."

And Twain stopped dead in his tracks, blessing Providence.

Because in the light of the next streetlamp he recognized the
decorous, satanic, three-named profile of Richard Watson Gilder,
publisher of the goddam *Century* magazine and common thief.

The next morning, promptly after breakfast, Twain took a taxi
up to East Sixty-sixth Street and had himself ushered into the
library, where Grant was sitting in one of his leather club chairs,
talking with his son Fred; and of course they were polite and
greeted him cordially, but the General was also in a businesslike
mood, and as Twain afterwards reported to his wife, Grant said in
substance something pretty much like: "Sit down and keep quiet
over there until I sign a contract." And he added, apparently so as
not to seem abrupt and impolite, that it was a contract for a book
of memoirs he was going to write.

This, of course, was what the Orphic prophets had referred to, and this was why they had appeared in the mystical darkness just when they did.

Twain sat down in his own club chair, lit a cigar, and waved the match imperially in the air to put it out. "Don't sign it yet, General," he said. "Let Fred read it out loud to me first."

Grant looked at Twain, then looked at Fred. When he didn't say anything, Fred cleared his throat and began to read. After two or three paragraphs Twain waved his hand again.

"They plan to pay you ten percent royalty, General?"

"Ten percent, yes."

"Fred, strike out ten percent. Put twenty percent instead." Fred lowered the sheet of paper and rubbed his jaw. "Better still," Twain said, "put seventy-five percent of the net returns in its place."

Grant demurred. He made little motions of discomfort that only served to prove to Twain that he was fundamentally the most modest and unassuming man in America. "They'll never pay those terms," he objected.

"Now, General, the *Century* company is a great magazine company, nobody can teach them anything about magazines. But they have about the same experience publishing *books* as I have flying backwards and they're offering you mighty poor terms in my experience. There's not a regular book publisher in the country who wouldn't do better."

Grant shook his head. They were going to run his articles about the war in the *Century* magazine, he said; they had been extremely kind and patient with him—they had come to him out of the blue, when he was in desperate need of money, and he thought he ought to sign the contract just as it stood.

"Well, the *other* problem I heard"—Twain crossed his legs, puffing smoke like a cannon—"was the clause that charges the publisher's office expenses against *your* ten percent royalty. They ought to pay that themselves."

He didn't want to rob them of their profits, the General said.

"To rob a publisher, bless your heart," Twain said with a little wink at Fred, "is an impossibility never yet achieved, and *if* achieved it ought to be rewarded with double halos in Heaven."

Fred put the contract down on the desk. Grant reached in his coat pocket as if for a cigar, but then stopped. "I guess you have a publisher in mind," he said.

"The American Publishing Company," Twain replied instantly, "of Hartford, of which your humble servant is a stockholder and director—"

"And a favorite author," Fred murmured, because the American Publishing Company had published Twain's first book, *The Innocents Abroad,* and almost all the others after that. He left the contract where it was on the desk and walked over to a row of uniformly bound gray books, lined up on a shelf next to an imported set of Dickens. He picked out one of them at random, *Tom Sawyer,* and handed it to his father.

"They are a subscription publisher," Grant said, but there was nothing in his tone to indicate disapproval, merely a fact. You could do business with two kinds of publishers in America, the high-toned literary ones like Ticknor & Fields in Boston that published Emerson and Longfellow and sold their books in bookstores only, and subscription publishers like the American Publishing Company that had an army of canvassers going door to door in every small town in the country, selling Bibles and cookbooks and popular writers like Mark Twain. Many ambitious writers looked down on subscription publishing. Grant had no such pretensions, he explained, but he didn't want to be disloyal either.

"Well, as to that," Twain said, "I guess you don't remember *I* proposed you write your memoirs three years ago—"

"He did," Grant said to Fred.

"At luncheon one day in that reptile den of Ward's. I said you ought to write it and *you* said you didn't need the money and you weren't a literary man."

Grant looked down at *Tom Sawyer* in his lap; opened it somewhere in the middle.

"And so," Twain said, "by all rights, General, I was first in the field and you wouldn't be disloyal in the least to let me telegraph Hartford and get their offer."

"You ought to have been a lawyer, I guess," said Fred, shaking his head in admiration.

Twain thought of several jokes he could make in reply, but this wasn't the time for jokes. One look at Grant's serious face told him that. His mouth pinched behind the beard, his eyes solemn and distant, the General did not look well, that was a fact; and another fact was that sometimes even Mark Twain, he thought to himself, knew when to be quiet.

"I believe," said Grant, "I can let this lie for twenty-four hours while we give it some thought."

TWAIN WAS SCARCELY ABLE TO WAIT THE TWENTY-FOUR HOURS. That night he gave another performance at Chickering Hall with Cable, who was even more irritating and incompetent than usual, but aside from the casual remark to a stagehand as he was going on that "Cable's way of reading would fatigue a corpse," Twain was in a strangely ebullient state of mind. Two weeks ago in St. Louis, he'd been so vexed by Cable's tardiness and general air of unforgivable Presbyterian piety, he had actually worked himself into a tantrum and clubbed a window shutter off its hinges with his fists. But this time he only nodded a pleasant good-night, went back to his hotel and drank three Scotches, and turned up precisely at nine the next morning at East Sixty-sixth Street.

"I talked to Sherman yesterday," was the first thing Grant said when Twain entered the library. "He told me his profits on his memoirs were twenty-five thousand dollars. Now, do you believe I could get that much from the American Publishing Company, as an advance payment?"

"I want you to forget the American Publishing Company." Twain beamed at Fred; he sat down in his leather chair and accepted a cup of coffee from Harrison, Grant's black valet who had a soft Missouri accent that was a comfort and a pleasure to hear. "In the first place, Sherman's book was published by Scribner's and it *ought* to have been published by subscription and then he would have made ten times that much. In the second place, I don't know what I was thinking, telling you to go to the American when I've just up and left them myself and started my own firm."

"Charles Webster Company," said Fred.

"I started it," Twain said firmly. "I set up my business manager Charley Webster in it, just to publish my own books on my own terms, that's all we do. First one comes out in February, called *Huckleberry Finn,* and the next book I want to publish after that is the *Memoirs of U. S. Grant.*"

Grant took his own coffee cup from Harrison and sipped and pursed his lips, as if at the taste, though the taste, Twain thought, was perfectly fine.

"That's *your* book, General," he said, risking a little humor.

But Grant's face was still solemn. He shook his head. He glanced at the tall window where the curtains were drawn back and a few stray snowflakes were starting to drift over the street. "I can't let a friend of mine take a risk of money," he said finally, and his voice was so low and scratchy that Twain knew he was thinking of Ward again, and Vanderbilt's famous Sunday loan, and all the sad, humiliating story of his finances that had been spelled out day after day in the papers. Grant was not outwardly dramatic, Twain thought, that was one of the impressive things about the man, to have accomplished what he had accomplished with so little fuss—but he could appreciate somebody else's sense of drama. Twain reached in his coat pocket and pulled out his cheque-book with a flourish, then his pen, and although he had originally intended to write $25,000, there was something so fine and touching about the sight of the grand old hero before him brought low by villainy, he doubled the sum on the spot.

There was more convincing to do, of course. Fred Grant wanted to talk with the *Century* again, the General himself insisted on sending for his friend George Childs from Philadelphia, who was an expert businessman, and he had to leave the house briefly in any case for an eleven o'clock appointment with his doctor. Twain waved aside all problems. He had no quarrel with the *Century*; indeed, they were about to run three chapters of *Huckleberry Finn* in the magazine. George Childs could come and pore over Webster's accounts like a Philadelphia bloodhound. Meanwhile, the $50,000 cheque would sit in escrow and the General could pull out his *own* pen and start the ink flying.

"You'll stay for lunch," Grant said as he put on his overcoat and limped to the door. "Lew Wallace is coming, and I'll be back in half an hour. Julia would like it."

"I'll wait right here and give young Fred one half-hour's worth of free moral counsel," Twain said.

In fact, he hoped that young Fred might say an unguarded word or two about the General's visits to the doctor, but all of the Grants, when they wanted, were a tight-lipped clan.

At twelve-thirty Lew Wallace arrived for lunch, former Union general and comrade at Shiloh, author now of the recent novel *Ben Hur,* one of Grant's oldest friends.

"Did you give Fred any moral counsel?" Grant asked as they all sat down to table.

"I told him a young person should not smoke, drink, or marry to excess," Twain said.

"Well, I must declare," said Julia Grant, smiling at everybody in turn, "there's many a woman in this land that would like to be in my place, and be able to tell her children she once sat elbow to elbow between two such great authors as Mark Twain and General Wallace."

Twain picked up the cigar he had carried to the table, but out of deference to Mrs. Grant not lighted. He rolled it between his fingers and cocked his face at Grant. "Don't look so cowed, General," he said in his slow, raspy drawl. "You're going to write a book too, and when it's published you can hold your head up and let on to be a person of consequence yourself." And winked at Fred.

CHAPTER FOUR

"Two or three times," said Elizabeth Cameron, "he's asked me where I've been, what I was doing."

"And you said you'd been having tea, of course, with Henry Adams."

If she heard the note of sarcasm in Trist's voice, she gave no sign of it. She shook her head and paused in the middle of the path to adjust her fur collar, and Trist (as if he were Boojum or Possum on a leash) paused obediently with her. Over the soggy black winter treetops of the Mall, not a quarter of a mile away, rose the gleaming white stone shaft of the Washington Monument. Its shape gave him sexual thoughts. He looked at Elizabeth Cameron in her trim, tight-fitting jacket, her full skirt like a swaying bell over her hips; anything in her presence gave him sexual thoughts.

"I don't know what could possibly be keeping them. I walked through once and there was nothing to see but old bones and buffalo skins." She wore a neat round fur hat to match the collar, something expensive, of Russian design. Her cheeks were flushed with the afternoon chill, her eyes bright with health and energy. It was the first time since the Adamses' celebration party two weeks ago that he'd managed to see her, and even so, respectable as mummies, they were only to walk along the frozen Mall while Maudie Cameron visited an exhibit with her school in the Smithsonian Institution.

"They're absolutely late." Elizabeth pulled out a beautiful little gold watch on a locket chain and frowned at it, prettily.

"We could meet in New York," Trist said. "The *Post* sends me there almost every week, or I could take a room in the Willard—"

"The Willard!" She laughed and tucked away the timepiece. "Where half my husband's friends spend their days in the bar, watching the lobby."

It was cold in the shadows of the Smithsonian's redbrick towers. They reached the end of the path and walked out onto the grass and into the sunshine. Clouds were building along the northern curve of the Potomac and the light was beginning to fail, but from the center of the Mall the newly completed Monument could still be seen in all its glory. Elizabeth had been in Pennsylvania with the Senator, so while they waited for the unpunctual Maudie, Trist described for her the pleasures of covering the story three days ago when the capstone of the shaft was officially put into place—rain had turned the ground at the base of the Monument into a freezing cauldron of mud, none of the speeches could be heard; the wind-speed indicator at its top had registered sixty miles an hour, though nobody had calculated it down at the bottom, next to the speaker's platform. He was conscious of trying to charm her, divert her, win her attention. When she turned to him and smiled her dazzling, distant smile, he felt like a trout on a hook.

"Clover Adams meant to come and photograph it." He ventured perversely onto the subject of Henry and Clover Adams again. In Lafayette Square, Emily Beale had told him, people now gossiped openly about Henry Adams's infatuation with *La Doña* Cameron. He would be damned if he would think of Henry Adams as a rival. "But the weather was so bad, she didn't come, of course. And now she's lost interest."

"Clover's not herself," Elizabeth said serenely. "Everybody says so."

"Her father isn't well." From the massive arched doors of the Smithsonian emerged a party of girls in blue-and-white school uniforms. Trist instantly picked out fifteen-year-old Maudie—

could it be true? fifteen?—unmistakable with Don Cameron's bushy dark hair and clumsy height.

"Clover's father," said Elizabeth. "I think you'd better go before Maudie sees us—her father is a kind of gentle, tyrannical monster. He lives for her alone. He came here last winter, and the two of them together, you should have seen them, inseparable. It's a wonder"—she turned to go, and her bland gaze swept past him like water over a stone—"a wonder Henry isn't jealous."

W HAT HE REALLY WANTS TO DO," SAID CLOVER ADAMS, "IS station a guard around these ruins."

"These ruins" were in fact the stone foundations and rising brick walls of the Hay and Adams houses, going up side by side next door to 1607 H Street, but proceeding so slowly that a full year after signing the contracts, the builders had only just now completed the second-story exterior walls. It was Clover's habit, she told Trist, to come out and practice her photography on the interesting contrasts of scaffolds and bricks left by the workmen at the end of the day. Henry preferred to watch the construction from his study window and rush out ten times a morning to offer advice and caution.

"And at night," she said, "he imagines noises, vandals, all sorts of catastrophes. I suppose," she added doubtfully, "we could put Boojum or Possum out as watchdogs."

Trist glanced over to the adjoining yard, where Boojum and Possum were lying fast asleep under a rosemary bush.

"I also like the juxtaposition," Clover said, adjusting her camera tripod, "of snow on top of the bricks." Together they stood behind the big black camera box and looked up at the array of intersecting gables and pointed turrets, lightly frosted with white, that made up the far wall of what would be John Hay's house on Sixteenth Street. The effect the architect Richardson had aimed at was evidently a mixture of Romanesque mass and Gothic height; the combination so far was about as American and modern as a medieval abbey. Trist couldn't imagine two structures more out of place in the prevailing redbrick and Federal styles of Lafayette Square. He was hardly surprised that a number of neighbors had already protested.

He walked a few steps farther into the muddy construction site. It was easy to see the truth of what Elizabeth Cameron had said. Clover Adams was not herself. Always thin, she had clearly lost weight. Her thick skirt enveloped her like a shapeless bag. Her dark bonnet seemed bigger, more concealing than ever. From time to time she stopped, even in the middle of a sentence, and simply fell silent. Silence, Trist thought, was not an Adams trait, husband or wife.

"I saw Emily Beale yesterday," Trist now said, to fill one such silence. Clover crossed her arms in contemplation of the snow and bricks. Trist rubbed the back of his neck and looked at the sinking sun beyond the trees on the Georgetown horizon. "Or Emily McLean, I should say. It's going to be hard to think of her as a married woman, I guess."

"She has taken to redoing her face so often," Clover said, "she looks like a ceiling by Michelangelo."

Trist frowned into the sun. "I understand you were in Massachusetts, seeing your father, when she was married."

"My poor father is not well at all. He has *angina pectoris*. My sister and brother do their best, but they're witless about medical care. He really needs *me*." She shook her head and turned back to her camera. "I took six photographs last week in the same kind of light, Mr. Trist, and none of them developed properly." She began to disassemble the bulky camera and tripod, and Trist came over to help as best he could. "At Beverly Farms I played the piano quite a good deal for my father," Clover said as they stooped together. Her hands moved quickly, decisively. "He always likes to hear me play, even though I'm not very good." She glanced up and smiled, and there was a momentary flash of her old gay irony. "We share the same high musical taste, I'm afraid—his favorite song and mine is 'Give My Chewing Gum to My Sister, I Shall Never Want It More.' "

Trist laughed and watched her shuffle her photographic plates into their carrying box, like big glass cards, and then place the camera and box on the child's red wagon she used for hauling things from her yard into the building area.

"Henry sent me over to the Smithsonian the other day," Clover said. "I was to study their collection of porphyry and jade, because Henry wants one or the other for our dining-room fireplace." She looked over her shoulder with a nod to indicate the space beside an unfinished retaining wall that was destined to be, Trist sup-posed, the dining room. "We spend *hours* each day contemplating the aesthetics of our house, you know. It reminds me of the months we spent when we lived in Boston years ago, helping Richardson design Trinity Church, which was his first big job, and we used to go inside and sketch where the stained-glass windows should go and how the clerestories ought to be placed, and all the paintings, day after day."

"Just like the novel *Esther*," Trist said without thinking. He instantly regretted it. He had been struggling to lift, awkwardly with his one hand, the last bundle of heavy photographic plates, and his mind had simply skipped a thought. In *Esther* the heroine helps an architect friend decorate the windows of a city church, her fiancé calls her a "second rate amateur." He felt his face grow hot. Clover pulled the wagon onto the sidewalk of H Street and appeared to take no notice.

"And I thought I saw you walking on the grounds with Elizabeth Cameron," she said, "by the Smithsonian, when I was there."

Washington was the smallest city on earth. "I ran into her on the Mall."

"Such a beautiful woman," Clover said, and it was impossible to be sure of her tone. "You men do 'run into her' so often, do you not?"

The construction gate closed with a loud metallic snap. Nearby, the first of the gas streetlamps on H Street flickered to life. Clover began to walk along the sloping brick sidewalk, tugging her wagon. Trist walked beside her in silence. He cradled the extra photographic plates in his arm. It was astonishing to him how quickly her mood had deteriorated at the mere mention of Elizabeth Cameron, *Esther*—who could say which? Her sadness, he thought, was nearly palpable, it showed in the slump of her tiny shoulders, the listless pace of her feet. At the front steps to her house they paused, but for once she made no motion to invite him in.

"I can carry these plates to your darkroom," he offered.

She took the plates from him. "I suppose Emily Beale will soon be producing little heirs and heiresses for the General," Clover said. Lights now glowed in the upper windows of Decatur House across the Square. "It's only natural." Then she gave him, scarcely visible between the folds of her winter bonnet, a soft, sweet, Clover smile and in a tone of unmitigated despair she added, "If any woman ever tells you that she doesn't want children, Mr. Trist, don't believe her. All women want children."

IT WAS A REMARK NOT EASILY FORGOTTEN, PARTLY BECAUSE IT was so unexpected, partly because her voice had cracked as she spoke, tears had all but sprung to her eyes. Three days later in New York City, on assignment again for the *Post*, Trist found himself pondering again The Question of Clover. Was she simply failing in spirit because of her father's illness? Or was there something else? She had read *Esther*, he knew. Had she also, like Emily, like himself—like who could say how many other people?—seen in the novel a strange, accidental *roman à clef*? a hostile reflection of her own life? The homely, unaccomplished woman overshadowed by the youthful beauty and charm of her friend, her Elizabeth Cameron rival? And why in the world had Henry Adams—who never read fiction—pressed the book into Clover's hands?

Who wrote *Esther*?

It was four P.M., February 3 of the gray, cold New Year of 1885 and Trist was seated at the window of an overheated diner on Second Avenue, sweating in his overcoat, drinking bad coffee, and watching the big illuminated clock on the sidewalk. The Question of Clover. Despite the bad coffee, which tasted like creosote and sugar, he yawned and rubbed his face. Clover. He had taken the last express train from Washington the night before in order to interview Thomas Edison once again first thing this morning, Stilson Hutchins's orders—the great man was rumored to be refining his miraculous phonograph machine; true—and he had telegraphed a long article back to the *Post* not more than half an hour ago. And now, in another ten minutes, about the time it would take him to walk to East Sixty-sixth Street, he was going to begin a second article, on his own initiative, with or without Hutchins's approval.

He spread the New York *World* on the counter and read the headline one more time: GEN. GRANT VERY ILL. The *World* was a scrappy, unreliable paper, with something of a vendetta against

Grant because of his friendship with Roscoe Conkling. Its editors had been among the first to suggest that the General himself had been part of the Grant & Ward criminal conspiracy and had fleeced his investors for his own secret profit, and no amount of protest from Grant's friends had done anything to change their story. But today at least the *World* seemed to have limited itself to verifiable facts. The article under the headline quoted a Philadelphia source as saying that "General Grant has been obliged to decline Mr. George W. Childs's invitation to visit him, on account of ill-health." It reminded readers that Grant's friend General Beale in Washington had also released a letter testifying to Grant's poor health and blaming it on the stress of the Grant & Ward debacle. And it added with some clinical precision that Grant was presently troubled, according to his doctors, with an "epithelial soreness at the root of the tongue, which causes him great pain when he swallows." Dr. John H. Douglas acknowledged that the General hadn't smoked a cigar since November 20th and was now receiving daily treatments at his office to clear away mucous obstructions in the throat.

Trist watched the clock's hands jerk toward four-fifteen. He paid for his coffee, braced his hand on the counter, and stood. The Question of Clover would have to wait. General Sherman had told him four-thirty sharp, and Trist had yet to meet anyone who didn't think Cump Sherman always meant, absolutely and ferociously, exactly what he said.

He walked four blocks up Second Avenue, under the bone-rattling screech of the Elevated Railway, and then turned west down Sixty-sixth Street. Here the sidewalks were still covered with inch-deep slush from a recent snowstorm. Edison's electric cables hadn't yet reached this far uptown. Trist passed beneath a series of hissing, flickering old-fashioned gas lamps, in a vague and shadowy black-and-white atmosphere that reminded him inevitably of Europe, of wet stone and foggy parks and the dank little flat off Primrose Hill in London that he had rented long-term and then impulsively abandoned, to become American again. As he neared Grant's well-publicized address at number 3, he was not entirely surprised to see a dozen or so silent figures hunched together under the nearest lamp. There was nobody in the world, Don Cameron liked to say, as famous as Grant. After the article that morning people would come, of course, just to stare at his house, at his empty front steps, just for the sheer morbid pleasure of his celebrity.

He passed by the nearest group of watchers and stopped a few feet from the corner. Grant's house was brightly lit on the lower floors, dark upstairs; curtains were drawn back. Through a second-story bay window he could see the library, a maid going past a shelf of shiny leather-bound books. On the third floor, peering down through a window, hands clasped behind his back, was a plump, unpleasant-looking man Trist identified after a moment as Adam Badeau, Grant's occasional assistant, Henry Adams's onetime friend. Then a handsome black barouche carriage came clopping and jingling through the slush up Sixty-sixth Street and wheeled to a skidding halt in front of Grant's door. A liveried coachman clambered out on the double.

"This is Trist," Cump Sherman said with his usual bounding energy as the three of them fumbled for seats five minutes later, four-thirty exactly, and the barouche swung smoothly back into traffic. "Dr. George Shrady. I forget your first name, Trist, don't matter—a reporter." He turned to Shrady and grinned a wicked yellow-toothed grin like Zeus or one of the Titans about to devour his own children. "*Normally,*" he declared, "I *hate* reporters."

"As all the world knows," murmured Shrady. He was a small, thin-shouldered man, clean-shaven except for a huge protruding moustache that resembled, Trist thought, the cowcatcher on a locomotive.

"But I like Trist, Trist writes straight."

Shrady gripped the side of the swaying carriage and looked at Trist's empty sleeve and nodded, and the word "veteran," Trist thought, might as well have formed in gold letters on his brow. They hurtled on down Fifth Avenue, in and out of traffic snarls, pockets of light, flurries of snow, while Sherman puffed fiercely at his cigar and kept up a running commentary on the streets, the theaters they passed, newspaper reporters, women with flat chests, anything and everything that occurred to his quick, cruel, entirely uninhibited brain.

At Gramercy Park the barouche came to a long, sliding halt, spraying two great white fans of snow onto the sidewalk. The liveried footman threw down portable steps, a doorman came rushing out to the General's carriage from the canopied entrance to the Player's Club, and in a matter of moments the three of them were seated in heavy comfortable chairs next to a fireplace in a secluded corner.

Sherman ordered—commanded—whiskeys and ice and stretched out his long legs to the fire.

"Now the doctor," he said to Trist, but aimed his cigar like a burning pike at Shrady, "agrees—at my reasonable, rational urging—to give you the medical diagnosis exactly, everything he knows, and you have his permission to go out tomorrow and print it in the *Post* or the *Times* or wherever the hell you like, just as long as you correct those goddam bloodsuckers at the *World*."

Shrady stroked his cowcatcher moustache and smiled faintly at Trist. "They weren't so far wrong," he murmured.

"Bloodsuckers." Sherman snapped his teeth as if he would bite the cigar in half. "Sam Grant never stole a cent in his life."

"The actual diagnosis is only tentative." Shrady smoothed a sheet of notes across his lap. "The ulcers in the throat are becoming very active and inflamed. General Grant is experiencing what most of us would call unbearable constant pain."

Sherman crossed his legs and stared bleakly into the fire.

"Dr. Douglas swabs his throat daily with anodyne mixtures. Three mornings ago we had a dentist in to extract two teeth, and that's been some help. As you might know, I'm a specialist in epithelial carcinomas. I've given a tissue sample from the throat to an expert microscopist—"

"Name?" Trist was writing as quickly as he could in his pocket notebook, but it was awkward, in the deep chairs, with one hand. Sherman reached over and held the notebook steady on Trist's knee.

"Dr. George B. Elliott. You'll find him in the Medical Directory."

"And what did he say?"

"He plans to communicate his results this month."

"And you asked him to look at what?"

"The capillary blood channels, also the anterior border of the tonsillar cavity, which may already be perforated."

There was much more, similarly technical and unusable in a general newspaper story, but under Sherman's prodding Shrady outlined the basic facts. The doctor suspected cancer of the throat—they wouldn't be certain until the microscopist reported—

if Grant had sought out proper medical attention in the summer, things might be better now, but this was probably wishful think- ing. If it was cancer, it was fatal, and the General was going to undergo—he was already suffering it—indescribable agony. The sheer pain was a nightmare for him. Almost worse was the unremitting feeling of choking and gagging, which made it nearly impossible for him to eat, drink, or sleep. They had considered a surgical operation to remove what they could of the ulcers and bring him some comfort, but the risk was great and the General insisted on having his faculties clear.

"Writing his memoirs." Sherman sat back and lit a new cigar off the old one. Trist nodded. Everybody remotely connected with the *Century* had heard the story of Grant's book and the pirate publisher Mark Twain. "Wants to save his family," Sherman grum- bled. "He won't take money from anybody, after all that *stuff* when he was President, turned me down when I offered him half my pension. Childs down in Philadelphia wanted to start a trust fund—no. What you boys don't appreciate"—in the smoky dark- ness of the club disembodied hands took away their glasses, deposited fresh ones—"is how goddam *hard* it is, in his *head,* for Sam Grant to write about the *past.* I hate reporters, *he* hates retracing his steps, oldest superstition he has, thinks it's like retreating. Nearly got him shot once at Vicksburg, he wouldn't ride back to his tent the way he'd come. Writing his memoirs—hell!"

"General Grant is a sensitive man," Shrady said.

Sherman snorted. Sherman leaned forward and drove a bony finger so hard into Shrady's shoulder that the little doctor jumped in his chair. "*Sensitive.* Back at Shiloh in '62, after the first day and we had taken such a beating you don't ever want to think about it, we were down about as far as an army can go, *I* wanted to retreat. So did every other officer on the staff. I went out looking for him, and when I found him, old sensitive Grant, he was standing under a tree in the rain, smoking a cigar, and I padded right up through the mud and got ready to tell him we had to turn tail or else lose the whole goddam army, that was what his staff thought. Then something made me stop, I didn't say a word—and you don't know how hard *that* is for *me*—and I just stood there under the tree, unnaturally quiet, smoking my cigar too. Finally I said, 'Well, Grant, we've had the devil's own day, haven't we?'

" 'Yes,' he said. He pulled at his cigar for a while and all I could see in the darkness was the little red glow at the tip. 'Yes,' he said. 'Lick 'em tomorrow, though.' "

Shrady smiled and shook his head. "You weren't at Shiloh?" he asked Trist.

"Cold Harbor."

"Our troops at Shiloh," Sherman said, "were so raw we had to walk around in the camp and show them how to load and aim. 'It's just like shooting squirrels,' Grant told them, 'only these squirrels have guns.' "

Shrady smiled again. "The General's a humorous man, if you stop and listen."

"Buckner came to see him yesterday," Sherman told Trist. "Man he defeated at Donelson. Made a special secret trip up from Kentucky. All the Confederates love Grant, you know. He could have humiliated them at Appomattox, he could have crushed them and slaughtered them like cattle, made old Bobby Lee strip down to ashes and sackcloth, and you know, as soon as it was won, he just said, 'Let there be peace,' and he stopped the killing." Sherman's cigar blazed like a flare. "*I* wouldn't have done it," he said.

"How long?" Trist asked Shrady.

"Anybody else," answered the little doctor, "would be dead in a matter of weeks. I think he keeps himself going by sheer willpower, to write his book."

The Question of Clover seemed a long way off. Elizabeth Cameron seemed a long way off, except that Cump Sherman had his niece's trick of lifting his chin when he spoke, a sensual flash of the eye that made Trist finish his whiskey in a gulp and hold out his glass for another.

"I did something the other night," said Shrady. He too had been drinking steadily. Only Sherman seemed unaffected, burning alcohol like air. Shrady leaned forward confidentially. "General Grant can't sleep because of the choking sensation in his throat, he wakes up gasping, terrified he's going to smother. When it got too bad, I went in his bedroom and rearranged his pillow and made him lie on his side, with his hand tucked under the bolster. And I stroked his head and told him to close his eyes and go to sleep the way he did when he was a baby."

Sherman groaned and turned away.

"The Butcher of Cold Harbor," Shrady said to Trist. Stilson

Hutchins would pay an enormous bonus for something like that, Trist thought, any paper in the country would, the old warrior reduced to babyhood, Grant's Last Battle. He thought of Mark Twain's Chicago speech: Grant in his cradle, clutching his toe. He looked at Sherman, still staring miserably into the fire. Somebody else could write it. He closed his notebook and slowly put it away.

CHAPTER FIVE

BY WEDNESDAY EVENING, TWO DAYS LATER, THE UNCERTAIN
snow that had fallen on New York had drifted lazily north across
New England, then blown eastward into the dreary Atlantic. At
Beverly Farms, Massachusetts, on the rugged coast above Boston,
the storm had barely touched down. The ground outside their
house, Clover Adams thought, looked like a brown cake, badly
frosted.

She repeated the description to her father, who was lounging
sleepily in his favorite chair by the fireplace. He had a plaid blanket drawn up to his chin, and on his head the battered black derby
hat he now insisted on wearing indoors and out, so that really all
she could see was his face, from chin to eyebrows. At her little joke
his jaw dropped and his mouth went slack in an invalid's half-
smile, but his eyes remained closed. For all she knew he hadn't
heard a single word, only the sound of her voice.

The sea coals in the fireplace crackled. Someone out in the
kitchen shifted a load of china, and she frowned at the clatter.
Otherwise, father and daughter sat together quietly side by side,
as they had all day, as they had for the last three days, and doubtless would again tomorrow until it was time to catch her train and
return to Henry and Lafayette Square.

Dr. Hooper began to snore. Clover studied his skin color, parchment pale, very bad even for winter. His big crow's beak of a nose, one of the few features they had in common, stood out more prominently than ever. Ugly blue veins mottled his cheeks. Her father was seventy-five years old and he had been the true anchor of her life since her mother had died when Clover was only five and he had retired from the practice of medicine to care for her, and now she was realist enough to know that he was failing; slowly, inexorably failing. Henry criticized her for not thinking logically through her figures of speech. Well, then. The true anchor was slipping, the good ship Clover was coming adrift.

She gripped the back of her neck with one hand and looked at the clock on the mantel and let her gaze travel restlessly over to the framed souvenir photograph beside it, the Gettysburg battlefield, Little Round Top. Her father had bought the photograph on a visit some years back, when a memorial to the doctors who served there was dedicated, and it was actually one of the earliest things that had sparked her interest in photography. She noted automatically the contrasts of light and shadow in the composition and the thin streaks of discoloration where the print had faded. She shuddered. She wondered, far from the first time, how her gentle, self-effacing, self-sacrificing father had stood it, how he had managed to keep his sanity in the Dantesque horrors of the army field hospital where he had worked, he once told her, thirty-six hours straight, performing amputations, removing bullets, nursing the dead.

The thought of Gettysburg reminded her of poor Nicholas Trist, and she stood up abruptly and paced a tight little circle on the carpet. Nicholas Trist, whose torn and wounded arm somebody like her father had once clasped hard and held down on a table with bloody surgeon's hands and started to cut—steel knife, white bone—and then to saw and then to *hack*; her mind coiled to shriek and she *made* it stop. The thought of Gettysburg also reminded her of the scene in that horrible novel *Esther* where the old father dies, and what was more horrible and more prophetic still, talks about Gettysburg in his last moments. She swept the photograph from the mantel with a crashing noise that woke her father, and an instant later she was pulling the bell cord over and over and over again to summon the nurse and servants.

Upstairs in her own room on the second floor, she took

her green velvet dress with the gold brocade and the label "M. Worth—Paris" and wrapped it herself in tissue paper. On the wall above her chest of drawers hung a small oil painting of her maternal grandfather Sturgis, who had been a merchant sea captain and travelled all over the world, three times to China. He had admired Andy Jackson when nobody else in New England did, he had lived a hard life. He had also been famous for the time a political opponent in the Massachusetts legislature mocked his lack of education by speaking on the floor in Latin, and Captain Sturgis had calmly stood up and replied in Algonquin.

The memory made her smile, and she decided she would tell the story to her father in the morning. She would also tell him the latest remark that was sweeping New York and Washington, where the antitobacco crusaders liked to stop men on the street and tell them how much they spent if they smoked just ten cigars a week, and then they would hold up a dollar bill and shout, "Put *that* in your pipe and smoke it!"

Her mood began to sink again. She caught herself in the mirror rubbing her right hand back and forth across her forehead, an obsessive gesture her older sister Nella had warned her against.

She stopped and lowered her hand to her side and simply stood in the center of the room. In the silence she could hear the wind and the sea in the distance. "Clover is as good as *pie,*" her grandfather Sturgis used to say. Her brain skipped to another association, sea captain, sea; *thalassa, thalassa,* the sea, the "wine-dark sea" in Greek that her grandfather had sailed across. She had been trying to learn Homeric Greek for years. On the table next to her bed this very moment was the little two-volume edition of the *Iliad* in Greek that she carried everywhere. Henry liked to laugh and say that she would never master it, that women were not rational and steady enough to learn Greek; not, she thought with a momentary flare of temper, that *he* could read it anymore himself, despite his lofty Harvard education. She had been denied Harvard altogether, of course, because she was a girl, but Nella's husband taught classics there and he was always willing to help.

She thought of Henry and Greek and the sea. His brother Charles Francis had told Henry not to marry her, she knew, because, as Charles said in his inimitable sarcastic way, "all the Hoopers are crazy as coots." On the chest of drawers was a little clay model of the boat she and Henry had taken up the Nile on their honeymoon. There, in the middle of all those sun-bleached and crumbling pagan temples she had experienced what she knew was a nervous collapse, though nobody ever said so. It was only her reaction . . . What was Henry's phrase? Her virginal reaction to "the brutalities of marriage."

For some reason she had left her letter box next to the little ship model. On top of the box was the letter she had received that very day from Henry, the first letter he had written her since they were married, because until now they had never in fact spent more than a night apart.

She picked it up and read the first few lines again.

> *Madam*
> *As it is now thirteen years since my last letter to you, possibly you may have forgotten my name. If so, please try and recall it. For a time we were somewhat intimate. . . .*

She smiled to herself and opened the box to put it away.

Inside the box, a slippery tooled-leather case with brass lock and key that she had bought on that same honeymoon, she saw all the other letters and scraps of paper she had saved, like a good New Englander, since girlhood. There was a letter she had jointly written with her grandfather Sturgis, with her four-year-old scrawl at the bottom of the sheet, CLOVER. There was another letter from about the same time: DEAR FATHER I LOVE YOU——CLOVER. Not on impulse, but observing her distant fingers as if they belonged to someone else, she watched herself rifle suddenly back toward the center of the box and pull out a handwritten document that she hadn't seen in years. It was addressed to her cousin Annie Hooper, and it was written in the form of a parody of a will, complete with detailed instructions for her funeral. Clover was thirteen when she wrote it. The first half consisted of her bequests—a ring and a tea caddy to Annie—the second half was an elaborate account of how she had died.

On the night of the sixth of January 1857, Clover Hooper passed the evening at Number 56, Beacon St. Her house was at 107, the same street. It was a bitter cold night and the wind howled most fearfully. As the time drew near for her departure, she felt a presentiment of death stealing up on her, and was loth to depart, but at last summoning up all her courage, she set forth, attended only by one of the masculine tribe. She had passed in safety the three first crossings below Charles Street when arriving at the last crossing a sudden gust of wind caught her nose—that being the most conspicuous feature of her body—and whirling her through the air dashed her upon the frozen waters of Back Bay. The servant was seized by a contrary wind and drowned in the waters of the River Charles. A milkman riding in from the country on Wednesday morning discovered her body laying upon the ice. On looking at the face, he discovered that it was minus a nose and whilst returning in perplexity to the land he perceived a nose minus a head. . . . A coroner's inquest will be held upon the body this afternoon at 3 o'clock precisely. Price of tickets 25 cts children half price viz 12 cts . . . A customary speech of hers was it's a weary world we live in, and her last speech just before reaching the 4th crossing was changed to it's a windy world we live in.

It had all been a girl's silly secret, of course, between her and her giggling cousin Annie, one of the two actual secrets Clover could remember ever having in her life. She was not a secretive person. Henry was. When Henry had written *Democracy* he only told four people in the world—herself, of course, John Hay, Clarence King, Henry Holt the publisher—and made them all swear to keep it a secret. Secrets made you feel superior, she thought now. Secrets let you make jokes of other people.

She started to fold the sheet of paper, but paused to look at her funny bold handwriting at the top, so unlike her present scrawl. "Will" was a curious word, it could be either noun or verb. Like Henry's irony, it had at least two meanings. A wife knows a husband's voice, she thought, anywhere. Clover replaced the sheet of paper in the box and closed it. Slowly, steadily, while the sea whispered in the distance, she rubbed her hand back and forth across her forehead.

LATE IN THE AFTERNOON OF FEBRUARY 27, MARK TWAIN came stepping briskly down the stairs, all business, from General Grant's second-floor library. At the front entrance hall he stopped and spoke to Grant's black valet Harrison, who gave a quick respectful bow and hurried off to find Twain's sealskin overcoat and giant fur hat. A little Irish maid stood solemnly to one side as Twain shot out his cuffs and patted his suit coat with both hands and came up with two cigars, which he placed on the hallway table, a miniature Bible that Cable had made him carry on the train up from Washington that morning, a stiff blue envelope of legal papers, a pocketknife with the blade missing, a set of girl's jacks, and finally a special reduced-size leather-bound copy of *Huckleberry Finn*, just published the week before.

"Now I forgot to give this to Colonel Fred," he told the maid. "But it's for his daughter."

The girl curtsied and vanished with the book.

Twain tugged his pockets back into shape and then peered into the mirror above the table and straightened his hair and smoothed his moustache. *He* looked fine, he thought, in the pink of health despite six months on the road with "The Twins of Genius"; but Grant upstairs—*Grant upstairs!*

Twain shook his head at the mirror. Only yesterday the lying and venomous and jackass New York newspapers had reported gleefully that the General was better, *much* better, *nearly well*— and so Twain had naturally come bouncing in with his hand stretched out and a grin on his face, full of noisy congratulations. And before he could shut himself up he realized that the object of all these congratulations was coughing and wheezing like a drowning man, and twenty pounds lighter, and pale as paper—"*De-lighted* to hear these reports of your good health!" he had blurted out before he could stop himself, and Grant had just smiled feebly up from his chair and murmured, "Well—if only they were true."

The shock must have showed on his face, Twain thought. Because while Grant was signing the official contracts that made Charles L. Webster & Company the sole publishers of his memoirs—the reason Twain had interrupted his lecture tour today— while all that legal rigamarole was going on, one of the doctors had taken him aside and said confidentially that the General was in fact extremely ill, and Fred Grant later at the top of the stairs had whispered in his ear that nobody had found the courage yet to tell his father the truth.

But he knew anyway. "I mean you shall have this book," Grant had said when he finished signing, and it wasn't about the contract, Twain understood, it was a pledge, a commitment, Grant's word to him that sick as he was he *would* finish what he had started, and Grant's word—well, you could go to the bank on Grant's word. Twain scowled at the mirror. Not the best possible phrase, in the home of Grant & Ward.

Harrison reappeared with his sealskin coat and helped him button it up. Then somebody rang a bell upstairs and Harrison scooted, and Twain was left to see himself out on his own.

Instead, he lingered. He pushed a vase of cut flowers from one corner of the table to the other. He fussed with his coat and patted its pockets too, and came up this time with a volume of Malory's *Morte d'Arthur,* which he had never read before, but Cable had recommended and which had already started him thinking about a new story, man dreams he's a knight in the Middle Ages, all the problems of suits of armor—no pockets for one thing. Can't scratch, can't blow your nose. Always getting struck by lightning. Make him a soldier like Grant.

He walked over to the front door, then stopped. He wished he had brought more copies of *Huckleberry Finn* as gifts, but (he certainly couldn't tell the General, who was as modest and chaste as a preacher) there had been a terrible to-do over one of the illustrations, and even he, the author, hadn't received his full allotment of books yet—because at the last minute some disgruntled engraver had inserted a large male sex organ in a picture of old Silas Phelps, chapter XXXII, and there was Aunt Sally smiling sweetly and asking, "Who do you reckon it is?" and they were having to cut out the offending page and replace it by hand, a book at a time, at J. J. Little's printing plant.

Well. Twain put his hand on the doorknob, but didn't turn it. Anybody with any sense would pull out of the deal with Grant. Anybody *sane* would wait to see how sick the General really was, if he *could* write a book in his condition. Anybody *sane* would march back upstairs and *revoke* the contract, since from what Twain had seen today, the General was still three or four long chapters away from the end of volume one, the siege and capture of Vicksburg. Without Vicksburg you couldn't have volume one, without Appomattox you couldn't have volume two.

He stood with his hand on the doorknob, listening to the thick, tense silence of an invalid's house, thinking furiously. The contract in his pocket meant more contracts, orders to presses, binders, shippers. He would have to commit to buying tons of paper, gallons of ink, his salesmen would need cash advances, and brochures and catalogues—if the book never arrived, lawyers would, *bankruptcy* would. What he had done, Twain thought, beginning to sweat in his heavy coat, was harpoon the Leviathan. Then he straightened his back, lifted his chin like a soldier. He told himself honor was a harder master than the law, Grant was a perfectly glorious man, and he turned the knob and opened the door.

The street outside was filled with curiosity seekers, dozens and dozens of them. They stood on the sidewalk and pavement for almost half a block down Sixty-sixth Street, just staring up at the house like morbid penguins. Some of the reporters recognized him and pushed their way forward, waving their notebooks and calling out his name, but for once Mark Twain hurried past the press without a word and climbed into the first free hansom cab he could hail.

H AD NICHOLAS TRIST ARRIVED HALF AN HOUR SOONER, HE
would have seen Mark Twain for himself.

As it happened, however, his train from Washington was late.
Consequently he had to stand on the sidewalk opposite Grant's
house, stamping his feet in the snow, and listen to three different
accounts of Twain's visit (including a brief and entirely fictitious
interview, described with a straight face and whiskey breath by the
man from the New York *World*).

Trist nodded politely. Peered as instructed at the two second-
floor bay windows, which the *World* assured him was Grant's
library and where, three days earlier, the General's silhouette
behind a curtain had been carefully analyzed to produce the
immortal headline: GRANT SMOKES A CIGAR!

By six-thirty snow had begun to fall and he was shivering with
cold. The crowd had dwindled to fewer than a dozen stalwarts,
standing like a mute glee club in a semicircle at the foot of Grant's
steps. The reporters closed their notebooks in boredom and began
to drift away. Against his better judgment Trist drank two brandy
smashes around the corner with a man he knew from the
Associated Press. He turned down a third because he was already
yawning and had to be up again first thing in the morning, on the
train back to Washington if need be.

"For the pension vote?" asked his friend, and Trist pictured the
tedious rattling train ride and sat down again and changed his
mind about the third brandy.

He had never quite intended to be a newspaper reporter, he
thought. He watched the waiter refill their glasses and set a
wooden bowl of pretzels on the table. His idea after the war, as he
recalled it, had been something more along the lines of a darkly
brooding one-armed Byronic poet, irresistible to women, prepos-
terously rich, forever twenty-three. But reality—poor old unimagi-
native reality—had turned into something else: pretzels, obscurity,
a job that, since he had thrown over his battlefields book, was in
danger of becoming routine. A small life.

And yet he had to give reality its due—the Grant story was far
from routine, the Grant story had suddenly blown up in the country's face like a delayed bombshell from the Civil War. Without

anyone's quite knowing how, Grant's Last Battle had become the biggest newspaper event since Appomattox.

The pension vote, for example—on February 16 the House of Representatives in a fit of partisan spite had turned down a proposal that the bankrupt Grant be restored to the retired army list and thereby given a pension. The outraged mood of Grant's friends—and Dr. George B. Elliott's official diagnosis of cancer, reported by Trist himself—had turned Congress upside down; a reconsideration vote was promised. Meanwhile, Henry West wanted Trist on the spot in New York.

"Where the circus is," said his friend from the AP with a weary grin.

"Reporter Finishes His Drink," Trist said and downed his brandy smash with one long swallow and hoped that reality wouldn't include a hangover.

The pension vote was put off. Next morning Trist was back at East Sixty-sixth Street, furry of tongue, shivering in the cold.

Meanwhile, the pressure of newspaper attention was forcing all kinds of changes. Because of the confusion over reports of Grant's health, his team of six doctors had decided that very morning to issue a daily bulletin to the press, something that hadn't been done since President Garfield had been shot in 1881. And to ensure complete fairness, three official "bulletin boys" were installed right in Grant's front hall—Trist and a crowd of some two or three hundred people watched them file in from the street—representing Western Union, the Associated Press, and the United Press. Any medical despatches would be handed to all three simultaneously, the door flung open at a signal, and all three would then presumably sprint away like crazy to their bosses.

Other arrangements were equally Barnumesque. On the east side of Madison Avenue, the eight major New York papers had pooled their resources and rented the basement of a small house. Here they were joined by a growing number of out-of-town papers like the *Post*. Special telegraph wires were strung to downtown desks and offices. A telephone line was promised. Reporters took turns going up to Sixty-sixth Street and monitoring the Grant home like sentinels.

On Trist's second day the police set up wooden sawhorse barriers at each end of the block in an effort to control the traffic. Yet despite the sawhorses, dozens of carriages squeezed past and waited alongside the curb, surrounded by people peering in the windows while the carriage occupants in turn stared up at the house. The bolder ones often got out and rang Grant's bell.

Those who were admitted—Mark Twain was a daily visitor, also Adam Badeau, said to be helping Grant write his book—were besieged by shouting reporters as they left. On March 1 Senator Jerome Chaffee, Buck Grant's father-in-law, caused a sensation by quoting the General as saying, "I am not better. I am going to die. Every moment is a week of agony." But General Horace Porter the next day denied that Grant ever complained of his illness at all, and General "Black Jack" Logan declared that Grant's suffering had wonderfully cleared his mind for writing.

On March 3, the day before Grover Cleveland was to be sworn in as President, the House of Representatives had still not managed to reconsider Grant's pension. Under heavy pressure from Cump Sherman and the press, the Speaker of the House announced at the last possible moment that they would convene again on March 4, but date all business as having been transacted on March 3. Trist caught the earliest train of the day from New York and raced up the steps of the Capitol well before nine A.M., but the House, despite the glowering presence of Sherman in the gallery, was still debating a series of minor questions—a change in rules, a disputed election in Iowa. A coterie of disgruntled Confederate veterans blocked all other matters.

At noon the House would be constitutionally unable to act. Grant supporters crowded the gallery, muttering ominously, and filled the corridors outside the chamber's doors. At quarter past eleven one of the Iowans abruptly took the floor and, pointing at the clock, declared that he would never stand in the way of the welfare of the country's Greatest Living Patriot—at which point a wild, tumultuous cheer broke out, the Speaker hammered the vote, and the whole room shook with repeated cries of "Aye!"

But the Senate had not yet convened that day. Worse still, the Capitol building was now in a state of roiling chaos, thanks to the inauguration ceremonies set to begin at noon, in the Senate chamber itself. Those Senators already inside scrambled for their seats, others fought their way up the steps and through the hallways in a mad rush—the President *pro tem* chased away carpenters still building the inaugural platform just below his podium, then banged his gavel and signaled for a voice vote on the amended retirement list for the army, just received from the House, and moments later, at exactly five minutes till twelve, at a desk in an adjacent room, outgoing President Chester A. Arthur signed the last bill of his administration. In New York, Mark Twain told reporters waiting on the stoop that Mrs. Grant had read the telegram to the General herself and then cried, "Our old commander is back!" and the whole household (the stern old commander excepted) had let out a whoop of joy!

Trist's story for the *Post* that day, featuring a rare interview with the journalist-hating Sherman, was picked up and reprinted by two hundred papers across the country, almost as many as his "Rum, Romanism, and Rebellion" story of the previous fall—when he reached New York again next morning he was greeted with champagne in the basement on Madison Avenue and, a few hours later, an invitation to interview Grant himself later in the week.

The invitation was Mark Twain's doing, and less an act of cordiality, Trist thought cynically, than of publicity for Grant's book, and in any event it was immediately postponed for a week, and then delayed indefinitely by Grant's fluctuating health.

By the middle of March, he was writing a daily report for the *Post* and two European press services, and the scene along East Sixty-sixth Street had settled into a colorful permanent uproar. Three or four times a day delivery carts fought their way through the crowds on the pavement and the parked carriages and unloaded crate after crate of gifts for the General—horse blankets, war bonnets, old swords, dozens of mailbags of letters with home remedies and herbal extracts. A fanatic named "Java John" tried to wrestle his way in the front door, and when the police pulled him away, he screamed to the press that Grant would be saved only if he stopped drinking coffee. Another man, dressed in a faded blue sergeant's uniform, dropped to his knees on the doormat and prayed at the top of his lungs till he, too, was hauled away. A reporter for the *Tribune* fell out of a tree in the yard next to Grant's and broke his arm and had to be treated by Grant's own doctors.

Yesterday [Trist wrote on March 17] in a kind of symbol of national reconciliation, the sons of Robert E. Lee and Albert Sidney Johnston, the Confederate general who died at Shiloh, came to offer their best wishes to General Ulysses S. Grant.

This morning telegrams arrived from Jefferson Davis and P.G.T. Beauregard. Later your reporter watched General Ely Parker go up the stairs just after Mark Twain and Senator Chaffee. Parker is a full-blooded Iroquois Indian, whom Grant promoted for bravery at Vicksburg and who stood by the General's side at Appomattox and was mistaken by Robert E. Lee for a black man.

The whole country, it might be said, or at least the generation of men who fought in the Civil War, seems to have taken Grant's struggles as the chance to review their own and the nation's past. Some days East Sixty-sixth Street looks like American History's own parade ground.

WHAT THE HELL EVER HAPPENED TO "GRANT THE BUTCHER"? Stilson Hutchins telegraphed Trist irritably from Washington.

"AND LAST BUT NOT LEAST," TWAIN SAID WITH THE SUBTLEST possible change of tone, "this is Adam Badeau, the General's personal research assistant."

"And also the friend of Henry Adams." Trist smiled and held out his hand. "I've heard him mention your Washington days together."

Badeau wore wire-rimmed glasses, a neat, closely trimmed beard, and slicked-back hair. His air of fussy precision was the exact and chilly opposite of Mark Twain's casual, cigar-puffing *bonhomie*. He shook hands with obvious distaste. "I haven't seen Henry Adams in a decade," he said.

"Trist is here to write about how the General writes." Twain was already holding the door open to Badeau's cubicle, where Trist could see a collection of reference books, two or three oversized cardboard portfolios of maps, and a typewriter. "Badeau checks facts," he told Trist, "and goes over the General's prose every day with a set of pruning shears."

This was so clearly not Badeau's idea of what he did that he turned away without a word and sat down at his desk. Twain was unruffled. He led Trist into Grant's bedroom, which adjoined the library and was separated from Mrs. Grant's room by folding doors; then into Fred Grant's study, facing onto East Sixty-sixth Street and furnished, like Badeau's, with reference books and maps. And finally, like a genial host in a country house, he took Trist's arm and opened the door again to the library.

It was, as Trist later informed his readers in the *Post*, a spacious, comfortable room, lined with books and paintings of military subjects. Two bay windows, stretching from floor to ceiling, looked down on the street and let in a full measure of afternoon sunlight. There were four or five leather club chairs arranged in one corner, a big globe on a stand, and vases of cut flowers on tables and shelves here and there, a weekly gift from George Childs, the Philadelphia tycoon.

Grant had placed his desk in the center, under a gas-chandelier, a simple mahogany rectangle bare of everything except stacks of notes in various categories and a green leather-framed blotter. Next to the desk, incongruously, was an old folding card table, rather battered and worse for the wear. On this the General kept manila writing paper, pens and ink, and a little box of children's wax crayons, which he used to mark Union and Confederate positions on his own set of maps. The only book on the desk or table was a well-thumbed copy of Sherman's *Memoirs*.

"Well, I think I remember you from Chicago," Grant said as they came up to him. He struggled to his feet, shook hands, and allowed his black valet to ease him back into the chair. "Cold Harbor."

"Yes, sir."

There was a long, not quite comfortable pause.

"I believe you're a friend of Senator Cameron."

"The Senator brought me over to report on the campaign in 1880."

"And his beautiful young wife," Grant said. He gestured with a small pale hand to a chair for Trist.

"I know her too, of course," Trist replied.

"Trist is a social butterfly," Twain said, sitting down and starting to tap one foot on the carpet. "He also knows Henry Adams down in Washington." He crossed his legs and waved his cigar in the presumed direction of Washington. "Just reminded me out in the hall. Only man I'm acquainted with, General, that goes harmlessly between Henry Adams and *you*."

Grant turned his head slowly toward Trist. "The Adams

family," he said in a voice raspier and scratchier than Twain's, "does not possess one noble trait of character that I ever heard of, from old John Adams down to Henry B. I don't mind if you write that down and print it, Mr. Trist."

"Illness," remarked Twain with a grin, "has made the General mellow."

Despite his pallor and weakness, Grant looked a little sheepish. "Well, I guess you'd better not print it. Henry's brother Charles Francis served three years in the cavalry and did just fine."

Twain pulled out a child's watch, attached to his white vest with a piece of blue ribbon. "I told young Trist you could give him exactly one hour for this momentous interview."

"I expect," Grant said after a moment, so softly that Trist could scarcely hear him, "we both of us have our deadlines."

But one hour turned into four, including dinner at the family table, and afterwards it was considered one of the most successful articles of the whole long Grant-watch saga. In three separate installments, published two days apart in the *Post* (but without any Adams reference), Trist described Grant's library, his weary, cancer-ridden appearance, his methods of composition (dictation to a stenographer in the morning, composition himself by pencil on a yellow tablet in the afternoon). Grant liked to sit sideways at his desk, legs crossed. He was an imaginative speller. He wrote so quickly and steadily that he never dotted his *i*'s or crossed his *t*'s. His concentration, despite the ravages of illness, was astonishing—in one day in March he had written fifty manuscript pages. His book, Trist thought—and wrote—was literally keeping him alive. He was bringing to it all the old qualities of his generalship, which had seemed to vanish during the dark days of his presidency—utter clarity, complete mastery of detail, singleness of purpose, a will that could apparently defy the fierce rebellion even of his own body.

On March 31, four days after Trist's visit, Grant suffered so terrible a fit of coughing that his doctors were summoned in the middle of the night and the Associated Press actually sent out on its wires a preliminary announcement of his death. But less than a week later he somehow struggled back to his desk and resumed his writing.

Once in early April Twain bought Trist a drink in a saloon near Webster & Company headquarters on Fourteenth Street. There

were more details to add, anytime Trist wanted to write again—
Twain had hired a sculptor to make a terra-cotta bust of the
General; the preacher who had baptized him on the terrible night
of the 31st was eager to have his profile written; even Badeau
would be glad to see Trist again.

Trist listened with amusement—Twain was in a wonderful
mood, frantic and buoyant at the same time—almost before they
had taken their seats he had managed to curse his incompetent
business manager Charley Webster, describe a surefire new invention (his own) for clamping infants in their bedclothes, and sing
out loud, beating time on the saloon table with his finger, the
words he had written that very morning to the old Methodist hymn
"There Is a Happy Land":

> *"There is a boarding house*
> *Far, far away,*
> *Where they have ham and eggs,*
> *Three times a day."*

He had brought Trist a present—proof sheets from the first volume of the *Memoirs*. Grant admired the way he, Trist, wrote,
Twain added; clean, crisp prose, not like the revolting verbal arabesques of people like Henry Adams.

"He didn't say 'arabesques,'" Trist said.

"Fred Grant told me the other day," Twain said, ignoring this,
"that the General was disturbed and disappointed because I was
reading the proofs for him, but I never expressed an opinion about
the literary quality. I was as much surprised as Columbus's cook
would have been to learn that Columbus wanted his opinion as to
how his navigation was going."

"What did you do?"

"I went up to the house next day and told him from what I had
read so far I would place his book on the same shelf with Caesar's
Commentaries. I told him his writing had the same high merits, it
was clear, just, candid, not a word wasted. You know, I carry
around in my wallet a copy of his letter to Buckner to surrender
Fort Donelson. 'I propose to move on your works immediately'—
that is soldierly, that is *frank*."

Trist listened to his monologue, jotted a few notes on his pad.
The truth was, he thought, General Grant and Private Twain

wrote alike: both had cleared the arabesques out of American prose. When he ventured something of this to Twain, the humorist was pleased and modest. "Well, maybe. You were right about his bad spelling, though, in the *Post*. Wonderful writer, can't spell worth a damn. I'm not any better. He was feeling bad about that the other day, looking at all Badeau's little corrections on the proofs. I told him sameness is tiresome, variety is pleasing. 'Kow' spelled with a large *K* is just as good as with a small one. Better. It gives the imagination a broader field. It suggests to the mind a grand, vague, impressive new kind of cow. The General was not convinced."

Twain puffed contentedly on his cigar and watched Trist write it down, word for word.

"Be sure you spell my name right," he said with a drawl.

On April 14, on his way to East Sixty-sixth Street, Trist read in the New York *Times* that Dr. Robert Hooper of Beverly Farms, Massachusetts, had died the day before of heart failure, after a long illness. The following week he travelled to Washington to call on Clover Adams and pay his respects, but Henry Adams met him at the door and simply shook his head. Mrs. Adams was not yet able to see anyone. The gift of additional Thomas Jefferson letters, found in a family trunk and mailed to Trist by a cousin, was received in grave silence. Adams made one of his nearly imperceptible bows and closed the door.

Across the Square Elizabeth Cameron was likewise not at home to visitors. Trist stood for half an hour in the gray Washington drizzle, next to the statue of Andrew Jackson, his stepfather's friend. Then he took the train back to New York, his work.

On April 29 the *World* reported under a blazing twelve-point headline that General Grant's celebrated *Memoirs*, to be published by the well-known publicity hound and buffoon Mark Twain, were in fact being written by Grant's former military aide Adam Badeau, from rough notes that the almost illiterate (or unconscious) General had scrawled. Two hours after this story appeared, a steaming, cursing, explosively red-faced Twain sought out Trist in the basement on Madison Avenue and handed him a sealed envelope. He had two things to say, Twain declared, and promptly said three.

The *World* was a daily issue of unmedicated closet paper.

He was suing it for libel.

Here was the General's reply, in the General's own hand.

The next day the Washington *Post* ran Grant's quiet, categorical denial of the story (CHARACTERISTIC DISCLAIMER TO FALSE STORY) and the day after that, in an uncharacteristic act of severity, Grant banished Adam Badeau from his house.

The weeks wore on. Toward the end of May, Stilson Hutchins decided abruptly that the *Post* needed a permanent bureau in New York, and not just for the Grant story alone, and Trist, correspondent in chief, was joined by two young staff reporters. He opened an office not far from Edison's Pearl Street station and began to write more and more about New York, less and less about the General. He mailed Elizabeth and Don Cameron a card with the address of his new rented rooms, another to Henry and Clover Adams. No reply or acknowledgment came back.

On June 16 Grant was moved by a special train (the loan, once again, of his friend Vanderbilt) to a cottage on Mount McGregor, a summer resort in the Adirondacks near Saratoga Springs, where it was thought the cool air would ease his pain, although in truth nobody now expected him to live much longer.

"He told me," Dr. Douglas remarked to Trist one day early in July when Trist came to his office in search of a statement, "the *World* has been trying to kill him off for the last year and a half, and one of these days they're bound to be right."

Trist laughed. "Well, he sounds as if he's actually better."

But Douglas only shook his head. "A hard man to understand, you know. Much humor under all that silence. We have to drain and swab his throat almost hourly, and we've cut away a great portion of the flesh in his mouth. Eating or swallowing must be sheer torture. The other day he told me, 'If you want anything larger in the way of a spatula, there's a man with a hoe out back.'"

"But he's still writing his book?"

"Twain came out to Mount McGregor last week and tried to take the manuscript for volume two away, talked a blue and yellow streak." Douglas was Scots and disapproving. "The General wrote him he wasn't satisfied yet, he intended to do it right, so his family would receive the money fairly."

Trist had been fumbling for a pencil in his coat pocket and now looked up, surprised. "Wrote him?"

"Most of the time, the General is in such excruciating pain he can't speak. It must be like having live burning coals jammed in

your throat. How he sits there and writes his book day after day I
don't know. When he can't bear to talk he writes notes to us. He
keeps a little pad and pencil in his lap and communicates that
way." Douglas paused and looked thoughtfully out his window at
the bright summer afternoon, then gave a short bark of a laugh.
"He says he needs another kind of doctor now, because he's caught
the writing bug."

Dr. Douglas, in fact, had carefully saved and dated every such
note that Grant had written him for the last three weeks. On condition that nothing was to be copied or reported, he allowed Trist
to read them at his desk, and for the rest of that day Grant, who
had been growing more and more remote as a figure in Trist's
mind, suddenly came forward as a presence again, almost a voice.

I have found so much difficulty in getting my breath this morning
that I tried laudanum a few minutes ago, but with the same result
as for some time past. The injection has not yet had any effect. The
douche has not acted well for some time. Do you think it worth the
experiment of trying. I imagine I feel the morphine commencing to
act.

July 3, 1885

In coughing a while ago much blood came up——Has Dr Sands
gone. He takes a much more hopeful view of my case than I
do——How old is he——I had to use the cocain several times in
quick succession this morning. I have not had to use it since.

July 4

I have been writing up my views of some of our generals, and of the
character of Lincoln & Stanton. I do not place Stanton as high as
some people do. Mr. Lincoln cannot be extolled too highly.

July 2

I must try to get some soft pencils. I could then write plainer and
more rapidly.

July 10

"This one"—Douglas handed him a longer slip of paper—"we were
talking Sunday about how he had been selling leather in Galena
in 1861, and the war came, and in all the confusion old Congress-

man Washburne, who kept an eye on all his constituents, pushed Grant's volunteer papers at the governor and had him restored to the army. And after that—I don't know. Grant told me when he sent Sherman off on his march to the sea he usually didn't know where he was, it was like trying to watch a mole under a lawn. Life is like that, he said, no pattern at all that he could see. An hour later he handed me this."

If I live long enough I will become a sort of specialist in the use of certain medicines if not in the treatment of disease. It seems that one mans destiny in this world is quite as much a mystery as it is likely to be in the next. I never thought of acquiring rank in the profession I was educated for; yet it came with two grades higher prefixed to the rank of General officer for me. I certainly never had either ambition or taste for a political life; yet I was twice president of the United States. If any one had suggested the idea of my becoming an author, as they frequently did I was not sure whether they were making sport of me or not. I have now written a book which is in the hands of the manufacturers. I ask that you keep these notes very private lest I become authority with treatment of diseases. I have already too many trades to be proficient in any. Of course I feel very much better from your application of cocain, the first in three days, or I should never have thought of saying what I have said above.

July 8, 1885, 4:00 A.M.

On July 16 Trist made the journey from New York to Mount McGregor himself. But Grant was by then too weak to see him or any other visitor except the closest of friends. For two or three hours Trist wandered the grounds—the "cottage" was a spacious ten-room house in the center of a pine forest—and observed the crowd of "death-watch tourists and relic-hunters," as the *World* called them, that stood on the road and the grass and stared - silently up at the shrouded windows. Two days before, Confederate General Simon Bolivar Buckner, the man who had lent Grant money after California and then surrendered Fort Donelson to him in 1862, had come for a final call. To the reporters gathered around him as he left, Buckner said his conversation with Grant had been private, but later in the afternoon Grant issued through his son a special statement to the press: *I feel that we are on the*

eve of a new era, when there is to be great harmony between the
Federal and Confederate. I cannot stay to be a living witness to the
correctness of this prophecy; but I feel within me that it is to be so.

At four o'clock Trist returned to the little spur-line railroad station that served the resort. He pulled out his watch to check the
time, and then as he stood waiting on the platform he heard his
name shouted. When he turned, Fred Grant was just scrambling
down from a still rolling carriage, in a cloud of dust, waving his
hands. Somebody in the house had told his father Trist was there,
outside in the crowd, Fred said when he caught up, and his father
had insisted that he bring this envelope down to the reporter.
When he opened it on the train, Trist found that it contained a
folded sheet of galley proofs from volume two of the book, now
completely finished and ready for the printer. Mrs. Grant had written Trist's name in ink across the top. Heavy black pencil marks in
another hand had underscored three sentences in the text.

I have always regretted that the last assault at Cold Harbor was ever
made. I might say the same thing of the assault of the 22d of May,
1863, at Vicksburg. At Cold Harbor no advantage whatever was
gained to compensate for the heavy loss we sustained.

DEATH COMING VERY NEAR, headlined the New York *Times.*

On July 21, in anticipation, the *World* began to trim its front
page with a thick black border.

On July 23 at eight-fifteen in the morning Trist was startled by
the sound of fire bells in the distance. He put down his pen and
rubbed his left shoulder. Church bells began to toll, nearby at first,
then, as it seemed, from every corner of the huge city, in slow,
mournful military cadence. Trist crossed the room to the window.
Down on the street, under a bruised gray sky, all traffic had
stopped. Nothing moved. On the sidewalks, in doorways, beside
their wagons and horses, men and women stood in small silent
groups, looking upward and listening. Automatically Trist began to
count, because days earlier the formula had been announced to
the whole country. A single peal every thirty seconds, sixty-three
peals in all, one for every year of U. S. Grant's life. North and
South, the air shook with the iron sound.

Afterwards, Dr. Douglas asked Trist to stop by his Fifth Avenue
office when he could. And a few days later he led Trist through his

examining rooms and back to his private desk and showed him the last in his collection of notes. It was dated simply "July, 1865."

I do not sleep though I sometimes dose off a little. If up I am talked to and in my efforts to answer cause pain. The fact is I think I am a verb instead of a personal pronoun. A verb is anything that signifies to be; to do; or to suffer. I signify all three.

CHAPTER EIGHT

"WHAT A PERSISTENT BURDEN GRANT WAS TO HIS GRATEFUL countrymen," said Clover Adams. She paused and rubbed her hand back and forth across her forehead and stared vacantly at the window, and had it been anyone else the group would no doubt have passed on quickly to some other topic or speaker. But Clover's distress was obvious, painful to see, it was unthinkable to hurry her or skip past her. Trist sat with the others around the little tea table in the parlor and waited for Clover to finish her thought.

"An extravagant *person*," she said after another long moment or two. "And a fool all his life about money."

"You mean the bankruptcy," ventured Rebecca Dodge, a middle-aged woman who lived around the corner from Lafayette Square. She had been in the house when Trist arrived, in some capacity between nurse and neighbor, and he had the impression she would be there when he left and there if he ever came again. "With all his Wall Street cronies?" she added after another pause.

"Yes," said Clover, and stopped, but this time the obsessive rubbing of hand across forehead was too much for Henry Adams's patience. He put down his teacup and nodded in a brisk, dismissive fashion to Trist.

"Bankruptcy," he said, getting to his feet, "or something else more disgraceful. I don't think that was ever quite settled. I admit, the rapidity with which the smallest stockbroker could clean out this man of action knocks my comprehension flat. In ordinary life I should say that a mind so easily deluded could never have marched a sergeant's guard out of a potato patch."

"I remember," Trist said dryly, "that you never thought much of his mind."

"*I* was thinking," said Clover, "of his funeral." As if someone had snapped his fingers and brought her out of a spell, she blinked and sat up straighter and gestured to the hovering black servant for more tea. "We're something of connoisseurs of funerals in Boston, you know, Mr. Trist. I always used to ask my father every spring for the latest tally of deaths and lunatics, and he would chide me for gloomy tastes, but of course Boston *is* one great charnel house." She watched her husband pace to and fro beneath the portrait of mad king Nebuchadnezzar. "I was referring to Grant's funeral, which must have cost the grateful nation an absolute fortune."

"The largest funeral in history." Rebecca Dodge was admiring. "Bigger than Lincoln's even—Mr. Trist wrote a wonderful account of it three days running." She coughed apologetically in Henry Adams's direction. "We take the *Post* at our house."

"Someone," said Adams from the fireplace, "must."

"Mr. Trist was quite eloquent about it."

Adams made a winding circle across the Persian carpet and returned. "It *is* November," he said, "the gloomy month, I believe Voltaire claimed, when all good Englishmen go out and hang themselves. But I'm sure Mr. Trist would prefer to talk about something more cheerful. Come next door, Mr. Trist, and see what our architect hath wrought in your absence."

There was no brooking the note of domestic command in Adams's voice. He tugged at the points of his vest, scowled at Rebecca Dodge and then his wife, and then held his arm out rigidly straight, like a miniature butler, to show Trist the way out of his home.

It was, in fact, very late in November, and outside on H Street the afternoon sun was no more than a distant orange lamp. Burning leaves somewhere farther off gave the day an autumnal tang. They had scarcely stepped from the porch to the sidewalk before Adams's scowl had cleared.

"In the company of women," he murmured as he held the gate for Trist.

"Your wife," Trist began, but Adams wagged his tiny hand in a peremptory cutting off of the subject.

"My wife," he interrupted, "is very glad to see you again. She likes your stories of journalistic derring-do. You made her smile, for which I'm grateful. The truth is, Mr. Trist, my wife and I are becoming green with mould. We're bored to death with ourselves, and since her father's death we see almost no one. At long intervals we chirp feebly to each other, then sleep and dream sad dreams. And that is enough of myself and my wife. Come, inspect the house."

Obedient, wryly amused at his obedience, Trist followed the little bobbing figure of Adams down the muddy, leaf-strewn sidewalk until they reached the corner of H and Sixteenth Streets, opposite St. John's church.

He had seen the house before, of course; all of Washington had been observing and criticizing for months the Hay-Adams Houses. But standing on the sidewalk next to Adams and looking up, he felt again how right Clover Adams had been when she said the architect inclined to the vastly monumental. The two buildings, each four stories high and seamlessly joined, were constructed of dark red bricks and massive cut blocks of gray quarried stone. John Hay's house was around the corner and hard to see, except for a tangle of pointed turrets on the roof. The roof of the Adams house directly above them was a simpler affair, steeply gabled at both ends. Beneath it, rows of undersized windows were set far back in the thick Romanesque walls. On the fourth floor the windows were rounded at the top to give a medieval effect. The whole great structure seemed to rest its weight on two arched bays at ground level, so low and flat that they almost concealed the relatively modest front door. Up close, Trist felt as if he were walking into a crypt.

"We plan to move in, Mr. Trist, at the end of December." Adams fumbled in his topcoat for keys. "At least *I* do. My wife is much less enthusiastic." He held up a brass key ring with a little pointlessly triumphant smile, and Trist remembered yet again how much he disliked Henry Adams, how much he liked his poor, distressed wife. "The architecture and design," Adams said while he selected his key, "have been altogether a masculine affair, I'm afraid, and Mrs. Adams doubtless feels left out. I would say I've interfered unforgivably with her female nest-making impulse, except, of course, the making of houses has always been in some sense the real province of men. You recall, of course, our mutual friend Saint Thomas of Monticello entertained himself in a similar way all his life."

"I once thought," Trist said as they entered the empty house, "we might all make an excursion together down to Monticello— Mrs. Cameron talked about it—the way the characters plan to do in *Democracy*."

"Your favorite novel, yes. Only the new Hebraic owner of Monticello has gutted the inside and rendered it almost unrecognizable, or so I'm told. This is the parlor-elect."

Trist stepped into a room at least twice as long as their present parlor at 1603 H Street. A huge arched fireplace, already furnished with two or three birch logs on a grate, occupied one end. Two diminutive Adams-sized wooden chairs were drawn up before it, in the center of an unswept bare stone floor. Light poured in from tall clear windows that opened onto a garden, now yellow mud. Adams led him down to the fireplace, out through a temporary plywood door, and up a set of stairs to the library. Room by room, heels clicking, hands gesturing like a schoolmaster's, he described his original aesthetic intentions, the architect Richardson's apostasies, the various compromises arranged, evaded. At the very top floor, where the clerestory windows still lacked glass, he motioned for Trist to lean out and enjoy the view and, at the southern end of Lafayette Square, the contrast with the plain columns and simple flat roof of the White House, dwarfed and almost literally in the shadow of Adams's creation.

"I like to think," Adams said as he thrust his own head out an adjoining window, so that from the ground they must have looked like two comical sparrows, "my ancestors would approve the irony of the location. It was down there that old John Adams, my great-grandfather, stormed out in a titanic fury after Saint Thomas defeated him in the election of 1800. And then, of course, my grandfather John Quincy Adams had to slink away in his own sullen fashion twenty-eight years later, when Saint Thomas's protégé the unspeakable Jackson defeated *him*."

"My stepfather worked for Jackson, for a time." Trist had no idea whether he meant to be informative or stupidly provocative.

He let his eye move from the White House over toward, he guessed, Don Cameron's roof. Then he stepped back from the window.

Adams lingered a moment longer. "The square is named Lafayette Square," he said with his bald head still framed in the open space. "But there's no statue of Lafayette in it, only Andrew Jackson, mounted on an implausible horse." He rubbed his hands together and turned back. "Yes, I remember—the Muse of Coincidence. I am a historian, after all. The Trists are well-connected to both Jefferson and Jackson. I wonder a little, Mr. Trist, that you never thought of entering politics yourself, after the war."

"Did you ever think of entering politics?"

"When I first came to Washington, in the early seventies, the idea was in my mind—in my blood, I suppose. An Adams is told in the cradle that he must be great. But I've always considered that the late lamented General Grant, by his sheer vulgarity and incompetence, wrecked my own life, and the last hope or chance of lifting society back to a reasonably high plane. Had someone else been President, I might have risked a run for office—as it is, Grant's administration is to me the dividing line between what we hoped for, and what we've got. But you're like my wife, Mr. Trist, I think. You consider our Civil War a success."

Trist had never been so conscious of his one arm, his awkward height in relation to Adams, his inarticulateness compared to Adams. He blinked against a sudden cold wind that swept through the room. "The war saved the country."

"I think not," Adams replied. "I think it gave birth to an entirely new nation. You don't like me very much, do you, Mr. Trist?" He gave his small, pointlessly triumphant smile again. "Come back downstairs," he said, "even so."

The huge fireplace in the living room contained, next to the birch logs, a tin box of wood shavings. Adams scattered a handful of these over the logs and struck a match. Then he stepped across to a built-in cabinet and removed a port decanter and two elegant leaded glasses.

"Did you ever, Mr. Trist, consider writing fiction instead of journalism?"

Trist was wary. He accepted his glass and sat down in one of the chairs, two men in a vast empty hall, faces barely lit by the windows and the glow from the little fire. Why bother to write fiction? "No," he answered.

"In my youth," Adams told him, "living in Berlin right after the war, I thought about writing a novel. I decided I would have a consumptive heroine, I would base her on a German girl I was flirting with then, and of course 'finish her off' in the most approved romantic style. Arsenic, I suppose, or drowning. Not marriage. As for bringing about a marriage, even in my novel, I would almost rather bring about a murder."

Something in the last sentence snagged at his memory. Trist looked sharply up. But Adams was merely shifting his posture in the wooden chair.

"I told myself," he added, "I would publish it in the year 1880. I have an odd fondness for the year 1880."

"And did you?"

Adams's face looked like a smiling mask of shadows. "I became an historian instead. But I liked the idea of fiction. I liked the idea of being able to express in fiction what one couldn't say directly."

Trist had the sensation of going blindfolded through a minefield. He sipped his port and twisted in the cramped Adams-sized chair. "Such as?"

Adams's hand moved negligently through the gray light. "Such as my view of Grant, other people, the aromatic state of American democracy. But I've grown too mellow for fiction now, I suspect. I regard this universe as a preposterous fraud, and human beings fit only for feeding swine. But when this preliminary understanding is conceded, I see nothing in particular to prevent one from taking a kindly view of one's surroundings." He sipped his port and appeared to lean back comfortably in the chair. "I'm instructed," he said, "by Mrs. Cameron to tell you that she doesn't wish to see you again."

CHAPTER NINE

"BRASS SPITTOON!" MARK TWAIN SAID WITH A CHUCKLE. "Steamboat pilot I knew on the Mississippi, absolutely true story—in the war he used to wear a brass spittoon on his head while he piloted the boat. Kind of a helmet, he thought, to protect him from flying bullets."

"Did he ever get hit?"

"Oh, hell, yes! Bullet hit him in the spittoon one day, his poor old head clanged like a bell—we all heard it. He damn near ran the boat aground, couldn't walk a straight line for a week!"

Henry West was almost doubled over with laughter. He took a deep, hacking breath, exhaled with a hee-haw honking sound, and wiped the tears from his eyes. Next to him, two other reporters were helplessly shaking their heads. Twain sipped his drink and looked benevolently around the newsroom.

"*You* were too young"—he pointed his cigar at West's scrawny chest—"to fight in the war."

"Yes, sir." West pulled a dirty white handkerchief out of one coat sleeve and touched his eyes, then his temples. "Age fourteen in '65."

"Did you ever fight, Mr. Twain?" Besides West and the two reporters sitting on his desk, six or seven others had taken up

places around Twain's chair, some with stacks of copy sheets cradled in their arms, some with notebooks and pencils, one or two
in hats and fur-collared topcoats, right off the street.

"I was a member," Twain answered with a solemn voice and a
deadpan expression, "of the illustrious Marion Rangers."

"Union?" somebody asked doubtfully.

"Confederate." Twain tapped his cigar against a little iron ashtray next to Henry West's typewriter; sipped his Scotch again;
engaged in one of his famous pauses. "Summer of 1861. I just happened to be visiting Hannibal, Missouri, Marion County, and a
few of us got all fired up by what we took to be the Union invasion
of our natal soil. So we came together in a secret place and formed
ourselves into a military company, fifteen of us, fifteen of the most
innocent, ignorant, good-natured, full-of-romance kind of fellows
you could ever hope to meet—remind me, Mr. West, to write up a
piece for you sometime on why the novels of Walter Scott ruined
the South. Gave us the most extravagant notions of aristocracy
and chivalry."

"You sound like a gang of Tom Sawyers," one of the younger
reporters ventured.

"*Exactly* what we were!" Twain was clearly pleased. "A regular
army colonel came over from Mississippi and swore us into the
service, and he commenced to *try* to train us, but it was really just
one long camping trip, nothing but idle nonsense. We would form
ourselves into lines of battle—all fifteen of us—and march a few
miles, and then find some shady and pleasant spot and set up our
tents. Lived off the local farmers till they were sick of us. Once or
twice we came near to landing in an honest-to-God battle, and
once or twice we did fire our weapons, but it was all Tom Sawyer
horseplay." Twain paused again and rolled his long cigar slowly
under a freshly lit match. "Nearly killed General Grant, of course."

Trist entered the newsroom from Stilson Hutchins's office just
in time to hear a shout of hilarious protest rise from the crowd
around West's desk. He stopped, transferred the papers he was
carrying to his jacket pocket. Mark Twain, naturally. He threaded
his way across the floor, through a mountainous jumble of cartons
and cabinets and packing boxes that were the sure signs Hutchins
was planning yet another move for the *Post*. Twain was seated in a
swivel chair with his back to the window, wearing, of all things for
the first day of December, a white suit. His bushy red hair was illu-

minated by an electric streetlamp just outside the window; his foxy face was almost obscured, as usual, by cigar smoke.

"We'd heard about an unknown Union colonel, you see, sweeping down our way with a regiment of troops—" Twain broke off to wave his cigar at Trist and smile. It was, Trist recognized at once, the story of the Marion Rangers in the Missouri woods. Twain had told it to Trist and Sherman in New York, two nights before Grant's funeral procession. It was Trist's strong impression that the humorist was working the story over, polishing it up, less for the lecture platform than for some personal reason hard to fathom.

The female reporter Calista Halsey beckoned him to stand beside her. Twain swiveled, paused, tapped cigar ash. He had already reached the point, Trist saw, where the Rangers had shot an innocent civilian stranger in the forest, and Private Twain had decided that was all he needed to see of war.

"After we fired our volleys at that perfect stranger," Twain said, modulating his speech to something soft, accentless, even maudlin, "we all crept stealthily out to see our victim. He was lying on his back in the moonlight, his chest was heaving, and his white shirtfront was splashed with blood. The thought went through me that I was a murderer, that I had killed a man—a man who had never done me any harm, and that was the coldest sensation that ever went through my marrow."

"Who was he?"

"We never knew. He muttered some words about his wife and child and died, and soon after I lit out for the Territories. In plain English, I deserted and went to live in Nevada."

"And Grant?"

"Well, the General and I used to talk—how it *might* have been *him* that night in the woods, just as easy as anybody else. You see, that unknown Union colonel that was coming after the Rangers turned out to *be* Grant. And Grant in those days didn't have a uniform yet, he was still in his civilian clothes, and he had just left his wife and child in St. Louis, fifty miles away. We used to talk, the General and I, about how mysterious it was, our two fates linked like that, how the course of human history would have been changed if he had come after the Rangers a day or two early." Twain paused, contemplated his smoke. "Not to mention the history of publishing."

Henry West was the first to laugh. He held up the copy of volume one of Grant's *Memoirs,* published that very week by Charles L. Webster & Company, for the rest of the room to see, and Twain himself leaned forward and opened a carton on the desk to reveal more books, a free copy for every reporter present.

In the ensuing scramble Twain worked his way over to Trist. "This man," he told Calista Halsey, shaking her hand, "wrote the best article anybody ever wrote on Ulysses S. Grant."

" 'The View from the Porch.' " Calista patted Trist's shoulder like a big sister. "Our boy does good work."

"Stole it from me, I'm sure," Twain said pleasantly, winking at Trist. "General Grant sitting on his porch at Mount McGregor, reviewing his life. If I didn't think of it, I *meant* to. You ought to write a biography of him, Trist, I'm serious, a full-length book—go see Charley Webster."

"He's writing a book on Edison," Calista informed him a little briskly, and then, because she was the unofficial hostess of the unofficial dinner the *Post* was giving him, she took Twain's arm and began to lead the chattering reporters out the door toward Willard's.

Leading newspapermen anywhere, as Henry West liked to say, was like herding cats. Twice they stopped off in neighboring bars; once, although it was almost six o'clock, they looked in a bookshop on Pennsylvania Avenue to see if the *Memoirs* were on display yet. Calista Halsey, now happily married, had come back to work a year and a half ago at the *Post.* But quite daringly, she still retained her maiden name—to his surprise Trist found he rather approved— and Twain evidently regarded her as at once exotic and alarming. In the lobby of Willard's, while the waiters were conferring about how and where to seat a party of sixteen men and one lady, he pulled Trist aside; asked her full name again; wondered aloud if she were one of those *radical* females.

"The Marion Rangers," Trist prompted. "In New York you told us something else, at the very end."

"Part about war." Twain nodded, glumly for once, and studied with an uncharacteristic frown the waiters and reporters across the lobby. "Part about how that man we shot wasn't in uniform, wasn't even armed. How I couldn't drive away the thought that taking that unoffending life was a wicked, wanton thing. And it seemed like the epitome of war to me, what war really was—killing strangers in cold blood, strangers you would help if you found them in trouble, or they would help you."

"Word for word," Trist said with a faint smile.

" 'It made me see,' " Twain recited, " 'I wasn't equipped for that awful business. It made me see the true nature of war, which is murder, and so I fled.' "

Calista Halsey was waving them over. A headwaiter carried a leather-bound menu over his head like a trophy. "And yet—" Trist's own mind was distracted, wrestling with other thoughts, but something in Twain's tone made him grip the older man's shoulder and hold him back for a moment. "And yet that was what Grant did, that was his trade."

"And we admired and worshipped him for it." Twain's smile was bleak. "He was a man and he faced up to the world, good and bad—and I was a child." A slow, melancholy pause. "I don't have a shred of religion. To a child, a grown-up man can look like a god."

"Mr. Twain—" An already drunken Henry West was tugging them both toward the open French doors of the dining room. "We voted, six of us at the table, to ask if you have any Advice for Youth?"

The showman's mask returned in a flash. The stage-prop cigar was produced, the drawl became a rich instrument of theater. "Well now, I would advise American Youth," he said with a deep Missouri rasp, throwing his shoulders back and walking toward his audience, white suit gleaming like a pearl under the new electric lights, "in the important matter of Lying, for instance, to be very, very careful." Pause, puff; wink. "Otherwise you might get caught."

It was three blocks from Willard's Hotel to Lafayette Square. By a quarter till eight Trist had slipped away from the dinner and was standing outside on the sidewalk, under the Willard's green-and-blue-striped awning, watching a cold rain come down.

A one-horse herdic rattled toward him, up from the Capitol. The driver slowed and peered through the rain over a swaying lantern, but Trist only shook his head and started to walk west. At the corner of the Treasury Department building he waited while an omnibus on rails made its noisy, iron-shredding turn down toward Pennsylvania Avenue. In his pocket he felt the note of dismissal Henry Adams had given him the day before, and for a moment he considered pulling it out to read again under the streetlamp. But in fact, for some things, he had a verbal memory almost as good as Mark Twain's.

Adams hadn't read the note, of course, no matter what smug pose of superiority he affected in his empty shell of a house, with his glass of port twirled between his tiny fingers. Adams hadn't been "instructed" to say a word. Henry Adams was simply a meddler, a self-appointed five-foot-tall stump of irony and malice and intuition.

Trist crossed the bottom of Lafayette Square, stepping around the carriages parked as usual at the gate to the White House. The single soldier posted as a sentinel glanced in his direction and yawned. The horse in front of the nearest carriage stamped its hoof with a splash. Even in the cold and the dark Trist could smell wet leather, the faint stench of rotting vegetation from piles of unburned leaves. At Don Cameron's house he rapped on the knocker hard, and when the black maid peeped in surprise around the edge of the door, he smiled and handed her his hat and walked straight in.

"Senator Cameron now, he's *out*," the maid protested unhappily, following him with quick little steps into the parlor. "Gone out late."

"At the Republican caucus, down at the Capitol." Trist went from one end of the familiar room to the other, stopped at the train-wreck photograph, still bizarre, he thought, and inexplicable. He felt his sleeve brush the tops of Cameron's quite formidable collection of crystal whiskey decanters, all full; resisted the impulse to pour himself a glass. "Mrs. Cameron's here, though?"

It was the same maid who had first greeted him in 1879, dressed as far as he could tell in the same starched white apron and gray cotton uniform dress. She straightened the decanters automatically and looked even more unhappy. "Mrs. Cameron's resting, Mr. Trist."

He walked over to the window and parted the curtains. "Well, I'm glad we're not in Cleveland anyway," he said, and the maid, whose name was Jewel, gave a nervous laugh and pushed the decanters farther against the wall. In the very late summer, after the enormous funeral procession for Grant the first week of August, Trist had travelled on some flimsy pretext or other to Cleveland, where the Camerons were visiting relatives. He had

waited three long days in the Western Terminus Hotel, next to a
seedy bar called the Cleveland Bunch of Grapes, hoping against
hope that Elizabeth could break free for two hours, an hour, anything. Love's old sweet song. Jewel had carried the note for him.
Jewel had shaken her head sadly when he had strolled by the family house at a prearranged time. Jewel, Trist thought, had gone
about as far as she was going to go.

"Mrs. Cameron's in the family way, Mr. Trist."

Trist nodded absently and squinted out through the rain at the
streetlamps in Lafayette Square. So many changes; so little
change. He had already known why Elizabeth was resting, thanks
to gossip at the *Post,* thanks to Henry West's infallible knowledge
of everything that went on in Washington.

"Is she in her dressing room?"

Jewel's eyes grew big with alarm. "No, sir."

"I'll just be a minute. You come too."

Feeling as though he ought to have malaria again, or at least
be shaking with fever, Trist started down the hallway, past the dining room; turned left at a corner; heard Jewel's shoes padding
uncertainly on the carpet behind him.

"This is the door?"

"No, sir."

Trist turned the knob.

"My semi-ancestor Jefferson," he said as he stepped across the
threshold and Elizabeth Cameron looked up from her *chaise
longue* with eyes as huge as Jewel's, "was fond of rejecting ladies
at long distance, by note if possible. He apparently broke the heart
of one Maria Cosway in Paris that way."

"Well." Elizabeth put down the book she held. The room was
alive with the hiss of gas lamps and heaters and the chuckle of rain
against the windowsill. "You're not a real descendant, I guess, so
the precedent doesn't apply. I knew you'd come. It's all right,
Jewel."

"No, ma'am. Yes, ma'am." Stubbornly, Jewel proceeded to the
foot of the *chaise longue* and busied herself with cushions.

"Can you walk to the parlor?" Trist asked. Elizabeth was
propped up against a mound of frilly stuffed pillows; her legs were
covered with a blanket; around her shoulders she wore, buttoned
modestly to the throat, a quilted bed jacket of exquisitely embroi-
dered Venetian silk that would have cost half a year's salary for

someone like Trist. A lady in her circumstances, a lady of wealth and station, would be largely confined to beds and *chaise longues*, of course, from now until the day of her lying-in, and for a month afterwards, and for another month after that confined entirely to her bedroom.

"You look well," she told Trist. "A healthy summer."

"You look wonderful."

"I'm very happy." She smiled for the first time, the wide, white, sharp-pointed smile that came from the Sherman side.

"Why send Henry Adams? Why dismiss me by messenger?"

The smile became smaller. "I can't, you see, go out."

"Is he the father?"

Jewel dropped an armful of cushions. Elizabeth laughed, a sensuous, full-throated laugh that made Trist's chest tighten. Despite the armor of quilts and silk he could still see the swell of her hips and the curve of her breast, and he felt his face as always flush with desire and his blood stir. Love's first moment after noon, he thought, is night.

"Is that what they say down at your newspaper?" Elizabeth shook her head through her laughter. "Just like the *Post*! No. No, Henry Adams is not the father. My husband is the father. Jewel, you're to go away right now."

"Yes, ma'am."

"There was never a time for us," Elizabeth told him, "not really," and smiled and shook her head more slowly, sweetly. Trist put his hand on the doorknob and his mind made one of those illogical, unconnected skips out of the present, back to Henry Adams the day before. As soon bring about a murder as a marriage, Adams had said about his book, which was a quotation from *Esther*. "Are you so very sad?" Elizabeth asked. "*Triste?*"

It took him a moment to answer. "I feel like the man in the story Lincoln used to tell, when he stubbed his toe. He was too big to cry, and it hurt too much to laugh."

"Lincoln," she murmured. "The war." She stretched languorously. In the mirror beside the *chaise* she seemed farther away. A trick of illusion. The first time he had ever seen her face was in a mirror. "Don't come again, Mr. Trist," she said.

CHAPTER TEN

DON CAMERON WAS ONE OF THOSE EXASPERATING MEN WHO
have no idea how long they take to think.

He hadn't always been that way. Age and alcohol would have
done their part, of course, along with the bout of lung fever he
claimed to have suffered last summer. Clover Adams regarded him
with a mixture of impatience and sympathy and considered that he
must have been standing for a full minute already, with his hat in
his hand, ready to go out the door, calculating with excruciating
slowness the complications of his social calendar.

"Well," he said finally, "this is December fourth. Just tell your
husband I might be free in a week. It all depends on when the
Senate adjourns." Then he looked around with a Cameronesque
scowl as if noticing for the first time that Henry Adams wasn't
present.

"My husband is at the German legation," Clover said, and it
cost her some effort to sit politely in the Cameron parlor and
explain to the Senator that Henry had gone off to his regular
Friday-evening diplomatic reception, but she, Clover, couldn't
bear the thought of so many clacking German tongues and so had
come over instead to visit Mrs. Cameron, which she ought to have
done anyway, long before. She made a gesture toward the bouquet

of Maréchal Niel roses that the maid was cutting and putting in a vase. She did not look at the window, where she knew her reflection would be small and tired and crowlike, and completely repellent to a man like Cameron.

"Well," he said again, "I guess I have to go to my own reception." He put on the hat and nodded to the maid. "Republican caucus at Willard's. Jewel can take you back to see my wife."

Jewel picked up the vase of roses and looked solemn. Together she and Clover listened to Cameron's heavy footsteps in the hallway, then the clatter of the door and chain. Frigid air from the outside swirled into the room and stirred the hem of her skirts. The little black maid cleared her throat; shifted the vase from one arm to the other. Slowly, as slowly as Don Cameron thought, as slowly as an arthritic old lady, Clover came to her feet and started to follow Jewel.

The Camerons had separate bedrooms, naturally. The half-open door to the Senator's revealed odd corners of heavy dark furniture and scattered objects masculine and leather. A smell of hair oil and bourbon just lingered in the air. Jewel swept past without a glance and knocked on the closed door on the left.

"I am," cried Elizabeth Cameron, bounding up straight on her *chaise longue* and holding out both her arms to Clover, "*so* glad you've come!"

And of course for the next five minutes Clover was *so* glad, too, did exactly what was expected of her, did it to the letter. Sat at the side of the *chaise* and admired the handsome new bed jacket Elizabeth wore, light green in color to match her eyes, a present from Don; handled the delicate little knitted stockings and slippers under way for the baby-to-be; listened to an unnecessarily intimate account of the complications of Elizabeth's "illness." Twice she caught herself rubbing her forehead, and once or twice, evidently, she lost track of the conversation for a moment.

"The roses," she explained in one of those awkward pauses, "came from Mrs. Bancroft's greenhouse."

"Dear Mrs. Bancroft," said Elizabeth. Discussion of Mrs. Bancroft's health, her eleven grandchildren, the prospects for more. Names were mentioned. The Camerons had gone all the way to California at the end of the summer, for the sake of the Senator's lungs, and some Western relatives had proposed the name Martha, if it were a girl, James for a boy.

"*We* meant to go to the new Yellowstone Park," Clover interrupted, more sharply than she intended, "in June. Henry made all the arrangements. Clarence King found us a guide, a mule train, six whole weeks of camping."

"But you didn't go," Elizabeth said kindly, "did you? I'm so sorry about your father. I wrote you a letter."

"I didn't think," Clover murmured, and must have said something else to finish the sentence, but her mind drifted off, her attention wandered. There was no point in trying to tell someone like Elizabeth Cameron how grief felt, how a void had simply opened up in her life, like an abyss at her feet. They had canceled Yellowstone because she couldn't bear the strain of the trip, and instead for a month they huddled in one of those empty, melancholy resorts in West Virginia, White Sweet Springs, riding sometimes, taking their meals in the hotel, reading. By early July neither she nor Henry could stand it a moment longer and so they had done what she swore not to do, gone back to Beverly Farms, where her father's house was, and all her girlhood and his grave and the cold ocean again, *thalassa, thalassa.* She was forty-two years old.

It was very hard, she thought, blinking at Elizabeth. It was a hard thing to ask her to come and visit such a beautiful young woman, about to become a mother, the Princess of Lafayette Square.

Her fingers rattled the teacup so badly the little black maid jumped forward nervously, as if to catch it when it fell. Clover set the cup down on the table. Automatically picked up the book beside it.

"General Grant's *Memoirs*," said Elizabeth, whose uncle and brother-in-law were generals too. "Just published this week. Mrs. Grant sent us a copy."

"He wrote it while he was dying of cancer," Clover said, to show she kept up, was *au courant.* "Practically the whole world was watching. He wrote it, so to speak"—she lifted her head and in the mirror looked defiant—"out in the open, to save his wife."

THE NEXT DAY WAS SATURDAY, DECEMBER 5. CLOVER MARKED IT on the calendar in her sitting room upstairs at 1607 H Street. The weather was dreary, cold. The great bulk of the two new unoccupied houses threw a shadow across her back garden, all the way to Mr. Corcoran's fence on the other side. At three o'clock Henry looked in to say good-bye—his tooth was still hurting, it had hurt him all night long, and his dentist had finally sent round a boy to say come and see him, even on a Saturday.

Clover heard the murmur of voices down below in the stable. The carriage rolled out, splashed away through the mud. On her desk in all sorts of uncooperative piles lay the papers she was supposed to put in order for their move. Her photographic records. Household receipts. Books of architectural drawings. The stiff cardboard folders with her father's letters, all the bank cheques, business letters, invitations, everything.

Everything. From a great distance, as if she were a cloud floating high above, she saw her hands sort through the envelopes and come to a stack labeled simply "Lafayette Square," tied with a red silk ribbon, which the hands, still small as a child's and far away, carefully untied with a will of their own. Notes from the Bancrofts, the Beales. Copies of notes sent, drafts of letters. Henry had the historian's horror of throwing away any single scrap of paper. *Dear Mrs. Cameron,* this one said, written in Henry's neat, careful hand, a draft but almost like printing, much clearer and more precise than Clover's messy scrawl, *December 7, 1884—*

> *Dear Mrs. Cameron—*
> *I shall dedicate my next poem to you. I shall have you carved*
> *over the arch of my stone door-way. I shall publish your vol-*
> *ume of extracts with your portrait on the title-page, I am mis-*
> *erable to think that none of these methods can fully express*
> *the extent to which I am*
>
> > *Yours   Henry Adams*

Of all things on earth, runs the line at the end of *Esther,* and Clover had no idea why her mind would remember it just now, *to be half married must be the worst torture.*

The smallest stack on her desk was the collection of letters, also tied with a red ribbon, from Thomas Jefferson to some forgotten ancestor of Mr. Trist in Philadelphia. No more than eight or nine letters in all, written on still crisp eighteenth-century French stationery. Henry had literally thrust them at her before he left, to give to Mr. Trist when he called. And of course, being curious, being a woman, being a historian's wife, had she not looked at them? Had she not turned the old sheets of paper over to read Jefferson's quaint old-fashioned handwriting? Had she not found in the center, misplaced surely somehow from Henry's business correspondence—but placed exactly where she must find it—a letter to Henry Holt the publisher in New York, dated January of this year while her father was sick and dying in the charnel house of Boston, and had she not taken the deepest breath of her life and read it and learned her husband's secret at last?

6 Jan. '85

My dear Holt,
My experiment has failed. The failure is disappointing
because it leaves the matter as undecided as ever to me. So far
as I know, not a man, woman or child has ever read or heard
of Esther. I wanted to see if my book would sell without any
advertising or reviews, by word of mouth only. My inference is
that America reads nothing—advertised or not—except maga-
zines.

My object in writing now is to ask you to make another
experiment. I want to test English criticism and see whether
it amounts to more than our own. Can you republish Esther
in England? I will supply you, privately, with the required
amount of money.

I see no reason for your giving yourself unnecessary trou-
ble to hide matters from your brother. The secret, though
interesting to me, is not so serious to you as to exact your
unnecessary labor. By all means let him know about it, if you
like. All I ask is that he should fully understand that no one
except yourself has been told it, and that it is to remain
absolutely between him and me.

Yrs as ever
Henry Adams

Henry was still away at the dentist when Mr. Trist arrived at four o'clock. Clover gave him tea and they sat together quietly in the parlor. They commented on the weather, he told her a complicated story about Thomas Edison's laboratory, and then she stood up abruptly, without thinking at all, and handed him the portfolio of

Jefferson's letters and insisted he examine them to be certain none was missing.

He demurred at first, of course; he was sure Mr. Adams had been scrupulously careful with the documents. But Clover was firm and repeated her insistence. He looked at her, she thought, strangely, but nodded and began to untie the ribbon.

For a minute or two there was nothing to hear but the crackling of logs in the fireplace. Nothing to see but his bowed head as he balanced the letters awkwardly on his lap and turned and glanced at the sheets of paper one by one. She rubbed her forehead so hard that it hurt. Trist came to the center of the stack and stopped. He read very slowly. Then he raised his head, and from the expression on his face she knew that he hadn't guessed either. They had both read *Esther,* she and Trist, but neither of them had guessed that Henry was the author.

Clover made herself lower her hand from her forehead. "I remember that we talked about that book, Mr. Trist. The heroine is rather inadequate, wouldn't you say?"

He murmured something she didn't hear.

"Inadequate," she repeated more loudly. "And unsatisfactory as a woman, to a man. The beautiful young girl in the book reminded me of Mrs. Cameron." Her hands had nothing to do. They made foolish wringing gestures. She looked over at the table by the end of the sofa where she had placed a vase of roses for herself, nobody had brought them. "Fiction is not always false," she added, pleased to be saying something intelligent, paradoxical. "A fiction is not always a lie. It can send a message. It can explain someone's feelings. Of course I knew that he liked her, all of you men like her. I even thought at one time, Mr. Trist, that you and Mrs. Cameron . . ."

Trist put the Jefferson letters in his jacket pocket, then slipped the letter from Henry Adams to his publisher back in its envelope. "What do you want me to do with this?" he asked quietly.

"We have a curious sympathy for one another, no, Mr. Trist? The company of the wounded." She held out her hand for the envelope, very calm, scarcely trembling. "I want you to do nothing with the letter. It's a secret, our secret, you must promise. Henry wrote a clever book in private, that's all." Her voice seemed to rise and crack. "The book has nothing at all to do with my marriage."

In the hallway Trist shrugged on his coat and prepared to say good-bye, but Clover, standing by the foot of the stairs, suddenly buckled at the knees and started to fall. She clutched the banister with both hands. As he hurried forward to help her she pushed him away with a shriek. "Please don't touch me, Mr. Trist—I should die if anyone touched me!"

A T NOON, SUNDAY THE 6TH OF DECEMBER, CLOVER AND HENRY finished a late breakfast in the morning room. The day was warmer, the sun was brighter. She had slept quite well, she told him, she was feeling much better than before. He looked at his watch; patted his lips with a napkin. He would just take a walk by himself, he said, for an hour or so.

Upstairs at her desk, where she used to write her Sunday letters to her father, Clover cleared a space in the papers and books and began a letter to her sister Ellen Gurney in Boston. *If I had a single point of character or goodness,* she wrote, *I would stand on that and grow back to life. Henry is more patient and loving than words can express—God might envy him. He fears and hopes and despairs hour after hour—Henry is beyond all words tenderer and better than all of you even.*

She read the letter over and stared for a long time at the blue sky over the garden. Then she folded the sheet of paper, unsigned, and placed it under the corner of her blotter.

Downstairs the packing men had not yet started work on her photographic darkroom. The little closet was just as crowded and jumbled as ever with frames and cameras and a whole table of nothing but tin basins and glass vials. From the cabinet next to the door she took a bottle of potassium cyanide that she used in developing her prints. She filled a vial with water and stirred in the colorless salts. Upstairs in her own room again she stood before the fireplace with the vial in her hand. The mixture had a strong bittersweet smell, like almonds. Three houses down and across the street the bells of St. John's church began to toll and she lifted the vial slowly and swallowed it all.

Paris   Late October 1891

AUTUMN DRIFTS DOWN TOWARD PARIS ALONG THE VALLEY OF the Seine, from the gray, wet coasts of Normandy, cooling the land, sending ripples of soft, sober-colored light and shadow southward. Most years the season changes in the calm leisurely fashion of a leaf falling gently from a tree.

In the first week of October 1891—Trist stopped writing and hastily shoved his pencil and notebook into his jacket pocket, but not before Sophie Liane Ledoiné stopped in front of him, folded her arms across her *décolleté*, and formed her lips into an exquisitely exaggerated, irresistibly kissable pout that, Trist assumed, Sophie had learned, like every French woman, as an infant.

"Do you know, Monsieur Trist, what the Duke of Gloucester said when Edward Gibbon gave him a copy of the *Decline and Fall of Rome*?"

"It's on the tip of my tongue."

Sophie stuck out the tiny pink tip of her own. "He said, 'Another damned thick square book—always scribble, scribble, scribble, eh, Mr. Gibbon?' "

"How is it, Madame Ledoiné, you know so much more about English literature than I do?"

"One," said Madame Ledoiné, "you're an American and not

expected to know anything except buffalo shooting and Indian fighting. Two, I spent every summer of my girlhood in Devonshire with a private tutor. My father had practical notions of female education. He thought a girl only needed to learn two things well—how to ride a horse and how to speak a foreign language. You're writing one of your witty articles about the *réception, n'est-ce pas?*"

Trist reluctantly took his eyes from her lips (and *décolleté*) and shook his head. At the other end of the *Grande Salle de Réception* of the Petit Palais museum, the President of the Third French Republic, M. Sadi Carnot, was standing with his ministers before a long line of foreign diplomats, many of them colorfully beribboned or becostumed, all of them shuffling forward for their bow, their handshake, their several well-chosen words of republican greeting and recognition. Three or four times a year, at irregular intervals, the President held this quite informal, for the French, reception of diplomats; his expression on each occasion never varied from the expression he wore now, the bland, professionally insincere smile of a headwaiter uncovering a dish.

"In the old days," remarked Madame Ledoiné rather wistfully, "when the Emperor received in the Tuileries palace, he always remained in the state room, beside the gold throne." They both looked at the empty space behind the President, where there was no throne at all, only a ceremonial tricolor flag in a stand. "And the Empress Eugénie always received separately, in the royal drawing room." They moved their eyes right, where instead of a royal drawing room there was a large open exhibit hall whose walls were covered with hundreds and hundreds of photographs of the American Civil War, an exposition organized by the museum staff, somewhat belatedly, in honor of the thirtieth anniversary of the war.

Madame Ledoiné sighed and snapped open an eighteenth-century silk fan the color of dusty roses. "You would have enjoyed the Empress; men did."

Trist nodded in respectful agreement—Madame Ledoiné was an acknowledged expert in what men enjoyed—and thought that people of a certain age in Paris talked about Eugénie and the days before the Commune in the same nostalgic way Americans talked about the vanished world before the war. Decline and Fall was

probably the oldest human topic in the world. Madame Ledoiné
touched the inside of his wrist lightly with two delicate fingers.
Second oldest, he corrected himself.

"Here approacheth your awful M. Hahr." She narrowed her
eyes and frowned prettily over the top of her fan. "Come and see
me, *mon cher,* five to seven, not Thursdays." She moved away,
leaving Trist to nod and shake hands briskly with Francis P.
"Frank" Hahr, First Secretary of the American Legation, a
Bostonian and a prude, and, Trist thought, one of President
Benjamin Harrison's more inexplicable diplomatic appointments.
Hahr spoke very little French, didn't drink, and like most prudes
had no sense at all of irony. Harrison might as well have sent him
to the moon as Paris.

"Found you," Hahr said when the handshake was done.
"Good. Was that Madame Ledoiné?"

"*Soi-même.*"

"Boucé's mistress, right? I heard her described the other day as
a *semi-castor*—a 'half-beaver.' Is that really the phrase?"

"Well, I wouldn't use it to her face. She's also called one of the
grandes horizontales, but I guess I wouldn't say that either."

"Beaver," Hahr said in a tone of wonderment. "What a country. I'm supposed to bring you over to the pictures, in case Reid
needs an expert comment in French."

Trist looked past Hahr to the exhibit hall, where the
Honorable Whitelaw S. Reid, former editor of the New York
Tribune, present United States Ambassador to France, was standing in the middle of a circle of diplomatic admirers. He wore an
elegant black swallowtail coat, white tie and shirt, and a brilliantly
colored ambassadorial sash of red, white, and blue across his
chest. Just beyond his bald head hung one of the featured photographs of the exhibit, nicely illuminated by a rank of suspended
Edison lights: U. S. Grant in scuffed boots and a rumpled old private's uniform, with his three stars sewn rather haphazardly on
one shoulder, leaning an arm against a shattered tree at City Point,
Virginia, in the fall of 1864. The juxtaposition was almost enough
to make Trist forget his resentment at being treated as an embassy
errand boy, because of all the unforgiving mugwump Republican
writers who had hated Grant and done their best to make his political life miserable; Whitelaw Reid was possibly the most virulent

and obsessive. Unless, of course, you counted his friend Henry Adams, who was also there, a full head shorter than Reid, holding a glass of champagne and blinking at the lights.

"We'll sneak up on them," Trist told Hahr, and started to cross the big room by way of the opposite wall.

"You remember the trouble he had with his speech," Hahr said, trotting beside him, hand diplomatically covering his mouth.

Trist nodded and pushed on through the crowd to the place on the left-hand side where the exposition began its chronological march: photographs of Fort Sumter; a young, raven-haired Lincoln; rows and rows of bloated Union corpses on the grassy fields of the First Bull Run, when Trist was still a student in New Haven, wondering what his duty was. At the opening of the exhibit Whitelaw Reid had attempted to give a speech in French, but had gotten so tangled in mispronunciations and stammers that he'd finally switched in desperation to English. Just as well. The French rather liked Grant, or their memory of him when he had visited Paris in 1877, after his second presidential term. But Reid had gone out of his way to describe the Union victory as the triumph of Northern manufacturing and numbers over Southern agriculture. Grant's role was merely incidental, he informed them. General Grant was nothing but a lucky blunderer.

They passed a map of Vicksburg, a picture of a Mississippi gunboat, more corpses; then a long stretch of photographs of the Army of the Potomac at Antietam and Gettysburg—all the illustrations for the battlefields book he should have written, Trist thought, long ago, but never had.

"He sees you," Hahr said with evident relief. And indeed Reid had made a half-turn with his glass and raised one eyebrow to signal, evidently, that Trist should stand close by. "His French really isn't very good, I'm afraid."

Trist took a glass of champagne from a passing waiter and remembered Mark Twain's description of his own bad French. He had hardly ever been taken for a Frenchman, Twain declared, except by horses.

"Mr. Adams seems to know you."

Trist nodded briefly and coolly to Henry Adams, whom he had already encountered two days ago, by accident, on the boulevard Haussmann.

"I *hear*," Hahr said, happily scandalized, "his wife committed suicide."

"I wouldn't say that to *his* face either," Trist said. The face in question was in fact rather sunburned—Adams had recently travelled all the way from Tahiti—but decades older, sharply creased and fixed in what seemed to be a perpetual melancholy. As far as Trist knew, since the day of Clover's funeral six years ago Adams had never mentioned her name or referred to her in any way whatsoever. He had commissioned the sculptor Saint-Gaudens to make an enigmatic yet strangely moving statue for her grave in Rock Creek Cemetery. People whispered he ought to have sought medical help for Clover when she first grew depressed, ought never to have left her alone in a house full of dangerous chemicals. The secret of *Esther* was still a secret—Trist's promise to Clover still a promise—but to his mind the book had always seemed as terrible and deadly to her in the end as cyanide.

"There is a question here about—Shiloh?" Henry Adams had strolled away to another corner of the hall, and Whitelaw Reid was holding his arm out rather helplessly to Trist.

"*Qui l'a posée?*" Trist asked, coming forward.

A Belgian consul, as it turned out, a whiskery little man bristling with notebooks and pencils and moustaches. Hadn't Monsieur the Ambassador actually been present at the Battle of Shiloh? Hadn't he himself seen the General Grant in one of his worst defeats?

When the question was translated for him, Reid smiled, hitched his shoulders, and led his group of attentive listeners to the right, toward a photograph of Union artillery units at Shiloh, and next to the photograph, framed under glass as a compliment to him, a copy of the article the Ambassador himself had written almost thirty years ago as a young reporter for the Cincinnati *Gazette*. Slowly, carefully, he began to read the article for his audience, pausing after every few sentences for Trist to translate. It was a famous article, Trist knew, and Reid was notoriously proud of it—*Fresh from the field of the great battle,* it began, *with its pounding and roaring of artillery and its keener voiced rattle of musketry still sounding in my wearied ears, I sit down to write my story.* . . . And the story thus begun was in fact one of the earliest and most widely reprinted attacks of the whole war on Grant—a lazy, stupid general, cruelly wasteful of human life, probably drunk on the first day of the battle. Reid wrote so well, Sylvanus Cadwallader had told Trist once, the "Butcher Grant" legend had started right there.

The little Belgian had another question. Trist translated automatically, scarcely paying attention. The truth was, when military historians, not newspapermen, had looked again, virtually every fact in Reid's story was wrong. Grant hadn't been beaten, he hadn't been drunk, he had actually done a superlative job of rallying his men and turning back the enemy, and if two of his subordinates had followed his orders, the Confederates would have probably been annihilated on the spot.

At the far end of the hall Henry Adams suddenly reappeared, with Elizabeth Cameron at his side.

"What do you think of the Ambassador's little speech?" Hahr whispered.

At the same moment someone asked Reid a question in English and Trist stepped back from the circle. "It reminds me," he told Hahr, "of Cuvier's remark about the French Academy's definition of a crab—brilliant, but not correct."

Hahr looked momentarily disconcerted. Then he followed Trist's gaze. Beside the ceremonial flag, Adams and Elizabeth Cameron were standing, two or three feet apart, watching the French President receive his guests. Even at this distance both seemed weary and sad. Neither of them spoke. Madame Ledoiné crossed in front of them and bowed to Adams, who didn't respond.

"They *say*," Hahr said, like all diplomats part feline, "Mrs. Cameron used to be Adams's mistress, but now she's thrown him over."

Trist's shoulder ached. He glanced at Reid, firmly back in English. Elizabeth Cameron had come to Paris a year ago, he had heard, without her husband, and promptly fallen into a minor scandal with a second-rate portrait painter named Helleu. Trist had seen her once or twice, they had talked, smiled, passed on. Life was like rocks and pebbles in a creek bed, he thought, time and feelings flowed ceaselessly over them into the past.

"She's very beautiful," Hahr said.

"She looks very fine in black and white."

Hahr touched his good sleeve. "Shall I introduce you? Or do you already know the lady?"

Trist shook his head. From around the corner, behind some potted palms, a string quartet began to play American Civil War tunes, in honor of the exposition. "If we had met," Trist said to Hahr, but the music was too close and Hahr probably didn't hear him, "I would certainly remember."

ABOUT THE AUTHOR

MAX BYRD is the award-winning author of many detective novels, including the Book-of-the-Month Club selection *Target of Opportunity*, and three bestselling historical novels. An authority on eighteenth- and nineteenth-century American history, he makes his home in Davis, California, where he is at work on a novel of historical suspense.

N O T E

NICHOLAS TRIST IS AN INVENTED CHARACTER AND HIS RELATIONSHIPS
with historical figures are, of course, fictitious, though his
romance with Elizabeth Cameron is loosely based on her real-life
affair with the poet Joseph Trumbull Stickney. Otherwise, historical characters do and say here pretty much what they actually did
and said. I have, however, moved John Sherman and the
Camerons about a little in 1880 and brought the Adamses home
early from Europe; for clarity I have modified the phrasing in one
of Henry Adams's letters, but not changed the meaning. Whenever
possible I have taken dialogue verbatim from letters, books,
diaries, etc. Clover Adams did commit suicide in the manner
described here. Scholars generally assert that she knew all along
about the authorship of *Esther*; as far as I know, there is no evidence whatsoever for that view. My version of her discovery is
speculative, but not inconsistent with the facts. Sylvanus
Cadwallader was a real person, but little is known of his life after
the Civil War; I have used his *Three Years with Grant,* not published until 1955, as the basis for his character.

Professor John Y. Simon, editor of the great *Papers of Ulysses
S. Grant,* published by the University of Southern Illinois Press,
was most kind and helpful to a perfect stranger. Professor Brooks

D. Simpson of Arizona State University has been similarly generous and good-natured. Celeste Walker and Richard Ryerson of the
Massachusetts Historical Society were unfailingly thoughtful,
learned, and patient.

Clover Adams's letters to her father were published in 1936,
but somewhat expurgated; the complete letters can be found in
the microfilm edition of the Adams Papers, reels 595–599. There is
a definitive three-volume life of Grant through 1865 by Lloyd
Lewis and Bruce Catton. The best one-volume complete life is by
Geoffrey Perret. Otto Friedrich's *Clover* is an outstanding biography, as is Arline Tehan's *Henry Adams in Love*. Adams's *Letters* are
edited by J. C. Levenson and Ernest Samuels, et al., and published
by Harvard University Press.

My wife Brookes has seen me through every page. I thank her
with love. My friend John Lescroart, a wonderful writer (and
reader) gave crucial help at the start. Diana Essert has typed my
manuscript with skill and good humor. Virginia Barber is a literary
agent *sans pareil*. And as for Kate Miciak—there just could not be
a more brilliant and supportive editor than Kate Miciak.